"When we come back, we'll be rich."

"You'll be rich, boss," Pancho said. "The rest of us'll still be employees."

Dan laughed. "You'll be rich, too. I'll see to that. You'll be rich."

"Or dead," Pancho countered.

"One minute," Amanda said. "I really think we should pay attention to the countdown."

"You're right," said Pancho.

Dan watched it all on the displays of the control board. The fusion reactor lit up as programmed. Star-hot plasma began generating energy. Through the MHD channel it roared, where a minor fraction of that heat energy was turned into electrical power. The ship's internal batteries shut off and began recharging. Cryonically-cold liquid hydrogen and helium started pumping through the rocket nozzles' cooling walls. The hot plasma streamed through the nozzles' throats.

"Ignition," Amanda said, using the traditional word even though it was now without physical meaning.

"Thrust building up." Pancho said. Dan watched the curves rising on the thrust displays, but he didn't need to; he could feel weight returning, feel the deck gaining solidity beneath his feet.

"We're off and running," Pancho announced. "Next stop, the Asteroid Belt!"

TOR BOOKS BY BEN BOVA

*forthcoming

THE
PRECIPICE

BOOK 1 OF THE ASTEROID WARS

BEN BOVA

A TOM DOHERTY ASSOCIATES BOOK
NEW YORK

This is a work of fiction. All the characters and events portrayed in this book are either products of the author's imagination or are used fictitiously.

THE PRECIPICE: BOOK 1 OF THE ASTEROID WARS

Edited by Patrick Nielsen Hayden

A Tor Book
Published by Tom Doherty Associates, LLC
175 Fifth Avenue
New York, NY 10010

www.tor.com

Tor® is a registered trademark of Tom Doherty Associates, LLC.

ISBN: 0-812-57989-5

First edition: October 2001
First mass market edition: December 2002

Printed in the United States of America

0 9 8 7 6 5 4 3 2 1

To Irving Levitt, a rare jewel among men
To Barbara, who adorns my life with beauty

ACKNOWLEDGMENTS

Special thanks to Jeff Mitchell, a real rocket scientist; to Chris Fountain, metallurgist and optimist; and to Lee Modesitt, an economist with imagination; true friends all.

The modern tropics and their fringes support more than half the world's population, numbered in the billions. Many already live at the fringe of survival, dependent on food aid transported from the grain belts of more temperate zones. Even a small climatic shift...would physically compress the geographical limits for cereal cropping....I leave it to your imagination what such a pace of climate change would entail for most people.

—Stephen Drury
*Stepping Stones: Evolving
the Earth and Its Life*

...some men have already embarked on a bold new adventure, the conquest of outer space. This is a healthy sign, a clear indication that some of us are still feral men, unwilling to domesticate ourselves by any kind of bondage, even that of the spatial limitations of our planet's surface.

—Carleton S. Coon
The Story of Man (Third Edition)

MEMPHIS

J esus," the pilot kept murmuring. "Jesus, Jesus, Jesus."

The helicopter was racing north, bucking, jolting between the shattered land below and the thick dark gray clouds scudding just above, trying to follow Interstate 55 from the Memphis International Airport to what was left of the devastated city.

You could not see the highway; it was carpeted from horizon to horizon with refugees, bumper to bumper traffic inching along, an unending stream of cars, trucks, vans, busses, people on foot swarming like ants, trudging painfully along the shoulders of the road in the driving, soaking rain, women pushing baby carriages, men and boys hauling carts piled high with whatever they could salvage from their homes. Flood water was lapping along the shoulder embankment, rising, still rising, reaching for the poor miserable people as they fled their homes, their hopes, their world in a desperate attempt to escape the rising waters.

Dan Randolph felt the straps of his safety harness cutting

into his shoulders as he stared grimly out the window from his seat behind the two pilots. His head throbbed painfully and the filter plugs in his nostrils were hurting again. He barely noticed the copter's buffeting and jouncing in the choppy wind as he watched the swollen tide of refugees crawling sluggishly along the highway. It's like a war zone, Dan thought. Except that the enemy is Mother Nature. The flooding was bad enough, but the earthquake broke their backs.

Dan put the electronically-boosted binoculars to his eyes once again, searching, scanning the miserable, soaking wet throng below for one face, one individual, the one woman he had come to save. It was impossible. There must be half a million people down there, he thought. More. Finding her will take a miracle.

The chopper bounced and slewed wildly in a sudden gust of wind, banging the binoculars painfully against Dan's brow. He started to yell something to the pilot, then realized that they had run into another blustery squall. Fat, pounding raindrops splattered thickly against the copter's windows, cutting Dan's vision down almost to nothing.

The pilot slid back the transparent sanitary partition that isolated Dan's compartment. Dan suppressed an angry urge to slam it back. What good are sterile barriers if you open them to the outside air?

"We've got to turn back, sir," the pilot yelled over the thrumming thunder of the engines.

"No!" Dan shouted. "Not till we find her!"

Half turning in his seat to face Dan, the pilot jabbed a finger toward his spattered windscreen. "Mr. Randolph, you can fire me when we land, but I ain't going to fly through *that.*"

Looking past the flapping windscreen wipers, Dan saw four deadly slim dark funnels writhing across the other side of the swollen Mississippi, dust and debris flying wherever they touched the ground. They looked like coiling, squirming snakes thrashing across the ground, smashing everything they touched: buildings exploded, trees uprooted, autos tossed into the air like dry leaves, homes shattered into splinters, RV parks, housing developments, shopping malls all destroyed at the flick of the twisters' pitiless, mindless malevolence, blasted as completely and ruthlessly as if they had been struck by an enemy missile attack.

The enemy is Mother Nature, Dan repeated silently, numbly, as he stared at the advancing tornadoes. There was nothing he could do about them and he knew it. They couldn't be bought, bribed, flattered, seduced, or threatened into obedience. For the first time since he'd been a child, Daniel Hamilton Randolph felt totally powerless.

As he locked the partition shut again and fumbled in his pockets for his antiseptic spray, the chopper swung away, heading back toward what was left of the international airport. The Tennessee National Guard had thrown a cordon around the grounds; the airport was the Memphis region's last link with the rest of the country. The floods had knocked out electrical power, smashed bridges, covered roads with thick muddy brown water. Most of the city had been submerged for days.

Then came the earthquake. A solid nine on the Richter scale, so powerful that it flattened buildings from Nashville to Little Rock and as far north as St. Louis. New Orleans had already been under water for years as the rising Gulf of Mexico inexorably reclaimed its shoreline from Florida to Texas. The Mississippi was in flood all the way up to Cairo, and still rising.

Now, with communications out, millions homeless in the never-ending rains, aftershocks strong enough to tumble skyscrapers, Dan Randolph searched for the one person who meant something to him, the only woman he had ever loved.

He let the binoculars drop from his fingers and rested his head on the seat back. It was hopeless. Finding Jane out there among all those other people—

The copilot had twisted around in his seat and was tapping on the clear plastic partition.

"What?" Dan yelled.

Instead of trying to outshout the engines' roar through the partition, the copilot pointed to the earpiece of his helmet. Dan understood and picked up the headset they had given him from where he'd dumped it on the floor. He had sprayed it when they'd first handed it to him, but now he doused it again with the antiseptic.

As he clamped it over his head, he heard the metallic, static-streaked voice of a news reporter saying, "... definitely identified as Jane Scanwell. The former President was found, by a strange twist of fate, on President's Island, where she was apparently attempting to help a family of refugees escape the rising Mississippi waters. Their boat apparently capsized and was swept downstream, but snagged on treetops on the island.

"Jane Scanwell, the fifty-second President of the United States, died trying to save others from the ravages of flood and earthquake here in what remains of Memphis, Tennessee."

LA GUAIRA

t was raining in Venezuela, too, when Dan Randolph finally got back to his headquarters. Another hurricane was tearing through the Caribbean, lashing Barbados and the Windward Islands, dumping twenty-five centimeters of rain on the island of La Guaira and Caracas, on the mainland, with more to come.

Dan sat behind his big, bare desk, still wearing the rumpled slacks and pullover that he had travelled in from the States. His office smelled musty, mildewed from the incessant rain despite its laboring climate control system. He wasn't wearing the protective nose plugs; the air in his office was routinely filtered and run past intense ultraviolet lamps.

Leaning back into the softly yielding caramel brown leather of his swivel chair, Dan gazed out at the windswept launch complex. The rockets had been towed back into the assembly buildings. In this storm they could not dare to launch even the sturdy, reliable Clipperships. The launch towers were visibly shaking in the gale-force wind, lashed by horizontal sheets of rain; roofs had already peeled off some of the smaller buildings. Beyond the launch towers, the sea was a wild madhouse of frothing whitecapped waves. The wind howled like a beast of prey, rattling even the thick double-paned windows of Randolph's office.

Third storm to hit us and it's not even the Fourth of July yet. Business isn't lousy enough, we've got these double-damned hurricanes to deal with. At this rate I'll be broke by Labor Day.

We're losing, Dan thought. We're in a war and we're losing it. Hell, we've already lost it. What's the sense of pretending otherwise?

The dampness made him ache deep in his bones, an arthritic-like reminder of his age and the dose of radiation sickness he'd contracted years earlier. I ought to get back to Selene, he told himself. A man with a broken-down immune system shouldn't stay on Earth if he doesn't have to.

Yet for hours he simply sat there, staring out at the pounding storm, seeing only the face of Jane Scanwell, remembering the sound of her voice, the touch of her fingers, the soft silkiness of her skin, the scent of her, the way she brightened a room, they way she had filled his life even though they were never really together, not more than a few quick hours now and then before they fell into bitter argument. There was so much separating them. After she had left the White House, they had managed to spend a couple of days together on a tropical atoll. Even that had ended in a quarrel.

But for once they had seen things the same way, had the same goal, fought the same fight on the same side. The greenhouse cliff meant war, a war pitting humankind's global civilization against the blind forces of nature. Jane understood that as well as Dan did. They were going to fight this war together.

And it killed her.

Should I go on? Dan asked himself. What's the use of it?

What's the sense of it? He wanted to cry, but the tears would not come.

Dan Randolph had always seemed larger than his actual physical size. He was a solidly-built welterweight, still in trim physical shape, although now, in his sixties, it took grueling hours in the gym to maintain his condition. His once-sandy hair was almost completely gray now; his staff people called him "the Silver Fox" behind his back. He had a fighter's face, with a strong stubborn jaw and a nose that had been flattened years ago by a fist, when he'd been a construction worker in space. Despite all the wealth he'd amassed since those early days, he'd never had his nose fixed. Some said it was a perverse sense of machismo. His light gray eyes, which had often glinted in amusement at the foolishness of men, were bleak and saddened now.

A chime sounded, and the sleek display screen of his computer rose slowly, silently out of the desktop surface.

Dan swiveled his chair to see the screen. His administrative assistant's young, somber face looked out at him. Teresa was a native of Caracas, tall, leggy, cocoa-cream complexion, deep brown almond eyes and thick lustrous midnight dark hair. Years earlier Dan would have tried to bed her and probably succeeded. Now he was simply annoyed at her intrusion into his memories.

"It's almost dinnertime," she said.

"So what?"

"Martin Humphries has been waiting all day to see you. He's the man Zack Freiberg wants you to meet."

Dan grimaced. Zack had been the first one to warn Dan of the impending greenhouse cliff.

"Not today, Teresa," he said. "I don't want to see anybody today."

The young woman hesitated a heartbeat, then asked, softly, almost timidly, "Do you want me to bring you a dinner tray?"

Dan shook his head. "I'm not hungry."

"You have to eat."

He looked at her image on his screen, so intent, so young and concerned and worried that the boss was going off the deep end. And he felt anger rising inside him, unreasoning blind blazing rage.

"No, goddammit to hell and back," he snapped. "*You* have to eat. I can do any goddamned thing I want to, and if you want to keep drawing your paycheck you'd better leave me the hell alone."

Her eyes went wide. Her mouth opened, but she said nothing. Dan snapped his fingers and the screen went blank. Another snap and it folded back into its niche in the desk's gleaming rosewood top.

Leaning back in his chair, Dan closed his eyes. He tried to close his mind against the memories, but that was impossible.

It was all going to be so damned great. Okay, a century or two of global warming would lead to a greenhouse cliff. Not a gradual warmup but a sudden, abrupt change in the world's climate. All that latent heat stored in the oceans would pour into the atmosphere. Ice caps in Greenland and Antarctica melting away. Sea levels shooting up over a decade or two. Big storms and lots of them. Climate shifts turning croplands into deserts.

So what? We'll use the resources of space to solve all those problems. Energy? We'll build solar power satellites, beam energy from space to wherever it's needed. Raw materials? We'll mine the Moon and the asteroids; there's more natural resources in space than the whole Earth can provide. Food production?

Well, that would be a tough one. We all knew that. But with enough energy and enough raw materials we could irrigate the croplands that were being desiccated by the climate shift.

Yeah, sure. And when half the world's major cities got

flooded out, what did we do? What could we do? When the electrical power grid got shattered, what did we do? When earthquakes and tsunamis wiped out the heart of Japan's industrial capacity, what did we do? Diddley-squat. When this quake flattened the midwest, what did we do? We tried to help the survivors and Jane got herself killed in the attempt.

The office door banged open and a huge, red-bearded man pushed in, carrying an ornately-carved teak tray laden with steaming dishes. In his massive hands the tray looked like a little child's toy.

"Teresa says you've got to eat," he announced in a high, sweet tenor as he set the tray on Dan's desk.

"I told her I'm not hungry."

"You can't fookin' starve yourself. Eat something."

Dan glanced at the tray. A steaming bowl of soup, a salad, a main course hidden under a stainless steel dome, a carafe of coffee. No wine. Nothing alcoholic.

He pushed the tray toward the red-haired giant. "You eat it, George."

Pulling one of the upholstered chairs up close to the desk, Big George looked his boss in the eye and pushed the tray back toward Randolph.

"Eat," he said. "It's good for ya."

Dan stared back at George Ambrose. He'd known Big George since he'd been a fugitive on the Moon, hiding out from the Selene City authorities with a handful of other free souls who styled themselves the Lunar Underground. Big George was Dan's personal bodyguard now; he wore custom-tailored suits instead of patched coveralls. But he still looked like a barely-tamed frontiersman: big, shaggy, the kind of man who could gleefully pound your head down into your ribcage with no personal malice at all.

"Tell you what," Dan said, feeling a reluctant smile bend his lips a little. "I'll split it with you."

George grinned back at him. "Good thinking, boss."

They ate in silence for several minutes, George gobbling

the entire main course, which turned out to be a thick slab of prime rib. Dan took a few spoonfuls of soup and nibbled at the salad.

"Better than the old days, huh?" George said, still chewing prime rib. "Fookin' soyburgers and recycled piss for water."

Dan ignored the younger man's attempt to jolly him. "Has Teresa gone home?" he asked.

"Nope."

Nettled, Dan glanced at his wristwatch. "She's not my nursemaid, double-damn it. I don't want her hovering over me like—"

"That Humphries bloke is still waitin' to see you," George said.

"Now? He's out there now? It's almost nine o'clock, for chrissakes. What's wrong with him? Is he stuck here because of the storm? Doesn't Teresa have the smarts to put him up in one of the guest suites?"

George shook his shaggy head. "He said he'll wait until you're ready to see 'im. He did have an appointment, y'know."

Dan let his breath out in a weary sigh. *I just got back from the funeral and they expect me to stick to a schedule made out weeks ago.*

"Teresa says he's makin' her nervous."

"Nervous?"

"He's comin' on to her. I can see it meself."

Frowning, Dan muttered, "Teresa can take care of herself."

"The voice of experience?" George grinned.

"He's been hitting on her all the time he's been waiting for me?"

"Want me to shoo 'im off?" George asked.

For a moment Dan relished the image of George hustling his visitor out of the building. But then he realized that the man would simply come back tomorrow. *I'll have to get back to business,* he told himself. *Can't avoid it forever.*

"Take the tray out," he said to Big George, "and show this Humphries guy in."

George smacked his lips. "I can bring in dessert and coffee."

"Fine," Dan said, unwilling to argue. "Do that."

Grinning, George scooped up the crumb-littered tray in one hand and started for the door. Dan saw that the desktop was sprinkled with crumbs, too. Annoyed, he brushed them to the carpet.

Teresa appeared at the door. "Mr. Martin Humphries," she announced. She looked tense, Dan thought. Humphries must have really rattled her.

Martin Humphries looked quite young. He was on the small side, a couple of centimeters shorter than Teresa, and he seemed soft, with rounded shoulders and a waistline that was already getting thick, despite the careful drape of his burgundy blazer. He seemed to radiate energy, though, as he strode confidently across the office toward Dan's desk.

Dan got to his feet and extended his hand across the desk.

"Sorry to keep you waiting," he said, making himself smile.

Humphries took Dan's hand in a firm grip. "I understand," he replied. "I'm sorry to intrude on your grief."

His eyes told Dan that the words were nothing more than an expected ritual. Martin Humphries's face was round, almost boyish. But his eyes were diamond-hard, cold and gray as the storm-lashed sea outside the window.

As they sat down, George re-entered the office bearing a tray of pastries and the same carafe of coffee, with a pair of china cups and saucers alongside it. For all his size, Big George walked with the lightfooted step of a dancer—or a cat burglar. Neither Dan nor Humphries said a word as George deftly deposited the tray on the desk and swiftly, silently left the office.

"I hope I haven't kept you from your dinner," Dan said, gesturing to the pastries.

Humphries ignored the tray. "No problem. I enjoyed chatting with your secretary."

"Did you?" Dan said thinly.

"She's quite a piece of work. I'd like to hire her away from you."

"Not a chance," Dan snapped.

With a careless shrug, Humphries said, "That's not important. I came here to talk to you about the current situation."

Dan waved toward the window. "You mean the greenhouse cliff?"

"I mean the way we can help the global economy to recover from the staggering losses it's sustained—and make ourselves a potful of profits while we're doing it."

Dan felt his brows hike up. He reached for one of the delicate little pastries, then decided to pour himself a cup of coffee first. Dan's firm, Astro Manufacturing Inc., was close to bankruptcy and the whole financial community knew it.

"I could use a potful of profits," he said carefully.

Humphries smiled, but Dan saw no warmth in it.

"What do you have in mind?" he asked.

"The Earth is in chaos because of this sudden climate shift," said Humphries.

"The greenhouse cliff, yes," Dan agreed.

"Selene and the other lunar communities are doing rather well, though."

Dan nodded. "On the Moon there's no shortage of energy or raw materials. They've got everything they need. They're pretty much self-sufficient now."

"They could be helping the Earth," said Humphries. "Building solar power satellites. Sending raw materials to Earth. Even manufacturing products that people down here need but can't get because their own factories have been destroyed."

"We've tried to do that," Dan said. "We're trying it now. It's not enough."

Humphries nodded. "That's because you've been limiting yourself to the resources you can obtain from the Moon."

"And the NEAs," Dan added.

"The near-Earth asteroids, yes." Humphries nodded as if he'd expected that response.

"So what are you suggesting?"

Humphries glanced over his shoulder, as if afraid that someone might be eavesdropping. "The Belt," he said, almost in a whisper.

Dan looked at Humphries for a long, silent moment. Then he leaned his head back and laughed, long and loud and bitterly.

They were gaining on her.

Still wearing the spacesuit, Pancho Lane zipped weightlessly through the lab module, startling the Japanese technicians as she propelled herself headlong down its central aisle with a flick of her strong hands against the lab equipment every few meters. Behind her she could hear the men yelling angrily.

If any of those dip-brains have the smarts to suit up and go EVA to head me off, she thought, I'm toast.

It had started out as a game, a challenge. Which of the pilots aboard the station could breathe vacuum the longest? There were six Astro Corporation rocket jockeys waiting for transport back to Selene City: four guys, Pancho herself, and the new girl, Amanda Cunningham.

Pancho had egged them on, of course. That was part of the sting. They'd all been hanging around the galley, literally floating when they didn't anchor themselves down with the footloops fastened to the floor around the table and its single pipestem-slim leg. The conversation had gotten around to vacuum breathing: how long can you hold your breath in space without damaging yourself?

"The record is four minutes," one of the guys had claimed. "Harry Kirschbaum."

"Harry Kirschbaum? Who the hell is he? I never heard of him."

"He died young."

They all had laughed.

Amanda, who had just joined the team fresh from tech school in London, had the face of an angelic schoolgirl with soft curly blonde hair and big innocent blue eyes; but her curvaceous figure had all the men panting. She said, "I had to readjust my helmet once, during a school exercise in the vacuum tank."

"How long did that take?"

She shrugged, and even Pancho noticed the way it made her coveralls jiggle. "Ten seconds, perhaps. Fifteen."

Pancho didn't like Amanda. She was a little tease who affected an upperclass British accent. One look at her and the men forgot about Pancho, which was a shame because a couple of the guys were really nice.

Pancho was lean and stringy, with the long slim legs of her African heritage. Her skin was no darker than a good tan would produce back in west Texas, but her face was just plain ordinary, with what she considered a lantern jaw and squinty little commonplace brown eyes. She always kept her hair cut so short that the rumor had gone around that she was a lesbian. Not true. But she had a man's strength in her long, muscled arms and legs, and she never let a man beat her in anything—unless she wanted to.

The transfer buggy that was slated to take them all back to Selene was running late. Cracked nozzle on one of the thrusters, and the last thing the flight controllers wanted was a derelict transfer vehicle carrying six rocket jocks; they would be rebuilding the buggy forty-five ways from Sunday while they coasted Moonward.

So the six of them waited in the galley and talked about vacuum breathing. One of the guys claimed he'd sucked vacuum for a full minute.

"That explains your IQ," said his buddy.

"Nobody's made it for a full minute."

"Sixty seconds," the man maintained stubbornly.

"Your lungs would explode."

"I'm telling you, sixty seconds. On the dot."

"No damage?"

He hesitated, suddenly shamefaced.

"Well?"

With an attempt at a careless shrug, he admitted, "Left lung collapsed."

They snickered at him.

"I could prob'ly do it for sixty seconds," Pancho announced.

"You?" The man nearest her guffawed. "Now, Mandy here, she's got the lung capacity for it."

Amanda smiled shyly. But when she inhaled they all noticed it.

Pancho hid her anger at their ape-man attitude. "Ninety seconds," she said flatly.

"Ninety seconds? Impossible!"

"You willin' to bet on that?" Pancho asked.

"Nobody can stand vacuum for ninety seconds. It'd blow your eyeballs out."

Pancho smiled toothily. "How much money are you ready to put against it?"

"How can we collect off you after you're dead?"

"Or brain-damaged."

"She's already brain-damaged if she thinks she can suck vacuum for ninety seconds."

"I'll put my money in an escrow account for the five of

you to withdraw in case of my death or incapacitation," Pancho said calmly.

"Yeah, sure."

Pointing to the phone on the wall, next to the sandwich dispenser, she said, "Electronic funds transfer. Takes all of two minutes to set up."

They fell silent.

"How much?" Pancho said, watching their eyes.

"A week's pay," snapped one of the men.

"A month's pay," Pancho said.

"A whole month?"

"Why not? You're so freakin' sure I can't do it, why not bet a month's pay? I'll put five months worth of mine in the escrow account, so you'll each be covered."

"A month's pay."

In the end they had agreed to it. Pancho knew that they figured she'd chicken out after twenty-thirty seconds and they'd have her money without her killing herself.

She figured otherwise.

So she used the galley phone to call her bank in Lubbock. A few taps on the phone's touchtone keypad and she had set up a new account and dumped five months' pay into it. All five of the other jocks watched the phone's tiny screen to make certain Pancho wasn't playing any tricks.

Then each of them in turn called their banks and deposited a month's pay into Pancho's new account. Pancho listened to the singsong beeping of the phone as she laid her plans for the coming challenge.

Pancho suggested they use the airlock down at the far end of the maintenance module. "We don't want some science geek poppin' in on us and gettin' so torqued he punches the safety alarm," she said.

They all agreed easily. So they floated through two lab modules and the shabby-looking habitat module where the long-term researchers were housed and finally made it to the cavernous maintenance unit. There, by the airlock, Pancho chose a spacesuit from the half-dozen standard models lined up against the bulkhead, size large because of her height. She quickly wriggled into it. They even helped her put on the boots and check out the suit's systems.

Pancho pulled the helmet over her head and clicked the neck seal shut.

"Okay," she said, through the helmet's open visor. "Who's gonna time me?"

"I will," said one of the guys, raising his forearm to show an elaborate digital wristwatch.

"You go in the lock," said the man beside him, "pump it down and open the outside hatch."

"And you watch me through the port," Pancho said, tapping the thick round window on the airlock's inner hatch with gloved knuckles.

"Check. When I say go, you open your visor."

"And I'll time you," said the guy with the fancy wristwatch.

Pancho nodded inside the helmet.

Amanda looked concerned. "Are you absolutely certain that you want to go through with this? You could kill yourself, Pancho."

"She can't back out now!"

"Not unless she wants to forfeit five months' pay."

"But seriously," Amanda said. "I'm wiling to call off the bet. After all—"

Pancho reached out and tousled her curly blonde hair. "Don't sweat it, Mandy."

With that, she stepped through the open airlock hatch and slid down her visor. She waved to them as they swung the hatch shut. She heard the pump start to clatter; the sound quickly dwindled as the air was sucked out of the metal-walled chamber. When the telltale light by the inner hatch turned red, Pancho touched the button that slid the outer hatch open.

For a moment she forgot what she was up to as she drank

in the overwhelming beauty of the Earth spread out before her dazzled eyes. Brilliantly bright, intensely blue oceans and enormous sweeps of clouds so white it almost hurt to look upon them. It was glorious, an overwhelming panorama that never failed to make her heart beat faster.

You've got work to do, girl, she reminded herself sternly.

Turning to the inner hatch, she could see all five of their faces clustered around the little circular port. None of them had the sense to find a radio, Pancho knew, so she gestured to her sealed helmet visor with a gloved finger. They all nodded vigorously and the guy with the fancy wristwatch held it up where Pancho could see it.

The others backed away from the port while the guy stared hard at his wristwatch. He held up four fingers, then three...

Counting down, Pancho understood.

...two, one. He jabbed a finger like a make-believe pistol at Pancho, the signal that she was to lift her visor *now*.

Instead, Pancho launched herself out the airlock, into empty space.

LA GUAIRA

Martin Humphries looked irked. "What's so funny about the Asteroid Belt?"

Dan shook his head. "Not funny, really. Just...I didn't expect that from you. You've got a reputation for being a hard-headed businessman."

"I'd like to believe that I am," Humphries said.

"Then forget about the Belt," Dan snapped. "Been there, done that. It's too far away, the costs would outweigh the profits by a ton."

"It's been done," Humphries insisted.

"Once," said Dan. "By that nutcase Gunn. And he damned near got himself killed doing it."

"But that one asteroid was worth close to a trillion dollars once he got it into lunar orbit."

"Yeah, and the double-damned GEC took control of it and bankrupted Gunn."

"That won't happen this time."

"Why not? You don't think the GEC would seize any resources we bring to Earth? That's the reason the Global Economic Council was created—to control the whole twirling Earth's international trade."

Humphries smiled coldly. "I can handle the GEC. Trust me on that one."

Dan stared at the younger man for a long, hard moment. Finally he shook his head and replied, "It doesn't matter. I'd even be willing to let the GEC run the show."

"You would?"

"Hell yes. We're in a global emergency now. Somebody has to allocate resources, control prices, see to it that nobody takes advantage of this crisis to line his own pockets."

"I suppose so," Humphries said slowly. "Still, I'm convinced there's a lot of money to be made by mining the Belt."

Nodding, Dan agreed, "There's a lot of resources out there, that's for sure. Heavy metals, organics, resources we can't get from the Moon."

"Resources that the Earth needs, and the GEC would be willing to pay for."

"Mining the asteroids," Dan mused. "That's a major undertaking. A *major* undertaking."

"That's why I'm here. Astro Manufacturing has the resources to do it."

"Astro Manufacturing is just about broke and you know it."

"I wasn't talking about financial resources," Humphries said, waving a hand in the air almost carelessly.

"Oh no?"

"No." Pointing a finger toward the window and the storm-battered launch facility outside, Humphries said, "You've got the technological know-how, the teams of trained personnel, the rockets and infrastructure to get us into space."

"And it's bleeding me white because there's less and less of a market for launch services. Nobody can afford to buy electronics manufactured on the Moon, not when they're being driven from their homes by floods and earthquakes."

Humphries's brows rose questioningly.

"I know, I know," Dan said. "There's the energy market. Sure. But how many solar-power satellites can we park in orbit? The double-damned GEC just put a cap on them. We're building the next-to-last one now. After those two, no more powersats."

Before Humphries could ask why, Dan continued, "The goddamned Greater Asia Power Consortium complained about the powersats undercutting their prices. And the double-damned Europeans sided with them. Serve 'em all right if they freeze their asses off when the Gulf Stream breaks up."

"The Gulf Stream?" Humphries looked startled.

Dan nodded unhappily. "That's one of the projections. The greenhouse warming is already changing ocean currents. When the Gulf Stream breaks up, Europe goes into the deep freeze; England's weather will be the same as Labrador's."

"When? How soon?"

"Twenty years, maybe. Maybe a hundred. Ask five different scientists and you get twelve different answers."

"That's a real opportunity," Humphries said excitedly. "Winterizing all of Europe. Think of it! What an opportunity!"

"Funny," Dan retorted. "I was thinking of it as a disaster."

"You see the glass half empty. To me, it's half full."

Dan had a sudden urge to throw this young opportunist out of his office. Instead, he slumped back in his chair and muttered, "It's like a sick Greek tragedy. Global warming is going to put Europe in the deep-freezer. Talk about ironic."

"We were talking about the energy market," Humphries said, regaining his composure. "What about the lunar helium-three?"

Dan wondered if his visitor was merely trying to pump him. Warily, he answered, "Barely holding its own. There's not that many fusion power plants up and running yet—thanks to the kneejerk anti-nuke idiots. And digging helium-three out of the lunar regolith ain't cheap. Fifty parts per million sounds good to a chemist, maybe, but it doesn't lead to a high profit ratio, let me tell you."

"So you'd need an injection of capital to start mining the asteroids," Humphries said.

"A transfusion," Dan grumbled.

"That can be done."

Dan felt his brows hike up. "Really?"

"I can provide the capital," Humphries said, matter-of-factly.

"We're talking forty, fifty billion, at least."

Humphries waved a hand, as if brushing away an annoyance. "You wouldn't need that much for a demonstration flight."

"Even a one-shot demo flight would cost a couple bill," Dan said.

"Probably."

"Where are you going to get that kind of money? Nobody's willing to talk to me about investing in Astro."

"There are people who'd be willing to invest that kind of money in developing the asteroid market."

For an instant Dan felt a surge of hope. It could work! Open up the Asteroid Belt. Bring those resources to Earth's needy people. Then the cost figures flashed into his mind again, as implacable as Newton's laws of motion.

"You know," he said wearily, "if we could just cover our own costs I'd be willing to try it."

Humphries looked disappointed. "Just cover your own costs?"

"Damned right. People need those resources. If we could get them without driving ourselves into bankruptcy, I'd go to double-damned Pluto if I had to!"

Relaxing visibly, Humphries said, "I know how we can do it and make a healthy profit, besides."

Despite himself, Dan felt intrigued. "How?"

"Fusion rockets."

By the seven cities of Cibola, Dan thought, this guy's a fanatic. Worse: he's an enthusiast.

"Nobody's made a fusion rocket," he said to Humphries. "Fusion power generators are too big and heavy for flight applications. Everybody knows that."

With the grin of a cat that had just finished dining on several canaries, Humphries replied, "Everybody's wrong."

Dan thought it over for all of half a second, then leaned both his hands on his desktop, palms down, and said, "Prove it to me."

Wordlessly, Humphries fished a data chip from his jacket pocket and handed it to Dan.

SPACE STATION *GALILEO*

Leaving her five fellow astronauts gaping dumbfounded at the airlock in the maintenance module, Pancho sailed weightlessly to the metal arm of the robotic cargo-handling crane jutting out from the space station. It was idle at the moment; with no mass of payload to steady it, the long, slim arm flexed noticeably as Pancho grasped it in both hands and swung like an acrobat up to the handgrips that studded the module's outer skin.

Wondering if the others had caught on to her sting, Pancho hand-walked along the module's hull, clambering from one runglike grip to the next. To someone watching from beyond the space station it would have looked as if she were scampering along upside down, but to Pancho it seemed as if the space station was over her head and she was swinging like a kid in a zero-gee jungle gym.

She laughed inside her helmet as she reached the end of the maintenance module and pushed easily across the connector section that linked to the habitation module.

"Hey Pancho, what the hell are you doing out there?"

They had finally gotten to a radio, she realized. But as long as they were puzzled, she was okay.

"I'm taking a walk," she said, a little breathless from all the exertion.

"What about our bet?" one of the men asked.

"I'll be back in a few minutes," she lied. "Just hang tight."

"What are you up to, Pancho?" asked Amanda, her voice tinged with suspicion.

Pancho fell back on her childhood answer. "Nothin'."

The radio went silent. Pancho reached the airlock at the end of the hab module and tapped out the standard code. The outer hatch slid open. She ducked inside, sealed the hatch and didn't bother to wait for the lock to fill with air. She simply pushed open the inner hatch and quickly sealed it again. A safety alarm shrilled automatically, but cut off when the module's air pressure equilibrated again. Yanking off the spacesuit's cumbersome gloves, Pancho slid her visor up as she went to the wallphone by the airlock hatch.

Blessed with perfect pitch and a steel-trap memory, Pancho punched out the numbers for each of the five astronauts' banks in turn, followed by their personal identification codes. Mother always said I should have been a musician, Pancho mused as she transferred almost the total amount of each account into her own bank account. She left exactly one international dollar for each of them, so the bank's computers would not start the complex process of closing down their accounts.

As she finished, the hatch at the other end of the habitation module swung open and her five fellow astronauts began to push through, one at a time.

"What's going on?" demanded the first guy through.

"Nothin'," Pancho said again. Then she dived through the hatch at her end of the long narrow module.

Into the Japanese lab module she swam, flicking her fingers along the equipment racks lining both sides of its central aisle, startling the technicians working there. Laughing to herself, she wondered how long it would take them to figure out that she had looted their bank accounts.

It didn't take very long. By the time Pancho had reached the galley once again, they were roaring after her, the men bellowing with outrage.

"When I get my hands on you, I'm gonna break every bone in your scrawny body!" was one of their gentler threats.

Even Amanda was so furious she lapsed back to her native working-class accent: "We'll 'ang you up by your bloody thumbs, we will!"

As long as I can stay ahead of them, I'm okay, Pancho told herself as she skimmed through the European lab module and into the observatory section, ducking under and around the bulky telescopes and electronics consoles. They were still yelling behind her, but she wondered if all five of them were still chasing. By now there'd been plenty of time for one or more of them to pop into a suit and cut across the top of the tee-shaped station to cut her off.

Sure enough, when she barged into the Russian hab module, two of the guys were standing at the far end in spacesuits, visors up, waiting for her like a pair of armored cops.

Pancho glided to a halt. One of the privacy unit screens slid back and a stubbled, bleary, puffy male face peered out, then quickly popped back in again and slid the screen shut with a muttered string of what sounded like Slavic cursing.

The other three—Amanda and two of the men—came through the hatch behind her. Pancho was well and truly trapped.

"What the fuck are you trying to pull off, Pancho?"

"You cleaned out our bank accounts!"

"We oughtta string you up, damn you!"

She smiled and spread her hands placatingly. "Now fellas, you can't hang a person in microgee. You know that."

"This isn't funny," Amanda snapped, back to her faux-Oxford enunciation.

"I'll make restitution, okay?" Pancho offered.

"You damned well better!"

"And you lost the bet, too, so we each get a month's pay from you."

"No," Pancho said as reasonably as she could. "We never went through on the vacuum breathing, so the bet's off."

"Then we want our money back from your goddamned escrow account!"

"Sure. Fine."

Amanda pointed to the wallphone by the hatch. "You mentioned restitution," she said.

Meekly, Pancho floated to the phone and tapped out her number. "You'll have to give me your account numbers," she said. "So I can put the money back in for you."

"We'll punch in the account numbers ourselves," Amanda said firmly.

"You don't trust me?" Pancho managed to keep a straight face, but just barely.

They all growled at her.

"But it was only a joke," she protested. "I had no intention of keeping your money."

"Not much you didn't," one of the guys snapped. "Good thing Mandy figured out what you were up to."

Pancho nodded in Amanda's direction. "You're the brightest one around, Mandy," she said, as if she believed it.

"Never mind that," Amanda replied tartly. To the men she said, "Now we'll all have to change our ID codes, since she's obviously figured them out."

"I'm going to change my account number," said one of the guys.

"I'm gonna change my *bank*," another said fervently.

Pancho sighed and tried her best to look glum, chastised. Inwardly, she was quivering with silent laughter. What a hoot! And none of these bozos realizes that the half hour or so they've spent chasing me means half an hour's worth of interest from each of their accounts into mine. It's not all that much, but every little bit helps.

She just hoped they wouldn't figure it out while they were all cooped up in the transfer buggy on the way to the Moon.

Well, she thought, if they try to get physical I'll just have to introduce them to Elly.

CHENGDU, SICHUAN PROVINCE

Dan had to shout through his sanitary mask to make himself heard over the din of construction.

"All I'm asking, Zack, is can he do it or can't he?"

He'd known Zack Freiberg for more than twenty years, since Zack had been an earnest young planetary geochemist intent on exploring asteroids and Dan had hired him away from his university post. Freiberg had taken flak from his friends in academia for joining big, bad Dan Randolph, the greedy capitalist founder and head of Astro Manufacturing. But over the years a mutual respect had slowly developed into a trusting friendship. It had been Zack who'd first warned Dan about the looming greenhouse cliff, and what it would do to the Earth's climate.

The greenhouse cliff had arrived, and the Earth's politicians and business leaders had sailed blindly over its edge as the planet plunged into catastrophic warming. Zack was no longer the chubby, apple-cheeked kid Dan had first met. His strawberry hair had gone iron gray, although it was still thick and tightly curled. The past few years had toughened him, made him leaner, harder, boiled away the baby fat in his body. His face had hardened, too, as he watched his equations and graphs turn into massive human suffering.

The two men were standing on the edge of a denuded ridge, looking out across a barren coal-black valley where thousands of Chinese workers toiled unceasingly. By all the gods, Dan thought, they really do look like an army of ants scurrying around. In the middle of the valley four enormously tall smokestacks of a huge electricity-generating plant belched dark gray fumes into the hazy sky. Mountainous piles of coal lay by the railroad track that ran alongside the power plant. Off on the horizon, beyond the farther stripped-bare ridge, the Yangzi River glittered in the hazy morning sunshine like a deadly boa constrictor slowly creeping up on its prey. A sluggish warm breeze smelled of raw coal and diesel fumes.

Dan shuddered inwardly, wondering how many billions of microbes were worming their way through his sanitary mask and nose plugs, eager to chew past his weakened immune system and set up homes for themselves inside his body.

"Dan, I really don't have time for this," Freiberg hollered over the roar of a huge truck carrying twenty tons of dirt and rubble down into the valley on wheels that dwarfed both men.

"I just need a few hours of your time," Dan said, feeling his throat going hoarse from his shouting. "Jeez, I came all the way out here to get your opinion on this."

It was a sign of the Chinese government's belated realization that the greenhouse warming would decimate China as well as the rest of the world that they had asked Freiberg to personally direct their massive construction program. At one end of the valley, Chinese engineers and laborers were building a dam to protect the electrical power-generating station from the encroaching Yangzi. At the other end, a crew from Yamagata Industries was constructing a complex pumping station to remove the carbon dioxide emitted by the power station's stacks and store it deep underground, in the played-out seams of the coal bed that provided fuel for the generators.

With an exasperated frown, Freiberg said, "Listen, I know I still get my paycheck from Astro, but that doesn't mean I can jump whenever you blow the whistle."

Dan looked into the other man's light blue eyes and saw pain there, disappointment and outright fear. Zack blames himself for this catastrophe, Dan knew. He discovered the greenhouse cliff and he acts as if it's all his fault. Instead of some fathead king shooting the messenger, the messenger wants to shoot himself.

"Look, Zack," he said, as reasonably as he could manage, "you have to eat a meal now and then, don't you?"

Freiberg nodded warily. He'd been sweet-talked by Dan into doing things he hadn't wanted to do often enough in the past.

"So I brought you lunch," Dan said, waving his arm in the direction of the oversized mobile home he'd arrived in. Its roof glittered with solar panels. "When the noon whistle blows, come in and break some bread with me. That's all I'm asking."

"You want me to look at this proposal over lunch? You think I can make a technical decision about this in an hour or less?"

Dan shrugged disarmingly. "If you can't, you can't. All I'm asking is that you give it a look."

Freiberg gave Dan a look that was far from happy.

Yet five minutes after noon he climbed up through the open door of Dan's big mobile home.

"I might have known," he muttered as he stepped past Big George, standing by the doorway.

The van was luxuriously fitted out. George was Dan's major domo and bodyguard. An attractive young Japanese woman, petite and silent, was stirring steaming vegetables in an electric wok. Dan was sitting in the faux-leather couch that curved around the fold-down dinner table, a suede jacket draped over his shoulders even though the van felt uncomfortably warm to Freiberg. Zack could see the crease across Dan's face that the sanitary mask had left.

"Drink?" Dan asked, without getting to his feet. A half-empty tumbler of something bubbly sat on the table before him.

"What are you having?" Freiberg asked, sliding into the couch where it angled around the table's end. The table was already set for two.

"Ginger beer," said Dan. "George turned me on to it. Non-alcoholic and it's even good for the digestion."

Freiberg shrugged his rounded shoulders. "Okay, I'll have the same."

George quickly pulled a brown bottle from the refrigerator, opened it, and poured Freiberg a glass of ginger beer.

"Goes good with brandy, y'know," he said as he handed the glass to Freiberg.

The scientist accepted the glass wordlessly and George went back to his post by the door, folding his heavy arms over his massive chest like a professional bouncer.

After a sip of his drink, Dan asked, "Might have known what?"

Freiberg waved a hand around the compartment. "That you'd be living in the lap of luxury, even out here."

Dan laughed. "If you've got to go out into the wilderness, you might as well bring a few creature comforts with you."

"Kind of warm in here, though," Freiberg complained mildly.

Dan smiled gauntly at him. "You're accustomed to living in the wild, Zack. I'm not."

"Yeah, guess so." Freiberg glanced at the painting above Dan's head: a little girl standing by a banyan tree. "Is that real?"

"Holoprint," said Dan. "A Vickrey."

"Nice."

"What're you living in, out here?"

"A tent," said Freiberg.

Nodding, Dan said, "That's what I thought."

"It's a pretty good tent, as tents go, but it's nothing like this." His eyes swept the dining area appreciatively. "How many other rooms in here?"

"Just two: office and bedroom. King-sized bed, of course."

"Of course."

"You like it, it's yours."

"The holoprint?"

"The van. The whole shebang. I'll be leaving later this afternoon. If you can find somebody to drive George and me to the airstrip you can keep this for yourself."

Surprised, Freiberg blurted, "Can you afford to give it away? From what I've heard—"

"For you, Zack," Dan interrupted, "my last penny. If it comes to that."

Freiberg made a wry face. "You're trying to bribe me."

"Yep. Why not?"

With a resigned sigh, the scientist said, "All right, let me see this proposal you want me to look at."

"Hey George," Dan called, "bring me the notebook, will you?"

Almost an hour later, Freiberg looked up from the notebook's screen and said, "Well, I'm no rocket engineer, and what I know about fusion reactors you could put into a thimble, but I can't find anything obviously wrong with this."

"Do you think it'll work?" Dan asked earnestly.

"How the hell should I know?" Freiberg snapped irritably. "Why in hell did you come all the way out here to ask my opinion on something you *know* is outside my expertise?"

Dan hesitated for several heartbeats, then answered, "Because I can trust you, Zack. This guy Humphries is too slick for me to believe. All the experts I've contacted claim that this fusion rocket is workable, but how do I know that he hasn't bought them off? He's got something up his sleeve, some hidden agenda, and this fusion rocket idea is just the tip of the iceberg. I think he wants to get his paws on Astro."

"That's a helluva mixture of metaphors," Freiberg said, grinning despite himself.

"Never mind the syntax. I don't trust Humphries. I do trust you."

"Dan, my opinion doesn't mean a damned thing here. You might as well ask George, or your cook."

Hunching forward over the table, Dan said, "You can talk the talk, Zack. You can contact the experts that Humphries has used and sound them out. You can talk to other people, the real specialists in these areas, and see what they think. They'd talk to you, Zack, and you'd understand what they're saying. You can—"

"Dan," Freiberg said icily, "I'm working twenty-six hours a day already."

"I know," Dan said. "I know."

Freiberg had thrown himself totally into the global effort to cut down on the greenhouse gas emissions given off by the world's fossil-fueled power-generating stations, factories, and vehicles.

Faced with disastrous shifts in climate due to the greenhouse warming, the nations of the world were belatedly, begrudgingly, attempting to remedy the cataclysm. Led by the Global Economic Council, manufacturers around the world were desperately trying to convert automobiles and other vehicles to electrical motors. But that meant trebling the global electricity-generating capacity, and fossil-fueled power plants were faster and cheaper to build than nuclear plants. There was still plenty of petroleum available, and the world's resources of coal dwarfed the petroleum reserves. Fission-based power plants were still anathema because of the public's fear of nuclear power. The new fusion generators were costly, complex, and also hindered by stubborn public resistance to anything nuclear.

So more and more fossil-fueled power plants were being built, especially in the rising industrial nations such as China and South Africa. The GEC insisted that new plants sequester their carbon dioxide emissions, capture the dangerous greenhouse gas and pump it safely deep underground.

Zachary Freiberg had devoted his life to the effort to mitigate the greenhouse disaster. He had taken an indefinite leave of absence from his position as chief scientist of Astro Manufacturing and criss-crossed the world, directing massive construction projects. His wife had left him, he had not seen his children in more than a year, his personal life was in tatters, but he was driven to do what he could, what he had to do, to help slow the greenhouse warming.

"So how's it going?" Dan asked him.

Freiberg shook his head. "We're shoveling shit against the tide. There's just no way we can reduce greenhouse emissions enough to make a difference."

"But I thought—"

"We've been working our butts off for...how long has it been? Ten years? Not even a dent. When we started, fossil fuel burning pumped six billion tons of carbon dioxide into the air every year. Know how much we're putting out now?"

Dan shook his head.

"Five point three billion tons," Freiberg said, almost angrily.

Dan grunted.

Pointing through the van's window to the massive trucks rumbling by, Freiberg grumbled, "Yamagata's trying to convert their whole fleet of trucks to electricity, but the Chinese are still using diesels. Some people just don't give a damn! The Russians are starting to talk about cultivating what they call the 'virgin lands' in Siberia, where the permafrost is melting. They think they can turn the region into a new grain belt, like the Ukraine."

"So something good might come out of all this," Dan murmured.

"My ass," Freiberg snapped. "The oceans are still warming up, Dan. The clathrates are going to break down if we can't stop the ocean temperature rise. Once they start releasing the methane that's frozen in them . . ."

Dan opened his mouth to reply, but Freiberg kept right on agonizing. "You know how much methane is locked up in the clathrates? Two times ten to the sixteenth tons. Twenty quadrillion tons! Enough to produce a greenhouse that'll melt all the ice in Greenland *and* Antarctica. Every glacier in the world. We'll all drown."

"All the more reason," Dan said, "for pushing out to the Asteroid Belt. We can bring in all the metals and minerals the Earth needs, Zack! We can move the world's industrial operations into space, where they won't screw up the Earth's environment."

Freiberg gave Dan a disbelieving look.

"We can do it!" Dan insisted. "If this fusion rocket can be made to work. That's the key to the whole damned thing: efficient propulsion can bring the cost of asteroid mining down to where it's economically viable."

For a long moment Freiberg said nothing. He merely glared at Dan, half angry, half sullen.

At last he mumbled, "I'll make a few calls for you, Dan. That's all I can do."

"That's all I ask," Dan replied, forcing a smile. Then he added, "Plus a ride to the airstrip for George and me."

"What about your cook?"

With a laugh, Dan said, "She goes with the van, old buddy. She only speaks Japanese, but she's terrific in the kitchen. And the bedroom."

Freiberg flushed deep red. But he did not refuse Dan's gift.

The customs inspector looked startled when he saw the plastic cage and the four live mice huddled in it among the loose food pellets.

He set his face into a scowl as he looked up at Pancho. "You can't bring pets into Selene."

The other astronauts had sailed through the incoming inspection without a hitch, leaving Pancho to face the grim-faced inspector alone. They had cruised to the Moon without incident, none of the others realizing that Pancho had milked each of their bank accounts for a half-hour's interest. Pancho figured that even if they eventually discovered her little scam, the amount of money involved was too small to fight over. To her, it wasn't the amount so much as the adroitness of the sting.

"They're not pets," she said coolly to the inspector. "They're food."

"Food?" The man's dark eyebrows hiked halfway to his scalp line.

"Yeah, food. For my bodyguard." Most of the customs inspectors knew her, but this guy was new; Pancho hadn't encountered him before. Not bad-looking, she thought. His dark blue zipsuit complemented his eyes nicely. A little elderly, though. Starting to go gray at the temples. Must be working to raise enough money for a rejuve treatment.

As if he knew he was being maneuvered into giving straight lines, the customs inspector asked, "Your bodyguard eats mice?"

Pancho nodded. "Yes, sir, she does."

The inspector huffed. "And where is this bodyguard?"

Pancho lifted a long leg and planted her softbooted foot on the inspector's table. Tugging up the cuff of her coverall trouser, she revealed what looked like a bright metallic blue ankle bracelet.

While the inspector gaped, Pancho coaxed Elly off her ankle and held her out in front of the man's widening eyes. The snake was about thirty-five centimeters long from nose to tail. It lifted its head and, fixing the inspector with its beady, slitted eyes, it hissed menacingly. The man flinched back nearly half a meter.

"Elly's a genetically-modified krait. She'll never get any bigger'n this. She's very well-behaved and wicked poisonous."

To his credit, the inspector swiftly recovered his composure. Most of it, at least.

"You...you can't bring a snake in," he said, his voice quavering only slightly. "That's against the regulations and besides—"

"There's a special exception to the regulations," Pancho said calmly. "You can look it up. Paragraph seventeen-dee, subclause eleven."

With a frown, the inspector punched up the relevant page on his palmcomp. Pancho knew the exception would be there; she had gone all the way up to the Selene health and safety executive board to get it written into the regs. It had cost her a small fortune in time and effort; many dinners with men old enough to be her grandfather. Funny thing was, the only overt sexual pass made at her was from the woman who chaired the executive board.

"Well, I'll be dipped in . . ." The inspector looked up from his handheld's tiny screen. "How in hell did you get them to rewrite the regs for you?"

Pancho smiled sweetly. "It wasn't easy."

"That little fella is poisonous, you say?"

"Her venom's been engineered to reduce its lethality, but she's still fatal unless you get a shot of antiserum." Pancho pulled a slim vial from her open travelbag and wagged it in front of the inspector's bulging eyes.

He shook his head in wonder as Pancho coaxed the snake back around her ankle. "And he eats mice."

"She," Pancho said as she straightened up again. "When I stay up here for more than a month I have to send Earthside for more mice. Costs a bundle."

"I'll bet."

"The mice never get out of their cage," Pancho added. "Once every other week I put Elly in with them."

The inspector shuddered visibly. He took Pancho's entry forms and passed them in front of the electronic reader. The machine beeped once. Pancho was cleared. The inspector put the transparent mouse cage back into her flight bag and zipped it shut.

"You're okay to enter Selene," he said, almost as if he didn't believe it himself.

"Thank you."

Before she could hoist her bag onto her shoulder, he asked, "Uh . . . what're you doing for dinner tonight?"

Pancho smiled her sweetest. "Gee, I'd love to have dinner with you, but I already have a date."

*   *   *

Dressed in a crisp white pantsuit set off by the flowery scarf she'd tied around her neck, Pancho followed the directions Martin Humphries had videomailed to her.

In Earthside cities, height meant prestige. In hotels and condo towers, the higher the floor, the higher the price. Penthouses were considered the most desirable, and therefore were the most expensive. On the Moon, where human settlements were dug into the ground, prestige increased with depth. The airless lunar surface was dangerous, subject to four-hundred-degree temperature swings between sunlight and shadow, bathed in hard radiation from deep space, peppered with meteoric infall. So in Selene and the other communities on the Moon, the deeper your living quarters, the more desirable it was, and the more expensive.

Martin Humphries must be rotten rich, Pancho thought as she rode the elevator down to Selene's lowest level. According to the biofiles on the nets Humphries was supposed to be one of the wealthiest men in the Earth/Moon system, but that could be public relations puffery, she thought. The tabloids and scandal sites had more on him than the biofiles. They called him "Hump," or "the Humper." He had a reputation as a chaser, married twice and with lots of media stars and glamour gals from the upper crust to boot. When Pancho looked up the pix of his "dates" she saw a succession of tall, languid, gorgeous women with lots of hairdo and skimpy clothes.

Pancho felt completely safe: the Humper wouldn't be interested in a gangly, horse-faced tomboy. Besides, if he tried anything Elly would protect her.

He had called her personally. No flunky; Martin Humphries his own self had phoned Pancho and asked her to come to his home to discuss a business proposition. Maybe he wants to hire me away from Astro, she thought. Astro's been a good-enough outfit, but if Humphries offers more money I'll go to work for him. That's a no-brainer. Go where the money is, every time.

But why did he call me himself, instead of having his personnel office interview me?

There were only a few living units carved into the rock this far underground. Big places, Pancho realized as she glided along the well-lit corridor in the practiced bent-kneed shuffle that you had to use to walk in the Moon's low gravity. The walls of the corridor were carved with elaborate low-relief sculptures, mostly astronomical motifs, but there were some Earthly landscapes in with the stars and comets. She counted about a hundred strides between doors, which meant that the living units on the other sides of the corridor walls were bigger than a whole dorm section on the floors above. The doors were fancy, too: most of them were double, all of them decorated one way or another. Some of them looked like real wood, for crying out loud.

But while all this impressed Pancho, she was totally unprepared for Martin Humphries's home. At the very end of the corridor was a blank metal door, polished steel from the look of it. More like an airlock hatch or a bank vault than the fancy-pants door she'd passed along the corridor. It slid open with a soft hiss as Pancho approached within arm's length.

Optical recognition system, she thought. Or maybe he's got somebody watching the corridor.

She stepped through the open doorway and immediately felt as if she'd entered another world. She found herself in a wide, high-ceilinged cavern, a big natural cave deep below the lunar surface. Flowers bloomed everywhere, reds and yellows and green foliage spread out on both sides of her. Trees! She gaped at the sight of young alders and maples, slim white-boled birches, delicately fronded frangipani. The only trees she'd seen in Selene were up in the Grand Plaza, and they were just little bitty things compared to these. After the closed-in gray sameness of Selene's warren of corridors and tightly-confined living quarters, the openness, the color, the heady scent of flowers growing in such profusion nearly over-whelmed Pancho. Boulders jutted here and there; the distant walls of the cave and the ceiling high above were rough bare rock. The ceiling was dotted with full-spectrum lamps, she saw. Jeez, it's like being in Oz, Pancho said to herself.

Like Oz, there was a path winding through the shrubbery, littered with flower petals. Pancho liked that much better than yellow bricks.

She realized that there were no birds singing in the trees. No insects buzzed among the flowers. There was no breeze sighing past. This ornate garden was nothing more than a big, elaborate hothouse, Pancho decided. It must cost a freaking fortune.

She glide-walked along the path until a final turn revealed the house set in the middle of the cavern, surrounded by still more trees and carefully-planted beds of roses, irises and pe-onies. No daisies, Pancho noted. No marigolds. Too ordi-nary for this layout.

The house was enormous, low but wide, with a slanted roof and walls of lunar stone, smoothed and glazed over. Big sweeping windows. A wide courtyard framed the big double doors of the front entrance, with a fountain gurgling busily in its center. A fountain! Pancho approached the door slowly, reached out her hand to touch its carved surface. Plastic, her fingertips told her, stained to look like wood. For several moments she stood at the door, then turned to look back at the courtyard again, the gardens, the trees, the foun-tain. What kind of a man would spend so much money for a private palace like this? What kind of a man would have that much money to spend?

"Welcome, Ms. Lane."

The sound of his voice made Pancho flinch. He had opened the door silently while her back had been turned as she surveyed the greenery. She saw a man apparently about her own age, several centimeters shorter than she, a little on the pudgy side. He was wearing an open-necked pale yellow tunic that came down to his hips. His slacks were cinnamon brown, perfectly creased. His feet were shod in fancy tooled leather boots. His skin was doughy white, his hair dark and slicked back.

"I'm here to see Mr. Humphries," she said. "I've been invited."

He laughed lightly. "I'm Martin Humphries. I gave my staff the night off."

"Oh."

Martin Humphries gestured Pancho to come into his house. Knowing Elly was comfortably wrapped around her ankle, Pancho stepped right in.

The house was just as luxurious as the grounds around it, perhaps even more so. Big, spacious rooms filled with the most beautiful furniture Pancho had ever seen. A living room long enough to hold a hockey rink, sofas done in gorgeous fabrics, holowindows showing spectacular Earthside scenery: the Grand Canyon, Mt. Fujiyama, Manhattan's skyline the way it looked before the floods.

The dining room table was big enough to seat twenty, but it was set for just the two of them: Humphries at its head, Pancho at his right hand. Humphries walked her past it, though, and into a book-lined library where the single holowindow showed the star-strewn depths of space.

There was a bar along one side of the library.

"What would you like to drink?" Humphries asked, gently guiding her to one of the plush-cushioned stools.

"Whatever," Pancho shrugged. A good way to judge a man's intentions was to let him select the drinks.

He looked at her for a fleeting, intense moment. Like being x-rayed, Pancho thought. His eyes were gray, she noted, cold gray, like lunar stone.

"I have an excellent champagne," he suggested.

Pancho smiled at him. "Okay, fine."

He pressed a button set into the bar's surface, and a silver tray bearing an opened bottle of champagne in a refrigerated bucket and two tall fluted glasses rose up to serving height with a muted hum of an electrical motor. Humphries pulled the bottle from its bucket and poured two glasses of champagne. Pancho noticed that the ice-cold bottle quickly beaded with condensation. The glasses looked like real crystal, prob'ly made at Selene's glass factory.

The bubbles tickled her nose, but the wine was really good: crisp and cold, with a delicate flavor that Pancho liked. Still, she merely sipped at it as she sat beside Martin Humphries on the softly-cushioned bar stool.

"You must be awful rich to have this place all to yourself," she said.

His lips edged into a thin smile. "It's not mine, really."

"It's not?"

"Legally, this building is a research center. It's owned by the Humphries Trust and operated jointly by a consortium of Earthside universities and the Selene executive board."

Pancho took another sip of champagne while she sorted that out in her mind.

Humphries went on, "I live here whenever I'm at Selene. The research staff uses the other end of the house."

"But they don't live here."

He laughed. "No, they live a few levels up, in . . . um, more ordinary quarters."

"And you get the whole place rent-free."

With a waggle of his free hand, Humphries said, "One of the advantages of wealth."

"The rich get richer."

"Or they lose what they've got."

Nodding, Pancho asked, "So what do they research down here?"

"Lunar ecology," Humphries replied. "They're trying to learn how to build Earthlike ecologies here on the Moon, underground."

"Like the Grand Plaza, up topside."

"Yes. But completely closed-cycle, so you don't have to put in fresh supplies of water."

"That's what all the flowers and trees are about."

"Right. They've been able to make a lovely garden, all right, but it's incredibly expensive. Very labor-intensive, with no birds or insects to pollinate the plants. The idiots running Selene's environmental safety department won't let me bring any up here. As if they could get loose! They're so stupidly narrow-minded they could look through a keyhole with both eyes."

Pancho smiled at him, remembering how hard it had been for her to get the approval to bring Elly and her food into Selene. I must be smarter than he is, she thought. Or maybe Selene's execs just don't like megazillionaires trying to push them around.

"And those full-spectrum lamps cost a fortune in electricity," Humphries went on.

"Electricity's cheap, though, isn't it?"

Humphries took a long draft of his champagne, then answered, "It's cheap once you've built the solar energy farm up on the surface...and the superconducting batteries to store electrical energy during the night. High capital costs, though."

"Yeah, but once you've got the equipment in place the operating costs are pitiful low."

"Except for maintenance."

"Keeping the solar farms clean, up on the surface, you mean. Yeah, I guess that ain't cheap."

"Any work on the surface is damned expensive," he grumbled, bringing his champagne flute to his lips.

"So how rich are you?" she asked abruptly.

Humphries didn't sputter into his champagne, but he did seem to swallow pretty hard.

Pancho added, "I mean, do you *own* any of this or are you just livin' in it?"

He thought a moment before answering. Then, "My grandfather made his fortune in the big dot-com boom around the turn of the century. Gramps was smart enough to get into the market while it was still rising and get out before the bubble burst."

"What's a dot-com?" Pancho asked.

Ignoring her question, Humphries went on, "My father took his degrees in biology and law. He bought into half a dozen biotech firms and built one of the biggest fortunes on Earth."

"What're your degrees in?"

"I have an MBA from Wharton and a JD from Yale."

"So you're a lawyer."

"I've never practiced law."

Pancho felt alarm signals tingling through her. That's not a straight answer, she realized. But then, what do you expect from a lawyer? She recalled the old dictum: How can you tell when a lawyer's lying? Watch his lips.

"What do you practice?" she asked, trying to make it sound nonchalant.

He smiled again, and there was even some warmth in it this time. "Oh...making money, mostly. That seems to be what I'm best at."

Glancing around the luxurious library, Pancho replied, "I'd say you're purty good at spendin' it, too."

Humphries laughed aloud. "Yes, I suppose so. I spend a lot of it on women."

As if on cue, a generously-curved redhead in a slinky metallic sheath appeared at the doorway to the dining room, a slim aperitif glass dangling empty from one manicured hand. "Say, Humpy, when is dinner served?" she asked poutily. "I'm starving."

His face went white with anger. "I told you," he said through clenched teeth, "that I have a business meeting to attend to. I'll be with you when I'm finished here."

"But I'm starving," the redhead repeated.

Glancing at Pancho, Humphries said in a low voice, "I'll be with you in a few minutes."

The redhead looked Pancho over from head to toe, grinned, and flounced off.

Visibly trying to contain his fury, Humphries said, "I'm sorry for the interruption."

Pancho shrugged. So I'm not invited for dinner, she realized. Should've known.

"Is that your wife?" she asked coolly.

"No."

"You are married, aren't you?"

"Twice."

"Are you married *now?*"

"Legally, yes. Our lawyers are working out a divorce settlement."

Pancho looked straight into his icy gray eyes. The anger was still there, but he was controlling it now. He seemed deadly calm.

"Okay," she said, "let's finish up this business meeting so y'all can get down to dinner."

Humphries picked up his glass again, drained it, and placed it carefully back on the bar. Looking up at Pancho, he said, "All right. I want to hire you."

"I already have a job," she said.

"As a pilot for Astro Manufacturing, I know. You've been working for them for more than six years."

"So?"

"You won't have to quit Astro. In fact, I want you to stay with them. The task I have in mind for you requires that you keep your position with Astro."

Pancho understood immediately. "You want me to spy on them."

"That's putting it rather crudely," Humphries said, his eyes shifting away from her and then back again. "But, yes, I need a certain amount of industrial espionage done, and you are ideally placed to do it."

Pancho didn't think twice. "How much money are we talkin' about here?"

Dan Randloph felt a wave of giddiness wash over him as he stood at his hotel window and looked down into the rugged gorge of the Júcar River.

This is stupid, he told himself. You've been in high-rises a lot taller than this. You've been on top of rocket launch towers. You've been to the Grand Canyon, you've done EVA work in orbit, for god's sake, floating hundreds of miles above the Earth without even an umbilical cord to hold onto.

Yet he felt shaky, slightly light-headed, as he stood by the window. It's not the height, he told himself. For a scary moment he thought it was one of the woozy symptoms of radiation sickness again. But then he realized that it was only because this hotel was hanging over the lip of the gorge, six stories down from the edge.

The old city of Cuenca had been built in medieval times along the rim of the deep, vertiginous chasm. From the street, the hotel seemed to be a one-story building, as did all the buildings along the narrow way. Inside, though, it went down and down, narrow stairways and long windows that looked out into the canyon cut by the river so far below.

Turning from the window, Dan went to the bed and unzipped his travel bag. He was here in the heart of Spain to find the answer to the world's overwhelming problem, the key to unlock the wealth of the solar system. Like a knight on a quest, he told himself, with a sardonic shake of his head. Seeking the holy grail.

Like a tired old man who's pushing himself because he doesn't have anything else left in his life, sneered a bitter voice in his head.

The flight in from Madrid had turned his thoughts to old tales of knighthood and chivalrous quests. The Clippership rocket flight from La Guaira had taken only twenty-five minutes to cross the Atlantic, but there was nothing to see, no portholes in the craft's stout body and the video views flashing across the screen at his seat might as well have been from an astronomy lecture. The flight from Madrid to Cuenca, though, had been in an old-fashioned tiltrotor, chugging and rattling and clattering across a landscape that was old when Hannibal had led armies through it.

Don Quixote rode across those brown hills, Dan had told himself. El Cid battled the Moors here.

He snorted disdainfully as he pulled his shaving kit from the travel bag. Now I'm going to see if we can win the fight against a giant bigger than any windmill that old Don Quixote tackled.

The phone buzzed. Dan snapped his fingers, then realized that the hotel phone wasn't programmed for sound recognition. He leaned across the bed and stabbed at the ON button.

"Mr. Randolph?"

The face Dan saw in the palm-sized phone screen looked almost Mephistophelean: thick black hair that came to a point almost touching his thick black brows; a narrow vee-shaped face with sharp cheekbones and a pointed chin; coal-black eyes that glittered slyly, as if the man knew things that no one else knew. A small black goatee.

"Yes," Dan answered. "And you are . . . ?"

"Lyall Duncan. I've come to take you to the test site," said the caller, in a decidedly Highland accent.

Dan puffed out a breath. They certainly aren't wasting any time. I'm not even unpacked yet.

"Are you ready, sir?" Duncan asked.

Dan tossed his shaving kit back onto the bed. "Ready," he said.

Duncan was short, rail-thin, and terribly earnest about his work. He talked incessantly as they drove in a dusty old Volkswagen van out into the sun-drenched countryside, past scraggly checkerboards of farms and terraced hillsides, climbing constantly toward the distant bare peaks of the Sierras. The land looked parched, poor, yet it had been under cultivation for thousands of years. At least, Dan thought, it's far enough from the sea to be safe from flooding. But it looks as if it's turning into a brown, dusty desert.

". . . tried for many a year to get someone to look at our work, *anyone*," Duncan was saying. "The universities were too busy with their big reactor projects, all of them sucking on one government teat or another. The private companies wouldn't even talk to us, not without some fancy university behind us."

Dan nodded and tried to stay awake. The man's soft Scottish burr was hypnotic as they drove along the winding highway into the hills. There were hardly any other cars on the road, and the hum of the tires on the blacktop was lulling Dan to sleep. Electric motors don't make much noise, he told himself, trying to fight off the jet lag. He remembered that auto makers such as GM and Toyota had tried to install sound systems that would simulate the *vroom* of a powerful gasoline engine, to attract the testosterone crowd. The GEC had nixed that; silent, efficient, clean electrical cars had to be presented as desirable, not as a weak second choice to muscle cars.

"...none of them wanted to see that a compact, lightweight, *disposable* fusion generator could work as well as the behemoths they were building," Duncan droned on. "No one paid us any attention until we caught the ear of Mr. Martin Humphries."

Dan perked up at the mention of Humphries's name. "How did you reach him? He's pretty high up in the corporate food chain."

Duncan smiled craftily. "Through a woman, how else? He came to Glasgow to give a speech. The anniversary of his father's endowment of the new biology building, or something of that sort. He took a fancy to a certain young lady in our student body. She was a biology major and had quite a body of her own."

With a laugh, Dan said, "So she did the Delilah job for you."

"One of the lads in our project knew her—in the biblical sense. He asked her if she'd help the cause of science."

"And she agreed."

"Willingly. 'Tisn't every day a lass from Birmingham gets to sleep with a billionaire."

"Oh, she was English?"

"Aye. We couldn't ask a Scottish lass to do such a thing."

Both men were still laughing as the car pulled into the test site's parking lot.

It wasn't much of a site, Dan thought as he got out of the car. Just a flat, open area of bare dirt with a couple of tin sheds to one side and a rickety-looking scaffolding beyond them. Rugged hills rose all around, and in the distance the Sierras shimmered ghostlike in the heat haze. The sun felt hot and good on his shoulders. The sky was a perfect blue, virtually cloudless. Dan inhaled a deep breath of clean mountain air; it was cool and sharp with a tang of pines that even got past his nose plugs. Dan thought about taking them out; it would be a relief to do without them. But he didn't remove them.

There were six people in the "office" shed, two of them women, all but one of them young, wearing shabby sweaters and slacks or jeans that hadn't known a crease for years. Dan felt overdressed in his tan slacks and suede sports jacket. One of the women was tall, with long, lank blond hair that fell past her broad shoulders. She looked like a California surfer type to Dan. Or maybe a Swede. The other was clearly Japanese or perhaps Korean: short and chunky, but when she smiled it lit up her whole face.

They all looked eager, excited to have Dan Randolph himself here to see their work, yet Dan caught a whiff of fear among them. Suppose it doesn't work today? Suppose something goes wrong? Suppose Randolph doesn't understand its value, its importance? Dan had felt that undercurrent in research labs all around the world; even on the Moon.

The one older man looked professorial. He wore baggy tweed trousers and a matching vest, unbuttoned. His long face was framed by a trim salt-and-pepper beard. Duncan introduced him as "Dr. Vertientes."

"I am delighted to meet you, sir," Dan said, automatically lapsing into Spanish as he took the man's hand.

Vertientes's brows rose with surprise. "You speak Spanish very well, sir."

"My headquarters is in Venezuela." Dan almost added that he'd once been married to a Venezuelan, but that had been too brief and too painful to bring into the conversation.

"We are a multinational group here," Vertientes said, switching to British English, overlaid with a Castilian accent. "We speak English among ourselves."

"Except when we curse," said the Japanese woman.

Everyone laughed.

Much to Dan's surprise, Duncan was the leader of the little group. The tall, distinguished Vertientes turned out to be the group's plasma physicist. Duncan was the propulsion engineer and the driving force among them.

"You know the principle of nuclear fusion," the Scotsman said as he led the entire group out of the office shack and toward the slightly larger shed that served as their laboratory.

Nodding, Dan said, "Four hydrogen atoms come together to form a helium atom and release energy."

"Nuclei," Duncan corrected. "Not atoms, their nuclei. The plasma is completely ionized."

"Yep. Right."

"Seven-tenths of one percent of the mass of the four original protons is converted into energy. The Sun and all the stars have been running for billions of years on that seven-tenths of one percent."

"As long as they're fusing hydrogen into helium," Dan said. To show that he wasn't entirely unlettered, he added, "Later on they start fusing helium into heavier elements."

Duncan gave him a sidelong glance from beneath his deep black brows, then said, "Aye, but it's only hydrogen fusion that we're interested in."

"Aye," Dan murmured.

The laboratory shed wasn't large, but the equipment in it seemed up-to-date. It looked more like a monitoring station to Dan's practiced eye than a research laboratory. Beyond it was a bigger building that couldn't be seen from the parking lot. The group trooped through the lab with only a perfunctory glance at its equipment, then went on to the other building.

"This is where the dirty work gets done," Duncan said, with his devilish grin.

Dan nodded as he looked around. It was a construction shack, all right. Machine tools and an overhead crane running on heavy steel tracks. The sharp tang of machine oil in the air, bits of wire and metal shavings littering the floor. Yes, they worked in here.

"And out there," Duncan said, pointing to a dust-caked window, "is the result."

It didn't look terribly impressive. Even when they stepped outside and walked up to the scaffolding, all Dan could see was a two-meter-wide metal sphere with a spaghetti factory of hoses and wires leading into it. The metal looked clean and shiny, though.

Dan rapped on it with his knuckles. "Stainless steel?"

Nodding, Duncan said, "For the outside pressure vessel. The containment sphere is a beryllium alloy."

"Beryllium?"

"The alloy is proprietary. We've applied for an international patent, but you know how long that takes."

Dan agreed glumly, then asked, "Is this all there is to it?"

With a fierce grin, Duncan said, "The best things come in the smallest packages."

They went back to the lab and, without a word, the six men and women took their stations along the bank of consoles that lined two walls of the shed. There was an assortment of chairs and stools, no two of them alike, but no one sat down. Dan saw that they were nervous, intense. All except Duncan, who looked calmly confident. He cocked a brow at Dan, like a gambler about to shuffle cards from the bottom of the deck.

"Are you ready to see wee beastie in action?" Duncan asked.

Tired from traveling, Dan pulled a little wheeled typist's chair to the middle of the floor and sat on it. Folding his arms across his chest, he nodded and said, "You may fire when ready, Gridley."

The others looked slightly puzzled, wondering who Gridley might be and what his significance was. Duncan, though, bobbed his head and grinned as though he understood everything.

He turned to Vertientes and said softly, "Start it up, then."

Dan heard a pump begin to chug and saw the readout

numbers on Vertientes's console start to climb. The other consoles came to life, display screens flickering on to show multi-colored graphs or digital readouts.

"Pressure approaching optimum," sang out the blonde. "Density on the curve."

"Fuel cells on line."

"Capacitor bank ready."

Duncan stood beside Dan, sweeping all the consoles with his eyes.

"Approaching ignition point," said Vertientes.

Leaning slightly toward Dan, Duncan said, "It's set to ignite automatically, although we have the manual backup ready."

Dan got to his feet and stared out the window at the stainless steel sphere out in the scaffold. There was a crackling air of tension in the lab now; he could feel the hairs on the back of his neck rising.

"Ignition!" Vertientes called.

Dan saw nothing. The metal sphere outside didn't move. There was no roar or cloud of smoke, not even a vibration. He looked at Duncan, then over to the six others, all of them standing rigidly intent at their consoles. Numbers flickered across screens, curves crawled along graphs, but as far as Dan could see or feel nothing was actually happening.

"Shutdown," Vertientes said.

Everyone relaxed, sagged back a bit, let out their breaths.

"Thirty seconds, on the tick," someone said.

"Power output?" Duncan asked.

"Design maximum. It reached fifty megawatts after four seconds and held it there right to cutoff."

Vertientes was beaming. He turned and clutched Duncan by both shoulders. "Perfecto! She is a well-behaved little lady!"

"You mean that's it?" Dan asked, incredulous.

Duncan was grinning too. They all were.

"But nothing happened," Dan insisted.

"Oh no?" said Duncan, grasping Dan's elbow and turning him toward the row of consoles. "Look at that power output graph."

Frowning, Dan remembered a scientist once telling him that all of physics boiled down to reading a bloody gauge.

"But it didn't go anywhere," Dan said weakly.

They all laughed.

"It isn't a rocket," Duncan said. "Not yet. We're only testing the fusion reactor."

"Only!" said the Japanese woman.

"Thirty seconds isn't much of a test," Dan pointed out.

"Nay, thirty seconds is plenty of time," Duncan rebutted.

"The plasma equilibrates in five seconds or less," said Vertientes.

"But to be useful as a rocket," Dan insisted, "the reactor's going to have to run for hours...even weeks or months."

"Si, yes, we know," Vertientes said, tapping a finger into the palm of his other hand. "But in thirty seconds we get enough data to calculate the heat transfer and plasma flow parameters. We can extrapolate to hours and weeks and months."

"I don't trust extrapolations," Dan muttered.

The blonde stepped between them. "Well, of *course* we're going to build a full-scale model and run it for months. For sure. But what Doc Vee is saying is we've done enough testing to be confident that it'll work."

Dan looked her over. California, he decided. Maybe Swedish ancestry, but definitely California.

"We intend to mate the reactor with an MHD generator," Vertientes said, earnestly trying to convince Dan. "That way the plasma exhaust from the reactor can provide electrical power as well as thrust."

"Magneto..." Dan stumbled over the word.

"Magnetohydrodynamic," Vertientes finished for him.

The blonde added, "The interaction of electrically-conducting ionized gases with magnetic fields."

Dan grinned at her. "Thank you." She's showing off, he thought. She wants me to know that she's a *smart* blonde, despite her surfer chick looks.

Then he caught Duncan watching him with that sly look in his glittering coal-black eyes, and remembered the student from Birmingham who had convinced Humphries to pay attention to their work. He shook his head ever so slightly, to tell Duncan that he wouldn't need to be convinced that way.

Once he would have scooped up a young available woman and enjoyed every minute of their brief fling together. But not now. He grimaced inwardly at the weird curves fate throws. When Jane was alive I chased every woman I saw, trying to forget her. Now that she's dead I don't want anyone else. Not now. Maybe not ever again.

D on't you intend ever to return to Earth?"
Martin Humphries leaned back in his exquisitely padded reclining chair and tried to hide the dread he felt as he gazed at his father's image on the wall screen.
"I'm working hard here, Dad," he said.

It takes almost three seconds for radio or light waves to make the round-trip between the Earth and the Moon. Martin Humphries used the time to study his father's sallow, wrinkled, sagging face. Even though the old man had made his fortune in biotech, he still refused rejuvenation treatments as "too new, too risky, too many unknowns." Yet he wore a snow-white toupee to hide his baldness. It made Martin think of George Washington, although George was alleged never to have told a lie and anyone who had ever dealt with W. Wilson Humphries knew that you had to count your fingers after shaking hands with the old scoundrel.

"I need you here," his father admitted grudgingly.

"*You* need *me?*"

"Those bastards from the New Morality are pushing more tax regulations through the Congress. They won't be satisfied until they've bankrupted every corporation in the country."

"All the more reason for me to stay here," Martin replied, "where I can protect my assets."

"But what about *my* assets? What about me? I need your help, Marty. I can't fight these psalm-singing fundamentalists by myself!"

"Oh, come on, Dad. You've got more lawyers than they do."

"They've got the whole damned Congress," his father grumbled. "And the Supreme Court, too."

"Dad, if you'd just come up here you'd be able to get away from all that."

His father's face hardened. "I'm not going to run away!"

"It's time to admit that the ship is sinking, Dad. Time to get out, while you can. Up here on the Moon I'm building a whole new organization. I'm creating Humphries Space Systems. You could be part of it; an important part."

The old man glared at him for much longer than it took his son's words to reach him. At last he growled, "If you stay up there too long your muscles will get so deconditioned you won't be able to come back to Earth."

He hasn't heard a word I've said, Humphries realized. He talks and he never listens.

"Dad, I'm in the middle of a very complicated deal here. I can't leave. Not now." He hesitated, then said, "I might never come back to Earth."

Once he heard that reply, his father's image went from its normal unhappy scowl to a truly angry frown. "I want you here, dammit! This is where you belong and this is where you're going to be. That's final."

"Father," said Martin, feeling all the old fear and frustration swirling inside him like a whirlpool pulling him down, drowning him. "Father, come here, come be with me. Please. Before it's too late."

His father merely glowered at him.

"Give it up, Dad," Humphries pleaded. "Earth is finished. Everything down there is going to crash; can't you understand that?"

The old man sputtered, "Dammit, Marty, if you don't listen to me . . ." He faltered, stopped, not knowing what to say next.

"Why can't you listen to me for a change?" Martin snapped. Without waiting for a response, he said, "I'm trying to build an empire up here, Dad, an empire that's going to stretch all the way out to the Asteroid Belt and beyond. I'm putting the pieces together right now. I'm going to be the wealthiest man in the solar system, richer than you and all your brothers put together. Maybe then you'll treat me with some respect."

Before his father could reply, Humphries sat up in his recliner and pressed the stud set into the armrest to terminate the videophone link. The old man's face disappeared from the wall, revealing a holowindow that showed a realtime view of Jupiter as seen by the twenty-meter telescope at the Farside Observatory.

For a long moment Humphries simply sat there, alone in the office he had set up for himself in the house deep below the lunar surface. Then he took a long slow breath to calm the furies that raged inside him. The old man has no understanding of the real world. He's still living in the past. He'd rather go down with the ship than admit that I'm right and he's wrong.

Unbidden, the memory of his drowning engulfed him again. Nine years old. His father insisting that the trimaran was in no trouble despite the dark storm winds that heaved the boat so monstrously. The wave that washed him overboard. The frothing water closing over him. Desperately clawing for the surface but sinking, sinking, can't breathe, everything going dark.

Martin Humphries died at the age of nine. After they revived him, he learned that it had been one of the crew who'd dived into the sound to rescue him. Watching the boy sink out of sight, his father had stayed aboard the trimaran and offered a bonus to any crewman who could rescue his son. Form that moment on, Humphries knew that there was no one in the world he could trust; he was alone, with only his inner fears and yearnings to drive him. And only his money to protect him.

Talking with his father always brought those terrible moments back to mind. And the gasping, choking paralysis that clamped his chest like a merciless vise. He reached into the top desk drawer for his inhalator and took a desperate whiff of the cool, soothing drug.

All right, Humphries thought, waiting for his breathing to return to normal, trying to calm himself. He's going to stay down there and try to fight the New Morality until they burn him at the stake. Nothing I say will budge him a millimeter. Very well, then.

I'll stay here in Selene where it's safe and everything's under control. No storms, no rain; a world built to suit me in every detail. From here I can pull the strings just as effectively as if I were down in New York or London. Better, really. There's no reason for me to go Earthside anymore.

Except for the divorce hearing, he remembered. I'm supposed to show up in the judge's chambers for that. But I can do even that from here, get my lawyers to make the excuse that I can't return to Earth, I've been on the Moon too long, it would be dangerous to my health. I can get a dozen doctors to testify to that. No sweat.

Humphries laughed aloud. I won't have to be in the same room with that bitch! Good! Wonderful!

He leaned back again and stared up at the ceiling. It was set to a planetarium display, the sky as it appeared above Selene. Briefly he thought about calling up a porno video, but decided instead to put on the latest informational release from the International Astronautical Authority about the microprobes searching through the asteroids in the Belt.

The IAA's motivation for investigating the asteroids was to locate rocks that might one day hit the Earth. They had good tracks on all the hundreds of asteroids in orbits that brought them close. Now they were sorting through the thousands of rocks out in the Belt big enough to cause serious damage if they were ejected from the Belt and impacted Earth.

The good news was that so far they had not found any asteroid in an orbit that threatened the homeworld—although the asteroids in the Belt were always being jostled by Jupiter and the other planets, perturbing their orbits unpredictably. A constant watch was a vital necessity.

The better news was that, as a byproduct of the impacter watch, the IAA was getting detailed data on the composition of the larger asteroids. Iron, carbon, nickel, phosphorus, nitrogen, gold, silver, platinum, even water was out there in vast abundance. Ripe for picking. Waiting for me to turn them into money, Humphries told himself, smiling happily.

Dan Randolph will send a team out to the Belt on a fusion rocket. The first mission will fail, of course, and then I'll have Randolph where I want him. I'll take control of Astro Corporation and we can put Randolph out to pasture, where he belongs.

Then a thought clouded his satisfaction. It's been damned near six months since I hired Pancho Lane to keep an eye on Randolph. Why haven't I heard from her?

A ren't you nervous?" Amanda Cunningham asked.

Sitting beside her as the Clippership returned to Earth, Pancho shook her head. "Nope. You?"

"A bit."

"Uh-huh."

"I mean . . . meeting the head of the corporation. It's rather exciting, don't you think?"

Pancho and Amanda had been summoned to Astro Manufacturing's corporate headquarters in La Guaira, on an island across the strait from Caracas. Something about a new assignment that Dan Randolph himself would decide.

"Well, meeting the big boss is important, I guess," Pancho said as nonchalantly as she could manage.

They were riding the Clippership down from the aging space station *Nueva Venezuela* to the landing field at La Guaira, riding comfortably in the nearly empty passenger cabin with a sparse handful of paying customers rather than in the cramped cockpit where the crew worked. Amanda reveled in the luxury of spacious seats and entertainment videos; Pancho figured that something important was waiting for them when they landed, something important enough for Astro to undergo the expense of letting them ride deadhead from Selene.

Well, she said to herself, the pilots up in the cockpit are really deadheading, too. Clipperships flew under control from the ground; they didn't need an onboard crew any more than a ballistic missile did. But even after all these years—decades, really—the politicians refused to allow spacecraft that carried passengers to fly fully automated. The pilots had to go along; there had to be a cockpit and full controls for them even though they had absolutely nothing to do.

Don't complain, she said to herself. If the aerospace lines didn't need to hire pilots you wouldn't have gotten a job in the first place. You'd still be sitting in front of a display screen in some cubicle back in Lubbock doing tech support and barely making enough money to keep Sis alive.

Amanda was flicking through the entertainment channels, eyes locked on her little pop-up screen. Pancho eased back in the comfortable passenger's chair and closed her eyes.

Why me? she asked herself. Why has the CEO of Astro Manufacturing called me all the way back from Selene to see him in person? Amanda I can understand. One look at her ID vid and the Big Boss prob'ly started panting like a dog in heat. Still, in the six months since they'd first met, Pancho had acquired a healthy respect for Amanda's piloting skills, boobs notwithstanding. This is her first job and she's already as good as I am . . . well, almost. I'm the best pilot Astro's got, flat out, but what's that got to do with seeing the CEO? Why does he want to see me?

Does Humphries have anything to do with this? He wants me to spy on Astro, which means he prob'ly wants me to spy on Randolph himself. So maybe he's worked things out so's

I get to see Randolph face-to-face. Is Humphries pulling strings inside Randolph's own company?

It never occurred to Pancho that Dan Randolph wanted to see her for reasons of his own.

The Clippership rode smoothly through re-entry, with only a few moments of turbulence as it plunged into the Earth's atmosphere like a squat, cone-shaped meteor, plummeting so fast that the very air outside the craft heated to incandescence. We're a falling star, Pancho told herself as she sat tightly buckled into her seat while the ship shuddered and jounced. She could hear the muted howl of the tortured air on the other side of the hull, mere centimeters from her seat. A falling star. Some kid down there's prob'ly making a wish on our trail.

The shaking and banshee wail of re-entry ended swiftly and the flight smoothed out.

"We'll be landing in four minutes," the captain's rich baritone voice announced over the intercom. "Don't be alarmed by all the banging and roaring. It's just the retrorockets and the landing struts deploying."

Pancho smiled. That's what we need the crew for: reassuring announcements.

It felt as if they were falling until the retros fired briefly, pushing Pancho deep into her seat. Another drop, so short she barely had time to feel it before the retros roared out a longer blast. Then everything went silent and still.

"We're on the ground," the captain said, sounding relieved.

Pancho had expected that she and Amanda would be sent directly to Randolph's office for their interview with the CEO, or at least to the personnel department for a briefing on what they should expect. Instead, once they cleared the access tunnel they were met in the terminal by a good-looking young Latino in a business suit who led them out to the garage and a sleek-looking sedan.

"Your luggage is being picked up and will be waiting for you in your quarters at the corporate housing center," he said in impeccable American English, opening the car's rear door for the two women.

As she and Amanda got into the back seat, Pancho saw there was a driver sitting behind the wheel. The young man slid in beside him.

She grinned. "What, no limo?"

The young man half-turned in his seat and said quite seriously, "Mr. Randolph doesn't believe in unnecessary frills. This is comfortable enough, isn't it?"

"Quite," said Amanda.

By the time they got to the test site Amanda had set up a dinner date for herself with their handsome young escort.

The test site was on the shoulder of a green hillside that sloped down into the warm Caribbean. Late afternoon sunshine slanted down from between massive cumulus clouds that were visibly growing, boiling up into towering thunderheads, getting darker and more menacing by the minute. Pancho smelled the salt tang in the air, heard the surf rolling in gently below, felt the warm steady breeze on her face. A tropical paradise, she thought.

Or it would be, if it weren't for all that danged hardware squatting in the middle of the field.

Following their Latino escort, they walked from the car to the small knot of people standing around what looked like a set of man-tall dewar flasks crusted with frost, a small crane, lots of plumbing and tubing, a medium-sized truck carrying what looked like a pair of major-league fuel cells on its bed, a smaller truck loaded with a bank of capacitors, and a corrugated-metal shed off to one side. Several automobiles and semivans were parked on the other side of the shed.

As they got closer, Pancho saw that the people were gathered around a small swept-winged aircraft that was resting on a pair of skids. It was an ancient cruise missile, she saw, an unmanned jet airplane. She knew they'd been outlawed by the disarmament treaties. Only the Peacekeepers had such weapons, and this one looked too old to be a Peacekeeper missile. The markings on it were faded, the serial number stenciled on its tail barely legible.

Before she could ask a question, a trim-looking man with silver hair and a rugged fighter's face stepped out of the crowd around the missile. He wore a light tan windbreaker zippered to the throat despite the warm sunshine, a baseball cap perched jauntily on his head, well-faded jeans, and cowboy boots. Their escort stiffened almost like a soldier coming to attention.

"Señor Randolph," he said, "may I introduce—"

"You must be Amanda Cunningham," said Dan Randolph, with a crooked smile. He put his hand out and Amanda took it briefly. "I'm Dan Randolph."

Then he turned to Pancho. "And you've got to be Priscilla Lane."

"Pancho," she corrected, taking his extended hand. His grip was firm, friendly. "Priscilla's too fussy, and anybody calls me Pru or Prissy, I'll belt him."

"Pancho," Randolph said, his smile widening. "I'll remember that."

"What's this all about?" Pancho asked. "Why've you brought us here?"

Randolph's eyes showed momentary surprise at her bluntness, but then he shrugged and said, "You're going to see some history being made...if this double-damned jury-rigged kludge works right."

He introduced Amanda and Pancho to Lyall Duncan and the others gathered around the missile. Almost all of them were male, engineers or technicians. One of the women was a tall blonde; competition for Amanda, Pancho thought. Duncan looked like a fierce little gnome, or maybe a troll, even when he smiled.

Puzzled, intrigued, Pancho allowed Randolph to usher her and Amanda to the shed. It was packed with instruments and consoles and one rickety-looking desk with a lopsided chair in front of it.

"You just stay here and watch," he said, with a curious grin. "If it works, you'll be witnesses. If it blows up, this ought to be far enough away to keep you from getting hurt."

The dark-haired troll called Duncan chuckled. "Experimental physics, you know. Always the chance of an explosion."

The crane was on its own caterpillar tractor. A pair of technicians used it to hoist the missile off the ground and trundle it out almost half a kilometer. They put the missile gently onto the grassy ground, pointing into the wind blowing steadily in from the sea.

Consoles were coming to life in the shed. Engineers were speaking to each other in their clipped jargon. Pancho watched Randolph. The man seemed outwardly relaxed as he stood with both hands jammed into his windbreaker pockets, watching the missile while the crane waddled back toward them.

Duncan buzzed around the shed like a bee in a flower bed. The tension built up; Pancho could feel it radiating from the backs of the crew standing by the consoles.

"Do you think it's going to rain?" Amanda whispered.

Pancho looked up at the looming thunderheads. "Sooner or later."

At last Duncan said to Randolph, "We're ready to launch."

"Okay," said Randolph. "Do it before it starts pouring."

Duncan said crisply, "Launch!"

Pancho turned her attention to the missile sitting out on the grass. For a moment nothing happened, but then its tail-end spurted flame and it lurched forward. Just as she heard the whining scream of the jet engine, another sound cut in: a deeper, more powerful roar. The missile leaped off the ground, angling sharply toward the cloud-filled sky, trailing a billow of smoke.

Something fell away from the climbing missile. A rocket pack, Pancho realized. They used it to get the bird off the ground.

The plane levelled off a scant hundred meters in the air and circled the field once.

"Nominal flight," one of the engineers called out.

"Fusion drive ready?" Duncan asked.

"Primed and ready."

"Light it."

The missile seemed to falter for a moment, as if it had stalled in mid-air. Pancho saw the slightly smoky exhaust wink out, heard the jet engine's screech die away. The missile glided for several moments, losing altitude.

Then it seemed to bite into the air, raising its nose and climbing steeply upward as it howled a thin, screeching ethereal wail.

"Programmed flight trajectory," Pancho heard someone call out. "On the money."

The bird flew out to sea until it was a barely visible speck, then turned back and rushed toward them, climbing almost to the base of the thunderheads, its ghostly wail barely audible, streaking past, heading inland. Then it turned again and headed seaward once more. Racetrack course, Pancho realized.

Lightning was flickering in the clouds now.

"Coming up on the two-minute mark," said one of the engineers. "*Mark!* Two minutes."

"Bring her in," Duncan commanded.

"Automatic trajectory," came the answer.

Pancho watched as the missile turned back toward them once again, dropped its flaps, slowed, and gracefully descended for a landing out in the area where it had taken off.

The grass was scorched out there from the takeoff rocket's hot exhaust.

Turning slightly, she saw that Randolph was standing just outside the door, eyes riveted to the approaching missile, mouth slightly open, fists clenched.

The missile was still moving fast when it touched the ground, bounced into the air again, wobbled back to the ground, and then plowed nose-first into the dirt, throwing a spray of grass clods and pebbles as it flipped over onto its back and banged down so hard one of the wings tore off. It sounded like a junkyard falling out of the sky.

But the engineers and technicians were all cheering, jumping up and down, pounding each other on the back, yelling and waving like a team that had just scored a gold medal in the Olympics. Randolph yanked off his cap and pegged it out toward the sea.

"Och, what a divot!" Duncan shouted. He raced through the open door to Randolph and launched himself into the older man's arms, wrapping his legs around Randolph's middle. Randolph staggered backward and they fell to the ground together, laughing like maniacs.

Pancho looked at Amanda. She seemed just as puzzled as Pancho felt.

With a shrug, Pancho said, "I guess any landing you can walk away from is a good landing."

Amanda shook her head. "I shouldn't think you'd walk away from that one if you'd been aboard it."

Randolph was disentangling himself from Duncan and getting to his feet. Brushing dirt from his windbreaker, grinning hugely, he walked over to Amanda and Pancho while Duncan scampered toward the shed.

"It works!" Randolph said. "You've just witnessed history, ladies. The first actual flight of a fusion-powered vehicle."

"Fusion?" Pancho gaped at him. "You mean that little bird had a fusion engine on her?"

Amanda said, "But I thought fusion generators were great immense things, like power stations."

Duncan raced back to them, waving a dark bottle in one hand. The rest of the crew gathered around. Pancho wondered why no one went to the poor little aircraft, smashed and crumpled on the grass.

Someone produced paper cups and Duncan began to splash liquor into them. At first Pancho thought it was champagne, but the bottle wasn't the right shape. Scotch, she realized. Scotland's gift to the world.

"Hey," said Randolph, "I need some ice with this."

Duncan actually shuddered. "Ice? With good whisky? You Americans!"

Pancho took a sip of hers, neat. "Wow!" she managed to gasp.

"To the Duncan Drive," Randolph toasted, lifting his paper cup.

"To the stars!" Duncan countered. "We'll ride this engine to Alpha Centauri one day!"

Randolph laughed. "The Asteroid Belt will be far enough, for now."

A couple of the men quaffed their drinks down in one gulp, then trotted out toward the wrecked cruise missile. Others headed for the shed.

"Check the cameras, too," Duncan called after them.

Pancho asked Randolph again, "That little ship has a fusion engine in it?"

Nodding, Randolph replied, "In place of its warhead."

"The engine's that small?"

"It's only a wee test engine," said Duncan. "Just to prove that it can provide controllable thrust."

"Now we can build one big enough to carry a real payload to the Belt," Randolph said.

"Once you raise the money," added Duncan.

With a glance at Amanda, Pancho asked Randolph, "But

why did you bring Mandy and me out here? Just to have a couple more witnesses?"

His grin growing even wider, Randolph answered, "Hell no. I wanted you to see this because you two are gong to pilot the first fusion rocket to the Asteroid Belt."

The Yamagata family estate was set on a rugged hillside high above the office towers and apartment blocks of New Kyoto. Built like a medieval Japanese fortress, the solid yet graceful buildings always made Dan think of poetry frozen into shapes of wood and stone. It had suffered extensive damage in the earthquakes, Dan knew, but he could see no sign of it. The repairs had flawlessly matched the original structures.

Much of the inner courtyard was given to an exquisitely maintained sand garden. There were green vistas at every turn, as well: gardens and woods and, off in the distance, a glimpse through tall old trees of Lake Biwa, glittering in the late afternoon sun.

The tiltrotor plane settled down, turbines screeching, in the outer courtyard. Dan pulled off his sanitary mask and unbuckled his safety belt. He was through the hatch before the pilot was able to stop the rotors. Squinting through the dust kicked up by the downwash, Dan saw Nobuhiko Yamagata waiting at the gate to the inner courtyard, wearing a comfortable kimono of deep blue decorated with white herons, the Yamagata family's emblem.

For an instant Dan thought he was seeing Saito Yamagata, Nobuhiko's father, the man who had been Dan's boss in the old days when Randolph had been a construction engineer on the first Japanese solar power satellite. Nobo had been ascetically slim when he was younger, but now his face and body had filled out considerably. He was tall, though, some thirty centimeters taller than his father had been, even several centimeters taller than Dan himself.

The two men bowed simultaneously, then grasped each other's shoulders.

"By damn, Nobo, it's good to see you."

"And you," Nobuhiko replied, smiling broadly. "It's been much too long since you've visited here." His voice was deep, strong, assured.

"You're looking well," Dan said as Yamagata led him past the flowering shrubbery of the inner courtyard, toward the wing of the old stone and wood house where the family lived.

"I'm too fat and I know it," Nobo said, patting his belly. "Too many hours behind a desk, not enough exercise."

Dan made a sympathetic noise.

"I'm thinking of taking a trip to Selene for a nanotherapy session."

"Aw, come on, Nobo," Dan said, "it's not that bad."

"My doctors nag me constantly."

"That's what the double-damned doctors always do. They learn it in medical school. No matter how healthy you are, they always find something to worry you about."

They walked along a winding path of stones set across the middle of the carefully-raked sand garden. Dan noticed the miniature olive tree off in one corner of the garden that he had given Nobo's father many years earlier. It looked green and healthy. Before the greenhouse cliff had struck, even in

June the tree would have been covered by a heated transparent plastic dome to protect it from the occasional frost. Now the winters were mild enough to leave the tree in the open all year long.

"What's your father's status?" Dan asked as they removed their shoes at the open door to the main house. Two servants stood silently just inside the door, both women, both in carnelian-red robes.

Nobuhiko grimaced as they walked down the hallway lined with shoji screens.

"The medical researchers have removed the tumor and cleaned father's body of all traces of cancerous cells. They are ready to begin the revival sequence."

"That can be tricky," Dan said.

Ten years earlier, Saito Yamagata had had himself declared clinically dead and then frozen in liquid nitrogen, preserved cryonically to await the day when his cancer could be cured and he would be revived.

"Others have been thawed successfully," Nobo said as they entered a spacious bedroom. It was paneled in teak, with bare floors of bleached pine, and furnished sparely: a western-style bed, a desk in the opposite corner, two comfortable-looking recliner chairs. One wall consisted of sliding shoji screens; Dan figured they covered a closet, built-in drawers, and the lavatory. Dan saw that his one travel bag had already been placed on a folding stand at the foot of the bed.

"Still," he said, "thawing must be pretty dicey."

Yamagata turned to face him, and Dan saw Saito's calm brown eyes, the certainty, the power that a long lineage of wealth and privilege can bring to a man.

"We have followed the research work very thoroughly," Nobo said. He smiled slightly. "We have sponsored much of the work ourselves, of course. It seems that Father could be revived."

"That's great!" Dan blurted. "Sai will be back with us—"

Nobuhiko raised a hand. "Two problems, Dan."

"What?"

"First, there are very strong political forces opposing revival of any cryonically-preserved person."

"Opposing . . . oh, for the love of Peter, Paul, and Peewee Reese. The New Morality strikes again."

"Here in Japan it's an offshoot of the New Dao movement. They call themselves the Flowers of the Sun."

"Flowers of crackpots," Dan grumbled.

"They have a considerable amount of political power. Enough to get nanotechnology banned in Japan, just as your New Morality people got it banned in the States."

"And now they're against reviving corpsicles?"

A reluctant grin cracked Yamagata's solemn expression. "Delicately put, Dan. My father is a corpsicle."

Waving a hand, Dan said, "You know I don't mean any disrespect."

"I know," Nobuhiko admitted. "But the unhappy fact is that these Flowers of the Sun are attempting to pass a law through the Diet that would forbid cryonics altogether and make it a crime to attempt to revive a frozen body."

"Why, for god's sake? On what grounds?"

Nobuhiko shrugged. "They say the resources should be spent in rebuilding our ravaged cities. They say that we don't need rich old people to be brought back among us, what we need are healthy young people who can work hard to rebuild Japan."

"Bullcrap," Dan muttered. Then he brightened. "Hey, I know how you can get around them! Fly your father up to Selene. They'll revive him there. They can even use nanomachines if they have to."

Nobo sat on the bed, his shoulders sagging. "I've thought of that, Dan. I'm tempted to do it, especially before the government bars removal of frozen bodies from the country."

"They can't do that!"

"They will, before the next session of the Diet is over."

"Goddammit to hell and back!" Dan shouted, pounding his fist into his palm. "Has the whole stupid world gone crazy?"

"There's something else," Nobo said, his voice barely above a whisper. "Something worse."

"What on earth could be worse?"

"The people who have been revived. Their minds are gone."

"Gone? What do you mean?"

With a helpless spread of his hands, Nobuhiko repeated, "Gone. The body can be revived, but apparently the freezing process wipes out the brain's memory system. Those we've revived are mentally like newborns. They even have to be toilet trained all over again."

Dan sank into one of the plush recliners. "You mean Sai's mind . . . his personality . . . gone?"

"That's what we fear. Apparently the neural connections in the brain break down when the body is frozen. The mind comes out a virtual *tabula rasa*."

"Shit," Dan muttered.

"We have our research scientists working on the problem, of course, but there's no point to reviving my father until we know definitely, one way or the other, how his mind has been affected by the freezing."

Dan hunched forward, forearms on his thighs. "Okay. I understand now. But get Sai's body to Selene. Now! Before these religious fanatics make it impossible to move him."

Nobuhiko nodded grimly. "I believe you're right, Dan. I've felt that way myself for some weeks now, but I'm glad that you agree."

"I'm heading up to Selene next week," Dan said. "If you like, I'll take him with me."

"That's very good of you, but this is a family matter. I'll take care of it."

Dan nodded. "Okay. But if you need any help—anything at all, just let me know."

Nobuhiko smiled again, and for the first time there was real warmth in it. "I will, Dan. I certainly will."

"Good."

The younger man rubbed at his eyes, then looked up at Dan again. "Very well, I've told you my problem. Now tell me yours. What brings you here?"

Dan grinned at him. "Oh, nothing much. I just need a couple of billion dollars."

Nobo's face remained completely impassive for a long moment. Then he said, "Is that all?"

"Yep. Two bill should do it."

"And what do I get in return for such an investment?"

With a chuckle, Dan replied, "A bunch of rocks."

LA GUAIRA

Pancho looked up, bleary-eyed, from her desktop screen. Across the room that she and Amanda were sharing, Mandy sat at her desk with virtual reality glasses and earphones covering half her face, peering intently at her own screen.

"I'm goin' for a walk," she said, loudly enough to get through Mandy's earphones.

Amanda nodded without taking off the VR glasses. Pancho squinted at the screen, but it was nothing but a jumble of alphanumerics. Whatever Mandy was studying was displayed on her glasses, not the computer screen.

Their dorm room opened directly onto the patio. Cripes, it's almost sundown, Pancho saw as she stepped outside. The late afternoon was still tropically warm, humid, especially after the air-conditioned cool of their quarters.

Pancho stretched her long arms up toward the cloud-flecked sky, trying to work out the knots in her back. Been settin' at that stupid ol' desk too damned long, she said to herself. Mandy can sit there and study till hell freezes over. She's like a dog-ass computer, just absorbing data like a friggin' machine.

Dan Randolph had put them to studying the fusion drive and working with the engineering team that was converting a lunar transfer buggy into the ship that would carry them out to the Belt. They saw Randolph rarely. The man was jumping all across the world like a flea on a hot griddle, hardly ever in the same place more than one night. When he was in La Guaira he drove the whole team hard, and himself hardest of all.

Peculiar place for a corporate headquarters, Pancho thought as she walked from the housing complex out past the swaying, rustling palm trees, toward the seawall. La Guaira was more suited to being a tourist resort than a major space launching center. Randolph had settled his Astro Manufacturing headquarters here years ago, partly because its location near the equator gave rockets a little extra boost from the Earth's spin, partly because he found the government of Venezuela easier to deal with than the suits in Washington.

Strange, though. Randolph was rumored to have been in love with President Scanwell. There were whispers about their being lovers, off and on, a stormy romance that only ended when the ex-President lost her life in the big Tennessee Valley earthquake.

It all seemed so far away. Pancho followed the winding path toward the seawall, her softboots crunching on the gravel. The Sun was just about touching the horizon, turning the Caribbean reddish gold. Massive clouds were piling up, turning purple and crimson in the underlighting. With the breeze coming off the sea, making the palms bow gracefully, this was as close to a tropical paradise as she could imagine.

But the seawall reminded her of a harsher reality. It was shoulder high, an ugly reinforced concrete barrier against the encroaching waters. It had originally been painted a pastel pink, but the paint had faded in the sun, and the concrete was crumbling here and there where storm tides had pounded against it. The old beaches were all underwater now, except at the very lowest tides. The surf broke out there, long combers tumbling and frothing with a steady, ceaseless growling hiss. And still the sea was rising, a little bit more every year.

"Looks pretty, doesn't it?"

Startled, she turned to see Randolph standing there, looking glumly out to sea. He was wearing a wrinkled white shirt and dark slacks that had gone baggy from long hours of travel.

"Didn't see you coming up the path, boss," said Pancho. "Come to think of it, I didn't even hear you on the gravel."

"I walked on the grass," Randolph said, quite seriously. "Stealth is my middle name."

Pancho laughed.

But Randolph said gloomily, "When Greenland melts down this will all go under."

"The whole island?"

"Every damned bit of it. Maybe some of the gantry towers will stick up above the surface. The hilltops. Not much else."

"Cripes."

"This used to be part of the mainland, you know. When I first brought the company here, that strait cutting us off from the hills didn't exist. The sea level's gone up that much in less than twenty years."

"And it's still goin' up," Pancho said.

Randolph nodded gloomily, then leaned his arms on the shoulder-high seawall and propped his chin on them.

"How's the job going?" he asked.

"We're workin' at it," she replied. "It's a lot to learn, all this fusion stuff."

With a tired nod, he said, "Yeah, but you've got to know every bit of it, Pancho. If anything breaks down out there, you've got to be able to diagnose it and fix it."

"We'll have an engineer on board," she said. "Won't we?"

"Maybe. But whether you do or not, *you've* got to know everything there is to know about the systems."

"Yeah. I guess."

"And you've got to get the new navigational technique down, too," he added.

"Point and shoot, yeah. Kinda weird."

With the thrust and efficiency of the fusion rocket, their spacecraft did not have to travel in an energy-conserving ellipse from Earth orbit to the Belt. Fusion-driven trajectories were almost straight lines: travel times would be days instead of months.

"It's a lot to learn, I know," Randolph said.

She saw the weariness in his eyes, and yet there was something else in them, something more. Hope, she thought. Or maybe just plain mulish stubbornness. He wants to make this fusion ship work. And he's trusting me to drive it. Me and Mandy.

"We could use a weekend off," she said. "Or even a night on the town."

The sun had sunk behind the mainland's mountains. They could see the lights on the mainland beginning to wink on.

"Sorry, kid, no can do," Randolph said. He started walking along the seawall. "I told you when you agreed to take this assignment, you stay here in the complex."

"Security, yeah, I know," Pancho said, following him.

"Your own security, too," Randolph said. "Not just the company's. You're very valuable now. You and Amanda are crucial to this entire operation. I don't want you running any risks."

Pancho thought it over. He's trusting us with this whole operation, right enough. Can't blame him for being careful. Still . . .

She looked across the strait again at the lights of the city. Then a new thought struck her. Does he know I'm supposed to be snooping on him? Is he keeping us bottled up here so's I can't get in touch with Humphries?

"Can I ask you somethin'?"

Randolph smiled tiredly at her in the fading light. "Sure, go right ahead."

"I've heard rumbles that you were—well, that Astro's got money problems."

Randolph hesitated a moment. Then, "Corporations always have money problems."

"I mean, like, you're purty close to broke."

"Pretty close," he admitted.

"Then why're you sinkin' all this money into the fusion ship?"

The light was dying fast. Pancho could barely see his face. But she heard the determination in his voice.

"Two reasons, kid," he said. "First, if it works, Astro can get first licks at the Belt. Our stock will zoom up, our profits will skyrocket, and the only money problem I'll have is how to spend all the cash flowing in."

Pancho said nothing, waiting for his second reason.

"And also," Randolph went on, "opening up the Belt is crucial for the human race's survival."

"You really think so?"

He stopped walking and turned toward her. "We can't take much more of this climate warming, Pancho. Millions have died already, tens of millions. But the worst is yet to come. If Greenland goes—"

"And Antarctica," she interjected.

"And Antarctica," he agreed. "If they melt down, civilization drowns. Billions will die, not just from the floods but from starvation and disease. We can't support the Earth's population now, for god's sake! There's famine in half the world, and it's getting worse, not better."

"You think the asteroids can help?"

"We need those natural resources. We have to rebuild our industrial base, rebuild our wealth."

"In space."

"Yep. Where we should've been building for the past half-century."

Pancho made a low whistle. "That's a big order, boss."

"You're damned right it is. But if we fail, the human race fails. Only a handful of people will live through this, and they'll be thrown back to a pre-industrial level. Subsistence farming. No electricity. No machinery. No medicines."

"The Middle Ages."

"More like the Stone Age," Randolph grumbled.

"That's why you're hangin' everything on this flight to the Belt."

She couldn't see his face in the deepening darkness, but she sensed him nodding.

"Everything I've got," he said flatly.

Everything he has. The enormity of it suddenly hit Pancho like an avalanche. He's risking everything he has on this flight, his whole company, his whole life. He's willing to gamble everything he's worked for and built up over his lifetime on this one mission. And he's trusting me to fly it for him. Me.

The responsibility felt like the weight of the world on her shoulders.

"Lemme ask you somethin' else," Pancho said, her voice trembling slightly. "Why'd you pick me to make this flight? You've got lots of other pilots with more experience."

Randolph chuckled softly. "More experience, sure. But they've got families to support. Spouses. Kids."

I've got a sister, Pancho thought. But she said nothing.

"Besides," Randolph went on, "none of them have your abilities."

"My abilities?"

"Listen, kid, I went through every scrap of data on every pilot in Astro's employ and quite a few who aren't on the company's payroll. You came out on top. You are the best we've got."

Pancho felt suddenly breathless. *Hell, I know I'm good, but am I really* that *good?*

"Before you ask for a raise," Randolph said, "I've got to tell you that my personnel people don't agree with me. They think you're a flake."

"Whattaya mean, a flake?" Pancho demanded.

"The rap on you, kid, is that you're not serious. You like to take risks, play games."

"Not with my flyin'."

"Oh no? Like the time you raced Wally Stinson from Selene to the Farside site?"

"Aw, c'mon, I was only havin' some fun," Pancho protested. "Wally let his testosterone do his thinkin' for him."

"And this bet a few months ago about vacuum breathing?"

"That was just a hoot."

He chuckled in the growing darkness, but then said, "You're a gambler, Pancho. That scared the hell out of the personnel gurus."

"I won't gamble with your fusion ship," she said firmly.

Randolph was silent for a few heartbeats, then he said, "I know you won't, Pancho. That's why I picked you to fly her."

"What about Amanda?" she heard herself ask. "She's better'n me, isn't she?"

"She's got more education, she's more cautious. But she's not better than you. Close, but not better. Anyway, if you go, I want you to have another woman pilot with you. Guys get funny ideas after a couple of weeks locked up in an aluminum can."

The plan was to carry an engineer/technician and at least one geologist or planetary astronomer on the flight. The mission was designed to be more than a mere test of the fusion drive; it was supposed to bring back results. It had to.

"I can handle the guys," Pancho said.

"Yep, I'm sure you can. But why bring up the problem?"

"You don't think Mandy'll cause a problem?"

Randolph laughed softly in the darkness. "I see your point. She can raise temperatures when she wants to."

"Even when she doesn't want to."

"I had a long talk with Amanda yesterday. She's going to be prim and proper during the flight. No bedroom eyes. No tight uniforms. She agreed to behave herself."

Pancho was shocked. *The little sneak never said a word to me about talking with the boss.*

"She'll be strictly business. She promised."

"I don't know if she can help herself," Pancho said.

"You think I should take her off the mission?"

Pancho blurted, "No, I think you should take me off it."

"You? Why?"

Don't do it! She raged at herself. *Don't go blabbing it out to him. He'll fire your butt out of here like a hot rocket and then make sure nobody'll ever hire you again. But he* trusts *me. He's hangin' his whole world on me because he trusts me to get the job done even when his personnel office doesn't.*

"Why should I take you off the mission?" Randolph insisted.

Cursing herself for six kinds of a fool, Pancho said, "Martin Humphries hired me to spy on you."

"He did, huh?" In the starlit darkness, Randolph sounded much less surprised than she thought he would. "When was this?"

"More'n six months ago," Pancho said, barely able to get the words out. "Last time I was up at Selene."

Randolph fell silent and resumed pacing slowly along the seawall. Pancho walked beside him, listening to the sighing of the wind, the grumble of the surf, waiting for him to explode or snarl or say *something.*

At last he started to laugh. Not loud, joyful laughter. Just a low, cynical snickering. "I knew the sonofabitch would try to plant snoops in my drawers, but I never figured he'd recruit you."

"You can fire me if you want to."

"What did he offer you?"

"Money."

"Is that all you're after?"

Pancho hesitated a heartbeat. "I got . . . family to take care of."

"Your sister, yes, I know."

"You know?"

"I told you, I went over every nanobit of data about you. I know about your sister."

"Well . . ." Pancho had to take a breath before she could repeat, "You can fire me, I guess." She was surprised at what an effort it was to say the words.

"Why would I do that?" Randolph sounded genuinely puzzled.

"'Cause I'm supposed to be spyin' on you."

"That's all right. No need to panic, kid. Go ahead and spy all you want. I knew he'd plant a few spooks into Astro. I'm glad you told me about it. I appreciate your honesty—and loyalty."

"But—"

"No, no it's okay," Randolph said, his tone almost bantering now. "You go ahead and report everything you're doing to him. I'll even make it easier for you. I'll transfer you and Amanda to Selene. That's where the sonofabitch is living, isn't it?"

"I think so, yeah."

"Good," Randolph said. "I ought to go there myself. It's a lot healthier there than here, that's for sure."

"Healthier?"

"Climate controlled. Decontaminated air. I don't need filter plugs stuffed up my nose when I'm there."

Before Pancho could ask why he needed filter plugs at all,

Randolph grasped her by the shoulder and turned her gently to look up into the darkening sky. A half-Moon rode among the scudding clouds, the unwinking brilliant beacon light of Selene visible along its terminator between night and day.

"That's where you're going, kid. To Selene."

Pancho wondered if Randolph was truly pleased with her confession, or if he was exiling her to the most remote spot he could find.

P ancho had no trouble getting through customs this time. The same inspector went through her bags perfunctorily, not even blinking at the mice in their sealed plastic cage.

But he paid elaborate attention to Amanda. Pancho groused to herself as the inspector carefully went through Amanda's travel bag, alternately grinning at Mandy and reddening as he saw her lacy underclothes.

He'd strip-search her if he could find the slightest excuse, Pancho thought, fuming.

Mandy simply stood on the other side of the table, looking wide-eyed and innocent while she kept up a constant nervous chatter.

"I don't know why they always go through my bag, Pancho. I really don't. You'd think that after all these times we've come to Selene they would simply let me pass through without all this bother."

"He went through my bag, too, Mandy," Pancho replied.

"Yes, but he didn't paw through your underwear."

Grinning with gritted teeth, Pancho said, "Yours are a lot purtier than mine."

The inspector kept his head down as he searched diligently through Amanda's one piece of luggage, but Pancho could see the back of his neck turn beet red.

"All the other passengers have already gone through," Amanda noticed. "We're the last ones."

"The rest of 'em are either up here to start a long-term work contract or they're tourists. We come and go all the time, so we could be smugglers."

"Smugglers?" Amanda looked shocked. "Us? *Me?*"

Pancho reached across the table and tapped the inspector on the shoulder. "Ain't that right? What're you looking for, dope or contraband seeds or maybe illegal bottles of air?"

The inspector mumbled something incomprehensible.

At last he finished and pushed the bag back across the table toward Amanda.

"There you go, Ms. Cunningham. Sorry to have delayed you. I'm just doing my job, miss."

Amanda thanked him politely as she zipped her bag shut and hefted it to her shoulder. Pancho saw that the inspector couldn't help but stare at Mandy's expansive chest. Even in a standard-issue flight suit she looked sexy.

Visibly working up his courage, the inspector said, "Um...Ms. Cunningham...could I take you out to dinner some time while you're here?" He made a sweaty smile. "To, uh, make up for inconveniencing you and all."

Mandy smiled sweetly at him. "Why, that would be lovely. Call me, won't you?"

"I sure will!"

Pancho seethed as the two of them left the customs station and headed for one of the electric carts that carried new arrivals through the tunnel from the spaceport into the underground city. He asked me to dinner when I was alone, but with bimbo boobs here he never even saw me. I could've carried the Eiffel Tower up here and he wouldn't have noticed.

The message light was blinking on their phone by the time they got to the quarters they were sharing. When Pancho had first come to work for Astro Manufacturing, six years earlier, pilots still got private quarters when they worked on the Moon. Not any more. The rumor back at La Guaira was that Randolph was going to rent a dormitory area for the spacecraft pilots and crews.

Why not just fire all of us? Pancho wondered. If Randolph had any real sense he'd talk the IAA into getting rid of their stupid regulations about keeping human crews aboard the ships.

Yeah, fine, she answered herself. Then what do you do? Get a job as a mission controller? Fat chance!

As soon as they opened the door to their quarters and saw the phone blinking on the nightstand between their two beds, Amanda dropped her bag on the floor; it landed with a gentle lunar thump as Mandy stretched out on the bed and put the handset to her ear.

With a surprised look on her face, Mandy held the phone out to Pancho. "It's for you," she said, as if she didn't really believe it.

Pancho took the handset and saw on the phone's tiny console screen that the caller was Martin Humphries. Rather than activate the speaker, Pancho put the handset to her ear.

"Pancho, is that you?" Humphries's voice said, sounding annoyed. "You're standing outside the camera view."

She stepped between the beds and swiveled the phone console. "It's me," she said, sitting on the bed opposite the one Mandy lay upon.

"I heard that Randolph sent you up here," Humphries said. "But I had to learn it from another source. I haven't heard a peep from you in months."

With a glance at Mandy, who was watching her with intense curiosity, Pancho replied guardedly. "Well, I'm here now."

"Who answered the phone? You're not alone, are you?"

"Nope, I'm here with Mandy Cunningham."

"She's an Astro employee too?"

"That's right."

Mandy was straining to see Humphries's face, but Pancho kept the phone turned away from her.

"Well, I've got to talk to you. I've been paying you for information but so far I've gotten nothing from you but a big, fat silence."

Pancho made a smile. "I'd love to see you, too. I've got a lot to tell you."

Humphries snapped, "All right, get down here right away."

"You want me to come to dinner?" Pancho replied pleasantly.

"Dinner?" Humphries glanced at his wrist. "All right. In two hours."

"Tonight?" Pancho cooed. "That'll be just fine. I'll see you at nineteen hundred. Okay?"

"Seven o'clock," Humphries said. "Sharp."

"I'll be there."

Pancho hung up the phone and said to Amanda, "I'll use the shower first, Mandy. I've got a dinner date."

She left Mandy standing by the bed, staring at her with wide-eyed astonishment.

Martin Humphries clicked his phone off and stretched back in his recliner. *Maybe she's smarter than I gave her credit for. She hasn't gotten in touch with me before this because she doesn't want to get caught. Okay, that's reasonable. She's being cautious. She's been surrounded by Randolph's people all the time. There's even somebody in her quarters with her.*

Humphries broke into a satisfied grin. Randolph's making his people double up, to save money. He's on the ropes, and he thinks *I'm* going to save him from bankruptcy.

He laughed aloud. "Me! The savior of Dan Randolph!"

He was still giggling when he put through his call to Nobuhiko Yamagata.

The head of Yamagata Industries was in his Tokyo office, from the looks of it. Humphries could see through the window behind Yamagata several construction cranes and the spidery steelwork of new towers going up. Rebuilding from the last earthquake. They'd better build stronger, he thought grimly. A lot stronger.

"Mr. Yamagata," Humphries said, nodding his head once in imitation of a polite bow. "It's good of you to take the time to talk with me."

He thought about putting Yamagata's image on the wallscreen, but that would make the Japanese look too big. He preferred the smaller desktop screen.

"Mr. Humphries," said Nobo, nearly three seconds later, barely dipping his chin. "It is always a pleasure to converse with you."

Blasted bullshit, Humphries thought. You can't come right out and say what you want with these Japs. You have to make polite fucking conversation for half an hour before you can get down to business.

To his surprise, though, Yamagata said, "Dan Randolph has asked me to invest in a new venture."

"Let me guess," Humphries said. "He wants to build a fusion rocket system."

Again the wait for the microwaves to reach Tokyo and return. "Yes, to go out to the Asteroid Belt and begin developing the resources there."

"And what will your answer be?"

Once Yamagata heard Humphries's question, his normally impassive face showed a tic of annoyance.

"I will be forced to tell him that Yamagata Industries is

fully committed to rebuilding the cities that were damaged so heavily by the tsunamis and earthquakes. We have no funds to spare on space developments."

"Good," said Humphries.

Yamagata seemed to freeze into stone. At last he murmured, "It will be as we agreed."

"You'd like to help him, wouldn't you?"

The seconds stretched. At last Yamagata said, "He is an old friend."

"You two were competitors at one time."

"Yamagata Industries no longer has any operations in space," the Japanese said slowly. "All of our energies are devoted to terrestrial developments."

"So I understand."

"But I agree with Dan. The resources from space can be of vital importance to our rebuilding efforts."

"I think so, too."

Yamagata seemed to be searching Humphries's eyes, trying to penetrate to his secret thoughts. "Then why do you insist that I refuse to help him?"

"You misunderstand me," Humphries said, putting on an expression of injured integrity. "I want Randolph to succeed. I intend to fund his fusion rocket venture myself."

"Yes, so I understand," said Yamagata, once Humphries's answer reached him. "What I do not understand is why you pressured me to refuse Dan."

"Could you help him if you wish?"

Yamagata hesitated, but at last replied, "I could put together two billion for him."

"Without hurting your rebuilding projects?"

The hesitation was longer this time. "There would be some ... repercussions."

"But I can provide the funding and you don't have to take a penny from your existing projects."

Yamagata said nothing for many long moments. Then, "You have put considerable pressure on the banks to make certain that I do not fund Dan Randolph. I want to know why."

"Because I believe the same as you do," Humphries replied, earnestly, "that all of Japan's resources of capital and manpower should be devoted to rebuilding your nation. This fusion rocket venture is very speculative. Suppose it doesn't work? The money will be wasted."

"Yet you are willing to risk your own money."

"I have the money to risk," Humphries said.

After an even longer pause, Yamagata said, "You could invest that two billion in Japan. You could help to house the homeless and feed the hungry. You could assist us to rebuild our cities."

Humphries worked hard to avoid grinning. Now I've got the little bugger, he told himself. To Yamagata he said, "Yes, you're right. Tell you what I'll do: I'll give Randolph one billion only, and invest the other billion in Yamagata Industries. How's that?"

The Japanese industrialist's eyes flickered when he heard Humphries's words. He sucked in a deep, shrill breath.

"Would you be willing to invest your billion in the Renew Nippon Fund?"

"That's essentially a charity, isn't it?"

"It is a nonprofit organization dedicated to helping those who have been displaced by our natural disasters."

This time Humphries hesitated, paused, let Yamagata believe that he was thinking it over before he came to a decision. The damned fool. Thinks he's so fucking smart, keeping me from putting any money into his own corporation. Okay, keep me shut out from your company. I'll get you sooner or later.

With as much of a show of concern as he could muster, Humphries said, "Mr. Yamagata, if you think that's the best way for me to help Japan, then that's what I'll do. One billion for Randolph, and one billion for the Renew Nippon Fund."

Yamagata was actually smiling as they ended their conversation. Once he had switched off the phone, Humphries burst into enormously satisfied laughter.

They're all so dense! So blind! Yamagata wants to rebuild Japan. Randolph wants to save the whole fricking world. Damned fools! None of them understand that the world is done for. Nothing's going to save them. The thing is to build a new civilization off-Earth. Build a new society where it's safe, where only the best people are allowed to live. Build it ... and rule it.

LONDON

The Executive Board of the Global Economic Council met in a spacious conference room on the top floor of the undistinguished neomodern glass-and-steel office tower that served as the GEC's headquarters. Originally, GEC's offices had been in Amsterdam, but the rising sea level and pounding storms that raged through the North Sea made that city untenable. The Dutch struggled in vain to hold back the IJsselmeer, only to see their city's narrow streets and gabled houses flooded time and again as the canals overflowed and the unrelenting sea took back the land that had been reclaimed by centuries of hard work. The GEC fled to London.

Not that London itself was immune to the rampaging storms and flooding. But the Thames was easier to control than the North Sea. And most of London was still above even the new, rising sea level.

Meetings of the Global Economic Council were usually restricted to the nine regular members and the privileged few who were invited to explain their positions or plead their causes. The news media were barred from the meetings, and there was no gallery for the public to attend.

Still, Vasily Malik dreaded this meeting of the Executive Board. Dan Randolph had demanded a hearing, and Randolph always made trouble.

Vasily Sergeivitch Malik was handsome enough to be a video star. He was tall for a Russian, slightly over one hundred eighty centimeters, broad-shouldered and heavily muscled. About the same age as Dan Randolph, Malik kept his body in good trim through a rigid schedule of daily exercise—and rejuvenation therapies that he kept secret from everyone except his doctors in Moscow. Most people thought he dyed his once-graying hair; no one knew that injections of telomerase had returned youthful vigor to him. Malik enjoyed his secret. His Arctic blue eyes sparkled with good humor.

Until he thought about Dan Randolph. Once they had been deadly enemies in politics, in business, even in romance. The catastrophic greenhouse cliff had forced them into a reluctant alliance. The old enmities were buried; not forgotten, but put aside while they each strove in their own way to save what remained of Earth's civilization.

We still don't think alike, Malik said to himself as he took his chair at the long committee table. He was serving as chairman for this session, so he knew that Randolph's principal fire would be directed at him. It's nothing personal, Malik repeated silently over and over. That was finished long ago. Our differences now are differences of attitude, differences of outlook and expectation.

Still, his stomach knotted at the thought of tangling with Randolph again.

The conference room was comfortable without being ostentatious. The carpeting was neutral gray, although thick and expensive. The sweeping windows that extended along one entire wall were discreetly curtained; a long sideboard of polished mahogany stood there, bearing a variety of drinks from spring water to iced vodka, and trays of finger foods. The table at which the board members sat was also mahogany; each place was set with a built-in computer and electronic stylus. The chairs were high-backed, luxuriously padded and upholstered in matte black leather.

Randolph had insisted, however, that the room be sprayed with disinfectant before the meeting began. Malik had been assured that the spray was necessary, and odorless. Still, his nose wrinkled as he took his chair in the exact middle of the table. Once all nine Board members were comfortably seated at the long table, Malik nodded to the uniformed guard at the door to admit the day's witnesses.

Dan Randolph came through the door and strode straight to the witness table. He looked firm and fit to Malik, dressed in a respectable business suit of dark blue. Randolph's chin was sticking out pugnaciously. He expects a fight, Malik thought.

Behind Randolph came two others. One was a gnomish, dark-haired man, Randolph's technical expert. Malik glanced at the agenda notes on the display screen built into the table before him: Lyall Duncan, an engineer. The other person was a tall blond woman who looked too young to be an expert at anything, except perhaps warming Randolph's bed. A few keystrokes and the display screen identified her as an electronics engineer from California.

Malik caught Randolph's eye as the American took his seat at the witness table. A slight crease across his face showed he had been wearing a sanitary mask. Randolph's usual cocky grin was absent. He looked determined, and deadly serious.

Suppressing a groan, Malik called the meeting to order.

They went through the standard agenda items first, while Randolph sat tensely, watching them like a leopard sizing up a herd of antelope. Finally they came to Randolph's item: *Request for funding new space propulsion system.*

Malik formally introduced Randolph to the other Board members, most of whom already knew Dan. Then, wishing he were elsewhere, Malik asked Dan to explain his proposal.

Randolph looked up at the Board and surveyed the long table from one end to the other. There were no notes before him, no slides or videos. Nothing on the little table except a silver carafe of water and a single crystal tumbler beside it. Slowly, he got to his feet.

"Ever since the greenhouse cliff hit," he began, "and our world's climate began to shift so drastically—no, actually, even *before* the greenhouse cliff came—it's been clear that the people of Earth need the resources that exist off-planet. Energy, raw materials, metals, minerals, all of the resources that Earth needs to rebuild its crippled economy lie in tremendous abundance in interplanetary space."

He paused for a heartbeat, then resumed. "In fact, if we have any hope of stabilizing the global climate and avoiding even worse warming than we've experienced so far, then a significant portion of the Earth's heavy industries must be moved off-planet."

"That's not possible," snapped the representative from North America, a dough-faced white-haired professor in an academic's tweed jacket.

Randolph stared at him bleakly. Once Jane Scanwell had been the North American on the Board.

"It's not economically feasible today," he replied softly. "But if you'll provide the funding, it will be possible within a year."

"One year?"

"Impossible!"

"How can you—"

Malik tapped lightly on the tabletop with his notebook stylus and their voices fell silent.

Randolph smiled tightly at him. "Thank you, Mr. Chairman."

"Please explain your statement," Malik said.

"The key to the economic development of space lies in the costs of acquiring the raw materials in the Asteroid Belt. With the metals and organic minerals from the asteroids, the people of Earth will have access to a pool of natural resources that's far greater than the entire planet Earth can provide."

"The people of the Earth?" questioned the representative from Pan Asia. "Or the corporations that reach the asteroids and begin mining them?"

"The people," Randolph said flatly. "If you provide the funding necessary for this, my corporation will do the work at cost."

"At cost?"

"No fees whatsoever?"

"At cost," Randolph repeated.

"We would certainly want our own accountants examining your cost figures," said the woman representing Black Africa, very seriously.

"Of course," Randolph replied with a wan smile.

"Wait a moment," Malik intervened. "Just what would our money be funding? You haven't told us what you actually propose to do."

Randolph took a deep breath, then said, "We have to develop a fusion rocket system."

Again the Board broke into querulous chatter. Malik had to tap his stylus sharply before they fell silent.

"A *fusion* rocket system?" he asked Randolph.

"We have developed and tested a small flight model of a fusion rocket," Randolph said. Turning slightly in his chair, he went on, "Dr. Duncan can explain it, if you like. We sent detailed notes to each of you when we applied for this hearing; I'm sure your own technical experts have gone over them."

Reluctant nods from the Board.

"I can show you a video of the flight tests we've done, if you wish."

"That won't be necessary," Malik said.

"The key to any and all operations in space is the cost of transportation," Randolph said. "The Clipperships that Masterson Aerospace developed have brought down the costs of going into Earth orbit. They opened up the Earth–Moon system for development."

"And encouraged Selene to thumb its nose at us," grumbled the representative from Latin America.

"Why do we need fusion rockets?" Malik asked, raising his voice enough to cut off any possible digression into the politics of the lunar nation's insistence on remaining independent of the GEC.

"Transportation costs," Randolph answered quickly. "Fusion rockets will cut the trip times and fuel costs for missions to the asteroids down to the point where they can be practical and profitable."

"Profitable for whom?"

"For the entire human race," Randolph snapped, looking slightly irked. "As I've already said, I'm willing to develop the fusion system and operate expeditions to the Asteroid Belt at cost."

"Under GEC management?"

Randolph visibly gritted his teeth. "No. That would be a bureaucratic disaster. But I'll agree to run the show under GEC oversight. You'll have complete access to our books. That's fair enough, I think."

Malik leaned back in his padded chair and allowed the other Board members to grill Randolph. Most of their questions were trivial, or repeated questions already asked and answered. Most of the Board members talked mainly to hear the beloved sound of their own voices, Malik knew.

He had seen the video of Randolph's flight tests. He had reviewed the technical data on the fusion rocket with the best scientists and engineers in the world. The Duncan Drive worked. There was no technical reason to believe that it would not work in a full-scale interplanetary spacecraft. It would cut the travel time to the Asteroid Belt from years to weeks, or less.

We should fund it, Malik thought. We should back Randolph to the hilt. But we won't, of course.

"But what's the fuel for this rocket?" one of the Board members was asking.

Patiently, Randolph replied, "The same as the fuel for the fusion powerplants that generate electricity here on the ground: isotopes of hydrogen and helium."

"Like the helium-three that's mined on the Moon?"

"Right." Randolph nodded.

"That is very expensive fuel," muttered the representative from Greater India. "Very expensive."

"A little goes a long way," Dan said, with a forced smile.

The representative from the League of Islam said irritably, "Selene has raised the price of helium-three twice in the past year. Twice! I have no doubt they are preparing to raise it again."

"We can get the fuel from space itself," Dan said, raising his voice slightly.

"From space itself?"

"How?"

"The solar wind blows through interplanetary space. It's the solar wind that deposits helium-three and hydrogen isotopes on the lunar soil."

"You mean regolith," pointed out the representative from United Europe.

"Regolith, right," Randolph admitted.

"How can you get the fuel from the solar wind?"

"The same way a jet airplane gets air for its engines," Randolph replied. "We'll scoop it in as we go."

Malik saw that the Scottish engineer, sitting off to Randolph's side, squirmed uncomfortably in his chair.

"Scoop it in? Really?"

"Sure," Randolph answered. "We'll use an electromagnetic scoop...a big funnel-shaped magnetic field. That way we'll be able to scoop in the fuel we need as we travel."

"How large a scoop will be necessary?"

Randolph made an exaggerated shrug. "That's for the tech people to work out. For the first missions to the Belt we'll carry the fusion fuel in tankage, just like other rockets. But eventually we'll be able to scoop fuel from the solar wind. That'll allow us to carry an even bigger payload, per unit of thrust." Turning slightly in his chair, Randolph asked, "Isn't that right, Lon?"

Duncan, the engineer, looked dubious, but he knew enough to answer, "Right."

With a glance at his wristwatch, Malik tapped his stylus again on the tabletop and said, "Thank you, Mr. Randolph, for a most interesting presentation."

Randolph fixed his gray eyes on Malik. The Russian went on, "The Board will discuss the question and inform you of its decision."

"Time is of the essence," Randolph said.

"We understand that," said Malik. "But we must have a full and thorough discussion of this concept before we can decide whether or not to commit any funding to it."

Reluctantly, Randolph got to his feet. "I see. Well, thanks for hearing me out. You have a tremendous opportunity here...and a tremendous responsibility."

"We are well aware of that," Malik said. "Thank you again."

Randolph nodded and headed out of the conference room, followed by the engineer and the blond Californian.

Malik now had to go through the formality of a discussion with the other Board members, but he already knew what the answer would be. He was framing the Board's reply to Randolph even while Dan was leaving the conference room:

Dear Mr. Randolph: While your proposal to develop a fusion rocket system appears to be technically feasible, the

Global Economic Council cannot devote such a significant portion of its resources to what is essentially a space-born venture. GEC funding is fully committed for the next five years to programs aimed at alleviating the effects of global climate shift and assisting national efforts at rebuilding and resettling displaced population groups.

SELENE

an went by tube train from the GEC Board meeting to the spaceport at old Heathrow. He rode a commercial Clippership to space station *Galileo*, then hitched a ride on a high-thrust Astro transfer buggy to Selene. He was in the offices that Astro Manufacturing rented in Selene by midnight, Greenwich Mean Time, of the day after the GEC meeting.

Duncan and his electronics engineer had gone back to Glasgow, hoping that the GEC Board would find the money to build at least a prototype spacecraft. Dan thought otherwise. He could see it in Malik's eyes: the GEC isn't going to spend diddley-squat on us.

Dan pushed through the empty office suite, ceiling lights flicking on as he entered each area and off as he breezed past, paying scant attention to the unoccupied desks and blank holowindows. He reached the private suite where he bunked down while he was in Selene, peeled off his jacket, tossed his travel bag onto the king-sized bed and stepped into the shower, still dressed in his pullover shirt and micro-mesh slacks. He kicked off his softboots and banged on the water. It came out at the preset temperature. He popped the plugs out of his nostrils and stripped off the rest of his clothes as the hot, steaming water began to ease the knots of tension in his back and shoulders.

It was an old and very personal indulgence of his: long, hot showers. Back when he'd been a kid working on the early construction projects in orbit and then on the Moon, a hot shower was an incredibly rare luxury. He'd had his nose broken for the second time over the right to a long shower. For years, before Moonbase became the independent nation of Selene, lunar shower stalls were rarer than ten-meter high jumps on Earth. Even when you did find an incredibly luxurious living unit with a real shower, back in those days the water shut of automatically after two minutes, and there was no way to get it to turn back on again until a full hour had elapsed.

Even now, Dan thought as he let the hot water sluice over him, being on Selene's water board carries more real political clout than being a member of the governing council.

He turned off the water at last and let the built-in jets of hot air dry him. Dan preferred old-fashioned towels, but the air blowers were cheaper.

Naked, he crawled into bed and tried to get some sleep. But his mind kept churning with his hopes, his plans, his frustrations.

Yamagata isn't going to put up any money, he realized. Nobo would have called me by now if he were going to come in with me. He hasn't called because he's reluctant to give me the bad news. Malik and the GEC are a lost cause. I shouldn't even have wasted the time to appear before them, but at least if and when we get this fusion drive going we can say we offered it to the double-damned bureaucrats and they turned us down. So they've got no claim on us whatsoever.

Astro's hanging on by the skin of its teeth, one jump

ahead of the bankruptcy courts, and I need to raise a couple of billion to make this fusion system work. Humphries is dangling the money at me, but he'll want a big slice of Astro in return. I need somebody else. Who can I turn to? Who the hell else is there?

Selene, he realized. They don't have the capital, but they've got trained people, equipment, resources. If I can talk them into coming in with me...

Then it hit him. Bypass Selene's governing council. Or, at least, end-run them. Douglas Stavenger still outvotes everybody else up here. And Masterson Aerospace is his family's company. If he'll go for this, Masterson will get behind it and Selene's council will fall in step with him.

Doug Stavenger.

He fell asleep thinking about the possibilities. And dreamed of flying past Mars, out to the Asteroid Belt.

"Who's your boyfriend?" Amanda asked.

She and Pancho were exercising in Selene's big gymnasium complex, working up a fine sheen of perspiration on the weight machines. Through the long window on one side of the room Pancho could see two men strapped into the centrifuge, both of them grimacing as the big machine's arms swung round and round, faster and faster. She knew one of the men, a maintenance tech out at the tractor garage, a thoroughly nice guy.

The gym was packed with sweating, grunting, grimacing men and women working the treadmills, stationary bikes, and weight machines. The only faces that didn't look miserable were the kids; they scampered from one machine to another, laughing, sometimes shrieking so loud the adults growled at them.

Every person in Selene, adult or child, citizen or visitor, had to follow a mandatory exercise regimen or be denied transport back to Earth. The low lunar gravity quickly deconditioned muscles to the point where facing Earth's gravity became physically hazardous. Daily exercise was the only remedy, but it was *boring*.

Pancho wore a shapeless T-shirt and faded old shorts to the gym. Amanda dressed as if she were modeling for a fashion photographer: brand-new gym shoes, bright pink fuzzy socks, and a form-fitting leotard that had men tripping over their own feet to gawk at her. Even the women stared openly.

"I don't have a boyfriend," Pancho replied, grunting as she pulled on the weighted hand grips. A favorite gambit of tourists was to have a picture taken while lifting a barbell loaded with enormous weights. What looked superhuman to Earth-trained eyes was merely ordinary in the one-sixth gravity of the Moon.

"You've gone out to dinner twice since we arrived here, and you're going out again tonight, aren't you?" Without waiting for an answer, Amanda added, "I have the impression it's been with the same fellow each night."

Mandy was sitting at the machine next to Pancho, doing pectoral crunches, her arms outstretched with her hands gripping the ends of two metal bars. Then she brought her hands together in front of her, pulling the weighted "wings" and thereby strengthening her chest muscles.

The rich get richer, Pancho thought.

"So?" Amanda insisted. "Who's your fellow?"

"It's strictly business," Pancho said.

"Really? And what business would that be, dear?"

Pancho suppressed a sudden urge to sock Mandy in her smirking face.

"Listen," she said, with some heat, "you go out just about every damned night, don't you? What's the matter with me havin' a date now and then?"

Mandy's expression softened. "Nothing, Pancho, really. I'm only curious, that's all. I think it's fine for you to have an enjoyable social life."

"Yeah, sure. You're just wonderin' who my date could be, 'cause you've got all the other men in Selene sewed up for yourself."

"Pancho, that's not true!"

"Like hell."

"I can't help it if men are attracted to me! I don't do any-thing to encourage them."

Pancho laughed out loud.

"Really, I don't."

"Mandy, all you have to do is breathe and the men swarm around you like flies on horseshit."

Amanda's cheeks flushed at Pancho's deliberate crudity. But then she smiled knowingly. "Well, it is rather fun to flirt. If men want to take me out to dinner, why not? I just bat my eyes at them and let them tell me how terrific they are."

"And then you bed down with 'em and everybody's happy."

Amanda flared with sudden anger. She started to reply, but stopped before saying a word. For several moments she stared down at her shoetops, then at last said in a lower voice, "Is that what you think?"

"It's the truth, ain't it?"

"Really, Pancho, I'm not a slut. I don't sleep with them, you know."

"You don't?"

"Well . . . once in a while. A great while."

Pancho looked at Amanda, really looked at her, and saw a very beautiful, very young woman trying to make her way in a world where a woman's physical appearance still catego-rized her in men's eyes. Jeez, she thought, Mandy prob'ly has to spend half her life keeping guys' hands off her. So she just smiles at them and jollies 'em along and splits before it gets serious. It's either that or carry a gun, I guess. Or a snake.

"Maybe we could ugly you up," Pancho muttered.

Amanda smiled ruefully. "That's what Mr. Randolph said."

"Huh? Randolph?"

"He told me that if I want to go on the mission with you I'll have to stop making myself so attractive to the men that go with us."

Pancho nodded. "We've gotta find you some big, bulky sweatshirts. Or maybe keep you in a spacesuit the whole damn trip."

The two women laughed together. But after a few moments, Amanda asked again, "So tell me, Pancho, who's your boyfriend?"

Exasperated, Pancho snapped, "You want to meet him? Come on along tonight."

"Really? Do you mean it?"

"Sure, why not?" Pancho said. "I bet he'd like to meet you."

Pancho knew that Humphries would go ballistic over Mandy. Good. The man had been pressuring her to find out more about what Dan Randolph was up to. Humphries had been getting downright nasty about it.

Humphries had snarled at her when they'd had dinner, Pancho's first night back at Selene. The man had seemed cordial enough when he'd ushered her into that big, formal dining room in the house down at Selene's lowest level. But once he had started asking Pancho what information she had for him, and she had been forced to reply that she had little to report, his mood swiftly changed.

"That's it? That's all you've got to tell me?" Humphries had snarled.

With a helpless shrug, Pancho had answered, "He's had us cooped up in La Guaira, studyin' the fusion system."

"I'm paying you a small fortune and I'm not getting a damned bit of information from you! Nothing! A big, fat zero!"

It was a pretty dinky fortune, Pancho thought. Still, she had tried to placate the man. "But Mr. Humphries, other than the flight tests with that beat-up ol' cruise missile, he hasn't been *doin'* anything."

"He's been flitting all around the fucking world," Humphries had snapped, "from Kyoto to New York to Geneva to London. He's been talking to bankers and development agencies—even to the GEC, and he *hates* the GEC!"

Pancho had tried to be reasonable. "Look, I'm just a rocket jockey. He says he wants me to test-fly the fusion drive once it's built but it might be years before that happens."

"So what does he have you doing in the meantime?" Humphries demanded.

Pancho shrugged. "Nothin' much. He's sent me and Mandy here to Selene. His personal orders. We're supposed to be learnin' about the asteroids out in the Belt. He's got an astronomer from the Farside Observatory tutoring us."

Humphries's expression grew thoughtful. "Maybe he knows you're working for me. Maybe he's just put you on ice for the time being, until he figures out how to get rid of you."

Pancho didn't want Humphries to think about the possibility that she had told Randolph everything.

"Wouldn't it be easier for him just to fire me?" she suggested mildly.

"He's on his way here right now, you know," Humphries muttered.

"He is?" Pancho couldn't hide her surprise.

"You don't even know where he is?"

"I'm not on the mailing list for his personal itinerary," Pancho retorted.

"Now you listen to me, lady. *I* got your name to the top of Astro's personnel list so that Randolph would take you into this fusion rocket program of his. *I'm* the one who's gotten you promoted. I want results! I want to know when Randolph goes to the toilet, I want to know when he inhales and when he exhales."

"Then get yourself another spy," Pancho had said, trying to hold on to her swooping temper. "Whatever he's up to, he hasn't even been on the same continent with me most of the time. I only saw him that once, at the first flight test in Venezuela. You hired the wrong person, Mr. Humphries. You want somebody who can be his mistress, not a pilot."

Humphries had glared at her over the dinner table. "You're probably right," he had muttered. "Still...I want you on the job. It might take a while, but sooner or later he's going to use you to test-fly the fusion drive. That's when you'll become valuable to me. I just hired you too soon, that's all."

He made a forced little smile. "My mistake, I guess."

Puffing and sweating at the weight machine, Pancho thought, Yep, it's time for Humphries to meet Mandy. That might solve all my problems.

She laughed to herself. What a setup! Humphries sends Mandy after Randolph and she doesn't know that I've already told Randolph I'm supposed to be spyin' on him for the Humper. And Mandy would go for it, too; she'd love to have Randolph in her bed.

And meantime, she thought, I can be spyin' on Humphries for Randolph! Whatta they call that? I'll be a double agent. Yeah, that's it. A double agent. Terrific.

But what if Humphries drops me altogether once he sees Amanda? That's a possibility. Then you won't be any kind of an agent; you'll be out in the cold.

Okay, so what? she told herself. So you won't be getting the extra money from Humphries, came the answer. So you'll have to maintain Sis on your Astro salary. Yeah, yeah, she argued back. I've been doin' that for years now, I can keep on doin' it.

Wait a minute, she said to herself. Humphries can't fire

me. If he tried to, he'd be afraid that I'd tell Randolph everything. The Humper has to keep me on his payroll—or get rid
of me altogether.

Pancho got off the weight machine and went to the exercise bike. Pedaling furiously, she thought, The trick is not to
get fired by both Humphries *and* Randolph. I don't want to
be left out in the cold. And I don't want Humphries to start
thinkin' he'd be better off if I happened to get myself killed.
No sir!

Y ou can't see them, Mr. Randolph."

Dan was startled by Douglas Stavenger's words.

"I was staring, wasn't I?" he admitted.

Stavenger smiled patiently. "Most people do, when they first meet me. But the nanomachines are all safely inside me. You can't get infected by them."

The two men were sitting in Stavenger's spacious office, which looked more like a comfortable sitting room than a business center. Wide windows made up two of the room's walls. No desk, not even a computer screen in sight; only up-holstered chairs and a small sofa off to one side of the room, with a few low tables scattered here and there. Dan had to re-mind himself that the windows were really transparent, not holoviews. They looked out on Selene's Grand Plaza, the only public greenspace within nearly half a million kilometers.

Douglas Stavenger's office was not buried deep under-ground. It was on the fifteenth floor of one of the three office towers that also served as supports for the huge dome that covered the Grand Plaza. Masterson Aerospace Corporation's offices took up the entire fifteenth floor of the tower.

Spread out beyond those windows was the six-hundred-meter-long Plaza itself, a grassy expanse with paved footpaths winding through it, flowered shrubbery and even small trees here and there. Dan could see people walking along the paths, stopping at the shopping arcades, playing lunar basketball in the big enclosed cage off by the orchestra shell. Kids were doing fantastically convoluted dives from the thirty-meter platform at one end of the Olympic-sized swimming pool, twisting and somersaulting in dreamlike slow motion before they splashed languidly into the water. A pair of tourists soared past the windows on brilliantly colored plastic wings, flying like birds on their own muscle power in the low lunar gravity.

"It's a pleasant view, isn't it?" Stavenger said.

Dan nodded his agreement. While most people on the Moon instinctively wanted to live as deep underground as possible, Stavenger stayed up here, with nothing between him and the dangers of the surface except the reinforced lunar concrete of the Plaza's dome, and a meter or so of rubble from the regolith that had been strewn over it.

And why not? Dan thought. Stavenger and his family had more or less created the original Moonbase. They had fought a brief little war against the old United Nations to win their independence—and the right to use nanotechnology even though it had been banned on Earth.

Stavenger was filled with nanomachines. Turning his gaze back to him, Dan saw a good-looking young man apparently in his thirties smiling patiently at him. Stavenger wasn't much bigger than Dan, though he appeared more solidly built. Smooth olive complexion, sparkling blue eyes. Yet Douglas Stavenger was at least his own age, Dan knew, well into his sixties. His body was filled with nanomachines, tiny, virus-sized mechanisms that destroyed invading microbes, kept his skin smooth and young, took apart plaque and fatty deposits in his blood vessels atom by atom and flushed them out of his body.

The nanomachines apparently kept him youthful as well. Far better than any of the rejuvenation therapies that Dan had investigated. There was only one drawback to the nanos: Douglas Stavenger was forbidden to return to Earth. Governments, churches, the media, and the mindless masses feared that nanomachines might somehow get loose and cause unstoppable plagues or, worse, might be turned into new genocidal bioweapons.

So Stavenger was an exile who lived on the Moon, able to see the bright beckoning Earth hanging in the dark lunar sky but eternally prohibited from returning to the world of his birth.

He doesn't look upset about it, Dan thought, studying Stavenger's face.

"Whatever they've done for you," he said, "you look very healthy. And happy."

Stavenger laughed softly. "I suppose I'm the healthiest man in the solar system."

"I suppose you are. Too bad the rest of us can't have nanos injected into us."

"You can!" Stavenger blurted. Then he added, "But you wouldn't be able to go back Earthside."

Dan nodded. "We can't even use nanomachines to help rebuild the damage from the flooding and earthquakes. It's outlawed."

Stavenger hunched his shoulders in a slight shrug. "You can't blame them, really. More than ten billion people down there. How many maniacs and would-be dictators among them?"

"Too damned many," Dan mumbled.

"So you'll have to rebuild without nanotechnology, I'm afraid. They won't even allow us to sell them machinery built with nanos; they're frightened that the machinery is somehow infected by them."

"I know," said Dan. Selene built spacecraft of pure diamond out of piles of carbon soot, using nanomachines. But they were allowed no closer to Earth than the space stations in low orbit. Stupid, Dan said to himself. Nothing but ignorant superstition. Yet that was the law, everywhere on Earth.

It also made more jobs for people on Earth, he realized. The spacecraft that Astro used to fly from Earth's surface into orbit were all made basically the same way Henry Ford would have manufactured them; no nanotechnology allowed. Typical politician's thinking, Dan thought: bow to the loudest pressure group, keep outmoded industries alive and turn your back on the new opportunities. Even with the greenhouse warming wiping out half Earth's industrial base, they still think the same old way.

Leaning back in his easy chair, Stavenger said, "I understand you're trying to raise the capital to develop a fusion drive."

Dan smiled crookedly at him. "You're well informed."

"It doesn't take a genius," Stavenger said. "You've had talks with Yamagata and most of the major banks."

"Plus the double-damned GEC."

Stavenger's brows rose slightly. "And now you're talking to me."

"That I am."

"What can I do for you, Mr. Randolph?"

"Dan."

"Dan, okay."

"You can help me save those ten billion people down there on Earth. They need all the help they can get."

Stavenger said nothing. He merely sat there, his face serious, waiting for Dan to go on.

"I want to open up the Asteroid Belt," Dan said. "I want to move as much of Earth's industrial base into orbit as we can, and we need the resources from the Belt to do that."

Stavenger sighed. "It's a pretty dream. I believed in it myself, once. But we found that it costs more than it's worth."

"Selene's sent spacecraft to the NEAs," Dan pointed out.

"Not for many years, Dan. It's just too expensive. We decided a long time ago that we can live on the resources that the Moon provides. We have to. No asteroids."

"But with fusion, it becomes economically feasible to extract resources from the NEAs. And even the Belt."

"Are you certain of that?" Stavenger asked softly.

"Positively," Dan agreed. "Same situation as the Clipperships. Your Clipperships brought down the cost of going into orbit to the point where it became economically feasible to build space stations and solar power satellites and full-scale factories."

"They're not *my* Clipperships, Dan."

"Masterson Corporation is your family's outfit, isn't it?"

Stavenger shifted uneasily in his chair, his smile fading. "Masterson was founded by my family, true enough. I still own a big slice of its stock, but I'm only the Chairman Emeritus. I'm not really involved in the company's operations any longer."

"But they still listen to you."

The smile returned, but it was more guarded now. "Sometimes," Stavenger said.

"So how would Masterson like to come in with me on this fusion system? It'll be a gold mine."

Stavenger hesitated before replying, "I've been told that Humphries Space Systems is backing your fusion program."

"Martin Humphries has offered to, that's true," Dan admitted.

"But you're not satisfied with his offer?"

"I don't know if I can trust him. He comes waltzing into my office and drops this fusion deal in my lap. Why? Why didn't he do it for himself? What's he want me for?"

"Maybe it's Astro Manufacturing that he wants," Stavenger said.

Dan nodded vigorously. "Yep, that's what scares me. The man has a reputation for being a grabber. He's built

Humphries Space Systems by swallowing up other companies."

Again Stavenger hesitated. At last he said, "He's on the verge of acquiring a majority of Masterson's stock."

"What?" A jolt of surprise flashed through Dan.

"I'm not supposed to know, really," Stavenger said. "It's all been very hush-hush. Humphries is on the verge of buying out two of our biggest shareholders. If he's successful, he'll have enough clout to load the board of directors with his own people."

"Damn," grumbled Dan. "Double dammit to hell and back."

"I'm afraid you'll have to play with Humphries whether you like it or not. In his court."

Suppressing an urge to get up and pound on the walls, Dan heard himself say, "Maybe not."

"No?"

"There's one other possibility."

"And what might that be?" Stavenger was smiling again, as if he knew precisely where Dan was heading.

"Selene."

"Ahh," said Stavenger, leaning back in his cushioned chair. "I thought so."

"Selene has trained technical personnel and manufacturing facilities. I could bring my fusion people up here and we could build the prototype together."

"Dan," said Stavenger gently, "who would pay Selene's technical personnel? Who would pay for using our facilities?"

"We could share the cost. I can divest a couple of Astro's operations and raise some cash that way. Selene could donate—"

The expression on Stavenger's face stopped him. It reminded Dan of the look that his geometry teacher would give him, back in high school, when he went off on the wrong tangent.

"You know something that I don't," Dan said.

Stavenger laughed gently. "Not really. You know it, too,

but you're not thinking of it. You're overlooking the obvious."

Dan blinked, puzzled.

"You are staring at the solution to your problem," Stavenger prompted.

"I'm looking at you and you say that I'm—" The light finally dawned in Dan's mind. "Oh for my sweet old Aunt Sadie! Nanomachines."

Stavenger nodded. "Nanotechnology can build your fusion engine for you, and do it faster and cheaper than the orthodox way."

"Nanotechnology," Dan repeated.

"It would mean your spacecraft could never get any closer to Earth than low orbit."

"So what?" Dan exclaimed. "The double-damned ship is for deep-space operations. It'll never touch down on Earth or any other planetary surface."

"Then you should have no problem," said Stavenger.

"You mean Selene will back us?"

Very carefully, Stavenger replied, "I believe the governing council will allocate personnel and facilities to demonstrate that a prototype fusion engine can be built by using nanotechnology."

Dan grinned widely. "Yep, and once the prototype proves out, Selene will have a major new product line to manufacture: fusion drives."

"And access to the asteroids."

"Damned right! And any comets that come waltzing by, too."

"Selene and Astro Manufacturing will be partners," Stavenger said.

"Partners!" Dan agreed, sticking out his hand. Stavenger gripped it firmly and they shook on the deal.

THE CATACOMBS

It had started as a temporary storage section, just off Selene's small hospital, up by the main airlock and the garage that housed the tractors and other equipment for work on the surface.

Bodies were stored along the blank corridor walls, sealed into protective metal canisters to await transport back to Earth. In earlier days, most of the people who died on the Moon were workers killed in accidents, or visitors who made fatal mistakes while outside on the surface. Hardly anyone died of natural causes until later, when people began settling at Selene to live out their lives.

So the bodies awaiting shipment back Earthside were stored in the corridor between the hospital and the garage, convenient to the tunnel that led to the spaceport.

Eventually, of course, people who had spent their lives on the Moon wanted to be buried there, usually in the farms that provided food and fresh oxygen for the community. But often enough families back Earthside demanded the bodies of their deceased loved ones, despite the deceased's wishes. Some legal wrangles took years to unravel. So the bodies were put into metal dewars filled with liquid nitrogen, frozen solid at cryogenic temperature while the lawyers argued and ran up their fees.

It took several years for Selene's governing council to realize that a new trend had started. Cryonics. People were coming to Selene to be declared legally dead, then frozen into suspended animation in the hope that they could one day be cured of the disease that killed them, thawed, and returned to life once more.

Cryonics had been banned in most of the Earth's nations. The faithful of many religions considered it an affront to God, an attempt to evade the divinely-mandated limits on human lifespan. While rejuvenation therapies could be done in relative secrecy, having one's body preserved cryonically was difficult to hide. With global warming causing catastrophes all over the world and many nations barely able to feed their populations, attempts to forestall death and elongate lifespan were frowned upon, if not banned altogether.

So those who wanted to avoid death, and had the money to reach the Moon, came to Selene for their final years, or months, or days. Thus the catacombs grew, row upon row of gleaming stainless steel dewars, each filled with liquid nitrogen, each holding a human body that one day might be revived.

Pancho Lane had brought her sister to Selene, back when the teenager had been diagnosed with an inoperable brain tumor. Sis was losing her memory, losing control of her body functions, losing her ability to speak or smile or even to think. Pancho had given Sis the final injection herself, had watched her younger sister's inert body being slid into the cold bloodless canister, watched the medical team seal the dewar and begin the long, intricate freezing process, her tears mingling with the cold white mist emanating ghostlike from the hoses.

Six years ago, Pancho thought as she walked slowly along the quiet corridor, looking for her sister's name on the long rows of metal cylinders resting along the blank stone walls.

She had heard rumors that a few people had actually been revived from cryonic immersion, thawed back to life. And other rumors, darker, that claimed those revived had no memories, no minds at all. They were like blank-brained newborns; they even had to be toilet-trained all over again.

Doesn't matter, Pancho said to herself as she stopped in front of Sis's dewar. I'll raise you all over again. I'll teach you to walk and talk and laugh and sing. I will, Sis. No matter how long it takes. No matter what it costs. As long as I'm alive, you're not going to die.

She stared at the small metal nameplate on the dewar's endcap. SUSAN LANE. That's all it said. There was a barcode next to her name, all Sis's vital information in computer-readable form. Not much to show for a human lifetime, even if it was only seventeen years.

Her wristwatch buzzed annoyingly. Brushing at the tears in her eyes, she saw that the watch was telling her she had one hour to get cleaned up and dressed and down to Humphries's place.

With Amanda.

Mandy wore virginal white, a sleeveless mandarin-collared dress with a mid-thigh skirt that clung lovingly to her curves. She'd done her hair up in the latest piled-high fashion: some stylist's idea of neoclassical. Pancho had put on her best pantsuit, pearl gray with electric blue trim, almost the same shade of blue as Elly. Next to Amanda, though, she felt like a walking corpse.

She'd phoned Humphries several times to tell him she was bringing Amanda, and gotten the answering machine

each time. It wasn't until she'd been on her way to the catacombs that Humphries had returned her calls, angrily de-
manding to know who this Amanda Cunningham was and
why Pancho wanted to bring her to their meeting.

It was tough holding a reasonable conversation through
the wristphone, but Pancho finally got across the information that Amanda was going to be her co-pilot on the mission
and she'd thought he might be interested in recruiting her to
help Pancho's espionage work.

In the wristphone's tiny screen it was almost impossible
to judge the expression on Humphries's face, but his tone
was clear enough.

"All right," he said grudgingly. "Bring her along if you
think she might be able to help us. No sweat."

Pancho smiled sweetly and thanked him and clicked the
phone off. No sweat, huh? she thought, laughing inwardly.
He'll change his mind once he gets a look at Mandy. He'll
sweat plenty.

Pancho spent the time on the electric stairways to Selene's
lowest level telling Mandy everything she knew about
Humphries. Everything except the fact that he'd hired her to
spy on Dan Randolph.

"He's actually a billionaire?" Amanda's big blue eyes
went wider than ever when Pancho described Humphries's
underground palace.

"Humphries Biotech," Pancho replied. "The Humphries
Trust, lord knows what else. You can look him up in the financial nets."

"And you're dating him!"

Frowning slightly at her incredulousness, Pancho replied,
"I told you, it's strictly business. He's...eh, he's tryin' to
hire me away from Astro."

"Really?" A suspicious, supercilious tone dripped from
the one word.

Pancho grinned at her. "More or less."

Once they stepped through the airlock-type door and into Humphries's underground garden, Amanda gasped with awe. "It's heavenly!"

"Pretty neat," Pancho agreed.

Humphries was standing at the open door to the house, waiting for them, eying Amanda as they came up the walk.

"Martin Humphries," Pancho said, as close to a formal introduction as she knew, "I would like you to meet—"

"Ms. Amanda Cunningham," Humphries said, all smiles. "I looked up your dossier when I got Pancho's message that you were joining us this evening."

Pancho nodded, impressed. *Humphries can tap into Astro's personnel files. He must have Dan's offices honeycombed with snoops.*

Humphries took Amanda's extended hand and bent over it, his lips barely touching her satiny white skin. Amanda looked as if she wanted to faint.

"Come in, ladies," Humphries said, tucking Amanda's arm under his own. "Come in and welcome."

To Pancho's surprise, Humphries didn't come on to Amanda. Not obviously, at least. A human butler served aperitifs in the library-cum-bar and Humphries showed off his collection of first editions.

"Pretty rare, some of them," he boasted mildly. "I keep them here because of the climate control system. Back home in Connecticut it would cost a considerable sum to keep the old family home at a constant temperature and humidity. Here in Selene it comes automatically."

"Or we breathe vacuum," Pancho commented. Amanda gave her a knowing look.

The butler showed them to the dining room, where the women sat on either side of Humphries. A pair of squat, flat-topped robots trundled back and forth from the kitchen carrying plates and glasses. Pancho watched intently as the robots' padded claws gripped the chinaware and crystal. They didn't drop a thing, although while clearing the salad plates one of them missed Pancho's dish by a fraction of a millimeter and almost knocked it off the table. Before anyone could react, though, it recovered, grasped the plate firmly and tucked it into its recessed storage section.

"That's a pretty good optical recognition system they've got," Pancho said.

"I don't believe it's optical," Amanda countered. To Humphries she asked, "Is it?"

"Very sharp, Amanda," he said, impressed. "Very sharp. The dishes have monomolecular beacons sprayed on their bottoms. The robots sense the microwave signals."

Pancho lifted up her water tumbler and squinted at its bottom.

"The chip's too small to see with the naked eye," Humphries said.

"What powers 'em?"

"The heat from the food or drink. They have trouble with iced drinks . . . and your salad."

Pancho thought it over for half a second. "Dishes pick up residual heat when we handle them, huh?"

"That's right."

Pancho smiled as the other robot placed a steaming plate of frogs' legs before her. Don't want Humphries to think Mandy's the only smart one here, she told herself.

All through dinner Humphries was charming, solicitous, all smiles. He paid almost as much attention to Pancho as he did to Amanda, up to the point where he encouraged Mandy to tell them about her early life. She began to talk, hesitantly at first, about growing up in London, winning a scholarship to the International Space University.

"It wasn't easy," Amanda said, with almost childlike candor. "All the men seemed to think I was better suited to be a photographer's model than an astronaut."

Humphries made a sympathetic murmur. Pancho nodded, understanding all over again that Mandy's good looks had been as much of a problem for her as an advantage.

"But I made it," she finished happily, "and here we all are."

"Good for you," said Humphries, patting her hand. "I think you've done wonderfully well."

As dessert was being served—fresh fruit from the botanical garden outside with soymilk ice cream—Amanda asked where the lavatory was.

Once she had left the room Pancho leaned closer to Humphries and asked in a lowered voice, "Well, whattaya think?"

He frowned with annoyance. "About what?"

"About Mandy." She almost added, *lunkhead,* but stopped herself just in time.

"She's wonderful," Humphries said, beaming. "Beautiful but brainy, too. You don't see that very often."

Pancho thought, Women don't let you see their brains very often, not if they can get by on their looks.

Aloud, she asked, "So d'you think she'd be any good cozyin' up to Dan Randolph?"

"No!" he snapped.

"No?" Pancho was astonished. "Why not?"

"I don't want her anywhere near Randolph. He'll seduce her in a hot second."

Pancho stared at the man. I thought that was the whole idea, she said to herself. Get Mandy into Randolph's bed. I thought that's what he'd want.

"She's much too fine a woman to be used that way," Humphries added.

Oh, for cryin' out loud, Pancho realized. He's fallen for her! This guy who picks up women like paperclips and dumps 'em when he feels like it, he doesn't just have the hots for Mandy. He's fallen in love with her. Just like that!

SELENE GOVERNING COUNCIL

Dan couldn't help contrasting in his mind this meeting of Selene's governing council with the meeting of the GEC's executive board he'd attended a few weeks earlier in London.

The meeting took place in Selene's theater, with the council sitting at student's desks arranged up on the stage in a semi-circle. Just about every seat on the main floor and the balconies was taken, although the box seats on either side of the stage were all empty. Maybe they've been roped off for some reason, Dan thought. Must be two thousand people out there, he thought as he peeked out at the audience through the curtains screening the stage's wings. Just about every voting citizen in Selene's showed up for this meeting.

As he stood in the wing of the stage, the council members filed past him, taking their seats. For the most part they looked young, vigorous. Six women, five men, none with white hair. A couple of premature baldies among the men; they must be engineers, Dan thought. He knew that membership on the council was a part-time task assigned by lottery; no one was allowed to duck their public service, although they could take time off their regular jobs to attend to their extra duties.

"Nervous?"

Dan turned at the sound of Doug Stavenger's voice.

Smiling, he answered, "When you've had to sit through as many board meetings as I have, you don't get nervous, you just want to get it the hell over with."

Stavenger patted Dan lightly on the shoulder. "This one will be different from all the others, Dan. It's more like an old-fashioned New England town meeting than one of your board of directors' get-togethers."

Dan agreed with a brief nod. Often in his mind he'd spelled it b-o-r-e-d meeting. This one would be different, he felt sure.

It was.

Stavenger served as non-voting chairman of the governing council, a largely honorary position. More pomp than circumstance, Dan thought. The chairman stood at the podium set up at one end of the stage, only a few meters from where Dan stood waiting for his turn to speak. The meeting agenda was displayed on a wallscreen along the back of the stage. Dan was dismayed to see that he was last on a list of nine.

The first five items went fairly quickly. The sixth was a new regulation tightening everyone's water allotment. Several people from the audience shot to their feet to make their opinions heard in no uncertain terms.

One of the council members was chairman of the water board, a chubby, balding, red-faced man wearing the coral-red coveralls of the Tourism Department. The student's desk at which he sat looked uncomfortably small for him.

"There's no way around it," he said, looking flustered. "No matter how efficiently we recycle our water, it's not a hundred percent and it never will be. The more people we allow in, the less water we have to go around."

"Then why don't we shut down tourism," came an angry voice from the floor.

"Tourism's down to a trickle anyway," the water chairman replied. "It's less than five percent of our problem. Immigration is our big difficulty."

"Refugees," someone said in a harsh stage whisper.

"Don't let 'em in!" an angry voice snapped.

"You can't do that!"

"Why the hell not? They made the mess on Earth. Let 'em stew in their own crap."

"Can't we find new sources of water?" a citizen asked.

Stavenger answered from the podium, "Our exploration teams have failed to locate any other than the polar ice fields we've been using all along."

"Bring up a few loads from Earthside," someone suggested.

"Yeah, and they'll gouge us for it."

"But if we need it, what else can we do?"

The audience stirred restlessly. A dozen conversations buzzed through the theater.

The water board chairman raised his voice to be heard over the chatter. "We're negotiating with the GEC for water shipments, but they want to put one of their own people onto the water board in return."

"Hell no!"

"Never!"

"Those bastards have been trying to get control of us since day one!"

The audience roared its angry disapproval.

Stavenger, still standing at the podium, pressed his thumb on a button set into its control panel and a painfully loud hooting whistle rang through the theater, silencing the shouters. Dan covered his ears until the shriek died away.

"We've got to maintain order here," Stavenger said in the numbed silence. "Otherwise we'll never get anywhere."

Reluctantly, they accepted the fact that water allotments would be decreased slightly. Then the water board chairman held out a potential carrot.

"We'll have the new recycling system on-line in a few

months," he said, drumming his fingers nervously on his desktop. "If it works as efficiently as the simulations show it should, we can go back to the current water allotments—at least for a year or so."

"And what happens if this recycling system fails?" asked a stern-faced elderly woman.

"It's being thoroughly tested," the water chairman answered defensively.

"This is just a way for the people running the damned hotel to put up their own swimming pool and spa," grumbled a lanky, longhaired citizen. He looked like a physicist to Dan. "Tourism is down so they want to fancy up the hotel to attract more tourists."

Dan wondered about that. Tourism is down because the world's going down the toilet, he thought. Then he admitted, But, yeah, people running tourist facilities will try their damnedest to attract customers, no matter what. What else can they do, except go out of business altogether?

In the end, the council decided to accept the water allotment restrictions until the new recycling system had been in operation for three continuous months. Then they would have a new hearing to decide on whether they could return to the old allotments.

Two more items were swiftly disposed of, then at last Stavenger said, "The final item on our agenda tonight is a proposal by Dan Randolph, head of Astro Manufacturing." He turned slightly and prompted, "Dan?"

There was some scattered applause as Dan stepped up to the podium. Astro employees, Dan thought. Stavenger moved off-stage.

He gripped the edges of the podium and looked over the crowd. He had no notes, no visual aids. For several moments he merely stood there, thinking hard. The audience began to murmur, whisper.

Dan began, "Halley's Comet will be returning to the inner

solar system in a few years. Last time it came by, Halley's blew out roughly thirty million tons of water vapor in six months. If I remember the numbers right, the comet lost something like three tons of water per second when it was closest to the Sun."

He waited a heartbeat, then asked, "Do you think you could use that water?"

"Hell yes!" somebody shouted. Dan grinned when he saw that it was Pancho Lane, sitting up in the first row of the balcony.

"Then let's go get it!" Dan said.

He spent the next fifteen minutes outlining the fusion rocket system and assuring them that it had performed flawlessly in all its tests to date.

"A fusion-driven spacecraft can bring in all the water you need, either from hydrate-bearing asteroids or from comets," Dan said. "I need your help to build a full-scale system and flight test it."

One of the women councilors asked, "Are you asking Selene to fund your corporation? Why can't you raise the money from the regular sources?"

Dan made himself smile at her. "This project will cost between one and two billion international dollars, Earthside. None of the banks or other funding sources that I've approached will risk that kind of money. They're all fully committed to rebuilding and mitigation programs. They've got their hands full with the greenhouse warming; they're not interested in space projects."

"Damned flatland idiots," somebody groused.

"I agree," Dan said, grinning. "They're too busy doing what's urgent to even think about what's important."

"Out of all the corporations on Earth," someone called out, "surely you can make a deal or two to raise the capital you need."

Dan decided to cut the discussion short. "Listen. I could

probably put together a deal that would raise the money we need, but I thought I'd give you a chance to come in on this. It's the opportunity you've been waiting for."

"Selene doesn't have that kind of money at its disposal," said one of the councilmen.

"No," countered Dan, "but you have the trained people and the facilities to build the fusion rocket with nanomachines."

A hush fell over the theater. Nanotechnology. They all knew it was possible. And yet . . .

"Nanomachines aren't magic wands, Mr. Randolph," said the councilor seated closest to Dan, a lean, pinch-faced young man who looked like a jogging fanatic.

"I understand that," said Dan.

"At one time we thought we could develop nanomachines to produce water for us by taking hydrogen from the incoming solar wind and combining it with oxygen from the regolith. It was technically feasible but in practice a complete failure."

Recognizing the councilman as one who loved the sound of his own voice, Dan said curtly, "If nanomachines can build entire Clipperships they can build fusion drives."

Another woman councilor, with the bright red hair and porcelain-white complexion of the Irish, spoke up. "I've been stuck with the job of treasurer for the council, the thanks I get for being an honest accountant."

Dan laughed, along with most of the audience.

"But it's a sad fact that we don't have the funds to spare on your program, Mr. Randolph, no matter how admirable it may be. The money just isn't in our hands."

"I don't want money," Dan said.

"Then what?"

"I want volunteers. I need people who are willing to devote their time to the greatest challenge of our age: developing the resources of the entire solar system."

"Ah, but that boils down to money, now, doesn't it?"

"No it doesn't," said a deep voice from the middle of the

theater. Dan saw a squat, heavily-built black man get to his feet.

"I'm Bernie James. I retired from the nanotech lab last year. I'm only a technician, but I'll work with you on this."

A few rows farther back, a taller man, blond hair cropped short, got to his feet. "Rolf Uhrquest, Space Transportation Department," he said, in a clear tenor voice. "I would be willing to take my accumulated vacation time to work on this fusion project."

Dan smiled at them both. "Thank you."

"And I believe," Uhrquest continued, "that Dr. Cardenas would be interested also." Turning slightly, he called, "Dr. Cardenas, are you here?"

No one answered.

"I will find her," Uhrquest said, very seriously. "It is a shame she is not present today."

Dan looked expectantly out at the audience, but no one else stood up. At last he said, "Thank you," and stepped away from the podium, back into the wings of the stage. Stavenger gave him a quick thumbs-up signal and returned to the podium for the final item on the meeting's agenda: a request from a retired couple to enlarge their living quarters so they could have enough space to start a new business for themselves.

Once the meeting broke up, Stavenger said, "If Kris Cardenas had been anywhere in Selene I would have introduced you to her. Unfortunately, she's in a space station in near-Earth orbit, working on developing nanomachines to bring down the costs of the Mars exploration centers."

"Which station?" Dan asked.

"The one over South America."

Dan grinned at him. "*Nueva Venezuela.* I helped build that sucker. Maybe it's time for me to pay a visit there."

Pancho watched the safety demonstration very carefully. No matter that she had put on a spacesuit and done EVA work dozens of times; she paid patient attention to every word of the demo. This was going to be on the surface of the Moon, and the differences between orbital EVAs and a moonwalk were enough to worry about.

The tourists in the bus didn't seem to give a damn. Hell, Pancho thought, if they're stinky-rich enough to afford a vacation jaunt to the Moon, they must have the attitude that nothing bad'll happen to them, and if it does they'll get their lawyers to sue the hell out of everybody between here and Mars.

They had all suited up in the garage at Selene before getting onto the bus. It was easier that way; the bus was way too tight for fourteen tourists to wriggle and squeeze into their spacesuits. They rode out to the Ranger 9 site in the hardshell suits, their helmets in their laps.

After all these years, Pancho thought, they still haven't

come up with anything better than these hard-shell suits. The science guys keep talking about softsuits and even nanomachine skins, but it's still nothing more'n talk.

Even the teenagers went quiet once they cleared the garage airlock and drove out onto the cracked, pockmarked surface of Alphonsus. A hundred and eight kilometers across, the crater floor went clear over the horizon. The ring-wall mountains looked old and weary, slumped smooth from eons of being sandpapered by the constant infall of meteoric dust.

It was the dust that worried Pancho. In orbital space you were floating in vacuum. On the surface of the Moon you had to walk on the powdery regolith, sort of like walking on beach sand. Except that the "sand" billowed up and covered your boots with fine gray dust. Not just your boots, either, Pancho reminded herself. She'd heard tales about lunar dust getting into a suit's joints and even into the life-support backpack. The dust was electrostatically charged from the incoming solar wind, too, and this made the freaking stuff cling like mad. If it got on your visor it could blind you; try to wipe it off with your gloves and you just smeared it worse.

They'd had some trouble finding Pancho a suit that would fit her comfortably; in the end they had to break out a brand new one, sized long. It smelled new, like pristine plastic. When the bus stopped and the guide told the tourists to put on their helmets, Pancho sort of missed the familiar scents of old sweat and machine oil that permeated the working suits she'd worn. Even the air blowing gently across her face tasted new, unused.

The tour guide and the bus driver both checked out each tourist before they let the visitors climb down from the bus's hatch onto the lunar regolith. Pancho's helmet earphones filled with "oohs" and "lookit that!" as, one by one, the tourists stepped onto the ancient ground and kicked up puffs of dust that lingered lazily in the gentle gravity of the Moon.

"Look how bright my footprints are!" someone shouted excitedly.

The guide explained, "That's because the topmost layer of the ground has been darkened by billions of years of exposure to hard radiation from the Sun and deep space. Your bootprints show the true color of the regolith underneath. Give 'em a few million years, though, and the prints will turn dark, too."

For all the years she'd worked in space, Pancho had never been out on a Moonwalk. She found it fascinating, once she cut off the radio frequency that carried the tourists' inane chatter and listened only to the prerecorded talk that guided visitors to the Ranger 9 site.

To outward appearances she was just another tourist from one of the three busloads that were being shepherded along the precisely-marked paths on the immense floor of Alphonsus. But Pancho knew that Martin Humphries was in one of the other buses, and her reason for being here was to report to him, not to sightsee.

She let the cluster of tourists move on ahead of her while she lingered near the parked buses. The canned tourguide explanation was telling her about the rilles that meandered near the site of the old spacecraft crash: sinuous cracks in the crater floor that sometimes vented out thin, ghostlike clouds of ammonia and methane.

"One of the reasons for locating the original Moonbase in Alphonsus's ringwall mountains was the hope of utilizing these volatiles for—"

She saw Humphries shuffling toward her, kicking up clouds of dust as if it didn't matter. It had to be him, she thought, because his spacesuit was different from the ones issued to the tourists. Not different enough to be obvious to the tenderfeet, but Pancho recognized the slightly wider, heavier build of the suit and the tiny servo motors at the joints that helped the wearer move the more massive arms and legs. Extra armor, she thought. He must worry about radiation up here.

Humphries had no name tag plastered to the torso of his suit, and until he was close enough to touch helmets she could not see into his heavily-tinted visor to identify his face. But he walked right up to her, kicking up the dust, until he almost bumped his helmet against hers. She recognized his features through the visor: round and snubby-nosed, like some freckle-faced kid, but with those cold, hard eyes peering at her.

Pancho lifted her left wrist and poised her right hand over the comm keyboard, asking Humphries in pantomime which radio frequency he wanted to use. He held up a gloved hand and she saw that he was holding a coiled wire in it. Slowly, with the deliberate care of a person who was not accustomed to working in a spacesuit, he fitted one end of the wire into the receptacle built into the side of his helmet. He held out the other end. Pancho took it and plugged into her own helmet.

"Okay," she heard Humphries's voice, almost as clearly as if they were in a comfortable room, "now we can talk without anyone tapping into our conversation."

Pancho remembered her childhood, when she and some of the neighborhood kids would create telephone links out of old paper cups and lengths of waxed string. They were using the same principle, linking their helmets with the wire so they could converse without using their suit radios. This'll work, Pancho thought, as long as we don't move too far apart. She judged the wire connecting their helmets to be no more than three meters long.

"You worried about eavesdroppers?" she asked Humphries.

"Not especially, but why take a chance you don't have to?"

That made sense, a little. "Why couldn't we meet down at your place, like usual?"

"Because it's not a good idea for you to be seen going

down there so often, that's why," Humphries replied testily. "How long do you think it would be before Dan Randolph finds out you're coming to my residence on a regular basis?"

Teasingly, Pancho said, "So he finds out. He'll just think you're inviting me to dinner."

Humphries grunted. Pancho knew that he had invited Amanda to dinner at his home twice since they'd first met. And he'd stopped asking Pancho to report to him down there. Now they met at prearranged times and places: strolling in the Grand Plaza, watching low-gravity ballet in the theater, doing a tourist moonwalk on the crater floor.

Pancho would have shrugged if she hadn't been encased in the suit. She said to Humphries, "Dan made his pitch to the governing council."

"I know. And they turned him down."

"Well, sort of."

"What do you mean?" he snapped.

"A couple of citizens volunteered to work on Dan's project. He's goin' down to the Venezuela space station to try to get Dr. Cardenas to head up the team."

"Kristine Cardenas?"

"Yup. She's the top expert at nanotech," Pancho said.

"They gave her the Nobel Prize," Humphries muttered, "before nanotechnology was banned on Earth."

"That's the one he's gonna talk to."

For several long moments Humphries simply stood there unmoving, not speaking a word. Pancho thought he looked like a statue, with the spacesuit and all.

At length he said, "He wants to use nanomachines to build the rocket. I hadn't expected that."

"It's cheaper. Prob'ly better, too."

She sensed Humphries nodding inside his helmet. "I should've seen it coming. If he can build the system with nanos, he won't need my financing. The sonofabitch can leave me out in the cold—after I gave him the fusion idea on a silver fucking platter!"

"I don't think he'd do that."

"Wouldn't he?" Humphries was becoming more enraged with every word. "I bring the fusion project to him, I offer to fund the work, but instead he sneaks behind my back to try to raise funding from any other source he can find. And now he's got a way to build the fucking rocket without me altogether! He's trying to cut my balls off!"

"But—"

"Shut up, you stupid bitch! I don't care what you think! That prick bastard Randolph thinks he can screw me out of this! Well, he's got another think coming! I'll break his back! I'll *destroy* the sonofabitch!"

Humphries yanked the wire out of Pancho's helmet, then pulled the other end out of his own. He turned and strode back to the bus that had carried him out to the Ranger 9 site, practically boiling up a dust storm with his angry stomping. If he hadn't been in the heavy spacesuit, Pancho thought, he'd hop two meters off the ground with each step. Prob'ly fall flat on his face.

She watched as he gestured furiously to the bus driver, then clambered aboard the tourist bus. The driver got in after him, closed the hatch, and started off for the garage back at Selene.

Pancho wondered if Humphries would allow the driver to come back out and pick up the other tourists, or would he leave them stranded out here? Well, she thought, they can always squeeze into the other buses.

She decided there was nothing she could do about it, so she might as well enjoy what was left of her outing. As she walked off toward the wreckage of the tiny, primitive Ranger 9, though, she thought that she'd better tell Dan Randolph about this pretty damned quick. Humphries was sore enough to commit murder, it seemed to her.

SPACE STATION *NUEVA VENEZUELA*

It was almost like coming home for Dan. *Nueva Venezuela* had been one of the first big projects for the fledgling Astro Manufacturing Corp., back in the days when Dan had moved his corporate headquarters from Texas to La Guaira and married the daughter of the future president of Venezuela.

The space station had lasted much better than the marriage. Still, the station was old and scuffed-up. As the transfer craft from Selene made its approach, Dan saw that the metal skin of her outer hulls was dulled and pitted from long years of exposure to radiation and mite-sized meteoroids. Here and there bright new sections showed where the maintenance crews were replacing the tired, eroded skin. A facelift, Dan thought, smiling. Well, she's old enough to need it. They're probably using cermet panels instead of the aluminum we started with. Lighter, tougher, maybe even cheaper if you consider the length of time they'll last before they need replacing.

Nueva Venezuela was built of a series of concentric rings. The outermost ring spun at a rate that gave the occupants inside it a feeling of normal Earthly gravity. The two other rings were placed where they would simulate Mars's one-third *g* and the Moon's one-sixth. The docking port at the station's center was effectively at zero gravity. The tech guys called it microgravity, but Dan always thought of it as zero *g*.

A great place to make love, Dan remembered. Then he chuckled to himself. Once you get over the heaves. Nearly everybody got nauseous their first few hours in weightlessness.

Dan went through customs swiftly, allowing the inspector to rummage through his one travelbag while he tried to keep himself from making any sudden movements. He could feel his sinuses starting to puff up as the liquids in his body shifted in response to weightlessness. No postnasal drips in zero *g*, Dan told himself. But you sure can get a beaut of a headache while the fluids build up in your sinuses before you adapt.

The main thing was to make as few head motions as possible. Dan had seen people suddenly erupt with projectile vomiting from merely turning their heads or nodding.

The inspector passed him easily enough and Dan gratefully made his way along the tube corridor that led "down" to the lunar-level wheel.

He dumped his bag in the cubbyhole compartment he'd rented for this visit, then prowled along the sloping corridor that ran through the center of the wheel, checking the numbers on each door.

Dr. Kristine Cardenas's name was neatly printed on a piece of tape stuck above her door number. Dan rapped once, and opened the door.

It was a small office, hardly enough room for the desk and the two plain plastic chairs in front of it. A good-looking young woman sat at the desk: shoulder-length sandy hair, cornflower blue eyes, broad swimmer's shoulders. She wore an unadorned jumpsuit of pastel yellow; or maybe it had once been brighter, but had faded after many washings.

"I'm looking for Dr. Cardenas," said Dan. "She's expecting me. I'm Dan Randolph."

The young woman smiled up at him and extended her hand. "I'm Kris Cardenas."

Dan blinked. "You . . . you're much too young to be *the* Dr. Cardenas."

She laughed. Motioning Dan to one of the chairs in front of the desk, she said, "I assure you, Mr. Randolph, that I am indeed *the* Dr. Cardenas."

Dan looked into those bright blue eyes. "You too, huh? Nanomachines."

She pursed her lips, then admitted, "It was a temptation I couldn't resist. Besides, what better way to test what nanotechnology can do than to try it on yourself?"

"Like Pasteur injecting himself with the polio vaccine," Dan said.

She gave him a sidelong look. "Your grasp of the history of science is a bit off, but you've got the basic idea."

Dan leaned back in the plastic chair. It creaked a little but accommodated itself to his weight. "Maybe I ought to try them, too," he said.

"If you don't have any plans to return to Earth," Cardenas replied, with a sudden sharpness in her voice.

Dan changed the subject. "I understand you're working with the Mars exploration program."

She nodded. "Their budget's being slashed to the bone. Beyond the bone, actually. If we can't develop nanos to take over the life-support functions at their bases, they'll have to close up shop and return to Earth."

"But if they use nanomachines they won't be allowed to come back home."

"Only if they use nanomachines in their own bodies," Cardenas said, raising a finger to emphasize her point. "The IAA has graciously decided they can be allowed to use nanotechnology to maintain and repair their equipment."

Dan caught the sarcasm in her tone. "I'll bet the New Morality was thrilled with that decision."

"They don't run the entire show. At least, not yet."

Dan huffed. "Good reason to live off Earth. I've always said, When the going gets tough, the tough get going—"

"—to where the going's easier," Cardenas finished for him. "Yes, I've heard that."

"I don't think I'd be able to live off-Earth forever," Dan said. "I mean . . . well, that's home."

"Not for me," Cardenas snapped. "Not for a half a dozen of the Martian explorers, either. They've accepted nanomachines. They have no intention of returning to Earth."

Surprised, Dan said, "I didn't know that."

"There hasn't been much publicity about it. The New Morality and their ilk have a pretty tight grip on the news media."

Dan studied her face for a long, silent moment. Dr. Cardenas was physically youthful, quite attractive, a Nobel laureate, the leader in her chosen field of study. Yet she seemed so indignant.

"Well, anyway," he said, "I'm grateful that you've taken the time to see me. I know you're busy."

She broke into a pleased smile. "Your message seemed kind of . . ." she fished for a word, ". . . mysterious. It made me wonder why you wanted to see me in person, rather than by phone."

Dan grinned back at her. "I've found that it's always easier to discuss matters face-to-face. Phones, mail, even VR meetings, they can't replace person-to-person contact."

Cardenas's smile turned knowing. "It's more difficult for someone to say 'no' to your face."

"You got me," Dan replied, raising his hands in mock surrender. "I need your help and I didn't want to tell you about it long-distance."

She seemed to relax somewhat. Easing back in her chair,

she asked, "So what's so important that you came up here to see me?"

"Down here. I came in from Selene."

"What's your problem? I've been so wrapped up with this Mars work that I haven't been keeping up with current events."

Dan took in a breath, then started, "You know I'm the head of Astro Manufacturing."

Cardenas nodded.

"I've got a small team ready to build a prototype fusion rocket, using nanomachines."

"A fusion rocket?"

"We've tested small models. The system works. Now we need to build a full-scale prototype and test it. We're planning a mission to the Asteroid Belt, and—"

"Spacecraft have gone to the Belt on ordinary rockets. Why do you need a fusion system?"

"Those were unmanned vehicles. This mission will carry a crew of four, maybe six."

"To the Asteroid Belt? Why?"

"To start prospecting for the metals and minerals that the people of Earth need," Dan said.

Cardenas's face turned stony. Coldly, she asked, "What are you trying to accomplish, Mr. Randolph?"

"I'm trying to save the Earth. I know that sounds pompous, but if we don't—"

"I see no reason to save the Earth," Cardenas said flatly.

Dan gaped at her.

"They got themselves into this greenhouse mess. They were warned, but they paid no attention. The politicians, the business leaders, the news media...none of them lifted a finger until it was too late."

"That's not entirely true," Dan said softly, remembering his own struggles to get the world's leaders to recognize the looming greenhouse cliff before it struck.

"True enough," Cardenas replied. "And then there's the New Morality and all those other ultraconservative cults. Why do you want to save them?"

"They're people," Dan blurted. "Human beings."

"Let them sink in their own filth," Cardenas said, her words dripping acid. "They've earned whatever they get."

"But..." Dan felt completely at sea. "I don't understand..."

"They exiled me." She almost snarled the words. "Because I injected nanomachines into my body, they prevented me from returning to Earth. Their fanatics assassinated anyone who spoke in favor of nanotechnology, did you know that?"

Dan shook his head mutely.

"They attacked Moonbase, back before it became Selene. One of their suicide killers blew up Professor Zimmerman in his own lab. And you want me to help them?"

Shocked by her vehemence, Dan mumbled, "But that was years ago..."

"I was there, Mr. Randolph. I saw the mangled bodies. And then, when we won and even the old United Nations had to recognize our independence, those hypocritical ignoramuses passed laws exiling anyone who had accepted nanomachines into her body."

"I understand that, but—"

"I had a husband," she went on, blue eyes snapping. "I had two daughters. I have four grandchildren in college that I've never touched! Never held them as babies. Never sat down at the same table with them."

Another woman might have burst into tears, Dan thought. But Cardenas was too furious for that. How the hell can I reach her? he wondered.

She seemed to recover herself. Placing both hands on her desktop, she said more mildly, "I'm sorry for the tirade. But I want you to understand why I'm not particularly interested in helping the people of Earth."

Dan replied, "Then how about helping the people of Selene?"

Her chin went up a notch. "What do you mean?"

"A working fusion drive can make it economical to mine hydrates from the carbonaceous asteroids. Even scoop water vapor from comets."

She thought about that for a moment. Then, "Or even scoop fusion fuels from Jupiter, I imagine."

Dan stared at her. Twelve lords a-leaping, I hadn't even thought of that. Jupiter's atmosphere must be loaded with hydrogen and helium isotopes.

Cardenas smiled slightly. "I presume you could make a considerable fortune from all this."

"I've offered to do it at cost."

Her brows rose. "At cost?"

He hesitated, then admitted, "I want to help the people of Earth. There's ten billion of them, less the millions who've already been killed in the floods and epidemics and famines. They're not all bad guys."

Cardenas looked away from him for a moment, then admitted, "No, I suppose they're not."

"Your grandchildren are down there."

"That's a low blow, Mr. Randolph."

"Dan."

"It's still a low blow, and you know it."

He smiled at her. "I'm not above a rabbit punch or two if it'll get the job done."

She did not smile back. But she said, "I'll spin this Mars work off to a couple of my students. It's mostly routine now, anyway. I'll be back in Selene within the week."

"Thanks. You're doing the right thing," Dan said.

"I'm not as sure of that as you are."

He got up from his chair. "I guess we'll just have to see where it all leads."

"Yes, we will," she agreed.

Dan shook hands with her again and then left her office.

Don't linger once you get what you want. Never give the other side the chance to reconsider. He had Cardenas's agreement, no matter that it was reluctant.

Okay, I've got the team I need. Duncan and his crew can stay Earthside. Cardenas will direct the construction job.

Now to confront Humphries.

SELENE

And he's madder'n hell," Pancho finished.

Dan nodded somberly as they rode an electric cart through the tunnel from the spaceport to Selene proper. Pancho had been at the spaceport to meet him on his return flight from *Nueva Venezuela,* looking worried, almost frightened about Humphries.

"I guess I'd be ticked off, too," he said, "if our positions were reversed."

The two of them were alone in the cart. Dan had deliberately waited until the four other passengers of the transfer ship had gone off toward the city. Then he and Pancho had clambered aboard the next cart. The automated vehicles ran like clockwork along the long, straight tunnel.

"What do you want to do?" Pancho asked.

Dan grinned at her. "I'll call him and arrange a meeting."

"At the O.K. Corral?"

"No," he said, laughing. "Nothing so grim. It's time he and I talked about structuring a deal together."

Frowning, Pancho asked, "Do you really need him now? I mean with the nanotech and all? Can't you run this show yourself and keep him out of it?"

"I don't think that would be the smart thing to do," Dan replied. "After all, he did start me off on this fusion business. If I tried to cut him out altogether he'd have a legitimate gripe."

"That's what he expects you to do."

Dan watched the play of shadows over her face as the cart glided silently along the tunnel. Light and shadow, light and shadow, like watching a speeded-up video of the Sun going across the sky.

"I don't play the game the same way he does," he said at last. "And I don't want this project tied up by lawyers for the next ninety-nine years."

Pancho grunted with distaste. "Lawyers."

"Humphries brought the fusion project to me because he wants to get into Astro. I know how he works. He figures that he'll finance the fusion work in exchange for a bloc of Astro's stock. Then he'll finagle some more stock, put a couple of his clones on my board of directors, and sooner or later toss me out of my own company."

"Can he do that?"

"That's the way he operates. He's snatched half-a-dozen corporations that way. Right now he's on the verge of taking over Masterson Aerospace."

"Masterson?" Pancho looked shocked.

Dan said, "Yep. Half the world drowning and the rest cooking from this double-damned greenhouse, and he's using it to snatch and grab. He's a goddamned opportunist. A vampire, sucking the life out of everything he touches."

"So what are you gonna do?"

"Keep his investment in the fusion project to a minimum," Dan said. "And keep the fusion project separate and apart from Astro Corporation."

"Good luck," she said glumly.

Dan grinned at her. "Hey, don't look so worried. I've been through this kind of thing before. This is what the corporate jungle is all about."

"Yeah, maybe, but I think he'll get rough if he doesn't get his way. Real rough."

With a brash shrug, Dan replied, "That's why I keep Big George around."

"Big George? Who's he?"

Dan had made his quick trip to *Nueva Venezuela* without George. He didn't feel the need for a bodyguard once he was off-Earth. In fact, he hadn't seen the Aussie since they'd arrived together in Selene for his meeting with Doug Stavenger.

"I'll have to introduce you to him."

The cart reached the end of the tunnel and stopped automatically. Dan and Pancho got off; he grabbed his travel-bag and they walked to the customs inspection station. Dan saw that the two uniformed inspectors were still checking the quartet of people who had arrived on his flight. On the other side of the area, by the entrance gate, an elderly couple was saying goodbye to a young family with two children, one of them a tot squirming in her mother's arms.

"So whattaya want me to tell Humphries?" Pancho asked. "He'll wanna know how you did with Dr. Cardenas."

"Tell him the truth. Cardenas is joining the team. She'll be here in a few days."

"Should I tell him you want to set up a meeting with him?"

Dan thought it over as they stepped up to the customs desk. "No," he said at last. "I'll call him myself as soon as we get down to our quarters."

Humphries seemed surprised when Dan called him, but he quickly agreed to a meeting the very next morning. He insisted on having the meeting in the Humphries Space System's suite of offices, up in the same tower on the Grand Plaza that housed Doug Stavenger's office.

Dan accepted meekly enough, laughing inwardly at Humphries's gamesmanship. He tried to phone Big George, got only his answering machine, and left a message for George to call him first thing in the morning. Then he undressed, showered, and went to bed.

He dreamed about Jane. They were together on Tetiaroa, completely alone on the tropical atoll beneath a gorgeous star-strewn sky, walking along the lagoon beach while the balmy wind set the palm trees to rustling softly. A slim crescent of a Moon rode past scudding silvery clouds. Jane was wearing a filmy robe, her auburn hair undone and flowing past her shoulders. In the starlight he could see how beautiful she was, how desirable.

But he could not speak a word. Somehow, no matter how hard he tried, no sound would come out of his mouth. This is stupid, Dan raged at himself. How can you tell her you love her if you can't talk?

The clouds thickened, darkened, blotted out the Moon and stars. Beyond Jane's shadowy profile Dan could see the ocean stirring, frothing, an enormous tidal wave rising up higher, higher, a mountain of foaming water rushing down on them. He tried to warn her, tried to shout, but the water crashed down on them both with crushing force. He reached for Jane, to hold her, to save her, but she was wrenched out of his arms.

He woke, sitting up and drenched with sweat. His throat felt raw, as if he'd been screaming for hours. He didn't know where he was. In the darkness of the bedroom all he could see was the green glowing numerals on the digital clock on the night table. He rubbed at his eyes, working hard to remember. Selene. I'm in the company suite in Selene. I'm going to see Humphries first thing in the morning.

And Jane's dead.

* * *

"You've been quite a busy fellow," Humphries said, with obviously false joviality.

Instead of meeting in his personal office, he had invited Dan to a small windowless conference room. Not even holoviews on the walls, only a few paintings and photographs of Martin Humphries with celebrities of various stripes. Dan recognized the current President of the United States, a dour-faced elderly man in black clerical garb, and Vasily Malik of the GEC.

Leaning back relaxedly in the comfortable padded chair, Dan said, "I guess I have been on the go quite a bit since we last met."

Sitting across the table from Dan, Humphries clasped his hands together atop its gleaming surface. "To tell you the truth, Dan, I get the feeling you're trying to screw me out of this fusion operation."

Laughing, Dan said, "I wouldn't do that, Marty, even if I could."

Humphries laughed back at him. It seemed more than a little forced to Dan.

"Tell me something," Dan said. "You didn't stumble across Duncan by accident, did you?"

Humphries smiled more genuinely. "Not entirely. When I started Humphries Space Systems I went out and backed more than a dozen small, long-shot research groups. I figured that one of them was bound to come through with something. You ought to see some of the kooks I had to deal with!"

"I can imagine," Dan said, grinning. He'd had his share of earnest zanies trying to convince him of one wild scheme or another over the years.

"I got lucky with Duncan and this fusion rocket," Humphries went on, looking pleased with himself.

"It was more than luck," Dan said. "You were damned smart."

"Maybe," Humphries agreed. "It only takes one swing to hit a home run."

"And it doesn't cost much, either, at the laboratory stage."

Nodding, Humphries said, "If more people backed basic research we'd get ahead a lot faster."

"I should've done it myself," Dan admitted.

"Yes, you should have."

"My mistake."

"Okay then, where do we stand?" Humphries asked.

"Well . . . you financed Duncan's original work."

"Including the flight tests that you saw," Humphries pointed out.

Dan nodded. "I've been trying to put together the financing for building a full-scale spacecraft and sending a team out to the Belt."

"I can finance that. I told you I'd put up the money."

"Yep. But it'd cost me a good chunk of Astro Corporation, wouldn't it?"

"We can negotiate a reasonable price. It won't cost you a cent out of pocket."

"But you'd wind up owning Astro," Dan said flatly.

Something flashed in Humphries's eyes for a moment. But he quickly put on a synthetic smile. "How could I take over Astro Manufacturing, Dan? I know you wouldn't part with more than fifteen-twenty percent of your company."

"More like five or ten percent," Dan said.

"Even worse, for me. I'd be a minority stockholder. I wouldn't even be able to put anybody on the board—except myself, I imagine."

Dan said, "H'mm."

Hunching closer, Humphries said, "I hear you're going the nanotech route."

"You hear right," Dan replied. "Dr. Cardenas is returning to Selene to head up the job."

"I hadn't thought about using nanomachines. Makes sense."

"Brings the cost down."

"Makes my investment smaller," Humphries said, straight-faced.

Tired of the fencing, Dan said, "Look, here's the way I see this. We bring Selene in as a third partner. They provide the facilities and nanotech personnel."

"I thought you were recruiting retirees," Humphries said.

"Some," Dan admitted, "but we'll still need Selene's active help."

"So we've got a third partner," Humphries said sullenly.

"I want to form a separate corporation, separate and apart from Astro. We'll each be one-third owners: you, me, and Selene."

Humphries sat up straighter. "What's the matter, Dan, don't you trust me?"

"Not as far as I can throw the Rock of Gibraltar."

Another man might have laughed grudgingly. Humphries glared at Dan for a moment, his face reddening. But then he got himself under control and shrugged nonchalantly.

"You don't want to let me have any Astro stock, do you?"

"Not if I can help it," Dan said pleasantly.

"But then what are you bringing into this deal? I've got the money, Selene's got the personnel and facilities. What do you offer?"

Dan smiled his widest. "My management skills. After all, I'm the one who came up with the nanotech idea."

"I thought it was Stavenger's idea."

Dan felt his brows hike up. And his respect for Humphries's sources of information. *He didn't get that from Pancho; I didn't tell her. Does he have Stavenger's office bugged? Or infiltrated?*

"Tell you what," said Dan. "Just to show you that I'm not such a suspicious sonofabitch, I'll chip in five percent of Astro's stock. Out of my personal holdings."

"Ten," Humphries immediately shot back.

"Five."

"Come on, Dan. You can't get out of this so cheaply."

Dan looked up at the paneled ceiling, took a deep breath, looked back into Humphries's icy gray eyes.

Finally he said, "Seven."

"Eight."

Dan cocked his head slightly, then murmured, "Deal."

Humphries smiled, genuinely this time, and echoed, "Deal."

Each man extended his hand across the table. As they shook hands, Dan said to himself, Count your fingers after he lets go.

SELENE NANOTECHNOLOGY LABORATORY

D an was watching intently as Kris Cardenas manipulated the roller dial with one manicured finger, her eyes riveted on the scanning microscope's display screen. The image took shape on the screen, blurred, then came into crisp focus.

The picture was grainy, gray on gray, with a slightly greenish cast. Dan could make out a pair of fuel tanks with piping that led to a spherical chamber. On the other side of the sphere was a narrow straight channel that ended in the flared bell of a rocket nozzle.

"It's the whole assembly!" he blurted.

Cardenas turned toward him with a bright California smile. "Not bad for a month's work, is it?"

Dan grinned back at her. "Kinda small, though, don't you think?"

They were alone in the nanotech lab this late at night. The other workstations were empty, all the cubicles dark, the ceiling lights turned down to their dim nighttime setting. Only in the corner where Dan and Cardenas sat on a pair of swivel stools were the overhead lights at their full brightness. The massive gray tubing of the scanning microscope loomed above them both like a hulking robot. Dan marveled inwardly that the big, bulky machine was capable of revealing individual atoms.

Cardenas said, "Size isn't important right now. It's the pattern that counts."

"Swell," said Dan. "If I want to send a team of bacteria to the Belt, you've got the fusion drive all set for them."

"Don't be obtuse, Dan."

"I was trying to be funny."

Cardenas did not appreciate his humor. Tapping a bright blue-polished fingernail against the microscope's display screen, she said, "We've programmed this set of nanos to understand the pattern of your fusion system: the tankage, the reactor chamber, the MHD channel, and the rocket nozzle."

"Plus all the plumbing."

"And the plumbing, yes. Now that they've learned the pattern, it's just a matter of programming them to build the same thing at full scale."

Dan scratched his chin, then said, "And the full-scale job will be able to handle the necessary pressures and temperatures?"

"Most of it's built of diamond."

That wasn't an answer to his question, Dan realized. Okay, so the virus-sized nanomachines could take individual atoms of carbon from a pile of soot and put them together one by one to build structures with the strength and thermal properties of pure diamond.

"But will that do the job?" he asked Cardenas.

Her lips became a tight line. She was obviously unhappy about something.

"Problem?" Dan asked.

"Not really," Cardenas said, "But..."

"But what? I've got to know, Kris. I'm hanging my *cojones* out in the breeze on this."

Raising both hands in a don't-blame-me gesture, she said, "It's Duncan. He refuses to come up here. None of his team will leave Earth."

Dan had known that Duncan, Vertientes, and the rest of the team had opted to remain Earthside and communicate with Cardenas and her nanotech people electronically.

"You talk to him every day, don't you?"

"Sure we do. We even have interactive VR sessions, if you can call them interactive."

Feeling alarmed, Dan asked, "What's wrong?"

"It's that damned three-second lag," Cardenas said. "You can't really be interactive, you can't even have a normal conversation when there's three seconds between your question and their answer every blasted time."

"Is it actually hindering your work?"

She made a face somewhere between a grimace and a pout. "Not hindering, exactly. It's just so damned inconvenient! And time-consuming. Sometimes we have to go over a thing two or three times just to be sure we've heard them right. It soaks up time and makes everybody edgy."

Dan thought it over. "Maybe I can talk them into coming up here."

"I've tried to, god knows. Duncan won't budge. Neither will any of his people. They're terrified of nanomachines."

"No!"

"Yes. Even Professor Vertientes. You'd think he'd know better, at his age."

"They're scared of nanomachines?"

"They won't admit it, of course," said Cardenas. "They say that they might not be allowed to return to Earth if the authorities know that they've been working with nanomachines. I think that's a crock; they're just plain scared."

"Maybe not," Dan said. "Those Earthside bureaucrats get

wonky ideas, especially about nanotechnology. I sure haven't told anybody that I'm dealing with nanomachines."

Her brows shot up. "But everybody knows—"

"Everybody knows that *you* and your staff are building a fusion rocket with nanos. As far as the general public is concerned, I don't come near 'em. I'm a bigshot tycoon, I don't get involved in the dirty work. I've never even been in your lab."

Cardenas nodded with newfound understanding. "That's why you sneak in here late at night."

"I don't sneak anywhere," Dan said, with great dignity. "I've never been here. Period."

She laughed. "Of course."

"Kris," he said, more seriously, "I think Duncan and the rest of them have legitimate reasons to be scared of coming up here and working with you. I'm afraid you're going to have to live with that three-second lag. It's their safety net."

Cardenas took a deep breath. "If I have to."

"You've accomplished a helluva lot in just four weeks," Dan pointed out.

"I suppose that's true. It's just... it'd be so much easier if we could all work together under the same roof."

Smiling gently, Dan said, "I never promised you a rose garden."

She was about to reply when the door to the corridor banged open, all the way across the mostly-darkened laboratory. Instinctively, Dan started to duck behind the big microscope tube, like a boy hiding from his mother.

Then he recognized the hulking, shaggy, red-bearded figure of Big George Ambrose.

"That you, Dan?" George called as he strode between workstations toward them. "Been lookin' everywhere for you, y'know."

Despite his size, George moved gracefully, light on his feet and perfectly at home in the low lunar gravity.

"I'm not here," Dan growled.

"Right. But if you were, I'd hafta tell you that Pancho Lane's missin'."

"Missing?"

"Not in her quarters," George said as he approached. "Not in any of the Astro offices. Not in the spaceport or the Grand Plaza. Not anyplace I've looked. Blyleven's worried about her."

Frank Blyleven was chief of Astro's security department. Dan glanced at Cardenas, then said to George, "She could be in someone else's quarters, you know."

George looked surprised at the idea. "Pancho? She doesn't have a guy and she doesn't sleep around."

"I wouldn't worry—"

"She didn't show up at the office t'day. She's never missed an hour of work, let alone a whole day."

That worried Dan. "Didn't show up at all?"

"I asked everybody. No Pancho, all day. I been lookin' for her all night. Nowhere in sight."

"Did you ask her roommate?"

"Mandy Cunningham? She was out havin' dinner with Humphries."

"She should be back by now."

George made a leering smirk. "Maybe. Maybe not."

Turning to Cardenas, Dan said, "I'd better look into this. George is right, Pancho's had her nose to the grindstone ever since she came up here."

"So maybe she's taking a little r and r," Cardenas said, unruffled.

"Maybe," Dan admitted. But he didn't think so.

PELICAN BAR

Pancho had spent the entire day being invisible.

The night before, she had gone to the Pelican Bar for a little relaxation after another long, grueling day of study and simulation runs in the Astro office complex.

The incongruously-named Pelican Bar had been started by a homesick Floridian who had come to Selene back in the days when the underground community was still known as Moonbase. Hired to be the base's quartermaster, he had developed a case of hypertension that kept him from returning to Earth until a regime of exercise and medication brought his blood pressure under control.

He took the pills, largely ignored the exercise, and started the bar in his own quarters as a clandestine drinking club for his cronies. Over the years he had grown into a paunchy little barrel of a man, his bald head gleaming under the ceiling fluorescents, a perpetual gap-toothed smile on his fleshy, tattooed face. He often told his patrons that he had found his true calling as a bartender: "A dispenser of cheer and honest advice," as he put it.

The bar was several levels down from the Grand Plaza, the size of two ordinary living suites, carved out of the lunar rock. And quiet. No music, unless someone wanted to sit at the synthesizer that lay dusty and rarely touched in the farthest, most shadowy corner of the room. The only background noise in the place was the buzz of many conversations.

Pelicans were everywhere. A holographic video behind the bar showed them skimming bare centimeters above the placid waters of the Gulf of Mexico against a background of condo towers and beachfront hotels that had long since gone underwater. Photos of pelicans adorned every wall. Statues of pelicans stood at each end of the bar and pelican mobiles hung from the smoothed-rock ceiling. A meter-tall stuffed toy pelican stood by the bartender's computer, dressed in garish, outlandish Florida tourist's garb and peering at the drinkers through square little granny sunglasses.

Pancho liked the Pelican Bar. She much preferred it to the tidy little bistro up in the Grand Plaza where the tourists and executives did their drinking. The Pelican was a sort of home away from home; she came often enough to be considered one of the steady customers, and she usually bought as many rounds as any of the drinkers clustered around the bar.

She exchanged greetings with the other regulars while the owner, working behind the bar as usual, broke away from an intense conversation with a despondent-looking little redhead to waddle down the bar and pour Pancho her favorite, a margarita with real lime from Selene's hydroponic fruit orchard.

Although a set of booths lined the back wall, there were no stools at the bar itself. You did your drinking standing up, and when you could no longer stand your buddies took you home. House rules.

Pancho had wedged herself into the crowd in between a

total stranger and a retired engineer she knew only as a fellow Pelican patron whose parents had hung the unlikely name of Isaac Walton around his neck. The word was he had originally come to the Moon to get away from jokes about fishing.

Walton's face always seemed slightly askew; one side of it did not quite match the other. Even his graying hair seemed thicker on one side than the other. Normally a happy drinker, he looked morose as he leaned both elbows on the bar and stared into his tall, frosted drink.

"Hi, Ike," Pancho said brightly. "Why the long face?"

"Anniversary," Walton mumbled.

"So where's your wife?"

He gave Pancho a bleary look. "Not my wedding anniversary."

"Then what?"

Walton stood up a little straighter. He was about Pancho's height, stringy and loose-jointed. "The eighth anniversary of my being awarded the Selene Achievement Prize."

"Achievement Prize?" she asked. "What's that?"

The bartender broke into their conversation. "Hey, Ike, don't you think you've had enough for one night?"

Walton nodded solemnly. "Yup. You're right."

"So why don't you go home to your wife," the bartender suggested. Pancho heard something more than friendliness in his tone, an undercurrent of—jeeps, she thought, he almost sounds like a cop.

"You're right, pal. Absolutely right. I'm going home. Whatta I owe you?"

The bartender waved a meaty hand in the air. "Forget it. Anniversary present."

"Thank you very much." Turning to Pancho, he said, "You wanna walk me home?"

She glanced at the bartender, who still looked unusually grim, then shrugged and said, "Sure, Ike. I'll walk you home."

He wasn't as unsteady on his feet as Pancho had thought he'd be. Once outside the bar Walton seemed more depressed than drunk. Yet he nodded or said hello to everyone they passed.

"What's the Achievement Prize?" Pancho asked as they walked down the corridor.

"Kind of a secret."

"Oh."

"I did the impossible for them, y'see, but I did it too late to be of any use and they don't want anybody to know about it so they gave me the prize as hush money and told me to keep my trap shut."

Confused, Pancho asked, "About what?"

For the first time that evening, Walton broke into a smile. "My cloak of invisibility," he answered.

Little by little Pancho wormed the story out of him. Walton had been working with Professor Zimmerman, the nanotech genius, when the old U.N. had sent Peacekeeper troops to seize Moonbase.

"Stavenger was in a sweat to develop nonlethal weapons so we could defend ourselves against the Peacekeepers when they got here without killing any of them," Walton said, growing steadier and gloomier with each step along the corridor. "Zimmerman promised Stavenger he'd come up with a way to make our guys invisible, but the bastards killed him when they attacked. Suicide bomber got down to his lab and blew the old man to smithereens."

"Himself, too?" Pancho asked.

"I did say 'suicide,' didn't I? Anyway, the so-called war ended pretty quick and we got our independence. That's when we changed the name from Moonbase to Selene."

"I know."

"For a while there I didn't have anything to do. I'd been Zimmerman's assistant and now the old man was gone."

Walton had doggedly kept working on Zimmerman's idea

of finding a method for making a person invisible. And eventually he succeeded.

"But who needs to be invisible?" Walton asked. Before Pancho could answer he went on, "Only somebody who's up to no damn good, that's who. Spies. Assassins. Crooks. Thieves."

Selene's governing council decided to mothball Walton's invention. Bury it so that no one would even know it existed.

"So they gave me the big fat prize to keep me quiet. It's a pension, really. I can live in comfort—as long as I stay in Selene and keep my mouth shut."

"Sounds cool to me," Pancho said, trying to cheer him up.

But Walton shook his head. "You don't understand, Pancho. I'm a freaking genius and nobody knows it. I've made a terrific invention and it's useless. I'm not even supposed to mention it to anybody."

Pancho said, "Aren't you taking a chance, talking to me about it?"

He gave her a sidelong glance. "Aw, hell, Pancho, I hadda tell somebody tonight or bust. And I can trust you, can't I? You're not gonna steal it and go out and assassinate anybody, are you?"

"'Course not," Pancho answered immediately. But she was thinking that it might be a hoot to be invisible now and then.

"Wanna see it?" Walton asked.

"The invisibility dingus?"

"Yeah."

"If it's invisible, how can I see it?"

Walton broke into a cackle of laughter. Clapping Pancho on the back, he said, "That's what I like about you, Pancho ol' pal. You're okay, with a capital oke."

Walton turned down the next cross-corridor and led Pancho up to the level just below the Grand Plaza, where most of Selene's life-support machinery chugged away, purifying the air, recycling the water, rectifying the electrical current coming in from the solar farms. Pumps clattered. The air hummed and crackled. The ceilings of these chambers were rough, unfinished rock. Pancho knew that on their other side was either the manicured lawn of the Grand Plaza or the raw regolith of the Moon's surface itself. And along a corridor not far from where they walked lay the catacombs.

"Isn't the dingus under lock and key?" Pancho asked as Walton led her past a long row of metal lockers.

"They don't even know it exists. They think I destroyed it when they gave me their lousy prize. Destroy it, hell! I'll never destroy it. It's the only one in the whole wide solar system."

"Wow."

He nodded absently. "And it's not a 'dingus,' it's a stealth suit."

"Stealth suit," Pancho echoed.

"Like a wetsuit, covers you from head to toe," he explained in a hushed voice, as if afraid someone would hear him. Pancho strained to listen to him over the background hum and chatter of the machinery.

Pancho followed Walton down the long row of metal lockers. The corridor smelled dusty, unused. The overhead lights were spaced so far apart that there were shadowy pools of darkness every few meters. Walton stopped in front of a locker identified by a serial number. Pancho saw that it had an electronic security lock.

Feeling uneasy, Pancho asked, "Don't they have any guards patrolling up here?"

"Nah. What for? There's cameras at the other end of the corridor, but this old tunnel's like an attic. People store junk up here, personal stuff they don't have room for down in their quarters."

Walton tapped out the security code on the electronic lock and pulled the metal door open. It squealed slightly, as if complaining.

"There it is," he said in a hushed voice.

Hanging inside the locker was a limp bodysuit, deep black.

"Ain't she a beauty?" Walton said as he carefully, lovingly, took the suit from the locker and held it up by its hanger for Pancho to admire.

"Looks almost like a wetsuit," Pancho said, wondering how it could make someone invisible. It glittered darkly in the feeble light from the overhead fluorescents, as if spangled with sequins made of onyx.

"The suit's covered with nanocameras and projectors, only a couple of molecules thick. Drove me nuts getting 'em to work right, lemme tell you. I *earned* that prize money."

"Uh-huh," Pancho said, fingering one of the gloved sleeves. The fabric felt soft, pliable, yet somehow almost gritty, like grains of sand.

"The cameras pick up the scenery around you," Walton was explaining. "The projectors display it. Somebody standing in front of you sees what's behind you. Somebody on your left sees what's on your right. Just like they're looking through you. To all intents and purposes you're invisible."

"It really works?" she asked.

"Computer built into the belt controls it," Walton said. "Batteries are probably flat, but I can charge 'em up easy enough." He pointed to a set of electrical outlets on the smoothed-rock wall of the corridor, opposite the lockers.

"But it really works?" she repeated.

He smiled like a proud father. "Want to try it on?"

Grinning back at him, Pancho said, "Sure!"

While Pancho wriggled into the snug-fitting suit Walton plugged the two palm-sized batteries into the nearby electrical outlet. By the time she had pulled on the gloves and fitted the hood over her head, he was snapping the fully-charged batteries into their slots on the suit's waist.

"Okay," Walton said, looking her over carefully. "Now pull the face mask down and seal it to the hood."

Narrow goggles covered Pancho's eyes. "I must look like a terrorist, Ike," she muttered, the fabric of the mask's lining tickling her lips.

"In a minute you won't look like anything at all," he said. "Unlatch the safety cover on your belt and press the pressure switch."

Pancho popped the tiny plastic cover and touched the switch beneath it. "Okay, now what?" she asked.

"Give it fifteen seconds."

Pancho waited. "So?"

With a lopsided grin, Walton said, "Hold your hand up in front of your face."

Pancho lifted her arm. A pang of shock bolted through her. "I can't see it!"

"Damn right you can't. You're invisible."

"I am?"

"Can you see yourself?"

Pancho couldn't. Arms, legs, booted feet: she could feel them as normally as always but could not see them.

"You got a full-length mirror in your locker?" she asked excitedly.

"Why the hell would I have a full-length mirror in there?"

"I want to see what I look like!"

"Cripes, Pancho, you don't look like anything. You're completely invisible."

Pancho laughed excitedly. She made up her mind at that moment to borrow Ike's stealth suit. Without telling him about it, of course.

Covered from head to toes in the stealth suit, Pancho crept slowly, silently along the corridor of Martin Humphries's palatial underground house. She had come down to the mansion with Amanda, although Mandy didn't know it.

For weeks Pancho had been dying to root around in Humphries's mansion. The man was so stinky rich, so ruthlessly powerful and sure of himself, Pancho figured that there must be plenty of dirt under his fingernails. Maybe she could find something that would help Dan. Maybe she could find something that would profit her. Or maybe, she thought, burglarizing Humphries's house would just be a hoot, a refreshing break from the endless hours of study that she and Mandy were grinding through. Besides, it'd be fun to wipe that smug smile off the Humper's face.

So she had borrowed the stealth suit from Walton's locker the very next morning after he'd shown it to her. Pancho had gone to bed that night arguing with herself over whether or not she should ask Ike's permission to use the suit. She had awakened firmly convinced that the less Ike knew the better off each of them would be. So, with a tote bag swinging from her shoulder, she'd gone to the catacombs instead of to work with Mandy, then detoured to the dusty, seldom-used corridor where Walton had stashed the suit. She remembered the singsong of the locker's electronic security code and tapped it out without a flaw.

With a glance at the tiny red eye of the security camera on the ceiling at the far end of the corridor, Pancho quickly bundled the suit into her tote bag. Security people can't watch every screen every minute, she told herself. Besides, even if one of 'em's watchin', I ain't doin' anything to rouse an alarm.

Pancho then went back to her quarters. Amanda was busily at work in the simulations lab; Pancho had the apartment to herself. Immediately she started putting on the stealth suit.

Once she got it on—and saw in the bedroom's full-length mirror that she was truly invisible—she went out to test the suit. It worked wonderfully well. Pancho walked slowly, carefully, through Selene's corridors, threading her way through the pedestrian traffic. Now and then someone would glance her way, as if they'd seen something out of the corner of their eyes. A stray reflection from the overhead lights, Pancho thought, an unavoidable momentary glitter off the array of nanocameras and projectors. But no one really saw her; she drifted through the crowds like an unseen phantom.

She spent the day wandering ghostlike through Selene, gaining confidence in the suit and her ability to use it. The suit fit her snugly, but the boots attached to its leggings were Ike's size, not her own. Pancho had solved that problem by wadding stockings into the boots. They weren't exactly comfortable, but she could walk in them well enough.

For kicks she lifted a soyburger from the counter of the fast-food cafeteria up in the Grand Plaza when no one was working the place except a dumbass robot. She immediately realized, though, that if anyone saw a soyburger floating in midair it would cause a fuss, so she dropped it into the recycler at the end of the counter before anyone noticed her.

By mid-afternoon Pancho returned briefly to her quarters, took off the suit, and dashed out for a quick meal. She was famished. Being invisible makes you hungry, she joked to herself. By the time Amanda returned from her day's work and began dressing for her dinner with Martin Humphries, Pancho was back in the stealth suit, standing quietly in a corner of the bedroom, waiting for Amanda to finish her damned primping and go out.

A cloak of invisibility, Pancho thought as she rode the escalators a few steps ahead of Amanda, down to Selene's bottom layer. What did they call those fancy suits the toreadors wear? A suit of lights, she remembered. Well, I'm wearing a suit of darkness. A cloak of invisibility.

She had to keep her distance from everyone. If somebody jostled into her they'd know she was there, invisible or not. Pancho felt glad that Selene did not allow pets. A dog would probably have sniffed her out easily.

The escalators got less and less crowded as she went down level after level. By the time she was riding down to the last level, she and Amanda were alone on the moving stairs. Once at the bottom, she waited for Amanda, then fell into step behind her. Mandy was heading for a private little dinner with Humphries. Just the two of them, they thought. Pancho smiled to herself. If the Humper tries anything Mandy doesn't like, I'll coldcock him. I'll be her guardian angel. Then she wondered just how far Mandy was willing to go with Humphries—and how far she could tease him without getting herself into real trouble. Well, she shrugged to herself, Mandy's a grownup, she knows what she's doing. Or she ought to.

Mandy looked like a princess in a fairy tale, wearing a short-sleeved frock of baby blue with a knee-length fringed skirt. Modest enough, Pancho thought, although on Mandy nothing could look really modest. Not in the eyes of a man like Humphries, anyway. Pancho couldn't recall seeing the dress before; Mandy must have bought it in one of Selene's shops. Everything cost a fortune there, except for stuff actually made on the Moon. Is Humphries buying her clothes? Pancho wondered. He hadn't given Mandy any jewelry, she was sure of that. Mandy would have showed it off if he had.

Amanda walked purposively down the length of the corridor and into the grotto that housed the Humphries Trust research garden and house. Humphries was at the front door to greet her, all smiles. Pancho slipped in behind her, nearly brushing Humphries's hand as he pulled the door shut. If the Humper felt anything, he didn't show it. Pancho was in the house and he didn't know it.

As Humphries guided Amanda off to the bar, Pancho stood stock-still in the foyer. A man like Humphries would have a state-of-the-art security system in his home, she reasoned. No matter that the house was in Selene; Humphries would insist on topflight security. He might give the human staff the night off for his dates, but he wouldn't turn off his alarm systems. Motion sensors were her big worry. Humphries obviously wouldn't have any working in the residential wing of the house. But the offices would be another thing altogether. She could see the long, spacious living room and the corridor that led to the formal dining room and, beyond it, the library/bar. That was the direction Humphries and Amanda had gone.

On the other side of the foyer was a single closed door. Pancho guessed that it opened onto the suite of offices and laboratories that the ecologists used. Would he have motion sensors set up in there? Probably not, she thought, but if he did . . .

There must be a central control for the security system. Most likely in Humphries's own bedroom or his office. His bedroom? Pancho grinned at the thought. That's one room in the house where he'd have any motion sensors definitely turned off!

Slowly, on tiptoes despite the thick carpeting, Pancho made her way up to the second floor. The master bedroom was easy to find: beautifully-carved double doors at the end of the hallway. She eased the door open. No sirens, no hooting klaxons. Could be silent alarms, she told herself, but if he's dismissed the servants for the night he'll have to come up here his own self, and I can handle that, easy.

The room was sumptuous, and Humphries's bed was enormous, like a tennis court. That bed could handle a whole squad of cheerleaders, she thought. Prob'ly has, Pancho told herself.

Through a half-open door she saw a desktop computer, its screen saver showing some old master's painting of a nude woman. As Pancho cautiously approached the door and eased it all the way open, the screen's image dissolved into another painting of another nude. Huh! she grunted. Some art lover.

Pancho sat at the desk and saw that the computer had a keyboard attached to it. Tentatively, she pecked at the ENTER key. The artwork vanished, and a honey-warm woman's voice said, "Good evening, Mr. Humphries. The time is eight-twelve and I'm ready to go to work anytime you are."

Frowning, Pancho turned the audio down to zero. The screen displayed a menu of options. Hell, he doesn't have any protection on his programs at all. She pictured Humphries at his computer, too impatient to deal with code words and security safeguards. After all, who'd have the balls to break into his home, his own bedroom?

Grinning from ear to ear, Pancho delved into Martin Humphries's computer files.

It turned out that most of the individual file names were indeed coded and incomprehensible to her. So he does have some security built into his programs, she realized. Many of the files required special keywords. One, though, was labelled BED. Curious, Pancho called it up. The screen went blank, except for the words INITIATING HOLOTANK. An eye-blink later the screen announced STARTING HOLOTANK. Then the screen went to a blank gray, except for a bar across its bottom that bore video commands.

Puzzled, Pancho saw a blur of color reflected off the blanked screen. Turning slightly in the desk chair, she saw that what had appeared to be a cylindrical glass *objet d'art* had metamorphosed into a hologram, a full-color three-dimensional moving picture of Humphries naked in bed with some woman.

Son of a bitch, Pancho said to herself. He vids his own sex life. She watched for a few moments. They weren't doing anything that unusual, or thrilling, for that matter, so Pancho touched the fast-forward button on the screen.

It was downright funny watching Humphries and his women in fast-forward. He's a Humper, all right, Pancho thought as she watched a succession of beautiful naked women performing arduously with him. She recognized the redhead from her first visit to the house. I wonder if they know they're being videoed, she asked herself.

After a half-dozen of Humphries's home videos, Pancho got a little bored. She cut the program and returned to the screen's menu of options, but she had new respect for the program labelled VR – PERSONAL. She looked into just one of its files for a few minutes, then angrily clicked it off, revolted.

The nasty S.O.B. uses his bedmates as models for his virtual reality fantasies, she realized. What he can't get them to do in real life he has them doing in his VR wet dreams. Creep!

With a disgusted shake of her head she decided to leave Humphries's sex life alone and started hacking into the other files.

When she glanced at the digital clock in the corner of the

screen, Pancho was shocked to realize that nearly two hours had elapsed. It had been a fruitful time, though. The Humphries Trust was now paying the rent on Susan Lane's cryonic storage unit, a big burden off Pancho's shoulders and a picayune pinprick in the Trust's multibillion funds.

Most of the files were incomprehensible to Pancho; some were technobabble and equations, lots of them were stock manipulations and business deals encoded in so much jargon and legalese that it would take a team of lawyers to decipher them. But now they all contained a new subroutine that allowed Pancho to tap into the files from a remote site. Codeword: Hackensack. Which was just what Pancho was preparing to do.

Got to be careful, though, she warned herself. Don't get greedy enough for him to recognize he's being hacked. A man like Humphries'll have you slapped into the slammer so fast it'll break the sound barrier. Or he'll just have somebody pay you a visit and rip out your arms.

Satisfied with her work, Pancho closed down the computer and left Humphries's office, careful to leave the door ajar just the way she'd found it. As she made her way downstairs, she wondered if Mandy and Humphries were still at dinner, after all this time.

They were. Peeking in on the dining room, Pancho saw the remains of some fancy dessert melting in their dishes, and half-empty flutes of champagne sparkling in the subdued light from the crystal chandelier above the table.

Mandy was saying, "...it's certainly beautiful, Martin, and I appreciate your thoughtfulness, but I can't accept it. Really, I can't."

Pancho crept closer, staring. Humphries held an open jewelry case in one hand. It contained a stunning sapphire necklace.

"I got it specially for you," he was saying, his voice almost pleading.

"Martin, you're a dear man, but I can't get myself involved in a relationship now. You of all people should understand that."

"But I don't understand," he said. "Why not?"

"I'll be heading off on the mission in a few months. I might never come back."

"All the more reason to grab whatever happiness we can now, while we can."

Amanda looked genuinely distressed. Shaking her head, she said, "I simply can't, Martin. I can't."

In a gentle whisper he said, "I could have you removed from the mission. I could see to it that you stay here, with me."

"No. Please..."

"I could," he repeated, stronger. "By god, that's what I'll do."

"But I don't want you to," Amanda said, alarmed.

"You don't have to go through with it," Humphries insisted. "I know it's dangerous. I had no idea that you're afraid of—"

"Afraid!" Mandy snapped. "I'm not afraid! Simply because I understand the risks involved does *not* mean that I'm afraid."

Humphries puffed out an exasperated breath. "Then you're using the mission as an excuse to keep your distance from me, is that it?"

"No!" Amanda said. "That's not it at all. I simply..." Her voice trailed off into silence.

"Then what's wrong?" Humphries asked. "What's the problem? Is it me?"

She stared down at the table for a long, miserable, silent moment. Pancho thought she saw tears glistening in Mandy's eyes. The expression on Humphries's face was somewhere between bafflement and anger.

"Martin, please," Amanda said at last. "We've only known each other for a few weeks. You're a very wonderful man in many ways, but I'm not ready for a meaningful relationship. Not now. Not with this mission coming up. Perhaps afterward, when I return, perhaps then."

Humphries pulled in a deep breath. It seemed obvious to Pancho that he was trying to control his temper.

"I'm not a patient man," he said, his voice low. "I'm not accustomed to waiting."

No, Pancho thought. What you're accustomed to is taking your women up to your bedroom and videoing the whole thing for playback. And then VR games.

"Please bear with me, Martin," Amanda whispered, her voice husky with tears. "Please."

If he tries to get rough with Mandy, Pancho told herself, I'll kick his balls into next week. She wished she'd brought Elly, but the stealth suit was too confining for the snake; she'd left Elly back at her quarters.

Humphries snapped the jewelry case shut with a click that sounded like a gunshot.

"All right," he said tightly. "I'll wait. I wish I'd never started this fusion business."

Amanda made a sad smile. "But then we'd never have met, would we?"

He conceded the point with a hopeless shrug, then got up and led Amanda to the front door of the house.

"Will I see you again?" he asked as he opened the door for her.

"It might be best if we don't, Martin. Not until after I return."

He nodded, grim-faced. Then he grasped both her wrists and said, "I love you, Amanda. I really do."

"I know," she said, and kissed him swiftly, lightly, on the cheek.

She hurried down the walk away from him so quickly that Pancho almost didn't make it through the door before Humphries slammed it shut.

Pancho had to sprint up the escalators to get back to the quarters she shared with Amanda before Mandy did. Twice she nearly stumbled and fell; it wasn't easy to run up moving stairs when you can't see your own feet.

It was late enough that the corridors were not crowded. Pancho easily dodged around the few people still up and about, leaving a couple of them bewildered as she brushed past them; they felt certain that someone had just rushed by, yet there was no one in sight. She got to their quarters well ahead of Amanda, powered down the stealth suit as soon as she slid the door shut behind her, stripped to her skivvies, and stuffed the suit under her bed. Elly was snoozing comfortably in her plastic cage, actually a box that still smelled faintly of the strawberries it had carried from China to Selene. Pancho had packed it with several centimeters of gritty regolith dirt, stuck in an artificial cactus, and kept a saucer of water in it for Elly's comfort.

She was kneeling beside the plastic box, pouring fresh water into the saucer when Amanda came in.

Pancho looked up at her roommate. Mandy's eyes were red, as if she'd been crying.

"How'd your date go?" she asked, innocently.

Looking troubled, Amanda said, "Oh, Pancho, I think he wants to marry me."

Pancho got to her feet. "He's not the marrying kind."

"He's been married. Twice."

"That's what I mean."

Amanda sat on her bed. "He... he's different from any other man I've ever met."

"Yeah. He's got more money."

"No, it isn't that," Amanda replied. "He's..." She searched for a word.

"Horny?" Pancho suggested.

Amanda frowned at her. "He's *powerful*. There's something in his eyes... he almost frightens me."

Thinking about Humphries's home videos, Pancho nodded.

"I can't see him again. I simply can't."

She sounded to Pancho as if she were trying to convince herself.

"He's so accustomed to getting whatever he wants," Amanda said, more to herself than Pancho. "He doesn't like being turned away, rejected."

"Nobody does, Mandy."

"But he..." Again her words faltered. "Pancho, with other men I could smile and flirt and let it go at that. But Martin won't be satisfied with that. He wants what he wants, and if he doesn't get it he can be... I just don't know what he'd do, but he frightens me."

"You think he wants to marry you?"

"He said he loves me."

"Aw hell, Mandy, guys have said that to me, too. All they want is to get into your pants."

"I think he really believes that he loves me."

"That's a strange way to put it."

"Pancho, I can't see him again. There's no telling what he might do. I've got to stay away from him."

Pancho thought that Amanda looked scared. And she's got plenty to be scared of, she told herself.

First thing the following morning, Pancho phoned Dan Randolph and asked to meet with him. One of Randolph's assistants, the big beefy-faced guy with the sweet tenor voice, said he'd call her back. In five minutes, he did. Randolph would see her in his office at ten-fifteen.

Astro Corporation's offices were just down the corridor from the living quarters that the company rented. In most corporations, executive country was conspicuously more luxurious than the regular troops' territory. Not so at Astro. There was no discernible difference along the length of the corridor. As she walked along the row of doors, looking for Randolph's name, Pancho decided that she wouldn't tell him about the stealth suit. She'd returned it first thing that morning to Walton's locker. Ike knew nothing of her borrowing the suit; if there was any bad fallout, he couldn't be blamed for anything.

Randolph looked tense when Pancho was ushered into his office by the big Aussie she'd talked to on the phone.

"Hi, boss," she said brightly.

It was a small office, considering it belonged to the head of a major corporation. There was a desk in one corner, but Randolph was standing by the sofa and cushioned chairs arranged around a coffee table on the opposite side of the room. Pancho saw that the walls were decorated with photos of Astro rockets launching from Earth on tongues of fire and billowing smoke. Nothing personal. No pictures of Randolph himself or anyone else. Pancho grinned inwardly when she saw that Randolph's desk was cluttered with papers, despite the computer built into it. The paperless office was still a myth, she realized.

Gesturing to the sofa, he said, "Have a seat. Have you had breakfast?"

Instead of sitting down, Pancho asked, "Is that a trick question? Astro employees are up at the crack of dawn every day, boss, and twice on Sundays."

Randolph laughed. "Coffee? Tea? Anything?"

"Can I use your computer for a minute?" she asked.

He looked puzzled, but said, "Sure, go ahead." Louder, he called, "Computer, guest voice."

Pancho went to the desk and leaned over the upright display screen. She gave her name and the computer came to life. Within a few seconds, she waved Randolph over to look at the screen.

He peered at the display. "What the hell's that?"

"Martin Humphries's personal menu of programs."

"Humphries?" Randolph sank into his desk chair.

"Yep. I hacked into his machine last night. You can tap in anytime you want."

Randolph looked up at Pancho, then back at his screen. "Without his knowing it?"

"Oh, he'll figger it out sooner or later, I guess. But right now he doesn't know it."

"How the hell did you do this?"

Pancho smiled at him. "Magic."

"H'mp," Randolph grunted. "It's a shame you couldn't do this a few days earlier."

"How come?"

"We're partners now."

"You and Humphries? Partners?"

"Humphries, Selene and Astro. We've formed a limited partnership: Starpower, Limited."

"Hot spit! Where can I buy stock?"

"It's not public. Duncan and his people will get a block of shares, but otherwise, it's Humphries, me, and the good citizens of Selene. It should help keep Selene's taxes down, if it works."

Feeling a bit disappointed, Pancho grumbled, "Oh, just the big boys, huh?"

Randolph gave her a sly grin. "I suppose," he said, running a finger across his chin, "that we'll award a few shares here and there, for exceptional performances."

"Like piloting a bird to the Belt and back."

Randolph nodded.

"Okay," Pancho said, with enthusiasm. "Meanwhile, you can poke into Humphries's files anytime you want to."

Randolph cleared the screen with a single, sharp, "Exit." To Pancho, he said, "You're wasting your time jockeying spacecraft. You make a mighty fine spy, kid."

"I'd rather fly than spy," she said.

Randolph looked at her. He's got really neat eyes, she thought. Gray, but not cold. Deep. Flecked with gold. Nice eyes.

"I'm not sure that I want to poke into Humphries's files," he said.

"No?"

"A man named Stimson was the U.S. Secretary of State back a century or more ago," Randolph said. "When he found out that the State Department was routinely intercepting the mail from the foreign embassies in Washington he stopped the practice. He said, 'Gentlemen do not read each other's mail.' Or something like that."

Pancho snorted. "Maybe you're a gentleman, but Humphries sure ain't."

"I think you're half right."

"Which half?"

Instead of answering, Randolph tapped a button on the phone console. The big Australian came through the door from the outer office almost instantly.

"You two know each other?" Randolph asked. Without

waiting for a reply from either of them, he said, "George Ambrose, Pancho Lane."

"Pleased," said Big George. Pancho made a quick smile.

"George, who do we have who can download a complete hard drive without letting the hard drive's owner know it?"

Big George glanced at Pancho, then asked, "You want this done as quiet as possible, right?"

"Absolutely right."

"Then I'll do it meself."

"You?"

"Don't look so surprised," George said. "I used to be an engineer, before I hooked up with you."

"You were a fugitive from justice before you hooked up with me," Randolph countered.

"Yeah, yeah, but before that. I came to the Moon to tele-operate tractors up on the surface. My bloody degree's in software architecture, for chrissakes."

"I didn't know that," Randolph said.

"Well now you do. So what needs doing here?"

"I'd like you to work with Pancho here. She'll explain the problem."

George looked at her. "Okay. When do we start?"

"Now," said Randolph. Then, to Pancho, he added, "You can tell George anything you'd tell me."

"Sure," Pancho agreed. But in her mind she added, Maybe.

FACTORY #4

This is more like it," said Dan.

He heard Kris Cardenas's nervous laughter in his helmet earphones.

There were five of them standing on the factory floor, encased in white spacesuits like a team of astronauts or tourists out for a jaunt on the Moon's surface. Before them, on the broad, spacious floor of the otherwise empty factory, stood a set of spherical fuel tanks, the smaller sphere of a fusion reaction chamber, and the unfinished channel of an MHD generator, all connected by sturdy-looking piping and surrounded by crates of various powdered metals and bins of soot: pure carbon dust. Dan, Cardenas and three of her nanotechnicians stood in a group, encased in their spacesuits, watching the results of the nanomachines' ceaseless work.

It was daylight outside, Dan knew. Through the open sides of the factory he saw the brilliant sunlight glaring harshly against the barren lunar landscape. But inside the factory, with its curved roof cutting off the glow from the Sun and Earth, the components of the fusion system looked dark and dull, like the unpolished diamond that they were.

"We start on the pumps next," Cardenas said, "as soon as the MHD channel is finished. And then the rocket nozzles."

Dan heard an edge in her voice. She did not like being out on the surface. Despite all her years of living on the Moon—or maybe because of them—being outside bothered her.

Selene's factories were built out on the Moon's surface, exposed to the vacuum of space, almost completely automated or run remotely by operators safe in control centers underground.

"You okay, Kris?" he asked.

"I'd feel better downstairs," she answered frankly.

"Okay, then, let's go. I'm sorry I dragged you out here. I just wanted to see for myself how we're doing."

"It's all right," she said, but she turned and started toward the airlock hatch and the tractor that had carried them to the factory.

"I know that the vacuum out here is great for industrial processing," she said, apologizing. "It just scares the bejesus out of me."

"Even buttoned up nice and cozy in a spacesuit?" Dan asked, walking across the factory floor alongside her.

"Maybe it's the suit," she said. "Maybe I'm a closet claustrophobe."

Contamination was something that flatlanders from Earth took for granted. Living on a planet teeming with life, from bacteria to whales, thick with pollution from human and natural sources, and deep within a turbulent atmosphere that transports spores, dust, pollen, smog, moisture and other contaminants everywhere, cleanliness for Earthsiders was a matter of degree. That was why Dan, with his immune system weakened by the radiation doses he'd been exposed to in space, wore filter plugs and sanitary masks when he was on Earth.

In the hard vacuum of the lunar surface, a thousand times better than the vacuum of low Earth orbit, not only was the environment clean of external pollution sources, the contaminants inside most materials could be removed virtually for free. Microscopic gas bubbles trapped inside metals percolated out of the metal's crystal structure and boiled off into the void. Thus Selene's factories were out on the lunar surface, open to the purifying vacuum of the Moon.

"We don't need to go through the carwash again," Dan said, touching the arm of Cardenas's suit. "We can go straight to the tractor."

He walked around the bulky airlock and hopped off the concrete slab that formed the factory floor, dropping in lunar slow-motion three meters to the regolith. His boots puffed up a little cloud of dust that floated lazily up halfway to his knees.

Cardenas came to the lip of the slab, hesitated, then jumped down to where Dan waited for her.

Like all the lunar factories, this one was built on a thick concrete platform to keep the factory floor above the dusty ground. With no winds, there was little danger of contaminants blowing in from the outside. A curving dome of honeycomb lunar aluminum protected the factory from the constant infall of micrometeoroids and the hard radiation from the Sun and deep space.

The most worrisome source of pollution came from the humans who occasionally entered the factories, even though they had to wear spacesuits. Before they were allowed onto the factory floor, Dan and the others had to go through the "carwash," a special airlock equipped with electrostatic scrubbers and special powdered detergents that removed the traces of oil, perspiration and other microscopic contaminants that clung to the spacesuits' outer surfaces.

As the tractor slowly trundled back to Selene's main airlock, Dan thought about what he had just seen. Before his eyes, the MHD channel was growing: slowly, he admitted, but it was visibly getting longer as the virus-sized nanomachines took carbon and other atoms from the supply bins and locked them into place like kids building a tinkertoy city.

"How much longer?" he asked into the microphone built into his helmet.

Cardenas, sitting beside him, understood his question. "Three weeks, if they go as programmed."

"Three weeks?" Dan blurted. "Looks like they're almost finished now."

"They've still got to finish the MHD channel, which is a pretty tricky piece of work. High-current-density electrodes, superconducting magnets and all. Then comes the pumps, which is no bed of roses, and finally the rocket nozzles, which are also complex: buckyball microtubes carrying cryogenic hydrogen running a few centimeters away from a ten-thousand-degree plasma flow. Then there's—"

"Okay, okay," Dan said, throwing up his gloved hands. "Three weeks."

"That's the schedule."

Dan knew the schedule. He had been hoping for better news from Cardenas. Over the past six weeks his lawyers had hammered out the details of the new Starpower, Ltd. partnership. Humphries's lawyers had niggled over every detail, while Selene's legal staff had breezed through the negotiation with little more than a cursory examination of the agreement, thanks largely to Doug Stavenger's prodding.

So now it was all in place. Dan had the funding to make the fusion rocket a reality, and he still had control of Astro Manufacturing. Astro was staggering financially, but Dan calculated that the company could hold together until the profits from the fusion system started rolling in.

Still, he constantly pushed Cardenas to go faster. It was going to be a tight race: Astro had already started construction of its final solar power satellite. When that one's finished, Dan knew, we go sailing over the disaster curve. No new space construction contracts in sight.

"Can't this buggy go any faster?" Cardenas asked, testily.

"Full throttle, ma'am," said the imperturbable technician at the controls.

To take her mind off her fears of being out in the open, Dan asked her, "Did you see this morning's news from Earthside?"

"The food riots in Delhi? Yeah, I saw it."

"They're starving, Kris. If the monsoon fails again this year there's going to be a monster famine, and it'll spread a long way."

"Not much we can do about," Cardenas said.

"Not yet," Dan muttered.

"They got themselves into this mess," she said tightly, "breeding like hamsters."

She's really bitter, Dan thought. I wonder how she'd feel if her husband and kids had decided to stay on the Moon with her. With a sigh, he admitted, She's got plenty to be bitter about.

Big George was waiting for Dan in his private office, sitting on the sofa, a sheaf of printouts scattered across the coffee table.

"What's all this?" Dan asked, sitting in the chair at the end of the coffee table. When George sat on the couch there really wasn't much room for anyone else.

"Stuff I lifted from Humphries's files," George said, his red-bearded face wrinkled with worry. "He's out for your balls, y'know."

"I know."

Tapping a blunt finger on the pile of printouts, George said, "He's buyin' every share of Astro stock he can get his hands on. Quietly. No greenmail, no big fuss, but he's pushin' his brokers to buy at any price."

"Great," Dan grunted. "Maybe the damned stock will go up a little."

George grinned. "That'd be good. Been in free fall long enough."

"You're not thinking of selling, are you?"

With a laugh, George replied, "The amount I've got? Wouldn't make any difference, one way or the other."

Dan was not amused. "If you ever do want to sell, you come to me first, understand? I'll buy at the market price."

"Humphries is buyin' at two points above the fookin' market price."

"Is he?"

"In some cases, where big blocks of stock are involved."

"Son of a bitch," Dan said fervently, pronouncing each word distinctly. "He knows I don't have the cash to buy out the minor stockholders."

"It's not all that bad," George said. "I did a calculation. At the rate he's acquiring Astro shares, it'll take him two years to buy up a majority position."

Dan stared off into space, thinking hard. "Two years. We could be making profits from the Asteroid Belt by then. Should be, if everything goes right."

"And if it doesn't go right?"

Dan shrugged. "Then Humphries will take control of Astro and throw me out on my butt."

"I'll take his head off his fookin' shoulders first," George growled.

"A lovely sentiment, pal, but then we'd have to deal with his lawyers."

George rolled his eyes toward heaven.

This is getting silly, Pancho thought. Humphries doesn't trust phones or electronic links, too easy to tap, he says. So we have to meet face-to-face, in person, but in places where we won't be noticed together. And he's running out of places.

He had stopped inviting Pancho to his home, down at the bottom level. Worried about somebody seeing her down there where she doesn't belong, he claimed. But Pancho knew he'd stopped inviting her down there once she'd introduced him to Mandy. So his house was now out.

Going outside on tourist jaunts is dumb, she thought. Besides, sooner or later some tourist is gonna recognize the high and mighty Martin Humphries on his bus. And how many times can an Astro employee take an afternoon off to go on a bus ride up on the surface? It's silly.

So now she was strolling along one of the paved paths that meandered through the Grand Plaza. Lots of grass and flowery shrubs and even some trees. Nothing as lush as

Humphries had down at his grotto, but the Plaza was pleasant, relaxed, open and green.

For a town that's only got about three thousand permanent residents, Pancho thought, there's an awful lot of people up here sashaying around. The walking paths weren't exactly crowded, but there were plenty of people strolling along. Pancho had no trouble telling the Selene citizens from the rare tourists: the locals shuffled along easily in the low gravity and dressed casually in coveralls or running suits, for the most part; the few tourists she spotted wore splashy tee-shirts and vacation shorts and hopped and stumbled awkwardly, despite their weighted boots. Some of the women had bought expensive frocks in the Plaza shops and were showing them off as they oh-so-carefully stepped along the winding paths.

The Selenites smiled and greeted each other as they passed; the tourists tended to be more guarded and uncertain of themselves. Funny, Pancho thought: anybody with enough money and free time to come up here for a vacation oughtta be more relaxed.

The outdoor theater was jammed, Pancho saw. She remembered a news bulletin about Selene's dance club performing low-gravity ballet. All in all, it seemed a normal weekday evening in the Plaza, nothing out of the ordinary.

All the paths winding through the greenery led to the long windows set into the far end of the Plaza dome. Made of lunar glassteel, they were perfectly transparent yet had the structural strength of the reinforced concrete that made up the rest of the dome's structure. It was still daylight outside, and would be for another two hundred-some hours. A few tourists had stopped to gape out at the cracked, pockmarked floor of Alphonsus.

"It looks so *dead!*" said one of the women.

"And empty," her husband muttered.

"Makes you wonder why anyone ever came up here to live."

Pancho huffed impatiently. You try growing up in Lubbock, or getting flooded out in Houston, see how much better the Moon looks to you.

"Good evening," said Martin Humphries.

Pancho had not seen him approaching; she'd been looking through the windows at the outside, listening to the tourists' comments.

"Howdy," she said.

He was wearing dark slacks with a beige pullover shirt. And sandals, no less. His "ordinary guy" disguise, Pancho thought. She herself was in the same sky-blue coveralls she'd been wearing all day, with an Astro Corporation logo over the left breast pocket and her name stenciled just above it.

Gesturing to a concrete bench at the edge of the path, Humphries said, "Let's sit down. There are no cameras out here to see us together."

They sat. A family strolled by, parents and two little boys, no more than four or five. Lunatics. Selenites. The kids might even have been born here, she thought.

"What have you been up to lately?" Humphries asked casually.

Truthfully, Pancho reported, "We've started the detailed mission planning. Randolph's picked out a couple of target asteroids for us to rendezvous with, and now Mandy and me are workin' out the optimum trajectory, trip times, supply needs, failure modes . . . stuff like that."

"Sounds boring."

"Not when your life hangs on it."

Humphries conceded the point with a nod. "The construction of the propulsion system is proceeding on schedule?"

"You'd know more about that than I would."

"It is," he said.

"That's what I figured. Dan'd go ballistic if there were any holdups there."

"Amanda refuses to see me," he said.

For a moment Pancho was jarred by the sudden change of

subject. Recovering quickly, she replied, "Mandy's got enough on her hands. This isn't the time for her to get involved with somebody... anybody."

"I want her off the mission."

"You can't do that to her!" Pancho blurted.

"Why not?"

"It'd ruin her career, that's why. Bounced off the first crewed mission to the Belt: how'd that look on her resume?"

"She won't need a resume. I'm going to marry her."

Pancho stared at him. He was serious.

"For how long?" she asked coldly.

Anger flared in Humphries's eyes. "Just because my first two marriages didn't work out, there's no reason to think this one won't."

"Yeah. Maybe."

"Besides," Humphries went on, "if it doesn't work out she'll get a very handsome settlement out of me. She'll never have to work again."

Pancho said nothing. She was thinking, If it doesn't work out he'll use every lawyer he's got to throw Mandy out into the cold without a cent. If it doesn't work out he'll hate her just as much as he hates his first two wives.

"I want you to help convince her to marry me," Humphries said.

Pancho's mind was spinning. You gotta be careful here, she warned herself. Don't get him mad at you.

"Mr. Humphries, that's something I just plain can't do. This isn't a business deal, I can't talk her into doin' something she doesn't want to do. Nobody can. Except maybe you."

"But she won't see me!"

"I know, I know," she said, as sympathetically as she could. "It's just too much pressure for her, what with the mission and all."

"That's why I want her off the mission."

"Don't do that to her. Please."

"My mind's made up."

Pancho sighed unhappily. "Well, you're just gonna have to talk to Dan Randolph about that. He's the boss, not me."

"Then that's what I'll do," Humphries said firmly.

"I wish you wouldn't. Whyn't you let us go out to the Belt. When we get back Mandy'll be able to give you her full attention."

"No." Humphries shook his head. "You might not get back."

"We will."

"You might not. I don't want to take the chance of losing her."

Pancho looked into his eyes. They were still cold, unreadable, like the eyes of a professional card shark she'd known once while she'd been supporting herself through the University of Nevada in Las Vegas by working at one of the casinos. Not the eyes of a lovesick swain. Not the eyes of a man whose heart might break.

"Better talk to Randolph, then," she said.

"I will."

Feeling weary and more than a little afraid of what was going to happen with Mandy, Pancho got to her feet. Humphries stood up, too, and she noticed that he was several centimeters shorter than she'd thought him to be. Glancing down at his sandals, she thought, The sumbitch must have lifts in his regular shoes.

"By the way," Humphries said, his voice hard-edged, "someone's hacked into my private files."

She was genuinely surprised that he'd found out so quickly. It must have shown on her face.

"Randolph is a lot smarter than I thought he was, but it won't do him any good."

"You mean he's the one who hacked you?"

"Who else? One of his people, obviously. I want you to find out who. And how."

"I can't do that!" Pancho blurted.

"Why not?"

"I'll get caught. I'm not a chip freak."

His eyes bored into her for a painfully long moment. "You find out who did it. And how it was done. Or else."

"Or else what?"

With a grim smile, Humphries answered, "I'll think of something."

f he finds the account I set up for him to pay the rent on my sister's dewar I'm toast," Pancho said as she paced across Dan's office.

Sitting behind his desk, Dan said, "I'll get George to scratch the program. Astro can pay the storage fees for your sister."

Pancho shook her head. "That'll just call attention to what I did."

"Not if we erase the subroutine completely. He'll never know."

"No!" Pancho insisted. "Don't go anywhere near it. It'll tip him off for sure."

Dan could see how agitated she was. "You just want to leave it there? He might stumble across it any minute."

"He knows I did it," Pancho said, crossing the room again in her long-legged strides. "I know he knows. He's just playin' cat-and-mouse with me."

"I don't think so. He's not the type. Humphries is more a sledgehammer-on-the-head kind of guy."

She stopped and turned toward Dan, her face suddenly white, aghast. "Jesus H. Christ . . . he might turn off Sis's life support! He might pull the plug on her!"

Dan knew she was right. "Or threaten to."

"That'd give him enough leverage to get me to do whatever he wants."

"What does he want?"

"He wants Mandy. He wants her scrubbed from the mission so he can talk her into marrying him."

Dan leaned back in his desk chair and stared at the ceiling. He'd had the office swept for bugs only an hour earlier, yet he had the uneasy feeling that Humphries knew everything that he said or did. Pancho's not the only Astro employee he's recruited, Dan reminded himself. My whole double-damned staff must be honeycombed with his snoops. Who can I trust?

He snapped forward in the chair and said into the phone console, "Phone, find George Ambrose. I want him here, now."

In less than a minute Big George came through the doorway from the outer office.

"George, I want this whole suite swept for bugs," Dan commanded.

"Again? We just did it an hour ago."

"I want you to do it this time. Yourself. Nobody else."

Scratching at his shaggy beard, George said, "Gotcha, boss."

It took a maddening half hour. Pancho forced herself to sit on the sofa while George went through the office with a tiny black box in one massive paw.

"Clean in here," he said at last.

"Okay," said Dan. "Close the door and sit down."

"You said you wanted the outer offices done, too," George objected.

"In a minute. Sit."

Obediently, George lowered his bulk into one of the cushioned chairs in front of Dan's desk.

"I've been thinking. Tonight, the three of us are going to move a dewar out of the catacombs," Dan said.

"Sis? Where—"

"I'll figure that out between now and then," Dan said. "Maybe somewhere else on the Moon. Maybe we'll move her to one of the space stations."

"You've gotta have the right equipment to maintain it," George pointed out.

Dan waved a hand in the air. "You need a cryostat to keep the nitrogen liquified. Not much else."

"Life support monitors," Pancho pointed out.

"Self-contained on the dewar flask," said Dan.

"Not the equipment," Pancho corrected. "I mean you need some people to take a look every few days, make sure everything's running okay."

With a shake of his head, Dan said, "That's a frill that you pay extra for. You don't need it. The equipment has safety alarms built in. The only time you need human intervention is when the flask starts to exceed the limits you've set the equipment to keep."

"Well, yeah . . . I guess," Pancho agreed reluctantly.

"Okay, George," Dan said. "Go sweep the rest of the place. We can all meet here for dinner at . . ." he called up his appointment screen with the jab of a finger, ". . . nineteen-thirty."

"Dinner?" Pancho asked.

"Can't do dirty work on an empty stomach," Dan said, grinning mischievously.

"But where are we taking her?" Pancho asked as she disconnected the liquid nitrogen feed line. Despite its heavy insulation, the hose was stiff with a rime of frost. Cold white vapor hissed briefly from its open end, until she twisted the seal shut.

"Shh!" Dan hissed, pointing to the baleful red eye of the security camera hanging some fifty meters down the corridor.

This late at night they were quite alone in the catacombs, but Dan worried about that security camera. There was one at each end of the long row of dewars, and although the area was dimly lit, the cameras fed into Selene's security office where they were monitored twenty-four hours a day. Pancho figured that, like security guards anywhere, the men and women responsible for monitoring the cameras seldom paid them close attention, except when a warning light flashed red or a synthesized voice warned of trouble that some sensor had detected. That's why they had hacked into the sensor controls on Sis's dewar and cut them out of the monitoring loop.

Dan and George were sweating with the effort of jacking up the massive dewar onto a pair of trolleys. Even in the low gravity of the Moon, the big stainless-steel cylinder was heavy.

"Where're we goin'?" Pancho repeated.

"You'll see," Dan grunted.

Pancho plugged the nitrogen hose into the portable cryostat they had taken from one of the Astro labs, several levels below the catacombs.

"Okay, all set," she whispered.

"How're you doing, George?" Dan asked.

The shaggy Australian came around the front end of the dewar. "Ready whenever you are, boss."

Dan glanced once at the distant camera's red eye, then said, "Let's get rolling."

The caster wheels on the trolleys squeaked as the three of them pushed the dewar down the long, shadowy corridor.

"Don't the security cameras have a recording loop?" Pancho asked. "Once they see Sis's dewar is missing, they'll play it back and see us."

"That camera's going to show a nice, quiet night," Dan said, leaning hard against the big dewar as they trundled along. "Cost me a few bucks, but I think I found an honest security guard. She'll erase our images and run a loop from earlier in the evening to cover the erasure. Everything will look peaceful and calm."

"That's an honest guard?" Pancho asked.

"An honest guard," Dan said, panting with the strain of pushing, "is one who stays bought."

"And I'll put an empty dewar in your sister's place," George added, "soon's we get this one settled in." Pancho noticed he was breathing easily, hardly exerting himself.

"But where're we takin' her?" Pancho asked again. "And why're we whisperin' if you got the guard bought?"

"We're whispering because there might be other people in the catacombs," Dan replied, sounding a bit irked. "No sense taking any chances we don't need to take."

"Oh." That made sense. But it still didn't tell her where in the hell they were going.

They passed the end of the catacombs and kept on going along the long, dimly-lit corridor until they stopped at last at what looked like an airlock hatch.

Dan stood up straight and stretched his arms overhead until Pancho heard his vertebrae crack.

"I'm getting too old for this kind of thing," he muttered as he went to the hatch and pecked on its electronic lock. The hatch popped slightly open; Pancho caught a whiff of stale, dusty air that sighed from it.

George pulled the hatch all the way open.

"Okay, down the tunnel we go," said Dan, unclipping a flashlight from the tool loop on the leg of his coveralls.

The tunnel had been started, he explained to Pancho, back in the early days of Moonbase, when Earthbound managers had decided to ram a tunnel through the ringwall mountains to connect the floor of Alphonsus with the broad expanse of Mare Nubium.

"I helped to dig it," Dan said, with pride in his voice. Then he added, "What there is of it, at least."

The lunar rock had turned out to be much tougher than expected; the cost of digging the tunnel, even with plasma torches, had risen too far. So the tunnel was never finished. Instead, a cable-car system had been built over the mountains. It was more expensive to operate than a tunnel would have been but far cheaper to construct.

"I've ridden the cable car up to the top of Mt. Yeager," Pancho said. "The view's terrific."

"Yep," Dan agreed. "They forgot about the tunnel. But it's still here, even though nobody uses it. And so are the access shafts."

The access shafts had been drilled upward to the outside, on the side of the mountain. The first of the access shafts opened into an emergency shelter where there were pressure suits and spare oxygen bottles, in case the cable-car system overhead broke down.

"And here we are," Dan said.

In the scant light from the flashlights that Dan and George played around the tunnel walls, Pancho saw a set of metal rungs leading up to another hatch.

"There's a tempo just above us," he said as George started climbing the ladder. "We'll jack into its electrical power supply to run the dewar's cryostat."

"Won't that show up on the grid monitors?" Pancho asked.

Shaking his head, Dan replied, "Nope. The tempos have their own solar panels and batteries. Completely independent. The panels are even up on poles to keep 'em out of the dust."

Pancho heard the hatch groan open. Looking up, she saw George squeeze his bulk through its narrow diameter.

"How're we gonna get Sis's dewar through that hatch?" she demanded.

"There's a bigger hatch for equipment," Dan said.

As if to prove the point, a far wider hatch squealed open over their heads. Dim auxiliary lighting from the tempo filtered down to them.

Even with the little winch from the tempo, it was a struggle to wrestle the bulky dewar and its equipment up through the hatch. Pancho worried that Sis would be jostled and crumpled in her liquid nitrogen bath. But at last they had Sis hooked up in the temporary shelter. The dewar rested on the floor and all the gauges were in the green.

"You'll have to come back here once a month or so to check up on everything. Maybe once every six or seven months you'll have to top off the nitrogen supply."

A thought struck her. "What about when I'm on the mission?"

"I'll do it," George said without hesitation. "Be glad to."

"How the hell can I thank you guys?"

Dan chuckled softly. "I'm just making certain that my best pilot isn't blackmailed by Humphries into working against me. And George..."

The big Aussie looked suddenly embarrassed.

"I used to live in one of the tempos," he said, his tenor voice softer than usual. "Back when I was a fugitive, part of the underground. Back before Dan took me under 'is wing."

Dan said, "This is a sort of homecoming for George."

"Yeah," George said. "Reminds me of the bad old days. Almost brings a fookin' tear to my eye."

Dan laughed and the Aussie laughed with him. Pancho just stood there, feeling enormously grateful to them both.

STARPOWER, LTD.

D an had offered space in Astro Corporation's office complex for the headquarters of the fledgling Starpower, Ltd. Humphries had countered with an offer of a suite in his own Humphries Space Systems offices. Stavenger suggested a compromise, and Starpower's meager offices opened in the other tower on the Grand Plaza, where Selene's governmental departments were housed.

Yet Stavenger had not been invited to this working meeting. Dan sat on one side of the small conference table, Martin Humphries on the other. The room's windowless walls were bare, the furniture strictly functional.

"I hear you've been having some problems with hackers," Dan said.

For just a flash of a second Martin Humphries looked startled. He quickly regained his composure.

"Whoever told you that?" he asked calmly.

Dan smiled knowingly. "Not much happens around here without the grapevine getting wind of it."

Humphries leaned back in his chair. Dan noticed that it was a personally fitted recliner, unlike the other chairs around the table, which were inexpensive padded plastic.

"The leak's been fixed," Humphries said. "No damage done."

"That's good," said Dan.

"Speaking of the grapevine," Humphries said lightly, "I heard a funny one just this morning."

"Oh?"

"There's a story going around that you and a couple of your employees stole a dewar from the catacombs last night."

"Really?"

"Sounds like something out of an old horror flick."

"Imagine that," Dan said.

"Curious. Why would you do something like that?"

Trying to find a comfortable position on his chair, Dan replied, "Let's not spend the morning chasing rumors. We're here to set our budget requirements."

Humphries nodded. "I'll get one of my people to track it down."

Or one of *my* people, Dan grumbled to himself. But it'll be okay as long as he can't find Pancho's sister. Only she and George and I know where we stashed her.

He said to Humphries, "Okay, you do that. Now about the budget..."

They spent the next hour going over every item in the budget that Humphries's staff had prepared for Starpower, Ltd. Dan saw that there were no frills: no allocations for publicity or travel or anything except building the fusion drive, testing it enough to meet the IAA's requirements for human rating, and then flying it with a crew of four to the Asteroid Belt.

"I've been thinking that it makes more sense to up the crew to six," Dan said.

Humphries's brows rose. "Six? Why do we need two extra people?"

"We've got two pilots, a propulsion engineer, and a geologist. Two geologists would be better...or a geologist and some other specialist, maybe a geochemist."

"That makes five," Humphries said warily.

"I want to keep an extra slot open. Design the mission for six. As we get closer to the launch, we'll probably find out we need another hand."

Suspicion showed clearly in Humphries's face. "Adding two more people means extra supplies, extra mass."

"We can accommodate it. The fusion system's got plenty of power."

"Extra cost, too."

"A slight increment," Dan said easily. "Down in the noise."

Humphries looked unconvinced, but instead of arguing he asked, "Have you picked a specific asteroid yet?"

Dan tapped at his handheld computer, and the wall screen that covered one entire side of the conference room displayed a chart of the Belt. Thousands of thin ellipsoidal lines representing orbital paths filled the screen.

"It looks like the scrawling that a bunch of kindergarten brats would make," Humphries muttered.

"Sort of," said Dan. "There's a lot of rocks moving around out there."

He tapped at the handheld again and the lines winked out, leaving the screen deep black with tiny pinpoints of lights glittering here and there.

"This is what it really looks like," Dan said. "A whole lot of emptiness with a few pebbles floating around here and there."

"Some of those pebbles are kilometers across," Humphries said.

"Yep," Dan replied. "The biggest one is—"

"Ceres. Discovered by a priest on New Year's Day, 1801."

"You've been doing your homework," Dan said.

Humphries smiled, pleased. "It's a little over a thousand kilometers across."

"If that one ever hit the Earth..."

"Goodbye to everything. Like the impact that wiped out the dinosaurs."

"That's just what they need down there," Dan muttered, "an extinction-level impact."

"Let's get back to work," Humphries said crisply. "There's no big rock heading Earth's way."

"None has been found," Dan corrected. "Yet."

"You know," Humphries said, musing, "if we were really smart we'd run a demo flight to Mars and do a little prospecting on those two little moons. They're captured asteroids, after all."

"The IAA has ruled the whole Mars system off-limits for commercial development. That includes Deimos and Phobos."

Hunching closer to the conference table, Humphries said, "But we could just do it as a scientific mission. You know, send a couple geologists to chip off some rock samples, analyze what they're really made of."

"They already have pretty good data on that," Dan pointed out.

"But it could show potential investors that the fusion drive works and there's plenty of natural resources in the asteroids."

Frowning, Dan said, "Even if we could get the IAA to allow us to do it—"

"I can," Humphries said confidently.

"Even so, people have been going to Mars for years now. Decades. Investors won't be impressed by a Mars flight."

"Even if our fusion buggy gets there over a weekend?"

Firmly, Dan said, "We've got to get to the Belt. That's what will impress investors. Show them that the fusion drive changes the economic picture."

"I suppose," Humphries said reluctantly.

"And we've got to lay our hands on a metallic asteroid, one of the nickel-iron type. That's where the heavy metals are, the stuff you can't get from the Moon or even the NEAs."

"Gold," Humphries said, brightening. "Silver and platinum. Do you have any idea of what this is going to do to the precious metals market?"

Dan blinked at him. I'm trying to move the Earth's industrial base into space and he's playing games with the prices for gold. We just don't think the same way; we don't have the same goals or the same values, even.

Grinning slyly, Humphries said, "We could get a lot of capital from people who'd be willing to pay us *not* to bring those metals to Earth."

"Maybe," Dan admitted.

"I know at least three heads of governments who would personally buy into Starpower just to keep us from dumping precious metals onto the market."

"And I'll bet," Dan growled, "that those governments rule nations where the people are poor, starving, and sinking lower every year."

Humphries shrugged. "We're not going to solve all the world's problems, Dan."

"We ought to at least try."

"That's the difference between us," Humphries said, jabbing a finger in Dan's direction. "You want to be a savior. All I want is to make a little money."

Dan looked at him for a long, silent moment. He's right, Dan thought. Once upon a time all I was interested in was making money. And now I don't give a damn. Not anymore. None of it makes any sense to me. Since Jane died—god, I've turned into a do-gooder!

Leaning forward again, toward Dan, his expression suddenly intense, earnest, Humphries said, "Listen to me, Dan. There's nothing wrong with wanting to make money. You can't save the world. Nobody can. The best thing we can do is to feather our own nests and—"

"I've got to try," Dan interrupted. "I can't sit here and just let them drown or starve or sink into another dark age."

"Okay, okay." Humphries raised both hands placatingly. "You go right ahead and beat your head against that wall, if you want to. Maybe the asteroids are the answer. Maybe you'll save the world, one way or the other. In the meantime, we can clean up a tidy little profit doing it."

"Yep."

"If we don't make a profit, Dan, we can't do anybody any good. We've got to make money out of this or go out of business. You know that. We can't do this mission at cost. We've got to show a profit."

"Or at least," Dan countered, "a profit potential."

Humphries considered the idea for a moment, then agreed, "A profit potential. Okay, I'll settle for that. We need to show the financial community—"

"What's left of it."

Humphries actually laughed. "Oh, don't worry about the financial community. Men like my father will always be all right, no matter what happens. Even if the whole world drowns, they'll sit on a mountaintop somewhere, fat and happy, and wait for the waters to go down."

Dan could barely hide his disgust. "Come on, let's get back to work. We've had enough philosophy for one morning."

Humphries agreed with a smile and a nod.

Hours later, after Dan had left the conference room, Humphries went back to his own office and sank into his high-backed swivel chair. As he leaned back and gazed up at the paneled ceiling, the chair adjusted its contours to accommodate his body. Humphries relaxed, smiling broadly. He missed it, he said to himself. The numbers are right there in the budget and Randolph went past them as if they were written in invisible ink.

It was so easy to distract Randolph's attention. Just get him started on his idiotic crusade. He blanks out to everything else. He wants to go to the Belt to save the world. Sounds like Columbus wanting to reach China by sailing in the wrong direction.

Humphries laughed out loud. It's right there in the budget and he paid no attention to it at all. Or maybe he thinks it's just a backup, a redundancy measure. After all, it's not a terribly large sum. Once the nanos have built one fusion system, it only costs peanuts to have them build another one. The real expense is in the design and programming, and that's all amortized on the first model. All the backup costs is the raw materials and the time of a few people to monitor the process. The nanos work for nothing.

He laughed again. Randolph thinks he's so fricking smart, sneaking Pancho's sister out of the catacombs. Afraid I'll terminate her? Or does he want to keep Pancho under his thumb? I won't be able to use her anymore, but so what, who needs her now? I'll be building a second fusion drive and he doesn't even know it!

P ancho stared across the desolate, blast-scarred expanse of the launch center and wrinkled her nose unhappily. "It sure looks like a kludge."

Standing beside her in the little observation bubble, Dan had to agree. The fusion drive looked like the work of a drunken plumber: bulbous spheres of diamond that sparkled in the harsh unfiltered sunlight drenching the lunar surface, the odd shapes of the MHD channel, the pumps that fed the fuel to the reactor chamber, radiator panels and the multiple rocket nozzles, all connected by a surrealistic maze of pipes and conduits. The entire contraption was mounted on the platform-like deck of an ungainly, spraddle-legged booster that stood squat and silent on the circular launch pad of smoothed lunar concrete.

The observation chamber was nothing more than a bubble of glassteel poking up above the barren floor of Alphonsus's giant ringwall. Barely big enough for two people to stand in, the chamber was connected by a tunnel to the control center of the launch complex.

"We didn't build her for beauty," Dan said. "Besides, she'll look better once we've mated her with the other modules."

Subdued voices crackled from the intercom speaker set into the smoothed wall of the chamber just below the rim of the transparent blister.

"Pan Asia oh-one-niner on final descent," said the pilot of an incoming shuttle.

"We have you on final, oh-one-niner," answered the calm female voice of a flight controller. "Pad four."

"Pad four, copy."

Dan looked up into the star-flecked sky and saw a fleeting glint of light.

"Retrorockets," Pancho muttered.

"On the curve," said the flight controller.

Another quick burst. Dan could make out the shuttle now, a dark angular shape falling slowly out of the sky, slim landing legs extended.

"Down the pipe, oh-one-niner," said the woman controller. She sounded almost bored.

It all seemed to be happening in slow motion. Dan watched the shuttle come down and settle on the pad farthest away from the one on which the fusion rocket was sitting, waiting for clearance to take off. The shuttle pilot announced, "Oh-one-niner is down. All thrusters off."

Pancho let out a puff of pent-up breath.

Surprised, Dan asked, "White knuckles? You?"

She grinned, embarrassed. "I always get torqued up, unless I'm driving the buggy."

Glancing at his wristwatch, Dan said, "Well, we ought to get clearance to launch as soon as they offload the shuttle."

With a nod, Pancho said, "I'd better get suited up."

"Right," said Dan.

The fusion system itself was the last part of their space-craft to be launched into orbit around the Moon. The propellant tanks and the crew and logistics modules were already circling a hundred kilometers overhead. Pancho would supervise the assembly robots that would link all the pieces together.

Dan went with her along the tunnel and into the locker room where the astronauts donned their spacesuits. Amanda was already there, ready to help check her out. Dan realized it had been a long time since he'd checked out anyone or donned a spacesuit himself. Spaceflight is so routine nowadays that you can come and go from the Earth to the Moon just like you ride a plane or a bus, he thought. But another voice in his head said, You're too old to be working in space. Over the years you've taken as big a radiation dose as you're allowed . . . and then some.

He felt old and pretty useless as he watched Pancho worm into the spacesuit while Amanda hovered beside her, checking the seals and connections. Like Pancho, Amanda was wearing light tan flight coveralls. Dan noticed how nicely she filled them out.

Well, he sighed to himself, at least you're not too old to appreciate a good-looking woman.

But he turned and headed for the tunnel that connected the spaceport to Selene proper, feeling useless, wondering if Humphries was right and he was butting his head against a stone wall.

As he started down the corridor that led to the connector tunnel, he saw Doug Stavenger coming up in the other direction, looking youthful and energetic and purposeful.

Dammitall, he thought, Stavenger's older than I am and he looks like a kid. Maybe I ought to get some nanotherapy.

"Going to watch the launch?" Stavenger asked brightly.

"Think I'll go to the launch center and watch it from there."

"I like to watch from the observation bubble."

"I was just there," Dan said.

"Come on, let's see the real thing instead of watching it on a screen."

Stavenger's enthusiasm was contagious. Dan found himself striding along the narrow tunnel again, out to the bubble.

They ducked through the open hatch and into the cramped chamber. Stavenger climbed the two steps and looked out, grinning. Dan squeezed in beside him, nearly bumping his head on the curving glassteel.

"I used to sneak out here when I was a kid to watch the liftoffs and landings," Stavenger said, grinning. "I still get a kick out of it."

Dan made a polite mumble.

"I mean, we spend almost our whole lives indoors, underground," Stavenger went on. "It's good to see the outside now and then."

"As long as the glass doesn't crack."

"That's what the safety hatches are for."

Dan said, "But you've got to get through them fast, before they shut themselves."

Stavenger laughed. "True enough."

They watched shoulder-to-shoulder in the cramped blister, listening to the flight controllers' crisp voices clicking off the countdown. Stavenger seemed as excited as a child; Dan envied him. A little tractor rolled noiselessly across the crater floor to the launch pad. Pancho's spacesuited figure jumped from it in dreamlike lunar slow-motion, stirring up a lazy puff of gray dust. Then she climbed up the ladder and sealed herself into the booster's one-person crew module.

"This is just an assembly mission, isn't it?" Stavenger asked.

"Right," said Dan. "She not a pilot on this flight, just baby-sitting the robots."

Strangely enough, Dan felt his palms going clammy as the countdown neared its final moments. Relax, he told himself silently. There's nothing to this.

Still, his heart began to thump faster.

"...three...two...one...ignition," said the automated countdown voice.

The spacecraft leaped off the launch pad in a cloud of smoke and gritty dust that evaporated almost as soon as it formed. One instant the craft was sitting on the concrete, the next it was gone.

"We have liftoff," said one of the human controllers in the time-honored tradition. "All systems in the green."

Pancho's voice came through the speaker. "Copy all systems green. Orbital insertion burn in ten seconds."

It was all quite routine. Still, Dan didn't relax until Pancho announced, "On the money, guys! I'm cruisin' along with the other modules. Time to go to work."

A controller's voice replied, "Rendezvous complete. Initiate assembly procedure."

Dan huffed. "She sounds more like a robot than a human being."

Just then the controller added, "Okay, Pancho. I'll see you at the Pelican tomorrow night."

Stavenger grinned at Dan. "Maybe she drinks lubricating oil."

They walked through the corridor to the tunnel that led back to Selene. As they climbed onto one of the automated carts that plied the kilometer-long tunnel, Stavenger asked, "How soon will you be ready for your flight to the Belt?"

"We've programmed a month of uncrewed flight tests and demo flights for IAA certification. Once we get the nod from the bureaucrats we'll be ready to go."

"Could your craft reach Jupiter?"

Surprised at the question, Dan replied, "In theory. But we won't be carrying enough propellant or supplies for that. Jupiter's almost twice as far as the Belt."

"I know," Stavenger murmured.

"Why do you ask?"

Stavenger hesitated. The cart trundled along the blank-walled tunnel smoothly, almost silently, its electrical motor purring softly. At last Stavenger answered, "Sooner or later we're going to have to go to Jupiter...or maybe one of the other gas giants."

Dan saw where he was heading. "Fusion fuels."

"Jupiter's atmosphere is rich in hydrogen and helium isotopes."

"Kris Cardenas mentioned that to me," Dan remembered.

"She and I have been talking about it. Fusion fuels could be a major trade commodity for Selene. And very profitable for Starpower, Ltd."

"Mining asteroids is a lot easier than scooping gases from Jupiter's atmosphere."

"Yes," Stavenger admitted, "but your idea of moving large segments of Earth's industry off the planet is only part of the solution to the greenhouse warming, Dan."

"I know, but it's a big part."

"The other half is to wean them off fossil fuel burning. They've got to stop pumping greenhouse gases into the atmosphere if they're going to have any chance of stopping the global warming."

"And fusion is a way to do that," Dan muttered.

"It's the only way," Stavenger said firmly. "Your solar power satellites can provide only a small fraction of the energy that Earth needs. Fusion can take over the entire load."

"If we can bring in enough helium-three."

"There are other fusion processes that could be even more efficient than burning deuterium with helium-three. But they all depend on isotopes that are vanishingly rare on Earth."

"But plentiful on Jupiter," Dan said.

"That's right."

Dan nodded, thinking, He's right. Fusion could be the answer. If we could replace all the fossil-fueled electricity-generating plants on Earth with fusion plants we could cut down the greenhouse emissions to almost nothing. Fusion power plants could generate the electricity for electric cars. That'd eliminate another big greenhouse source.

He looked at Stavenger with new respect. Here's a man who's exiled from Earth, yet he wants to help them. And he sees farther than I do.

"Okay," he said. "After the flight to the Belt, we make a run out to Jupiter. I'll start the planning process right away."

"Good," said Stavenger. Then he added, "Will this be a Starpower project or will you keep it for Astro Corporation?"

For a moment Dan was dumbstruck. When he found his voice, it was a shocked whisper. "You want to cut out Humphries?"

"He's maneuvering to get a stranglehold on asteroidal resources," Stavenger said, as cold as steel. "I don't think it would be wise to let him control fusion fuels as well."

By all the gods that ever were, Dan thought, this guy is ready to go to war with Humphries.

BOARD MEETING

The filters in his nostrils were giving Dan a headache; they felt as big as shotgun shells. He had come back to Earth reluctantly for this quarterly meeting of his board of directors. Dan always felt he could run Astro Manufacturing just fine if the double-damned board would simply stay out of his way. But they always had to poke their noses into the corporation's operations, complaining about this, asking about that, insisting that he follow every crackbrained suggestion they came up with.

It was all so unnecessary. Dan held a controlling interest of the corporation's outstanding stock; not an absolute majority of the shares, but enough to outvote the other board members if he had to. The board could not throw him out of his seat as corporate president and chief executive officer. All they could do was nibble away, waste his time, drive up his blood pressure.

To top it off, now Martin Humphries had joined the board, smiling, making friends, chatting up the other members as they milled around the sideboard scarfing up drinks and tea sandwiches before sitting in their places at the long conference table. Humphries was out to get an absolute majority, that was as clear to Dan as a gun aimed at his head.

Through the sweeping window that ran the length of the board room Dan could see the surging waters of the Caribbean sparkling in the morning sun. The sea looked calm, yet Dan knew it was inching ever higher, encroaching on the land, patiently, inexorably. Humphries kept his back to the window, deep in intense discussion with a trio of elderly directors.

Dan had flown back to La Guaira specifically for this meeting. He could have stayed in Selene and chaired the meeting electronically, but that three-second lag would have driven him crazy. He appreciated how Kris Cardenas felt, dealing from the Moon every day with Duncan and his team in Scotland.

Dan stood at one end of the sideboard, beneath the big framed photograph of Astro's first solar-power satellite, glinting in the harsh sunlight of space against the deep black background of infinity. He sipped on his usual aperitif glass of Amontillado, speaking as pleasantly as he could manage with the people closest to him. Fourteen men and women, most of the men either gray or bald, most of the women looking youthful, thanks to rejuvenation treatments. Funny, he thought: the women are taking rejuve therapy but the men are holding back from it. I am myself, he realized. The ultimate machismo stupidity. What's wrong with delaying your physical deterioration? It's not like a face-lift; you actually reverse the aging of your body's cells.

"Dan, could I speak to you for a moment?" asked Harriett O'Banian. She'd been on the board for more than ten years, ever since Dan had bought out her small solar-cell production company.

"Sure, Hattie," he said, walking her slowly to the far corner of the big conference room. "What's on your mind?"

Hattie O'Banian was a trim-looking redhead who had consummated her buyout by Astro Manufacturing with a month-long affair with Dan. It had been fun for them both, and she'd been adult enough to walk away from it once she realized that no matter who shared his bed, Dan Randolph was in love with former President Jane Scanwell.

Glancing over her shoulder to make certain no one was within eavesdropping range, O'Banian half-whispered, "I've been offered a damned good price for my Astro shares. So have half a dozen other board members."

Dan's eyes flicked to Humphries, at the other end of the room, still chatting with the directors gathered around him.

"Who made the offer?" he asked.

"A straw man. Humphries is the real buyer."

"I figured."

"The trouble is, Dan, that's it's a damned good offer. Five points above the market price."

"He's gone up to five, has he?" Dan muttered.

"With the stock in free-fall the way it is, the offer is awfully tempting."

"Yep, I can see that."

She looked up at him and Dan realized that her emerald green eyes, which could be so full of delight and mischief, were dead serious now.

"He can buy up enough stock to outvote you," O'Banian said.

"That's what he's trying to do, all right."

"Dan, unless you're going to pull some rabbit out of your hat at the meeting today, half your board is going to cash out."

Dan tried to grin. It came out more as a grimace. "Thanks for the warning, Hattie. I'll see what kind of rabbits I've got for you."

"Good luck, Dan."

He went to the head of the conference table, tapped the computer stylus against the stainless steel water tumbler there, and called the meeting to order. The directors took their seats; before he sat down, Humphries complained of the glare from the window and asked that the curtains be closed.

The agenda was brief. The treasurer's report was gloomy. Income from the company's final solar-power satellite construction project was tailing off as the project neared completion.

"What about the bonus for finishing the job ahead of schedule?" asked a florid-faced graybeard. Dan thought of him as Santa Claus with hypertension.

"That won't be paid until the sunsat is beaming power to the ground," said the treasurer.

"Still, it's a sizeable amount of money."

"It'll keep us afloat for several months," Dan said, waving the treasurer to silence.

"Then what?"

"Then we have to live off the income from existing operations. We have no new construction projects."

"That's the last of the power satellites?" asked the board member that Dan had privately nicknamed Bug Eyes. His eyes were even wider than usual, as if this was the first time he'd heard the bad news.

Dan clasped his hands as he answered carefully, "Although there are several orbital slots still available to accommodate solar power satellites, the GEC refuses to authorize any new construction."

"It's those damned Chinese," growled one of the older men.

"China is not alone in this," said a plump oriental woman sitting halfway down the table. Dan's name for her was Mama-San. "Many nations prefer to build power stations on their own ground rather than buy electrical power from space."

"Even though the price for that electricity is more than twice as high as our price," Dan pointed out. "And even higher, if you count the costs of sequestering their greenhouse gas emissions."

"Their governments subsidize the greenhouse amelioration," the treasurer pointed out.

"The people still have to pay for it, one way or another."

"What about beaming power from the Moon?"

"You wouldn't need the GEC to allocate any orbital slots for that, by god!" Santa Claus thumped the table with his fist.

"It's a possibility," Dan admitted, "and we've talked about it with the officials of Selene—"

"Selene doesn't own the whole damned Moon! Go off and build solar energy farms in the Ocean of Storms. Cover the whole expanse with solar cells, for god's sake!"

"We've looked into it," Dan said.

"And?"

"The problem is that no matter where the electricity is generated, it's got to be beamed to the ground here on Earth."

"We know that!"

Holding on to his temper, Dan went on, "The Pan-Asia bloc doesn't want to import energy, whether it comes from orbit or the Moon or the Lesser Magellanic Cloud. They won't allow us to build receiving stations on their territory. The Europeans have gone along with them and, between the two blocs, they have the GEC all wrapped up."

"How can we generate electricity from the Lesser Magellanic Cloud?" asked Bug Eyes. "That's quite a long distance away, isn't it?"

Give me strength, Dan prayed silently.

He got them through the various departmental reports at last, fielding what seemed like seventeen thousand questions and suggestions—most of them pointless, several absolutely inane—and went on to new business.

"At least here I have something positive to report," Dan said, smiling genuinely. "Our prototype fusion drive has been assembled in lunar orbit and test-flown successfully."

"You are ready to go to the Asteroid Belt?" asked Mama-San.

"As soon as we get the required crew-rating from the IAA."

From the far end of the table, Humphries spoke up. "We should have IAA approval in two to three weeks, barring any unforeseen setbacks."

"Setbacks?"

"An accident," Humphries said lightly. "Failure of the equipment, that sort of thing."

Or an IAA inspector on the take, Dan added silently. It happened only rarely, but it happened.

"How much is this mission to the asteroids costing us?" asked the sprightly, dapper Swiss gentleman whom Dan had dubbed The Banker.

"The mission is being fully funded by Starpower, Limited," Dan replied.

"Astro owns one-third of Starpower," Humphries pointed out.

"And you own the rest?" The Banker asked.

"No, Humphries Space Systems owns a third, and the other third is owned by Selene."

"How can a city own part of a corporation?"

"All the details are in the reports before you," Dan said, tapping his stylus against the computer screen built into the tabletop.

"Yes, but—"

"I'll explain it after the meeting," Humphries said, full of graciousness.

The Banker nodded but still looked unsatisfied.

"The point is," Dan told them, "that once this flight to the Asteroid Belt is accomplished, Astro's stock is going to rise. We'll have taken the first step in opening up a resource base that's enormous—far bigger than all the mining operations on Earth."

"I can see that Starpower's stock will go up," Santa Claus challenged.

"Astro's will, too," Dan said. "Because we have the corner on building the fusion engines."

"Not Humphries Space Systems?" They all turned to Humphries.

He smiled gently, knowingly. "No, this is going to be Astro's product. My corporation is merely supplying the capital, the funding."

Dan thought that Humphries looked like a cat eyeing a helpless canary.

SELENE

So there you have it," Dan said to the IAA inspector. "The system performs as designed."

They were sitting in Starpower, Ltd.'s one and only conference room, a tiny cubicle with an oval table that felt crowded even though only five people were sitting around it. The display screens on all four smartwalls showed data from the test flights of the fusion drive. The first half-dozen flights had been run remotely from the control center underground in Armstrong spaceport. The second string of six flights had been piloted by Pancho and Amanda.

Pointing to the screens, Dan said, "We've demonstrated acceleration, thrust, specific impulse, controllability, shutdown and restart . . . every facet of the full test envelope."

The inspector nodded solemnly. He was a young man with Nordic fair skin and pale eyes, dressed rather somberly in a plain gray pullover shirt and darker slacks. His hair was a thick dirty-blond mop that he wore long, almost down to his shoulders. Despite his conservative outfit, though, he wore several small silver earrings, silver rings on his fingers, a silver bracelet on his right wrist, and a silver chain around his neck. There was a pendant of some sort hanging from the chain but most of it was hidden beneath his shirt.

Pancho and Amanda sat flanking Dan; Humphries was on the other side of the small oval table, next to the inspector. For some long moments there was silence in the conference room. Dan could hear the background hum of the electrical equipment and the soft breath of the air circulation fans.

At last, Dan asked, "Well, what do you think, Mr. Greenleaf?"

"Dr. Greenleaf," the IAA inspector replied. "I have a doctorate in sociology."

Dan felt his brows hike up. Why would the IAA send a sociologist to check out a new spacecraft propulsion system? And why this particular little prig of a sociologist?

Greenleaf steepled his fingers in front of him. "You're surprised that a sociologist is evaluating your test data?"

"Well ... yes, actually I am," Dan said, feeling decidedly uncomfortable.

"I can assure you, Mr. Randolph—"

"Dan."

"I can assure you, Mr. Randolph, that your data has been examined by the best engineers and physical scientists that the IAA has at its command," Greenleaf said. "We are not taking your application lightly."

"I didn't mean to imply anything like that," Dan said, thinking, This guy is out for blood.

Greenleaf shifted his gaze from Dan to the wall screen before him. "I can see that your device has performed within your design criteria quite reliably."

"Good," said Dan, relieved.

"Except in one respect," Greenleaf went on.

"What? What do you mean?"

"Long-term reliability," said Greenleaf. "The longest flight in your testing program was a mere two weeks, and even then it was at low power."

"I wouldn't call a constant acceleration of one-tenth *g* low power," Dan said, testily. "And the IAA seemed very happy with the data we got from that test flight."

Pancho and Amanda had flown the test rig on a parabolic trajectory that took them around Venus. The ship carried a full panoply of instrumentation for making observations of the planet as it flew by a scant thousand kilometers above Venus's glowing clouds. A team of planetary astronomers had provided the equipment and monitored the flight, all of them from universities that belonged to the IAA, all of them ecstatically happy and grateful for the data that the flight brought back—for free.

"Two weeks is not a sufficient endurance test," Greenleaf said flatly.

Pancho snapped, "It's long enough to get us to the Belt."

"Under full power."

"What else?"

"I cannot authorize a crewed flight to the Asteroid Belt until you have demonstrated that your propulsion system can operate reliably at full power for the time it would take to complete the mission."

Dan felt burning anger rising in his throat. Pancho looked as if she wanted to reach across the table and sock the guy. But then he realized that Amanda was looking not at Greenleaf, but at Humphries, who sat calmly in his chair, his face as expressionless as a professional card shark, his hands in his lap.

"Even your flight past Venus was an infraction of IAA regulations," Greenleaf said, as if justifying himself.

"We filed the flight plan with the IAA," Dan responded hotly.

"But you didn't wait for authorization, did you?"

"It was a test flight, dammit!"

Greenleaf's face flashed red. And Dan finally realized what he was up against. Oh, by all the saints in New Orleans, he said to himself, he's a New Morality bigot. They've infiltrated the IAA.

"I am not going to argue with you," Greenleaf said flatly. "You will be required to fly your device for four weeks at full power before you can receive approval for a crewed mission to the Asteroid Belt."

He pushed his chair back and got to his feet, stumbling in the low lunar gravity despite the weighted boots he wore.

"Four weeks!" Dan blurted. "We can fly to the Belt and back in four weeks under full power."

"Then do so," said Greenleaf, smugly. "But do it under remote control. Without any crew."

He headed for the door, leaving Dan sitting at the table, angry, stunned, and feeling betrayed.

"I'd better go after him," Humphries said, getting up from his chair. "We don't want him angry at us."

"Why the hell not?" Dan grumbled.

Humphries left the conference room. Dan sagged back in his chair. "Flying an uncrewed mission to the Belt doesn't make a dime's worth of sense," he muttered. "It's just an exercise that costs us four weeks' time and almost as much money as a crewed mission."

Pancho said, "Four weeks isn't so bad. Is it?"

"It's four weeks closer to bankruptcy, kid. Four weeks closer to letting that Humper take over my company."

In a very small voice, Amanda said, "It's my fault, actually."

Dan looked at her.

"Martin . . ." she hesitated, then said, "Martin doesn't want me to go on the mission. I'm sure he's had some influence on Dr. Greenleaf's position."

Pancho explained, "He's bonkers about Mandy."

Dan asked, "And how do you feel about him, Amanda?"

"Trapped," she replied immediately. "I feel as though

there's nowhere on Earth I can go to get away from him. Or the Moon, for that matter. I feel like a trapped animal."

Dan left the two women and went to his office. As he slipped into his desk chair he commanded the phone to locate his chief counsel, the woman who headed Astro's corporate legal department.

The phone computer system found her on the ski slopes in Nepal. Her image was faint and wavered noticeably. She must be holding her wrist communicator in front of her face, Dan thought. He could see a bit of utterly blue sky behind her. She was in ski togs, polarized sun goggles pushed up on her forehead, and not at all happy about being buzzed by the boss.

"What in the nine billion names of God are you doing in Nepal?" Dan asked, irritated. Then he had to sit, fuming, for the few seconds it took for his message to reach the lawyer and her reply to get back to him.

"Trying to get in some skiing while there's still snow left," she snapped, equally irked.

"Skiing?"

"I do get some vacation time now and then," she said, after the usual pause. "This is the first time I've taken any since lord knows when."

Through gritted teeth, Dan explained the IAA inspector's decision to her.

"You could appeal," she said, once she understood the situation, "but that would take longer than running the un-crewed test flight he wants you to do."

"Couldn't we ask for another hearing, a different inspector?" Dan demanded. "This guy's a New Morality fanatic and they're dead-set against space exploration."

The lawyer's face hardened when she heard Dan's words. "*Mr.* Randolph," she said, "I am a member of the New

Morality and I'm not a fanatic. Nor am I against space exploration."

Feeling surrounded by enemies, Dan said, "Okay, okay. So I exaggerated."

She said nothing.

"Can we claim an asteroid with an uncrewed spacecraft?"

"No one can claim ownership of any body in space," her reply came back. It was what Dan had expected. Then she went on, "No planet, moon, comet, asteroid—no celestial body of any kind. That's been international law since the Outer Space Treaty of 1967, and subsequent amendments and protocols."

Trust a lawyer to use two dozen words when one will do, Dan groused to himself.

She went on, "Individuals are allowed to have exclusive use of part or all of a celestial body, for the purpose of establishing a human habitation or extracting natural resources. In that instance, corporations are regarded as individuals."

"So could Astro Corporation claim *use* of an asteroid that an uncrewed spacecraft rendezvouses with?"

Nearly three seconds later she replied, "No. Such a claim can only be made by humans on the scene of the claim itself."

"But the double-dipped spacecraft would be under human control, remotely, from Selene."

Again the lag, and again the answer, "No, Dan. It's not allowed. Otherwise corporations would be able to send miniprobes all over the solar system and claim everything in sight! It would be like the efforts to patent segments of DNA and living organisms, back around the turn of the century."

"So an uncrewed test flight wouldn't do us any good at all," he said.

Once she heard his question, the lawyer answered, "That's a decision that you'll have to make, Dan. I'm just a lawyer; you're the CEO."

"Thanks a lot," Dan muttered.

*   *   *

Martin Humphries had not bothered to chase after the IAA inspector. What was the point? The young bureaucrat had done precisely what Humphries had wanted. Barely able to hide his satisfaction, he rode the moving stairs down to his home deep below the Moon's surface.

It's all working out very neatly, he congratulated himself as he walked along the corridor toward the cavern. Just enough delay to break Randolph's back. Astro's stock is in the toilet, and the other major shareholders will be glad to sell once they hear that the asteroid mission has to be postponed for more testing. By the time they finally get the mission going, I'll own Astro and Dan Randolph will be out on his ass.

And better yet, he thought, once I'm in charge I'll make certain that Amanda stays here on the ground. With me.

She looks better now, doesn't she?" Dan asked as their jumper coasted toward the fusion-powered spacecraft.

Pancho nodded her agreement. The ship was still utilitarian, not sleek, but now the starkness of the bare engine system by itself was dwarfed by six huge, gleaming spherical propellant tanks. Big white letters stenciled along the cylindrical crew module identified the craft as STARPOWER 1; the logos of Astro Corporation, Humphries Space Systems and Selene adorned one of the propellant tanks.

The jumper was little more than an ordinary lunar transfer buggy with an extra set of tankage and a bigger rocket engine for ascents from the Moon's surface into lunar orbit and descents back to the ground again. Dan and Pancho wore tan Astro coveralls as they rode in the bulbous glassteel crew module, standing with their booted feet anchored in floor loops because seats were not needed for this brief, low-*g* flight. An instrument podium rose at the front of the module, its controls standing unused, since the vessel was being handled by the flight controllers back at Armstrong. Still, Dan felt good that Pancho was a qualified pilot. You never know, he thought.

As they approached the fusion-powered vessel, Pancho whistled at the size of the propellant tanks.

"That's a lot of fuel."

"Tell me about it," Dan said ruefully. "I've had to default on two helium-three contracts with Earthside power utilities to fill those double-damned tanks."

"Default?"

Nodding, Dan said grimly, "Two steps closer to bankruptcy."

Pancho decided to change the subject slightly. "So what've you decided to do about the long-duration test?" Pancho asked.

Dan shook his head. "I've spent the past four days pulling every wire I know."

"And?"

"Nothing so far. Zip. Nobody's going to lift a finger to go against the IAA."

"So you'll have to do the test flight?"

Running a finger across his chin, Dan said reluctantly, "Looks that way."

"Then why are we takin' this ride?"

The shadow of a smile crossed Dan's face. He was thinking of the time, many years earlier, when he had briefly become a privateer, a pirate, hijacking uncrewed spacecraft for their cargoes of ore. It had started as a desperation ploy, the only way a frustrated Dan Randolph could force open the space markets that had been closed by monopolists. He had won his war against monopoly and opened the solar system to free competition among individuals, corporations and governments. But at a price. His smile faded as he remembered the people who had died fighting that brief, unheralded war. He himself had come to within a whisker of being killed.

"So?" Pancho prodded, "Is this a joyride or what?"

Putting his thoughts of the past behind him, Dan replied, "I want to see the crew module for myself. And we're going to meet the planetary geologist that Zack Freiberg's picked out for us."

"The asteroid specialist?"

"Yep. He's aboard the ship now. Came up to Selene yesterday and went straight to the ship. He slept aboard last night."

Pancho huffed. "Eager beaver. College kid, I bet."

"He's got a mint-new degree from Zurich Polytech."

The flight controllers brought the jumper to a smooth rendezvous with *Starpower 1*. While Dan and Pancho stood watching, the little transfer buggy linked its airlock adapter section to the hatch of the bigger vessel. They floated through the womb-like adapter to the fusion ship's airlock hatch.

The airlock opened into the midsection of the crew module. To their left, Dan saw the accordion-fold doors of a half-dozen privacy compartments lining the passageway. Further up were the galley, a wardroom with a table and six small but plush-looking chairs, and—past an open hatch—the bridge. To their right was the lavatory and a closed hatch that led to the equipment and storage bays.

Dan headed left, toward the galley and the bridge.

"Chairs?" Pancho asked, looking puzzled, as they pushed weightlessly past the wardroom, floating a few centimeters above the deck's carpeting.

"You'll be accelerating or decelerating most of the way," Dan pointed out. "You won't be spending much time in zero-*g*."

She nodded, looking disappointed with herself. "I knew that; it just didn't latch."

Dan understood how she felt. He'd seen the layout of the crew module hundreds of times, viewed three-d mockups and even walked through virtual reality simulations. But being in the real thing was different. He could smell the newness of the metal and fabric; he could reach his hand up and run his fingers along the plastic panels of the overhead. The bridge looked small, but shining and already humming with electrical power.

"Where's our college boy?" Pancho asked, looking around.

"That would be me, I suppose," said a reedy voice from behind them.

Turning, Dan saw a husky-looking young man gripping the edges of the open hatch with both hands. He was a shade shorter than Dan, but broad in the shoulders, with a thick barrel chest. The build of a wrestler. His face was broad, too: a heavy jaw with wide, thin lips and small, deepset eyes. His hair was cropped so close to his skull that Dan couldn't be sure of its true color. He wore a small glittering stone in his left earlobe, diamond or zircon or glass, Dan could not tell.

"I heard you enter. I was in the sensor bay, checking on the equipment," he said in a flat midwestern American accent, pronounced so precisely that he had to have learned it in a foreign school.

"Oh," said Pancho.

"I am Lars Fuchs," he said, extending his hand to Dan. "You must be Mr. Randolph."

"Pleased to meet you, Dr. Fuchs." Fuchs's hand engulfed his own. The young man's grip was strong, firm. "This is Pancho Lane," Dan went on. "She'll be our pilot on the flight."

Fuchs dipped his chin slightly. "Ms. Lane. And, sir, I am not Dr. Fuchs. Not yet."

"That's okay. Zack Freiberg recommends you highly."

"I am very grateful to Doctor Professor Freiberg. He has been very helpful to me."

"And my name is Dan. If you call me Mr. Randolph it'll make me feel like an old man."

"Oh, I wouldn't want to offend you, sir!" Fuchs said, genuinely alarmed.

"Just call me Dan."

"Yes, sir, of course. And you must call me Lars." Turning to Pancho, he added, "Both of you."

"That's a deal, Lars," said Pancho, sticking out her hand.

Fuchs took it gingerly, as if not quite sure what to do. "Pancho is a woman's name in America?"

She laughed. "It's *this* woman's name, Lars old buddy."

Smiling uneasily, Fuchs said, "Pancho," as if testing out the name.

"You handle weightlessness very well," Dan said. "From what Zack told me, this is your first time off-Earth."

Fuchs said. "Thank you, sir...Dan. I came up last night so I could adapt myself to microgravity before you arrived here."

Pancho smiled sympathetically. "Spent the night makin' love to the toilet, huh?"

Looking flustered, Fuchs said, "I did retch a few times, yes."

"Ever'body does, Lars," she said. "Nothin' to be ashamed of."

"I am not ashamed," he said, his chin rising a notch.

Dan moved between them. "Have you picked out which cabin you want for yourself? Since you were first aboard you get first pick."

"Hey," Pancho griped, "I've been aboard this buggy before, you know. So has Amanda."

"The privacy compartments are all exactly alike," Fuchs said. "It doesn't matter which one I get."

"I'll take the last one on the left," Dan said, peering down the passageway that ran the length of the module. "It's closest to the lav."

"You?" Pancho looked surprised. "Since when are you comin' on the mission?"

"Since about four days ago," Dan said. "That's when I made up my mind...about a lot of things."

PELICAN BAR

S o here's my plan," Dan said, with a grin.

He and Pancho were hunched over one of the postage-stamp-sized tables in the farthest corner of the Pelican bar, away from the buzzing conversations and bursts of laughter from the crowd standing at the bar itself. Their heads were almost touching, leaning together like a pair of conspirators.

Which they were. Inwardly, Dan marveled at how good he felt. Free. Happy, almost. The double-damned bureaucrats have tried to tie me up in knots. Humphries is behind it all, playing along with the IAA and those New Morality bigots. Those uptight psalm-singers don't want us to reach the asteroids. They like the Earth just the way it is: miserable, hungry, desperate for the kind of order and control that the New Morality offers. This greenhouse warming is a blessing for them, the wrath of God smiting the unbelievers. Anything we do to try to help alleviate it, they see as a threat to their power.

Vaguely, Dan recalled from his childhood history lessons something about a group called the Nazis, back in the twentieth century. They came to power because there was an economic depression and people needed jobs and food. If he remembered his history lessons correctly.

So the New Morality has its tentacles into the IAA now, Dan thought. And the GEC too, I'll bet. And Humphries is playing them all like a symphony orchestra, using them to stymie me long enough so he can grab Astro from me.

Well, it's not going to be that easy, partner.

"What's so funny?" Pancho asked, looking puzzled.

"Funny?"

"You say, 'Here's my plan,' and then you start grinnin' like a cat in a canary's cage."

Dan took a sip of his brandy and dry, then said, "Pancho, I've always said that when the going gets tough, the tough get going—to where the going's easier."

"I've heard that one before."

"So I'm going with you."

"You?"

"Yep."

"To the Belt."

"You need a flight engineer. I know the ship's systems as well as anybody."

"Lordy-lord," Pancho muttered.

"I'm still a qualified astronaut. I'm going with you."

"But not until we do the uncrewed test flight," she said, reaching for her beer.

Leaning across the table even closer to her, Dan said in a hoarse whisper, "Screw the test flight. We're going to the Belt. You, Amanda, Fuchs and me."

Pancho nearly choked on her mouthful of beer. She sputtered, coughed, then finally asked, "What're you drinkin', boss?"

Happy as a pirate on the open sea, Dan said, "We'll let 'em think we're doing exactly what they've told us to do, except that the four of us will happen to be aboard the bird when she breaks orbit."

"Just like that?"

"Just like that. We'll calculate a new flight plan once we're underway. Instead of accelerating at one-sixth *g*, as we've planned, we'll goose her up to one-third *g* and cut the flight time by more than half."

Pancho looked unconvinced. "You better bring an astrogator aboard."

"Nope." Pointing a finger at her, Dan said, "You're it, kid. You and Amanda. I'm not bringing anybody into this that we don't absolutely need."

"I'm not so sure about this," Pancho said warily.

"Don't go chicken on me, kid," Dan said. "You two have been studying this point-and-shoot technique for a lot of weeks. If you can't do it, I've been wasting money on you."

"I can do it," Pancho said immediately.

"Okay, then."

"I'd just feel better if you had a real expert on board."

"No experts. Nobody else except the four of us. I don't want anybody tipped off about this. And that includes Humphries."

Pancho waved a hand nonchalantly. "He hasn't said a word to me since we moved Sis."

"I don't think he knows were we stashed her," Dan said, reaching for his drink.

"He knows about ever'thing."

"Not this flight," Dan said firmly. "*Nobody* is going to know about this. Understand me? Don't even tell Amanda or Fuchs. This is just between you and me, kid."

"And the flight controllers," Pancho muttered.

"What?"

"How're you goin' to get the flight controllers to go along with this? You can't just waltz aboard the *Starpower* and light her up without them knowin' it. Hell's bells, Dan, you won't even be able to hop up to the ship if they don't let you have a jumper and give you clearance for takeoff."

Sipping at his brandy-laced ginger beer, Dan admitted, "That's a problem I haven't worked out yet."

"It's a toughie."

"Yep, it is," Dan said, unable to suppress a grin.

Pancho shook her head disapprovingly. "You're *enjoying* this."

"Why not?" Dan replied. "The world's going to hell in a handbasket, the New Morality is taking over the government, Humphries is trying to screw me out of my own company—what could be more fun than hijacking my own spacecraft and riding it out to the Belt?"

"That's weird," Pancho murmured.

Dan saw that his glass was empty. He pressed the button set into the table's edge to summon one of the squat little robots trundling through the crowd.

"Don't worry about the flight controllers," he said casually. "We'll figure out a way around them."

"We?"

"You and me."

"Hey, boss, I'm a pilot, not a woman of intrigue."

"You made a pretty good spy."

"I was lousy at it and we both know it."

"You hacked into Humphries's files."

"And he found out about it in half a minute, just about."

"We'll think of something," Dan said.

Pancho nodded, then realized that she had already thought of something.

"I'll fix the flight controllers," she said.

"Really?" Dan's brows rose. "How?"

"Better that you don't know boss. Just let me do it my way."

Dan looked skeptical, but he shrugged and said nothing.

MISSION CONTROL CENTER

The timing had to be just right.

Nervous despite being invisible, Pancho edged cautiously into the Armstrong spaceport's mission control center. It was nearly two a.m. The center was quiet, only two controllers on duty and both of them were relaxed, one leaning back in his chair while the other poured coffee at the little hotplate off by the door to the lav.

Pancho hadn't told anyone about this caper. She thought it best to borrow the stealth suit and get the job done without bringing anyone else into the picture, not even Dan Randolph. The fewer people who knew about the stealth suit, the better.

No landings or takeoffs were scheduled at this hour; the skeleton crew was in the control center strictly because prudent regulations required that the center always be manned, in case an emergency cropped up.

How could there be an emergency? Pancho asked herself as she slowly tiptoed to the console farthest from those being used by the pair of controllers. Spacecraft don't just zoom in on the spur of the moment; even a max-thrust flight from one of the space stations orbiting Earth takes six hours to reach the Moon. Plenty time to rouse the whole crew of controllers if they were needed. The only possible emergency would be if one of the teams at a remote outpost on the lunar surface ran into a jam. Maybe if an astronomer at the Farside Observatory suddenly developed a case of appendicitis and their radio was out so they sent the poor boob on a ballistic lob to Selene without being able to alert anybody first. That was just about the only emergency Pancho could think of.

Or if an invisible woman sneaked in and jiggered the flight schedule for tomorrow's launches. No, Pancho thought, not tomorrow's. It's already past two in the morning. Today's schedule.

She sat at one of the unattended consoles, as far from the human controllers as possible, and waited for the woman at the coffee urn to return to her post. The overweight guy sitting at his console looked half asleep, feet up on the consoles, eyes closed, a pair of earphones clamped over his head. They weren't the regulation earphones, either. The guy was listening to music; Pancho could see the rhythmic bobbing of his head.

Hope it's a lullaby, she said to herself.

The woman controller took a sip of her coffee and made a sour face. Then she looked straight at Pancho. Inside the stealth suit, Pancho froze. The moment passed. The woman's gaze shifted and she started back toward her console, her steaming coffee mug in one hand. Pancho began to breathe again.

The woman came back to her console, next to the guy, gave him a disapproving frown, then sat down and clapped a regulation earphone and pin-mike set to her head.

Good, thought Pancho. The big chamber was too quiet to suit her. Normally the rows of consoles would be filled with controllers talking to the traffic coming in and out of Selene. There would be plenty of background chatter to hide her pecking at a keyboard. But then there wouldn't be any empty consoles to use; they'd all be occupied during normal working hours.

Pancho tentatively tapped on the keyboard before her, once to silence the voice system, then again to call up the status board. The woman at her console did not hear the faint clicks. Or if she did, she paid no notice. The guy was definitely asleep, Pancho thought, his head lolling on his shoulders now, his bulging belly rising and falling in deep, slow breathing.

Only one craft on the schedule, Pancho saw from the status display. Due to land in five hours. Plenty of time for her to do what she had to and get out before more controllers began filing in for the morning shift.

Slowly, cautiously, with one eye on the bored woman sitting on the other side of the room, Pancho tapped out a set of instructions for the morning's schedule. Then she got up, quietly left the control center, and returned the stealth suit to Ike Walton's locker up in the storage area near the catacombs. She wondered if she'd ever need it again. Maybe I ought to keep it, she thought. But then Ike would discover it was gone, sooner or later, and that would raise a stink. Better to let it stay here and just hope Ike doesn't change the combination on the lock.

Sudden panic hit Pancho. Elly was not in the locker, where she had left her. Pancho had thought that the krait would snooze away in the chilly air of the storage area; she had fed Elly a mouse only a day earlier, and that usually left the snake in a pleasantly drowsy state of digestion. But moving her to Walton's locker must have disturbed Elly's torpor. The snake had slithered through one of the air slits in the bottom of the locker door.

For several frantic minutes Pancho searched for the krait. She found her at last, curled on the floor in front of a heating vent. But when she tried to pick Elly up, the krait reared and hissed at her.

Pancho got down on both knees and frowned at the snake. "Don't you go hissy on me," she said sternly. "I know I disturbed your nap, but that's no reason to get sore."

The snake's tongue flicked in and out, in and out.

"That's right, take a good sniff. It's me, and if you'll just calm yourself down, I'll wrap you around my nice warm ankle and we can get back home. Okay?"

Elly relaxed and sank back into a tight little coil of glittering blue. Pancho slowly extended her hand and when Elly didn't react, she stroked the krait's head gently with one finger.

"Come on, girl," she crooned, "we're gonna take you home where you can sleep nice and comfy."

But not for long, Pancho added silently.

HUMPHRIES TRUST RESEARCH CENTER

artin Humphries was awakened from a dream about Amanda by the insistent shrill of his personal phone.

It wasn't a sexual dream. Strangely, when he dreamed of Amanda it was never sexual. They were on a yacht this time, sailing across a calm azure sea, standing up by the prow and watching dolphins leaping across the ship's bow wave. He felt nervous on the water, unable to shake the fear of drowning even in this idyllic setting.

Amanda stood by the rail, wearing a lovely pale blue dress, the soft breeze tousling her hair. She gazed at him with sad eyes.

"I'll be leaving soon," she said unhappily.

"You can't leave me," Humphries said to her. "I won't let you leave."

"I don't want to, darling. But they're forcing me to. I must go. I have no choice."

"Who?" Humphries demanded. "Who's forcing you?"

"You know who, dearest," said Amanda. "You know. You're even helping him."

"It's Randolph! He's taking you away from me!"

"Yes," Amanda said, her eyes pleading with him to help her. To save her.

And then the damned phone woke him up.

He sat up in his bed, blazingly angry. "Phone!" he called out. "On the art screen."

A reproduction of a Picasso cubist nude disappeared to reveal the somber face of his security chief.

"Sorry to wake you, sir," the man said, "but you said you wanted to be personally informed of Ms. Cunningham's movements."

With a glance at the digital clock on the nightstand, Humphries demanded, "Where's she going at four in the fricking morning?"

"She's apparently asleep in her room, sir, but—"

"Then what are you bothering me for?" Humphries bellowed.

The security man swallowed visibly. "Sir, her name has just appeared on a flight manifest."

"Flight manifest?"

"Yessir. She and three other people are scheduled to go to the Starpower ship, up in orbit."

"Now? Today?"

"Scheduled for eight this morning, sir."

Four hours from now, Humphries realized. "And this flight manifest just came up on the launch schedule?"

"About an hour ago, sir."

"Why are they going to *Starpower 1*?" Humphries wondered aloud.

"That vessel is scheduled for launch on a test flight at nine o'clock, sir."

"I know that," Humphries snapped. "It's an unnamed long-duration flight."

"Perhaps they're going up for a last-minute checkout, before the ship is launched out of orbit."

"Three other people going with her, you say? Who are they?"

The security chief read off the names. "P. Lane, command pilot; L. Fuchs, mission scientist; and C. N. Barnard, flight surgeon."

"I know Lane," Humphries said. "Who are the other two?"

"Fuchs is a graduate student from Zurich Polytechnical Institute. He just arrived in Selene a few days ago. Barnard is apparently a medic of sort."

"Apparently?"

Looking uncomfortable, the security chief replied, "He's an Astro employee. We have no background data on Barnard, sir. No ID photo, either. All that we've been able to pull up from Astro's files are his name, his position, and his fingerprints and retinal scan."

"Dan Randolph," Humphries growled. "It's an alias for Randolph!"

"Sir?"

"Check those prints and retinal scan against Dan Randolph's file."

"Yessir."

"And send a couple of men to Amanda Cunningham's quarters. Bring her here, to me."

"Right away, sir."

The wall screen went blank for an instant, then the Picasso image reappeared. Humphries paid no attention. He leaped out of bed, snarling aloud, "That fucking Randolph thinks he's going to zip off to the Belt and take Amanda with him. Like hell he will!"

Dan was already up and dressed in a white flight suit, the kind of coveralls worn by members of Selene's medical staff. "C. N. Barnard" was one of the extra identities he had stored in Astro's personnel files, a hangover from the days when he'd been up to his armpits in international skullduggery. He still had modest bank accounts scattered here and there on Earth under various aliases, just in case he ever needed to disappear for a while.

He grinned to himself as he started for the tunnel that led to the spaceport. I'm going to disappear for a while, all right. Completely out of the Earth–Moon system. Past Mars. Out to the Asteroid Belt. The IAA will go apeshit when they find out we're on board *Starpower 1*. Humphries'll have a fit.

And Astro's stock ought to shoot up when we claim mining rights to a nice, rich asteroid or three. The lawyers may squabble over the details, but a few billion dollars worth of high-grade ores will start a feeding frenzy among the brokers. And the publicity will help, too.

His grin disappeared as he reached the entrance to the tunnel. An electric cart sat waiting to take him to the spaceport, but neither Pancho nor Amanda was in sight. Dammit—all to hell and back, Dan fumed. They were supposed to meet me here at five sharp. Women!

"Come on, Mandy," Pancho urged. "Dan's prob'ly waitin' for us already!"

"One more minute," Amanda said, from the lav. "I've just got to—"

Somebody pounded impatiently on the door.

"Oh, hell!" Pancho said.

Amanda came out of the lavatory. "I'm ready, Pancho. Sorry to keep you waiting."

Pancho opened the door. Instead of Dan Randolph, two strangers stood out in the corridor. Both were men, wearing identical dark gray business suits. One with long blond hair and a nice full moustache, the other a taller, darker man with a military crew cut. Both were big-shouldered and stone-faced. They looked like cops to Pancho.

Shit! Pancho thought. They know I hacked into the flight schedule.

But the blond said, "Amanda Cunningham? Come with us, please."

Pancho hiked a thumb over her shoulder. "That's her. And she's not goin' anywhere with you. We're late for work already."

They pushed past Pancho and entered the room. "You'll have to come with us, Ms. Cunningham," the blond said.

"Why? On whose authority?"

"Mr. Humphries wants to see you," the buzz cut said. His partner frowned at him.

Pancho said, "Now wait a minute—"

"Don't interfere," the blond said sharply. "Our orders are to bring Ms. Cunningham to Mr. Humphries's residence. That's what we're going to do."

"Call security, Mandy," Pancho said. "These guys are workin' for Humphries."

Amanda started around the bed to the phone on the night table between their two beds, but the blond moved faster and blocked her way.

"We don't want to get physical," he said to Amanda, "but we've got a job to do and we're going to do it."

"How rough we get depends on you," said the darker man, grinning at Amanda.

She stared at them, wide eyed, somewhere between confusion and terror.

The blond took another step toward Amanda. "Come along now, honey. We don't want to hurt anybody."

Mandy stumbled back, away from him. Pancho saw that both men were focused on her. She swiftly bent down and peeled Elly from her ankle.

"Here, wiseass," Pancho said as she hurled the bright blue snake at the blond.

He turned just fast enough to see the krait sailing in lunar slow motion toward his face. Instinctively he raised his arm to shield himself.

"What the hell!"

Elly bounced off the guy's arm and fell to the floor. She reared up, hissing angrily.

"Jesus Christ, what is it?"

The buzz cut was tugging at something inside his jacket. Pancho chopped at the back of his neck and he sagged to the floor. Elly slithered toward him. The blond seemed frozen with fright, staring at the snake.

Pancho gestured to Amanda, who stepped past the goggle-eyed blond and came to her side.

The guy on the floor pushed himself up on one elbow and saw the snake rearing a bare ten centimeters in front of his face, its beady eyes staring at him.

"Aaaggh," he moaned.

The blond pulled a small pistol from the holster beneath his jacket. Pancho saw that his hand was shaking badly.

"Loud noises annoy her," she said. "Just be quiet and don't move."

The blond glanced at her, then returned his stare to the snake. The buzz cut was sweating as Elly stood before him, her tongue flicking in and out.

"D-do something," he whispered hoarsely.

"Better drop your gun on the bed," said Pancho to the blond. "If you shoot and miss her, she'll bite him for sure."

The blond tossed the gun onto the bed. "Get it out of here," he pleaded.

Pancho started to lean forward, slowly, carefully, bending toward Elly. But the buzz cut's nerve broke. He swung blindly at the snake and tried to scramble to his feet. Elly sank her fangs into the meaty side of his hand.

He screamed and sagged back to the floor, unconscious. Pancho bent over and scooped Elly up, careful to hold her so the krait couldn't twist and bite her.

"He'll be dead in an hour 'less you get the antiserum into him," Pancho said quickly.

The blond stared at his partner helplessly.

"Take him to the hospital!" Pancho shouted.

She headed for her travel bag, still on her bed, next to the blond's discarded gun. Still holding Elly, she rummaged in the bag until she found the vial of antiserum and tossed it to the blond.

"Get him to the hospital! Now! Tell 'em what happened and give 'em this. It's the antiserum."

Then she grabbed her still-open travel bag and headed for the door. Amanda came right behind her, then rushed back in to get her own bag. As they hurried down the corridor together, Pancho glanced back over her shoulder and saw the blond lugging his unconscious partner in the other direction, toward the hospital.

"Good girl, Elly," she said. The krait had wrapped itself contentedly around Pancho's wrist.

When they got to the spaceport tunnel Dan Randolph was pacing angrily.

"Where the hell have you been? We're running late."

"I'll tell you all about it, boss," Pancho said as they climbed aboard the cart.

"It's Martin," Amanda said, her voice low.

"Humphries?" asked Dan.

"He wants Mandy, and I think he knows we're tryin' to get out of here."

"What the hell happened?" Dan demanded.

Pancho told him as the automated cart rode down the tunnel to the spaceport.

Martin Humphries sat at his desk, staring coldly at the frightened, worried face of the blond security agent. The man was sweating and nervously brushing at his moustache with a fingertip.

"So you let her get away," Humphries said, after the man had explained his failure for the third time.

"My partner was dying!" the blond said, his voice ragged. "That motherfucking snake bit him!"

"And you let Ms. Cunningham get away," Humphries repeated, icily.

"I had to take him to the hospital. He would've died otherwise."

"You didn't phone me, or security, or anyone who might have prevented her leaving."

"I'm phoning you now," the blond said, with some heat. "They're just about making their rendezvous with the *Starpower* ship. You can call the control center and have them abort the mission."

"Can I?"

"There's still time."

Humphries clicked off the connection. Stupid clod, he thought. I send him to do one simple thing and he fucks it up completely.

"Abort the mission," he said aloud. Then he shook his head. I should call the control center and tell them that Dan Randolph is hijacking my vessel and taking the woman I love alone with him. That would be a lovely item for the scandal nets. Everyone would laugh themselves sick at me.

He leaned back in his contoured chair, but its softly yielding padding failed to soothe him. Amanda's running off with Randolph. He's probably been hot for her all the time, just waiting to get her away from me. Well, now they can be together. She prefers him to me. So she can die with him.

His teeth hurt. With some surprise, Humphries realized that he'd clamped his jaw so tight it was making his whole head ache. His neck and shoulders were painfully stiff with tension. His fists were clenched so tightly he could feel his fingernails cutting into his palms.

Amanda's gone off with him. I'll acquire Astro, but I've lost her forever. They'll die together. It's not my fault. I didn't want to kill anybody. They're doing it to themselves. She's killing herself.

He wished he could cry. Instead, he glanced at the list of major Astro stockholders that was displayed on his desktop screen. And he punched his right fist into the screen, exploding it in a shower of sparks and plastic shards.

STARPOWER 1

uchs met them at the spaceport, wondering why the four of them were going to the ship a bare hour before it was due to leave orbit and head out to the Belt.

"There's been a change in plans, Lars," Dan told him. "We're going along, too."

The young man's dark brows lifted halfway to his scalp. "The IAA has approved this?"

"That doesn't make any difference," Dan said as Amanda and Pancho clambered into the tractor waiting to take them to the jumper out on the launch pad. "We're going."

Fuchs hesitated, standing in the open airlock hatch of the tractor.

"We're going," Dan repeated. "With you or without you."

A slow smile spread across Fuchs's broad face. "With me," he said, and hopped up into the tractor, clearing its six steps with ease.

Dan grinned and resisted the urge to imitate the younger man's athleticism. Amanda and Pancho had taken the two rear seats, Fuchs the one next to the hatch. Dan sat behind the driver's seat as the driver herself closed the airtight hatch and then checked out the cab's pressurization. She got behind the wheel and slipped on her headset.

She's waiting for authorization from the controller to go out, Dan knew. If they're going to stop us, this'd be the easiest time for them to do it.

But after a few moments' wait, she put the tractor in gear and rolled to the garage's airlock. A few minutes later they were at the jumper, connecting the flexible access tube from the tractor's hatch to the airlock hatch on the jumper's crew module. In their flight coveralls, the four of them stepped carefully along the springy plastic of the narrow tube, hands touching the walls, heads bent slightly to keep from brushing the low ceiling.

Small as it was, the jumper's hab module was better than the claustrophobic tube. It was little more than a few square meters of metal deck enclosed in a glassteel bubble. A control console stood up front on a waist-high pedestal. Pancho went to the control console and pulled on one of the headsets hanging there; Amanda took up her post on Pancho's right.

"Better use the foot loops," Dan said to Fuchs. "We'll be in zero-g for a few minutes."

Fuchs nodded. He looked tense, expectant, his thin lips tightly closed.

They can stop us at any time, Dan told himself. But as each second ticked by, he felt better and better.

"Five seconds and counting," Pancho told them. She hadn't bothered to turn on the speaker built into the console.

Just as Dan reached out to clasp one of the handgrips along the curving inner surface of the bubble, the jumper leaped off the ground with a single short, sharp bang of its ascent rocket. Dan's knees flexed, but Fuchs nearly buckled. Dan grabbed his arm to steady him.

"I . . . I'm sorry," Fuchs apologized. "I didn't expect it."

"It's okay," said Dan, impressed by the hard muscle he felt. "This is only your second launch, isn't it?"

Fuchs looked pale. "My second from the Moon's surface. I also rode the shuttle from the Zurich aerospace port."

Dan saw that zero-*g* was making Fuchs queasy. "Are you going to be okay?" he asked. Nothing worse than having the guy next to you upchucking all the way to rendezvous.

With a weak smile, Fuchs pointed to his well-muscled biceps. "I took the precaution of wearing a medicinal patch."

"Good," Dan said.

"And also these." He pulled a thick wad of retch bags from the thigh pocket of his coveralls.

"Smart man," Dan said, hoping that Fuchs wouldn't have to use them.

Under control from the ground, the jumper made rendezvous with *Starpower 1* and docked with the fusion ship's main airlock hatch. Dan felt the slightest of thumps as the jumper's adapter section locked onto the ship's hatch.

"Confirm docking," Pancho said into her pin-mike. "You guys did a good job. I didn't have to touch the controls once."

Whatever the controller said back to her made Pancho laugh. "Yeah, I know; that's why you drag down the big bucks. Okay, we're goin' aboard now."

Turning to Dan, Pancho said, "I'll set her up for automatic separation and return to Selene."

"Right," said Dan, lifting free of his foot restraints and floating to the hatch. As far as the controllers back at Armstrong spaceport were concerned, the four of them were to be aboard *Starpower 1* only for a final checkout before the ship was launched out of orbit. They were expected to return to Selene on the jumper.

"They're gonna be kinda surprised when this li'l buggy lands and nobody's in it," Pancho said with a mischievous grin.

Dan went through the jumper's hatch and into the coffin-sized adapter section. He tapped out the entry code to open the fusion ship's airlock hatch.

"Okay," he said, once the hatch had swung open. "Let's get aboard the Beltline express."

"You first, boss," said Pancho. "You're the owner."

He grunted. "One-third owner. I imagine at least one of the other two is going to be mighty slammed once he figures out what we're doing,"

"But he must have figured that out already," Amanda said.

"Right," Pancho agreed. "Why else would he send those goons after Mandy?"

Dan felt his brow furrow. "Then why isn't he raising a howl? Why isn't he trying to stop us?"

Fuchs looked back and forth from Amanda to Pancho to Dan, clearly baffled by their conversation.

"Well, let's get aboard before he does start hollerin'," Poncho said, making a shooing motion toward Dan with both her hands.

Feeling suddenly uneasy, Dan sailed through the hatch and entered *Starpower 1*. He hovered at the airlock's inner hatch as Pancho came through and pushed off straight toward the bridge. Amanda started through the hatch, but stumbled slightly. Fuchs grasped her by the shoulders, steadying her.

"Thank you, Lars," Amanda said.

Dan thought the kid's face turned red for a moment. He let her go and Amanda sailed through both hatches without needing to use her hands or feet. Fuchs, still a newcomer to zero-g, gripped the edges of the hatch with both his meaty hands and cannonballed through. He thumped painfully against the far bulkhead. Dan said nothing, suppressing his laughter at the young man's attempted display of athletic prowess.

But as he sealed the hatches Dan's mood darkened. *I warned Amanda about coming on to a guy.* He realized that she was wearing ordinary coveralls, but still—I'll have to play chaperon between her and Fuchs, Dan told himself.

He headed up to the bridge, "swimming" in zero gravity by flicking his fingertips against the passageway bulkheads to propel himself weightlessly forward.

Pancho had strapped herself into the command pilot's chair, busily working both hands across the control board. Through the wide glassteel ports above the board, Dan could see the dead gray curve of the Moon's limb and, beyond it, the beckoning bright crescent of the glowing Earth.

"I just disconnected ground control," she said. "They oughtta start squawkin' about it just about . . . now."

"Put them on the speaker," said Dan.

Amanda glided into the co-pilot's chair and buckled the safety harness. Fuchs came up behind her and slid his feet into the restraint loops on the floor.

"We have a disconnect signal, S–1," came a man's voice from the speaker. He sounded more bored than annoyed.

Pancho looked over her shoulder toward Dan, who placed a finger before his lips. "Run silent, run deep," he whispered.

Cupping her pin-mike with one hand, Pancho said, "I'm ready to separate the jumper."

"Do it," Dan replied.

"Jumper separation sequence initiated," Pancho said into her mike.

"Are you aboard the jumper?" asked the controller. "We can't launch S–1 as long as that disconnect is in effect. We've lost command of the vehicle."

A red light flashed on the control panel, then winked off.

"Jumper separated," Pancho said.

"Repeat, are you aboard that jumper?" the controller asked, his voice rising with irritation.

"Where else would we be?" Pancho asked innocently. And she disconnected the radio link with Selene.

Amanda worked on the launch sequence program, her manicured fingers tapping dexterously on the touchscreen.

"Three minutes to launch," she said calmly.

"Gotcha," said Pancho.

Despite himself, Dan felt his palms go sweaty. Standing there behind the two pilots, ready to ride a man-made star out farther than any sane man had ever gone before, he said to himself, *Everything I've got is riding on this bird. If we don't make it, I've got nothing to come back to. Not a double-damned thing.*

He looked at Fuchs. The kid was smiling fiercely, like an old-time warrior watching the approach of an enemy army, waiting for the battle to begin, eager to get into it. *He's got guts,* Dan thought admiringly. *We picked the right guy.*

"Two minutes," Amanda called out.

"They must be goin' apeshit down there by now," Pancho said, grinning.

"Nothing they can do about it," said Dan. "They can't shoot us down."

"Couldn't they send a Peacekeeper vessel after us?" Fuchs asked.

"Once we light the fusion rocket," Dan answered, "*nothing* in the solar system will be able to catch us."

"Till we come back," said Pancho.

Dan frowned at the back of her head. Then he relaxed. "*When* we come back, we'll be rich."

"You'll be rich, boss," Pancho said. "The rest of us'll still be employees."

Dan laughed. "You'll be rich, too. I'll see to that. You'll be rich."

"Or dead," Pancho countered.

"One minute," Amanda said. "I really think we should pay attention to the countdown."

"You're right," said Pancho.

Dan watched it all on the displays of the control board. The fusion reactor lit up as programmed. Star-hot plasma began generating energy. Through the MHD channel it roared, where a minor fraction of that heat energy was turned into electrical power. The ship's internal batteries shut off and began recharging. Cryonically-cold liquid hydrogen and helium started pumping through the rocket nozzles' cooling walls. The hot plasma streamed through the nozzles' throats.

"Ignition," Amanda said, using the traditional word even though it was now without physical meaning.

"Thrust building up," Pancho said, Dan watched the curves rising on the thrust displays, but he didn't need to; he could feel weight returning, feel the deck gaining solidity beneath his feet.

"We're off and running," Pancho announced. "Next stop, the Asteroid Belt!"

SPACEPORT ARMSTRONG

lanked by his chief of security and the head of his legal department, Martin Humphries arrived at the spaceport just in time to see *Starpower 1* light up and break orbit.

He stood at the rear of the control center, arms folded across his chest, and watched the telescopic view of the fusion ship displayed on the main wallscreen. It was not a spectacular sight: *Starpower 1*'s four rocket nozzles glowed slightly, and the ship drifted away so slowly that Humphries had to check the numbers running along the right edge of the screen to be certain that it was moving at all.

A smaller screen on the side wall showed a lunar jumper approaching the spaceport.

Four rows of consoles took up most of the control center; only three of the consoles were occupied, but Humphries could sense the consternation and confusion among the controllers.

"Jumper Six, answer!" the controller on the left was practically shouting into his headset mike.

The ponytailed, bearded man sitting in the middle of the trio was whispering heatedly with the woman on his other side. Then he whipped around in his swivel chair and grabbed his own headset from the console.

"Pancho!" he yelled in a rumbling basso voice. "Where the hell are you people? What's going on?"

Humphries knew perfectly well what was going on.

The woman controller looked up and saw Humphries standing there. She must have recognized him. Her face went white and she jabbed the chief controller's shoulder, then pointed in Humphries's direction.

The chief literally jumped out of his chair, sailing high enough almost to clear the console behind his station. But not quite. He banged his shins painfully on the top edge of the console and went sprawling in lunar slow motion into the unoccupied chair behind it, ponytail flying. He was enough of a lunik to reflexively put out his hands and grab the chair's arms to break his fall. But the chair rolled backward into the last row of consoles, and the chief controller crashed ungracefully to the floor with a loud thud and an audible, "Ooof!"

Humphries's security chief instinctively hustled down to the fallen controller and yanked him to his feet while Humphries himself and his lawyer stood impassively watching the idiotic scene.

The security man half-dragged the controller, limping, to Humphries.

"Mr. Humphries," the controller babbled, "we don't know what's going on—"

"Isn't that *Starpower 1* accelerating out of its orbit?" Humphries asked frostily.

"Yessir, it is, but it wasn't scheduled to launch for another half-hour yet and I think Pancho Lane and three other people are *aboard* it and they don't have the authorization for a crewed flight. The IAA is going to—"

"Is there any way to get them back?" Humphries asked, deadly calm.

The chief controller scratched his beard, blinking rapidly. "Well?"

"Nosir. No way in hell, Mr. Humphries."

"Who else is aboard her?"

"That's just it, we don't know if they're aboard the vessel! They might be on the jumper but they're not answering our calls. Maybe their radio broke down."

"They are aboard *Starpower 1*," Humphries said flatly. "Who else was with Pancho Lane?"

"Um..." The chief controller turned to his two assistants, wincing.

The woman called, "Amanda Cunningham, co-pilot; Lars Fuchs, planetary astronomer; and C. N. Barnard, flight surgeon."

"And you allowed them to go aboard my ship?" Humphries asked, his voice sharp as an icepick.

"They had proper authorization," the chief controller said, sweating noticeably. "IAA approval." The other two controllers, still standing at their stations, nodded their agreement.

"Amanda Cunningham was definitely with them?"

All three nodded in unison.

Humphries turned and started out of the control center. The chief controller exhaled a relieved sigh. His coveralls were stained with sweat.

But Humphries stopped at the doorway and turned back toward him. "I want you to know that the so-called Dr. Barnard is actually Dan Randolph."

All three of the controllers looked stunned.

"You never bothered to check their identifications, did you?"

"We never..." The controller's deep voice dwindled into silence under Humphries's furious glare.

"I know you work for Selene, and not for me. But I'm going to do my best to see to it that you three incompetent morons never get within a thousand kilometers of a control center again."

Then he went through the door and headed for the tunnel that led back to Selene proper.

"Shall I start the proceedings for the Astro takeover?" Humphries's lawyer asked him.

He nodded grimly.

With a satisfied smile, the lawyer said, "He won't have any part of the corporation by the time he gets back here."

"He's not coming back," Humphries said darkly. "None of them are."

Sitting in the tiny wardroom behind *Starpower*'s bridge, Dan Randolph felt truly relaxed for the first time in months. The ship was accelerating smoothly. Fuchs looked a lot better now, with the feeling of weight that came from the acceleration. No more floating in zero-*g;* they could sit in chairs without having to strap themselves down.

He marveled at his good mood. The Earth's melting down, your corporation is going broke, you've busted every regulation the IAA ever wrote, Humphries is after your scalp, you're heading out for parts unknown, and you're sitting here with a grin on your face.

He knew why.

I'm free, he told himself. Maybe for only a couple of weeks, but I'm free of all of them, free of all their crap. We're on our own and nobody can bother us.

Until we come back.

Pancho ducked through the hatch and went straight to the juice dispenser.

"How's it going?" Dan asked casually.

"All systems working jus' fine," she said, filling a mug and coming to the table to sit next to Dan.

"Must be okay if you feel good enough to leave the bridge."

"Mandy's up there, keepin' an eye on ever'thing. The bird will actually fly on her own; we don't need to be on the bridge every minute of the day."

"Any incoming calls?" Dan asked.

She shrugged. "Only about six or seven million. Ever'-body from Doug Stavenger to the Global News Network wants to talk to you."

"Global News?" Dan's ears perked up.

"Lots of news media. They all want to interview you."

Dan stroked his chin thoughtfully. "Might not be a bad idea. If we're going to do an interview it'll have to be before we get so far away the time lag makes it impossible to have a real-time conversation."

"Better do it quick, then," Pancho said. "Once we goose this bird to one-third *g*, we'll really be sprintin' fast."

Dan nodded his agreement. Pointing to the phone console built into the bulkhead, he asked, "Can you patch me through?"

"Easy."

"Okay . . . lemme talk to La Guaira."

The head of Astro's corporate public relations staff was a sweet-faced brunette who was older—and much tougher—than she looked. Dan asked her if she could arrange a news conference with the world's major news networks.

"It has to be today," he pressed. "We're zipping out so fast that by tomorrow we won't be able to talk back and forth without a four-to-five-minute lag."

"Understood," said the PR woman.

"Can you do it?"

She arched a carefully-drawn brow. "Arrange a major news conference with the man who's hijacked his own su-perduper spaceship to go out past Mars and start mining the asteroids? Just get off the line, boss, and let me get to work."

Dan laughed and obliged. He was glad that he had de-cided to keep his public relations team intact, despite the layoffs in other corporate departments. Fire the accountants and the lawyers, he reminded himself. Get rid of the paper shufflers and bean counters. But keep the people who polish your public image. They're the last to go—except for the people who do the *real* work: the engineers and scientists.

Pancho watched him as she sipped at her juice. When Dan ended his call to La Guaira, she asked, "So now what happens?"

"Now we wait while my PR people do their jobs."

"Uh-huh. How long do you think it'll take?"

"We'll know in an hour or so," Dan said. "If it takes longer than that, it's not going to go down."

Pancho nodded. "I could hear it. The lag between you and her's already longer than the usual Earth–Moon delay."

Dan got to his feet and went to the coffee dispenser. He really wanted a pleasant glass of amontillado, but there was no alcohol on the ship.

Remembering the story the two women had told him about the goons Humphries had sent after Amanda, Dan asked, "Whatever happened to your snake?"

"Elly?"

"Is that the snake's name?"

"Yup."

"So what'd you do with her?"

Pancho reached down to her ankle and came up with the glittering blue krait.

Dan flinched back. "You brought that thing aboard?"

Shrugging, Pancho said, "I was gonna leave it with Pistol Pete, he's the guy who owns the Pelican Bar. But with those goons and all, I didn't have the time."

"We've got a poisonous snake on the ship!"

"Relax, boss," Pancho said easily. "I've got four mice in my travel bag. That's enough to keep Elly fat and happy for more'n a month."

Dan stared at the snake. Its beady eyes stared back at him.

He started to shake his head. "I don't want that thing on this ship."

"Elly won't be a problem," Pancho insisted. "I'll keep her in a nice, cool spot. She'll sleep most of the time." Then, with a smirk, she added, "And digest."

"But if something should happen..."

Pancho's face went deadly serious. She seemed to Dan to be struggling with herself.

He suggested, "Maybe we could freeze the snake for the duration of the flight. Thaw her out when we get back to Selene."

"She's not poisonous," Pancho blurted.

"What?"

"I don't like to admit it, but Elly's not really poisonous. I just tell people that to keep 'em respectful. You think Selene's safety board would let a poisonous critter into the city?"

"But you said..."

Looking almost apologetic, Pancho said, "Aw, you can't believe ever'thing I say, boss. A gal's got to protect herself, doesn't she?"

"But what about that guy she bit?"

"Elly was gengineered. They modified her toxin so she produces a tranquilizer, not a lethal poison."

Dan gave her a hard look. Can I believe anything she says? he wondered.

"The science guys wanted to use Elly to trank animals in the wild that they wanted to study. It never worked."

"And you got the snake for a pet."

"A bodyguard," Pancho corrected.

"What about the antiserum?"

She laughed. "Saline solution. Just a placebo. The guy would've woke up whether they used it or not."

Dan broke into a chuckle, too. "Pancho, you're something of a con artist."

"I suppose," she admitted easily.

Amanda's voice came through on the intercom. "I've got an incoming call from La Guaira."

"I'll take it here," Dan said.

It took several frenzied hours, but Dan's PR director finally set up an interactive news conference with reporters from virtually every major media network on Earth, plus Selene's own news director, Edith Elgin, who happened to be Mrs. Douglas Stavenger when she wasn't on the air.

Dan sat back in the little plastic chair in *Starpower*'s wardroom and smiled into the camera of the phone console set into the bulkhead. His PR director acted as moderator, choosing which reporter was allowed to ask a question, and a backup. Dan found that the time lag from the ship to Earth worked in his favor; it gave him time to think before the next question arrived.

It's always smart to think before you talk, he told himself. Engage brain before putting mouth in gear.

THE INTERVIEW

Cable News: Why did you hijack your own ship?

    Dan Randolph: How can you call it a hijacking if it's my own ship? And it's only partially mine, by the way. *Starpower 1* is owned by Starpower, Ltd., which in turn is owned by three organizations: Humphries Space Systems, Astro Manufacturing, and the people of Selene. Far as I know, neither Humphries nor Selene is complaining, so I don't see this as a hijacking.

Cable News: But the International Astronautical Authority says you have no right to be aboard *Starpower 1*.

Dan Randolph: Bureaucratic [DELETED]. There's no reason why a human crew can't ride in this vessel. The IAA is just trying to strangle us in red tape.

BBC: Why do you think the IAA refused to give permission for a human crew to fly in your vessel?

Dan Randolph: I'll be double-dipped in hot chocolate fudge if I know. Ask them.

BBC: Surely you have some opinion on the matter.

Dan Randolph: Paper shufflers tend to be conservative souls. There's always a risk in allowing somebody to do something new, and bureaucrats hate risk-taking. Much safer for them to say no, you need more testing or another round of approvals. Buck the responsibility upstairs and don't stick your own neck out. If the IAA had been running America's expansion westward back in the nineteenth century, they'd still be trying to decide whether to build Chicago or St. Louis.

Nippon News Agency: What do you hope to achieve by this flight?

Dan Randolph: Ah, a substantive question for a change. We intend to stake out a claim to one or more asteroids. Our goal is to open up the vast resources of the Asteroid Belt for the human race.

Nippon News Agency: Have you determined which asteroids you will investigate?

Dan Randolph: Yes, but I'm not at liberty to reveal which they are. I don't want anyone or anything to cloud our claim.

Several questioners simultaneously: What do you mean by that? What are you afraid of? Who would make a rival claim?

Dan Randolph: Whoa! Hey, one at a time. Basically, I fear that if I announce that we're aiming for a certain asteroid, the IAA will find a reason to declare it off-limits to development, just as they've declared the Near-Earth Asteroids and the moons of Mars closed to development.

Network Iberia: But the NEAs have been closed to development because there is the chance that their orbits could be perturbed and they would crash into the Earth, isn't that so?

Dan Randolph: That's the IAA's excuse for keeping the NEAs off-limits, right. Bureaucrats can always find a good excuse to prevent progress.

Network Iberia: Are you saying, then, that the IAA has other motives in this? A hidden agenda?

Dan Randolph: If they do, their agenda isn't hidden terribly well. They've denied the resources of the NEAs to the needy people of Earth. If they could, they'd deny the resources of the Belt, as well. Why? Ask them, not me.

Lunar News: You seem to be implying that the IAA is working against the best interests of Earth.

Dan Randolph: I'm not implying it, I'm saying it loud and clear: The IAA is working against the best interests of Earth.

Lunar News: If that's the case, who do you think they are working for?

Dan Randolph: The status quo, of course. That's what bureaucrats always support. Their goal is to keep tomorrow exactly like today, or yesterday, even—no matter how lousy today or yesterday may have been.

Pan Asia Information: You cast yourself in the position of helping the needy people of Earth. Yet isn't your true goal to make billions in profits for your corporation?

Dan Randolph: My true goal is to open up the resources of the Asteroid Belt. We are running this mission on a shoestring; we don't intend to make a profit from this flight.

Pan Asia Information: But you hope to make profits from future missions, don't you?

Dan Randolph: Certainly! But more important than that, we'll have shown that the people of Earth can tap the enormous treasures of resources waiting for us in the Belt. We'll be glad to see other companies coming out to the Belt to find and develop those resources.

Columbia Broadcasting: You'd be glad to see competitors going to the Belt, but only after you yourself have claimed the best asteroids.

Dan Randolph: That's real flatland thinking. There are millions of asteroids in the Belt. Hundreds of millions, if you count the boulder-sized ones. We could claim a thousand of them and that wouldn't even begin to put a dent into the total number available.

Columbia Broadcasting: You say "claim" an asteroid. But isn't it illegal to claim any object in space?

Dan Randolph: It's been illegal since 1967 to claim sovereignty over any body in space. But since the founding of Selene, it has been perfectly legal to claim *use* of the natural resources of a celestial body.

Euronews: Weren't you accused of piracy at one time? Didn't you hijack shipments of ore on their way from the Moon to factories in Earth orbit?

Dan Randolph: That was a long time ago, and all those legal issues have been resolved.

Euronews: But aren't you doing the same thing now? Stealing a ship and going out to claim resources that rightfully belong to the entire human race?

Dan Randolph: Look, pal, I *own* this ship, One-third of it, at least. And those resources out in the Belt won't do the entire human race one diddley-squat [DELETED] iota's worth of good if somebody doesn't go out there and start developing them.

Anzac Supernet: Is it true that *Starpower 1* runs on fusion rockets?

Dan Randolph: Yes. For more about the Duncan Drive you should talk to Lyle Duncan, who headed the team that built this propulsion system. He's at the university in Glasgow.

Anzac Supernet: Are you really going to be able to reach the Asteroid Belt in two weeks?

Dan Randolph: If we accelerate at one-sixth *g* halfway and then decelerate to our destination, yes, two weeks.

Global News: Do you think this stunt will help the price of Astro Manufacturing stock?

Dan Randolph [grinning]: You must be a stockholder. Yes, if we're successful I think Astro's price should climb considerably. But that's just my guess. I'm in enough trouble with the IAA; I wouldn't want the GEC's regulators on my back, too.

Global News: How many people are on the ship with you? Could you introduce them?

Leaning back in his reclining chair as he watched the interview, Martin Humphries felt whipsawed by emotions. Try as he might to remain calm, he seethed inwardly with cold fury at Dan Randolph and Amanda Cunningham.

Yet when Amanda appeared on the wallscreen, sitting at the ship's control panel alongside Pancho Lane, looking properly businesslike in her flight coveralls and her hair pinned up, his anger melted in the light from her eyes.

How could you? He silently asked Amanda. I offered you everything and you turned your back on me. How could you?

After hardly a minute of seeing her on-screen he abruptly snapped the broadcast off. The wallscreen went blank.

It's over and done with, he told himself as he called up his appointments calendar on his desk screen. Put it behind you. Grimly he searched for the date of the next quarterly meeting of Astro Manufacturing's board of directors. He marked the date in red. Randolph will be dead by then. I'll be able to pick his bones and snap up Astro for a song. They'll all be dead by then. Her too.

Furious at the way his hands trembled, Humphries called up his most reliable dating service and began scrolling through the videos of the women who were available and ready to please him.

None of them were as desirable as Amanda, he realized. But he began making his choices anyway.

OUTWARD BOUND

A n adenoidal woman lamented lost love as country music twanged softly in the bridge of *Starpower 1*.

"That was some performance you put on," said Pancho.

She was sitting in the command-pilot's seat at the instrument panel. Dan was in the right-hand seat, beside her, separated by a bank of control knobs and rocker switches. He saw that half the touchscreens on the panel had been personalized by Pancho: they showed data against backgrounds of the Grand Canyon, sleek acrobatic aircraft, even muscular male models smilingly reclining on sunny beaches.

"The interview?" Dan laughed softly. "I could've predicted three-quarters of the questions they asked. Maybe more."

He stared out at the view through the wide glassteel port that ran the length of the instrument panel and wrapped around its sides. To his left, behind Pancho, was the Sun, its brilliance toned down by the port's heavy tinting but still bright enough to dominate the sky. It made Pancho look as if she had a halo ringing her close-cropped hair. The zodiacal light stretched out from the Sun's middle clear across the width of the port; dust motes scattered the sunlight, leftovers from the solar system's early days of creation. Beyond was darkness, the deep black infinity of space. Only a few of the brightest stars shone through the port's tinting.

"You really think the stock price'll go up?" Pancho asked, her eyes shifting back and forth among the displays on the panel.

"Already has, a couple of points," Dan said. "That's one of the reasons I did the interview."

She nodded. "From what I heard afterward, the IAA wants to slap your butt in jail the instant you get back into their jurisdiction."

"Wouldn't be the first time I've been in jail," Dan muttered.

"Yeah, but that wouldn't do the stock any good, would it?"

"Pancho, you talk like a worried stockholder."

"I'm a stockholder."

"Are you worried?"

"What, me worry?" she joked. "I got no time for worryin'. But I would like to know exactly where we're heading."

"Would you?"

"Come on, boss, you can razzle-dazzle the reporters but I know you got an asteroid all picked out. Maybe a couple of 'em."

"I want to get to three of them."

"Three?"

"Yep. One of each type: stony, metallic, and carbonaceous."

"How deep into the Belt will we hafta go?"

'We'd better bring Fuchs into this; he's the expert."

In a few minutes the four of them were seated around the table in the ship's wardroom: Amanda and Fuchs on one side, Pancho and Dan on the other. A computer-generated chart of the Asteroid Belt was displayed on the bulkhead screen, a ragged sprinkling of colored dots between thin yellow circles representing the orbits of Mars and Jupiter.

"So you can see that the metallic asteroids," Fuchs was saying, in an almost pedantic drone, "lie mostly in the outer areas of the Belt. This is a region that hasn't been explored as well as the inner zones."

"Which is why we haven't picked a specific metallic rock as yet," said Dan.

"What're we talkin' here?" Pancho asked. "Three AUs? Four?"

"Four astronomical units," Amanda replied, "give or take a fraction."

"And you want to head out there and scout around?" Pancho clearly looked incredulous.

"We have enough fuel for some maneuvering," Dan said.

Pulling her palmcomp from her coverall pocket, Pancho said, "Some maneuvering. But at that distance, not a helluva lot."

"I need a nice chunk of nickel-iron," Dan said. "Doesn't have to be big: a few hundred meters will do just fine."

Fuchs broke into a smile. It made his heavy-featured, normally dour face light up. "I think I understand. A nickel-iron piece a few hundred meters across would contain enough iron ore to feed the world's steel industry for a year or more."

Dan jabbed a forefinger in his direction. "You've got it, Lars. That's what I want to show them, back home."

Amanda spoke up. "Didn't someone bring a nickel-iron asteroid into the Earth–Moon vicinity?"

"Gunn did it," Fuchs answered. "He even named the asteroid Pittsburgh, after the steel-producing center in the United States."

"Yeah, and the double-damned GEC tossed Gunn off the rock and damned near ruined him," Dan recalled sourly.

"You simply can't have people bringing potentially dangerous objects into the Earth–Moon region," Amanda said. "Suppose this Pittsburgh thing somehow was perturbed into an orbit that would impact Earth? It could have been devastating."

Dan scowled at her. "It's been more than four centuries since Newton figured out the laws of motion and gravity. We can calculate orbits with some precision. Pittsburgh wasn't going to endanger anything. It was just the double-damned GEC's way of maintaining control."

Pancho looked up from her palmcomp. "We've got fuel enough to maneuver for three days, out at the four AU range."

"Good enough," Dan said. "We'll be scanning all the way out there. Maybe we'll get lucky and find a nickel-iron baby right away."

Fuchs shook his head gloomily. "There is vast emptiness out there." Pointing to the wallscreen display, he went on, "We think of the Belt as crowded with asteroids, but really they are nothing but infinitesimal bits of matter floating in an enormous sea of emptiness. If that chart was drawn to true scale, the asteroids would be too small to see, except in a microscope."

"A few needles in a tremendous haystack," Amanda added.

Dan shrugged carelessly. "That's why we have radar and telescopes and all the other sensors."

Pancho brought the conversation back to practicality. "Okay, so we have to go huntin' to find a metallic rock. What about the others you want, boss?"

"Lars has already picked them out."

Tapping on his own palmcomp, lying on the table before him, Fuchs highlighted two particular asteroids on the wall display. Bright red circles flashed around them. With another touch of his stylus on the palmcomp's tiny keyboard, the trajectory of *Starpower 1* appeared on the display, with the ship's current position outlined by a flashing yellow circle.

"The closer object is 26–238, an S–type asteroid."

"Stony," Amanda said.

"Yes," Fuchs agreed, smiling at her. "Stony asteroids are rich in silicates and light metals such as magnesium, calcium and aluminum."

Dan stared at the display. The dot showing *Starpower 1*'s position was noticeably moving. Christ, we're going like a bat out of hell. He had known the facts and figures of the fusion-driven ship's performance, but now, seeing the reality of it on the chart, it began to hit him viscerally.

"Our second objective," Fuchs was going on, "will be 32–114, a C–type, chondritic object. Chondritic asteroids contain carbon and hydrates—"

"Water," said Pancho, getting up from the narrow table and heading for the food freezer.

"Yes, water, but not in the liquid form."

"The water molecules are linked chemically to the other molecules in the rock," Amanda said. "You have to apply heat or some other form of energy to get the water out."

"But it's water," Dan said, watching Pancho as she pulled a foil-wrapped prepackaged meal from the freezer. "Selene needs water. So does anybody working in space."

"'You will do your work on water,'" Amanda murmured. "'An' you'll lick the bloomin' boots of 'im that's got it.'"

"What's that?" Dan asked, puzzled.

She looked almost embarrassed. "Oh . . . Kipling. Rudyard Kipling."

"'Gunga Din,'" Fuchs added quickly. "A very fine poem."

"By a white European male chauvinist," Pancho quipped as she slid her meal into the microwave oven.

"How can you be hungry?" Amanda asked. "You had a full meal only a few hours ago."

Pancho grinned at her. "I don't have to watch my figure. I burn off the calories just like that." She snapper her fingers.

"But those prepackaged meals," Amanda said. "They're so . . . prepackaged."

"I like 'em," said Pancho.

"Anyway," Dan said, raising his voice slightly to cut off any disagreements, "those are the two rocks we're going after. We'll take some samples to solidify our claim and then head for the outer region of the Belt and find ourselves a metallic body."

"I've been wondering," Amanda said slowly, "about the legal status of any claims we make. If the IAA considers this flight to be illegal...I mean, if we're deemed to be outlaws—"

"They could disallow our claims to the asteroids," Dan finished for her. "I've thought about that."

"And?"

A single, sharp, clear *ping* sounded from the open hatch to the bridge. Pancho sprinted from the microwave oven and ducked through the hatch.

She came back into the wardroom a moment later, her face taut. "Solar flare."

Amanda got to her feet and pushed past Pancho, into the bridge. Fuchs looked concerned, almost alarmed.

Dan said, "I'll check out the electron guns."

"Might not hit us," Pancho said. "The plasma cloud's still too far away to know if it'll reach us or not."

"I'll check out the electron guns anyway," Dan said, getting up from his chair. "I've taken enough radiation to last me a lifetime. I don't need any more."

EARTHVIEW RESTAURANT

The instant Martin Humphries saw Kris Cardenas, he realized that she was suffering pangs of guilt. Big time. The scientist looked as if she hadn't slept well recently; dark circles ringed her eyes, and her face looked bleak.

He rose from his chair as the maitre d' escorted her to the table and smiled as the dark-clad man held Cardenas's chair for her while she sat down. Cardenas was not smiling.

Gesturing with an outstretched arm, Humphries said, "The finest restaurant within four hundred million kilometers."

It was an old joke in Selene. The Earthview was the only true restaurant on the Moon. The other two eateries were cafeterias. Ten years earlier, the Yamagata Corporation had opened a top-grade tourist hotel at Selene, complete with a five-star restaurant. But Yamagata was forced to shut down their restaurant as the greenhouse warming throttled the tourist trade down to a trickle. Now they sent their few guests to the Earthview.

At least Cardenas had dressed properly, Humphries saw.

She wore a sleeveless forest-green sheath decorated tastefully with accents of gold jewelry. But she looked as if she were ready to attend a funeral, not an elegant dinner.

Without preamble, she leaned across the table so intently she almost touched heads with Humphries. "You've got to warn them," she whispered urgently.

"There's plenty of time for that," he said easily. "Relax and enjoy your meal."

In truth, the Earthview was a fine restaurant by any standard. The staff were mostly young, except for the stiffly formal maitre d', who added an air of grave dignity to the establishment. Carved out of the lunar rock four levels below the surface, the restaurant lived up to its name by having broad, sweeping windowalls that displayed the view from the lunar surface. It was almost like looking through windows at the barren, gauntly beautiful floor of the great ring-walled plain of Alphonsus. The Earth was always in the dark sky, hanging there like a splendid glowing blue and white ornament, ever changing yet always present.

There were no robots in sight at the Earthview restaurant, although the menus and wine list appeared on display screens built into the tabletops. Instead of tablecloths, each place setting rested on a small mat of glittering lunar honeycomb metal, as thin and flexible as silk.

Humphries ordered wine from their waiter. As soon as the young man walked away from their table, Cardenas hunched forward again and whispered, "Now! Tell them now! The sooner they know the safer they'll be."

He gave her a hard look. Apparently the nanobugs in her bloodstream can't deal with the effects of too little sleep, he thought. Or maybe she has nightmares. She's on a royal guilt trip, that's certain.

"We agreed, Dr. Cardenas," he said softly, "that we would warn them just as they approached the outer fringes of the Belt. That won't happen for another day and a half."

"I want you to warn them now," she insisted. "I don't care what we agreed on."

With the barest shake of his head, Humphries said, "I'm afraid I can't do that. We must stick to our plan."

"I was insane ever to agree to this," Cardenas hissed.

"But you did agree," Humphries pointed out. "In the long run, you'll be glad that you did."

It had been so easy to turn her. Humphries considered that his one major talent was finding the weak spot in other people's personalities, and then playing on their weaknesses to get what he wanted. It worked with Dan Randolph and his ridiculous crusade to save the Earth. It worked with Dr. Cardenas and her burning anger against the Earth and the people who had separated her from her husband and family.

The wine came. Humphries tasted it and sent it back. There was nothing really wrong with it, but Humphries simply felt like asserting himself. Subtly. Cardenas probably doesn't understand what's going on, not at the conscious level, he thought. But down in her guts she's got to know that I'm the one in charge here. I make the decisions. I mete out the rewards and the punishments.

She sat in stony silence while the embarrassed waiter took away the wine and swiftly returned with another bottle. Humphries sipped at it. Not as good as the first one, really, but he had established his point.

"This is fine," he murmured. "You may pour."

They ordered dinner. Cardenas barely picked at hers as, course by course, the dishes came and were taken away again. Humphries ate heartily. He was almost enjoying Cardenas's discomfort.

At last, after the waiter had left their desserts and walked away from the table, Cardenas said, "Well, if you won't tell them, I will."

"That's not what we agreed on," Humphries said tightly.

"To hell with what we agreed on! I don't know why I let you talk me into it."

"You let me talk you into it because I can get you back to Earth, back to your ex-husband and your children and grandchildren."

"He's remarried," she said bitterly. "There's no point in messing up his life any more than I have already."

Humphries almost smiled. She's really riding the guilt train, he said to himself.

Aloud, he coaxed, "But your grandchildren. You do want to see them, don't you? If you prefer, I could arrange to have them come up here, you know."

"I've asked them to come up, just for a visit. Begged them," Cardenas said. "They won't do it. They're terrified that they'll be refused re-entry back to Earth. That they'll be exiled here, just as I am."

Smoothly, Humphries said, "I can arrange a visit for them. Outside normal channels. I can guarantee that they'll be allowed to return to their homes."

He saw new hope kindled in her eyes. "You could?"

"No sweat."

She sat in silence while her dessert slowly melted. Humphries spooned his up, watching her, waiting.

"But don't you understand how dangerous it is?" she blurted at last. "They're going out past Mars, for god's sake. There's no one out there to help them."

"Randolph's no fool," he said sharply. "When the ship's systems start to fail he'll turn around and come back here. In a big hurry."

"I don't know . . ."

"And his pilot's an expert. She won't do anything foolish."

Cardenas either wasn't listening to him or not hearing. "Once those nanos kick in," she said, "there's no stopping them. They'll take the radiation shield apart, atom by atom, and then—"

"They won't have the time," Humphries insisted. "You

forget how fast *Starpower* goes. They'll zip back here in a few days."

"Still . . ." Cardenas looked utterly unconvinced.

Trying to sound unconcerned, Humphries said, "Look, I know this is a dirty trick to play on Randolph. But that's the business world. I want his mission to fail so I can buy out his company on the cheap. I don't want to kill him! I'm not a murderer."

Not yet, he added silently. But I'm going to be. And I'm going to have to silence this woman before her guilt trip makes her warn Randolph.

Unbidden, the thought of Amanda came to him. It only hardened his resolve. *He's* making me kill her. Randolph deserves to die. He's forced me to kill Amanda.

As he looked across the table at Kris Cardenas, so troubled, her eyes focused on god-knows-what, Humphries nodded to himself. If I leave her alone she'll warn Randolph. She'll ruin everything. I can't let her do that.

SOLAR STORM

The Apollo missions to the Moon in the mid-twentieth century were timed to avoid periods when the Sun was likely to erupt with a flare that would drench the solar system with killing levels of hard radiation.

Later, spacecraft shuttling between the Earth and the Moon simply scurried for shelter when a solar storm struck. They either returned to the protection that the Earth's magnetic field provides against the storm's lashing hail of protons and electrons, or they landed on the Moon and their crews sought shelter underground.

The earliest spacecraft to carry humans beyond the Earth–Moon system had no such options available to them, for their transit times to Mars were so long that they would inevitably encounter a solar storm while weeks or months away from a safe haven. Thus they were outfitted with storm shelters, special compartments in which the crew could be protected from the intense radiation spewed out by a solar flare. The first explorers sent to Mars spent days on end cooped up in their spacecraft's cramped "storm cellar," until the high-energy particles of the storm's plasma cloud finally passed them by.

Starpower 1 had no storm cellar. The entire crew module was protected in the same manner that a storm shelter would have been. The module was lined with thin wires of an exotic yttrium-based compound that formed a superconducting magnet which generated a permanent magnetic field around the crew module, a miniature version of the Earth's magnetic field. Yet the superconductor could not produce a magnetic field strong enough to deflect the solar storm's most dangerous killers, the high-energy protons.

When faced with a vast cloud of deadly subatomic particles blasted out by a solar flare, the ship was charged to a high positive electrostatic potential by a pair of electron guns. The energetic protons in the cloud were repelled by the ship's positive charge. The magnetic field was strong enough to deflect the cloud's lighter, less energetic electrons—and thus keep the negatively-charged electrons from ruining the ship's positive charge.

Safely cocooned inside the protective magnetic field, the crew of *Starpower 1* watched the swift approach of the storm's plasma cloud.

"Be here in another six hours," Pancho announced, pulling off her headset as she swiveled the command pilot's chair to face Dan.

He frowned at the news. "That's for certain?"

"Certain as they can be. Early-warning spacecraft in Mercury co-orbit have plotted out the cloud. Unless there's a great big kink in the interplanetary field, it's gonna roll right over us."

Nodding, Dan said, "The electron guns are ready to go."

"Better start 'em up," she said. "No sense waitin' till the last minute."

"Right." Dan stepped through the hatch, into the empty wardroom, and headed aft, where the electron guns were housed. Pancho could control them from the bridge, but Dan wanted to be there in case any problems cropped up.

"And send Amanda up here, will you?" Pancho called to him. "I gotta take a break."

"Right," Dan shouted back, over his shoulder.

Where is Amanda? He asked himself. The wardroom was empty. The doors to the privacy compartments along the passageway were closed. And where is Fuchs? he wondered, starting to feel nettled.

He found them both in the sensor bay, where Fuchs was explaining something about the x-ray projector.

"It would be more helpful if we could use a small nuclear device," the planetary astronomer was saying, totally serious. "That would be the most convenient way of generating x-rays and gamma rays all at the same time. But of course, nuclear devices are banned."

"Of course," Amanda said, looking just as intent as Fuchs.

"Pancho needs you on the bridge, Mandy." Dan said.

She looked startled for a flash of a second, then said, "Right."

As she hurried toward the bridge, Dan asked Fuchs, "What in the name of the nine gods of Sumatra do you want a nuke for?"

"I don't!" Fuchs said. "They're illegal, and justly so."

"But you just said—"

"I was explaining to Amanda about x-ray spectroscopy. How we use x-rays to make an asteroid fluoresce and reveal its chemical composition. The x-rays from this solar flare would have been very helpful to us if we were only close enough to the Belt."

"But a nuke?"

Fuchs spread his hands. "Merely an example of how to produce x-rays and gamma rays on demand. An example only. I have no intention of bringing nuclear explosives into space."

"I don't know," Dan said, scratching his chin. "You might

be onto something. Maybe we could talk the IAA into letting us use nukes as sources for spectroscopic studies."

Fuchs looked aghast. Dan laughed and slapped him on the shoulder. Fuchs saw the joke and grinned weakly back.

Dan's mood darkened as he edged down the narrow walkway in the aft end of the module. He did not like the thought of being exposed to hard radiation. He had taken a lifetime's worth of radiation back in his earlier days, working in space. Much more of a dose would kill him, he knew. It wouldn't be an easy way to go, either.

As he lifted the covers protecting the electron guns' innards and checked them for the eleventh time since they'd launched out of lunar orbit, Dan thought, Maybe Stavenger's right. Get a jolt of nanomachines, let them clean up the damage the radiation's done, rebuild me from the inside. So I won't be able to go back to Earth. So what? What's down there that I'd miss so much?

He knew the answer even as he asked the question. Sea breezes. Blue skies and soft sunsets. Birds flying. Flowers. Huge ugly brutal cities teeming with life. Vineyards! Dan suddenly realized that no one had yet tried to grow wine grapes off-Earth. Maybe that's what I'll do when I retire: settle down and watch my vineyards grow.

The intercom speaker set into the narrow walkway's overhead carried Pancho's voice. "Dan, you ready for me to light up the guns?"

The electron guns were just as good as they'd been all the other times he'd inspected them. Closing the cover on the one on his right, Dan answered, "You may fire when ready, Gridley."

Pancho retorted, "I don't know who this Gridley guy is, but I can't rev up the guns till you close both their covers and seal 'em right and proper."

"Aye, aye, skipper," Dan said.

By the time he made it back to the bridge, Pancho was nowhere in sight. Amanda sat alone in the right-hand seat, and the bridge was rocking to the beat of high-intensity pop music. As soon as she saw Dan come through the hatch, Amanda snapped the music off.

"Pancho's in the loo," she said as Dan slid into the command-pilot's seat.

"How's the storm?"

"Precisely on track." Amanda tapped at one of her touch-screens; it displayed a simplified map of the inner solar system, the orbits of Earth and Mars shown as thin lines of blue and red, respectively; the position of *Starpower 1* was a blinking bright yellow dot. A lopsided gray miasma was almost touching the dot.

Dan's mouth went dry. "I hate these things," he mumbled.

"It missed the Earth completely. Mars, as well."

"But it's going to swamp us."

"Actually," Amanda said, "we'll merely be brushed by it. A few hours, that's all."

"That's good."

"Our own velocity is helping a lot, you know. An ordinary spacecraft, coasting along the way they do, would be in the cloud for days on end."

Dan had no desire to be in the cloud for even ten minutes. He changed the subject, as much to get away from the fear building up inside him as any other reason. "How friendly are you and Fuchs?"

Amanda's brows shot up. "Lars? He's very earnest—about his work. Nothing more."

"That's all there is to it?"

"Yes."

Dan thought it over. Two healthy young people locked in this sardine can for a couple of weeks. Of course, there's Pancho and me to chaperon them. Dan grinned to himself. Damn, it's like being a teenager's father.

Pancho returned to the bridge. "Hey boss, get outta my chair."

"Yes'm," said Dan.

The plasma cloud hit them less than an hour later. There was no buffeting, no clanging of alarms, nothing to tell them that they were being engulfed in the cloud of killing radiation except the rising curves of fire-engine red on the radiation monitoring screens.

Pancho did not consider the storm so dangerous that someone had to be on the bridge at all times. She came into the wardroom and joined the others for dinner. Dan ate mechanically, not really tasting his food, not really hearing the conversation. Double-damned radiation, he kept thinking. I hate this. Despite two steaming mugs of coffee, he felt cold inside.

But the others seemed completely unfazed by the storm. After the meal Dan said good-night to them all and went to his compartment. He dreamed of floating helplessly in space, slowly freezing as the Sun glowered at him.

NANOTECHNOLOGY LABORATORY

ong past midnight, Kris Cardenas sat alone in her office in Selene's nanotechnology lab. The rest of the lab was empty, darkened to its nighttime lighting level.

She had agreed to have dinner with Martin Humphries because she wanted to get the man to warn Dan Randolph about the nanomachines that she had planted in his vessel, virus-sized disassemblers that once were known as "gobblers."

They were the reason that nanotechnology was banned on Earth—and under careful supervision at Selene.

Quis custodiet ipsos custodes? she asked herself. Who will watch the watchmen? Some Roman asked that question more than two thousand years ago, Cardenas knew.

All nanotech work was under very strict control in Selene. No one was allowed to work with gobblers: they had killed people. They had even been used to commit murder. If they ever got loose they could destroy all Selene. The medical work had to be supervised down to the nanometer because the therapeutic nanobugs that took apart plaque in a person's arteries or destroyed tumors atom by atom were forms of gobblers, nothing less. If they ever got loose, if their programming was ever-so-subtly altered...

That was why Kris Cardenas's primary duty as head of all nanotech work at Selene was to protect against such a catastrophe. She watched over every aspect of the work done in the nanotech lab.

But who will watch the watchmen? She had produced a microscopic batch of gobblers for Humphries, specifically tailored to damage *Starpower 1* enough so Dan would have to turn the ship around and limp back to Selene. Humphries had promised that he would obtain permission for her to visit Earth again, to see her daughters and her grandchildren.

Now he was offering to bring them up here. Even better. But the price! Dan Randolph and the other people on that ship could get killed.

Is that what Humphries really wants? She asked herself. If I warned Dan now he'd have to return to Selene. Flat and simple. But Humphries wants to wait another day or so, let Dan get to the inner fringes of the Belt and then tell him that his ship's going to fail.

Or maybe he won't warn Dan at all!

Cardenas sat up straight in her desk chair. That's it, she told herself. He wants to kill Dan and the rest of the crew. She knew it with the certainty of revealed truth.

What can I do about it?

Warn Dan, she answered her own question. Warn him *now*.

But how? She wondered. I can't just pick up a phone and put a call through to him. They're out past the orbit of Mars by now.

I've got to get to someone in the Astro office. Someone who can put me through to Dan. Maybe that big Australian bodyguard of his. What's his name? George something.

*   *   *

Martin Humphries could not sleep, despite the exertions he'd been through with the raven-haired woman lying beside him. Nominally an environmentalist on the consulting staff of Humphries Trust, the young woman's favored environment seemed to be a bedroom with plenty of furniture to play on, as far as Humphries could determine.

She was sleeping peacefully. He was wide awake.

Dr. Cardenas. Humphries was worried about her. Even the lure of seeing her grandchildren wasn't going to outweigh her overdeveloped sense of honor, he thought. She wants to warn Randolph; she's probably figured out that I want the sonofabitch dead.

He sat up in the bed and glanced at the woman sleeping beside him. Slowly, carefully, he pulled the silk sheet down from her shoulders. Even with no lights in the room except the green glow from the digital clock, he could see that her body was smooth, flawless, perfectly proportioned. Too bad she's heading back to Earth in a few days.

Cardenas, he reminded himself sternly.

She's going to try to warn Randolph, he felt certain. Maybe that's a good thing. If Randolph turns back now, Amanda will come back with him. With *him*. She won't be coming back to me. She doesn't want me, that's why she ran off with him. If Cardenas warns them, they'll come back here together to gloat at me.

He squeezed his eyes shut and tried to drive out the mental images of Randolph and Amanda together. I've got to think this through carefully. Logically.

For Cardenas to warn Randolph she'll have to get somebody here in Selene to set up the message for her. She'll probably go to Astro; that's where Randolph's people are. And if she asks them to let her put through a call to Randolph they'll ask her why. Sooner or later she'll tell them why: Martin Humphries has bugged the *Starpower* ship with nanomachines. And then they'll know all about it.

Conclusion: For my own protection, I've got to stop her

from talking to anyone at Astro. I've got to stop her from even trying to warn Randolph. I've got to stop her. Period.

When Dan awoke from his troubled sleep the solar storm had passed. Pancho was in the wardroom when he shambled in, bleary-eyed.

"Top o' the mornin', boss," she said cheerily, hefting a mug of steaming coffee.

"How's the weather out there?" Dan asked, heading for the juice dispenser.

"Clear and calm, except for a few rocks we should be passin' by this afternoon."

That made Dan smile. "We're at the Belt."

"Will be, by sixteen hundred hours. Right on *shedyule,* as Mandy would say."

"Good. Great. Where's Fuchs? We've got to make some course adjustments."

Ten minutes later the four of them were seated around the table in the wardroom.

"I want to get a metallic nugget first," Dan said.

Fuchs lifted his heavy shoulders slightly. "The metallic bodies are more heavily concentrated towards the outer area of the Belt."

"So we go to the outer edge of the Belt," Dan replied, "and search for a lump of iron. We can pick up the stony and carbonaceous rocks on the way back."

"We'll have to go more than four astronomical units, then," Amanda pointed out. "No one's gone that far before."

Dan said, "We've got the supplies for it. And the fuel. Everything's running all right, isn't it?"

"No major problems," said Pancho.

His brows rising, Dan asked, "What are the minor problems?"

She grinned at him. "The coffee's pretty awful. A couple of li'l maintenance chores to do. You know, a cranky pump, one of the fuel cells is discharging when it shouldn't. Nigglin' stuff. Mandy and I are takin' care of it."

Amanda nodded. Dan looked from her back to Pancho. Neither woman seemed worried. Well, he thought, if the pilots aren't worried, no reason for me to sweat.

"The sensor suite is in perfect working order," Fuchs volunteered. "I'm already recording data."

"We'll have to do the turnaround maneuver soon," said Amanda.

Gesturing vaguely toward infinity, Dan asked Fuchs, "Have you picked a destination point out there?"

"A general area only," he replied. "The outer Belt has not been mapped well enough to pick a precise asteroid. Most of them are not even numbered yet."

"Have you given Pancho the coordinates?"

Fuchs's face colored slightly. "I gave them to Amanda."

"I've put the data into the nav computer," Amanda said quickly, looking at Pancho.

Pancho nodded. "Okay. I'll go check it out."

"Onward and upward," said Dan, rising from his chair. "We'll be breaking distance records, if nothing else."

"Four AUs," Pancho muttered, getting to her feet also.

She headed for the bridge. Dan followed her, leaving Amanda and Fuchs still sitting at the table.

Pancho slid into the pilot's chair and tapped on her main touchscreen, the one showing the hunk on the beach. Standing behind her, Dan saw the navigation computer program come up over the muscles and teeth.

But Pancho was looking at one of the smaller screens, where an amber light was blinking slowly.

"What's that?" Dan asked.

"Dunno," said Pancho, working the screen with her fingers. "Running a diagnostic . . . h'mmph."

"What?"

Without turning her head from the display screens, Pancho muttered, "Says there's a hot spot on one of the super-conducting wires outside."

A jolt of alarm surged through Dan. "The superconductor? Our storm shield?"

She glanced up at him. "Don't get frazzled, boss. Happens all the time. Might be a pinhole leak in the coolant line. Maybe a micrometeor dinged us."

"But if the coolant goes—"

"The rate of loss ain't much," Pancho said calmly. "We're due for turnaround in six hours. I can angle the ship then so's that side's in the shade. If the hot spot doesn't go away then, Mandy and me will go EVA and fix the leak."

Dan nodded and tried to feel reassured.

STAVENGER THEATER

K ris Cardenas marveled at the crowd's willingness to leave their comfortable homes and jam themselves cheek-by-jowl into the cramped rows of narrow seats of the outdoor theater. A considerable throng of people was flowing into the theater. It was built in the Grand Plaza, "outdoors." Exactly one thousand seats were set in a shallow arc around the graceful fluted shell that backed the stage.

Even with three-dimensional interactive video and virtual reality programs that were nearly indistinguishable from actuality, people still went to live performances. Maybe it's because we're mammals, Cardenas thought. We crave the warmth of other mammals. We're born to it and we're stuck with it. Lizards have a better deal.

There was one particular mammal Cardenas wanted to see: George Ambrose. That morning she had phoned the Astro corporate office trying to find him, only to reach his video mail. Late in the afternoon he returned her call. When she said she had to talk to him in person as soon as possible, and preferably in a public place, George had scratched at his thick red beard for a moment and then suggested the theater.

"I've got a date comin' with me," he said cheerfully, "but we can get together in the intermission and chat for a bit. Okay?"

Cardenas had quickly agreed. Only as an afterthought did she ask what the theater was playing.

George sighed heavily. "Some fookin' Greek tragedy. This date of mine, she's a nut for th' classics.".

Usually the theater was sold out, no matter what the production might be. In the days before the greenhouse cliff, when tourism was building up nicely, Selene's management invited world-class symphony orchestras, dance troupes, drama companies to come to the Moon. Now, most of the performances were done by local amateur talent.

Medea, performed by Selene's very own Alphonsus Players. Cardenas would have shuddered if it had mattered to her at all. Still, the theater was fully booked. Only Cardenas's status as one of Selene's leading citizens wheedled a ticket out of the system, and she had to go all the way up to Doug Stavenger for that. He smilingly admitted that he wasn't going to use his.

She barely looked at the stage during the first half of the performance. Sitting on the aisle in the fourth row, Cardenas spent most of her time scanning the crowd for a glimpse of George Ambrose's shaggy red hair.

When the first half ended, she trudged with the slow-moving throng along the central aisle as they chatted about the play and the performances. Cardenas felt surprised to see so many gray and white heads among the theater-goers. Selene is aging, she thought. And very few of our people are taking nanobugs or other therapies to stop it. Finally she saw Big George, like a fiery beacon bobbing head and shoulders above the others.

Once past the last row of seats, most of the crowd scattered to the concession stands spread among the plaza's flowering shrubbery. A maintenance robot trundled slowly along the periphery of the crowd, patrolling for litter.

George was at the jam-packed bar. Cardenas hung back, waiting for him to get his drink and work his way out of the crowd. When he did, he had a plastic stein of beer decorated with Selene's logo in one hand and a skinny, hollow-eyed redhead on his other arm. She was pretty, in a gaunt, needy way, Cardenas thought. Nice legs. The drink in her hand was much smaller than Ambrose's.

Big George spotted Cardenas and, leaving his date standing by a flowering hibiscus bush, walked toward her.

"Dr. Cardenas," he said, with a polite dip of his head. "What can I do for you?"

"I've got to get a message to Dan Randolph," she said. "As quickly as possible."

"No worries. Pop over t' the office tomorrow morning. Or tonight, after th' show, if you like."

"Is there some way I could talk to Dan without coming to your offices? I think I'm being watched."

George looked more puzzled than alarmed. "You could phone me, I suppose, and I'll patch you through to the radio link." He took a pull from his stein.

"Can we do it tonight?"

"Sure. Right now, if you like. I wouldn't mind an excuse to leave this show. Pretty fookin' dull, don'tcha think?"

"Not now," she answered. "That would attract attention. After the show. I'll drop in at friend's place and call your office from there."

For the first time, George showed concern. "You're really scared, are you?"

"I think Dan's life is in danger."

"You mean someone's out to kill 'im?"

"Humphries."

George's face hardened. "You certain of that?"

"I'm ... pretty sure."

"Sure enough to want to warn Dan. From a safe place, where the phone won't be bugged."

"Exactly."

George took a big breath. "All right. Instead of all this pussyfootin' around, you come with me after the show's finished and I'll put you in an Astro guest suite. That way I can protect you."

Cardenas shook her head. "That's kind of you, but I don't think I'm in danger."

"Then why th' cloak and dagger stuff?"

"I don't want Humphries to know that I'm warning Dan. If he knew, then maybe I would be in trouble."

George thought that over for a few moments, a huge red-maned mountain of a man towering over her, scratching his head perplexedly.

"All right," he said at last. "Back to Plan A, then. I'll go to the office after this fookin' show and you call me there. Okay?"

"Yes. Fine. Thank you."

"Sure you don't want some protection?"

She considered his offer for several heartbeats, then said, "Thanks, but I won't need it. And I've got my work to consider. I can't run the lab from an Astro guest suite."

"Okay," said George. "But if you change your mind, just holler."

Martin Humphries was reclining in his favorite chair, watching a home video of his own performance, when the phone buzzed. Irked, he glanced at the console and saw that it was his emergency line. He snapped his fingers, and the wallscreen lit up to show the woman he'd sent to follow Cardenas. She was a nondescript clerk from Astro Corporation's communications department who needed extra money to bring her younger sister up from the ravaged ruins of Moldavia.

"Well?" Humphries demanded.

"She talked with George Ambrose and then went back to the show."

"You have video?"

"Yes, of course."

"Well let me see it," he snapped.

The woman's face was replaced by a slightly jittery video of Cardenas talking earnestly with Randolph's body-guard, that big Australian.

"They went back to the show together?"

The woman's face reappeared on the screen. "No, separately. He had another woman with him."

Glancing at the digital clock on his desk, Humphries asked, "When does the show end?"

"I don't know."

Stupid cow, he fumed silently. Aloud, he commanded, "Stay with her. I'm going to send a couple of men to pick her up. Keep your phone on and they'll home in on the signal. That way, even if they don't get there before the show's over they can find you—and her."

"It is not allowed to keep the phone on during the performance," the woman replied.

"I don't care what's allowed and what isn't! Keep your phone on and stay with Dr. Cardenas or I'll have you shipped back to Moldavia!"

Her eyes widened with sudden fear. "Yes, sir," she said. Sullenly.

"How's the leak?" Dan asked.

He'd been fidgeting around in the wardroom for hours, trying not to pop into the bridge and bother the pilots. But a leak in the superconductor's coolant scared Dan. Without the superconductor they could be fried by the next solar storm.

So when Amanda left the bridge, Dan asked about the leak.

She looked surprised at his question. "Leak?"

"In the coolant line."

"Oh, that. It's nothing much. Pancho will go EVA after turnaround and patch it."

"Just Pancho?" Dan asked. "By herself?"

"It's only a tiny leak," Amanda said lightly. "Pancho decided it won't need both of us out there."

Dan nodded and got up from his chair. "Think I'll go aft and see what Fuchs is doing." *If I just sit here I'll turn myself into a nervous wreck,* he added silently.

Fuchs was back in the sensor bay, humming tunelessly to himself as he bent over a worktable strewn with parts from an infrared scanner.

"Did it break down?" Dan asked.

Fuchs looked up at him, a pleased smile on his broad face. "No, no," he said. "I decided to upgrade its sensitivity so we could get better data at long range."

"We're going to turn around soon. You'll have to get all these loose parts stowed away safely or they'll slide off the table."

"Oh, I should be finished by then."

"Really?"

With a glance that was part surprise at having his word questioned, and part pride in his abilities, Fuchs said, "Of course."

He bent over his work again, stubby thick fingers handling the delicate parts with the precision of a well-trained mechanic. Dan watched him for a while, then quietly left the man to himself. As he started back to his privacy cubicle, he saw Amanda heading along the narrow passage toward him.

"Going to help Pancho suit up?" he asked. "I can—"

"Oh, there's plenty of time for that," Amanda said brightly. "I thought I'd pop in on Lars for a few minutes and help him get prepared for turnaround."

Dan felt his brows inch upward. "Something going on between you two?" he asked.

She looked genuinely surprised. "Lars is a complete gentleman," Amanda said with great dignity. "And even though you may not believe it, I know how to behave like a lady."

She brushed past Dan, chin high, radiating disdain.

Dan grinned at her retreating back. Something's going on, all right, even if Fuchs doesn't know it yet.

O n my mark," Pancho's voice came through the intercom, "turnaround in thirty minutes. *Mark.*"

Dan sat up in his bunk. He had just drifted to sleep, it seemed, after staring at the compartment's overhead for what had felt like hours.

We're well inside the Belt, he thought. The ship's working fine. We're heading for the outer reaches to scout around for a good, solid M–type body.

And there's a leak in the coolant that keeps the superconductor cooled down enough to maintain the magnetic field around us that protects us from the hard radiation of solar storms. Sounds like the house that Jack built, he said to himself, trying to shake the feeling of foreboding that plagued him.

He grabbed a fresh pair of coveralls and marched to the lav. I need a shower and a shave, he thought. And you need to get that leak fixed, a voice in his head reminded.

He wished it didn't bother him so much. Pancho wasn't worried about it; neither was Amanda.

Damned good-looking woman, Amanda, he thought. Even in loose-fitting coveralls she's dynamite. Better make it a cold shower.

The only tricky part of the turnaround maneuver was that they had to shut down the main thrusters. Not the fusion reactor itself; the procedure was to kill the ship's thrust during turnaround, and use the reactor's exhaust gases to turn the ship by venting a fraction of the exhaust through maneuvering jets set into the sides of the propulsion module.

Dan headed up to the bridge after his shower. Both pilots were in their places. No music was playing.

"All systems ready for turnaround," Amanda murmured.

"Check, all systems go," Pancho replied.

Standing behind their chairs, Dan asked, "Where's Fuchs?"

"Prob'ly still in the sensor bay," Pancho said, "playin' with his toys."

Amanda frowned slightly as she touched the comm screen. "Turnaround in five minutes," she announced.

Glancing over her shoulder, Pancho said, "Boss, you oughtta find a chair."

He scowled at her. "I've been in micro-*g* before, kid." Before you were born, he almost added.

He could see Pancho grinning in her reflection on the port in front of her. "Okay, you're the boss. Footloops on the deck and handgrips on the overhead."

"Aye-aye, skipper," Dan said, grinning back at her.

"Thrust cutoff in two minutes," Amanda called out.

"Two minutes. Check."

When the main thrusters cut off, Dan felt completely at ease. The feeling of gravity dwindled away to nothing, and he floated off the deck slightly. Grabbing one of the handgrips, he hung there and watched the pilots working their touchscreens.

"How's Fuchs doin' back there?" Pancho asked.

Amanda tapped the central screen and it showed Fuchs strapped into the fold-up chair in the sensor bay, looking a little pasty-faced but otherwise okay.

"Maneuver thrust in two minutes," Amanda said.

"Check," Pancho replied.

Dan worked his feet into the loops on the deck without letting go of the overhead handgrips. The maneuvering jets fired and he felt as if somebody suddenly shoved him from one side. He remembered from childhood his first ride in a people-mover at some airport: he'd been standing facing the doors, and when the train lurched into movement he'd nearly toppled over sideways. Only the grownups crowded around him had prevented him from falling.

"Phew," Pancho said, "this bird turns like a supertanker: slow and ugly."

"You're not flying a little flitter now," Dan said.

"Turn rate is on the curve," Amanda pointed out, tracing the curve on the touchscreen with a manicured fingertip. Her screen's background showed the white cliffs of Dover.

"Uh-huh," said Pancho. "Still feels like we're pushin' freight."

Amanda said, "We are: all that deuterium and helium-three."

The fuel weighs a lot, Dan realized. Funny. You think of hydrogen and helium as being light, almost weightless. But we've got tons of the stuff in our tanks. Dozens of tons.

There was nothing much to see through the port. No panoply of stars swinging past. No asteroids in sight. Nothing but emptiness.

"Where's the Sun?" Dan heard himself ask.

Pancho chuckled. "It's there, boss. Hasn't gone away. We're just angled up too much to see it through the windshield, that's all."

As if in confirmation, a stream of light glowed through the port.

"Sunrise in the swamp," Pancho called out.

Dan felt another sideways surge of thrust, pushing from the opposite direction.

"Turnaround maneuver complete," said Amanda.

"Flow to main thrusters," Pancho said, working the touchscreens.

"Main thrusters, confirmed."

Weight returned to the bridge. Dan settled back onto the deck.

Amanda smiled happily. "On course and on velocity vector."

"Hot spit!" Pancho exclaimed. "Now let's see how that leak is doin'."

Kris Cardenas almost made it back to her own apartment before two young men in dark business suits caught up with her.

"Dr. Cardenas?"

She turned. The man who had called her name was taller than his partner, slim and lithe, sallow complexion, his dark hair cropped into a buzz cut. The other was huskier, blond, pink-cheeked.

"Come with us, please," said the dark one.

"Where? Why? Who are you?"

"Mr. Humphries wants to see you."

"Now? At this hour? It's—"

"Please," said the blond, slipping a dead-black pistol from inside his jacket.

"It fires tranquilizing darts," said the dark one. "But you wake up with a bitching headache. Don't make us use it on you."

Cardenas looked up and down the corridor. The only other person in sight was a mousy little woman who immediately turned away and started walking in the opposite direction.

"Now," said the blond, pointing his pistol at her.

With a resigned droop of her shoulders, Cardenas nodded her surrender. The blond put his gun away and they started along the corridor toward the escalators.

"At least this one doesn't have a snake," the blond whispered hoarsely to his partner.

The other man did not laugh.

EVA

Pancho felt an old excitement bubbling up inside her as she wormed her arms through the spacesuit's sleeves. After more than five days of being cooped up in the ship, she was going outside. It was like being a kid in school when the recess bell rang.

Standing by the inner airlock hatch where the spacesuits were stored, she popped her head up through her suit torso's neck ring, grinning happily to herself. This is gonna be fun, she thought.

Dan looked uptight, though, as he held her helmet in his arms and watched her pull on the gloves and seal them to the suit's cuffs.

"Jealous?" she teased.

"Worried," he replied. "I don't like the idea of you going out alone."

"Piece of cake, boss," Pancho said.

"I ought to go with you. Or Amanda, maybe."

With a shake of her head, Pancho countered, "Mandy's

gotta stay at the controls. Shouldn't have both pilots out at the same time, if you can help it."

"Then I'll suit up—"

"Whoa! I've seen your medical record, boss. No outside work for you."

"The safety regs say EVAs should be performed by two astronauts—"

"Whenever possible," Pancho finished for him. "And since when did you start quotin' IAA regulations?"

"Safety is important," Dan said.

Inside the spacesuit, with its hard-shell torso and servomotor-amplified gloves, Pancho felt like some superhero out of a kids' video confronting a mere mortal.

"I'll be fine," she said as she took the helmet from Dan's hands. "Nothin' to worry about."

"But if you run into trouble..."

"Tell you what, boss. You suit up and hang out here at the airlock. If I run into trouble you can come on out and save my butt. How's that?"

He brightened. "Okay. Good idea."

They called Amanda down from the bridge as Dan struggled into the lower half of his suit and tugged on the boots. By the time he was completely suited up, backpack and all, except for the helmet, Pancho was feeling antsy.

"Okay," she said as she pulled the bubble-helmet over her head and sealed it to the neck ring. "I'm ready to go outside."

Amanda hurried back to the bridge while Dan stood there grinning lopsidedly at her, his head sticking out of the hard suit like some kid posing for a photograph from behind a cardboard cutout of an astronaut.

Pancho opened the inner hatch of the airlock and stepped through. The airlock was roomier than most, big enough to take two spacesuited people at a time. Through her helmet she heard the pump start to clatter, and saw the telltale on the control panel switch from green to amber. The sound dwindled to nothing more than a slight vibration she felt through her boots as the air was pumped out of the chamber. The light flicked to red.

"Ready to open outer hatch," she said, unconsciously lapsing into the clipped argot of flight controllers and pilots.

Amanda's voice came through the tiny speaker set into her neck ring, "Open outer hatch."

The hatch slid up and Pancho stared out at an infinite black emptiness. The helmet's glassteel was heavily tinted, but within a few seconds her eyes adjusted and she could see dozens of stars, then hundreds, thousands of them staring solemnly at her, spangling the heavens with their glory. Off to her left the bright haze of the zodiacal light stretched like a thin arm across the sky.

She turned her back to the zodiacal light's glow and attached her safety tether to one of the rungs just outside the hatch.

"Goin' out," she said.

"Proceed," Amanda replied.

"Gimme the location of the leak," Pancho said as she clambered out and made her way up the handgrips set into the crew module's side.

"On your screen."

She peered at the tiny video screen strapped to her left wrist. It showed a schematic of the module's superconducting network of wires, with a pulsating red circle where the leak was.

"Got it."

Although she knew the ship was under acceleration and not in zero-g, Pancho still felt surprised that she actually had to climb along the handgrips, like climbing up a ladder, toward the spot marked on the schematic. Deep in her guts she had expected to float along weightlessly.

"Okay, I'm there," she said at last.

"Tether yourself," Dan's voice commanded sternly.

Pancho was still tethered to the rung next to the airlock

hatch. Grinning at Dan's fretfulness, she unreeled the auxiliary tether from her equipment belt and clipped it to the closest grip.

"I'm all tucked in, Daddy," she quipped.

Now to find the leak, she thought. She bent close and played her helmet lamp on the module's skin. The curving metal was threaded with thin wires running along the module's long axis. There was no obvious sign of damage: no charred spot where a micrometeor might have hit, no minigeyser of escaping nitrogen gas.

It can't be more than a pinhole leak, Pancho told herself.

"Am I at the right spot?" she asked.

No answer for a few moments. Then Amanda replied, "Put your beacon on the wire you're looking at, please."

The radio beacon was strapped to Pancho's right wrist. She laid her right forearm on the wire.

"How's that?"

"You're at the proper spot."

"Can't see any damage."

"Replace that section and bring it in for inspection, then."

She nodded inside her helmet. "Will do."

But she felt silly, cutting out what looked to be a perfectly good length of wire. Something's wonky here, Pancho thought. This ain't what we think it is, I bet.

Behind his unkempt beard, Big George was frowning with worry as he sat at one of the consoles in the spaceport's control center. This little cluster of desks was occupied by Astro employees, monitoring *Starpower 1*'s flight. They sat apart from the regular Selene controllers, who handled the traffic to and from Earth.

George wanted to send his message to Dan in complete privacy. The best the Astro controllers could do was to hand him a handset and tell him to keep his voice down.

Wishing they had worked out a code before Dan had impetuously sailed off, George pulled the pin-mike to his lips and said hurriedly, "Dan, it's George. Dr. Cardenas has disappeared. She told me last night she was worried that Humphries wants to kill you. When I called her this morning she wasn't in her office or in her quarters. I can't find her anywhere. I haven't told Selene security about it yet. What do you want me to do?"

He pulled off the headset and nudged the controller who had given it to him. The man had been studiously keeping his back to George.

He swiveled his chair to face the Aussie. "Finished so soon?"

"How long will it take to get an answer?"

The controller tapped at his keyboard and squinted at the display on his console's central screen. "Seventeen minutes and forty-two seconds for your message to reach them. Same amount of time for their answer to get back here, plus a couple additional seconds. They're moving pretty damned fast."

"Thirty-five minutes," George said.

"Got to allow some time for them to hear what you've got to say and decide what to say back to you. Probably an hour, at least."

"I'll wait."

Martin Humphries unconsciously licked at the thin sheen of perspiration beading his upper lip. He hated talking with his crotchety sour-faced father, especially when he had to ask the old man for advice.

"You kidnapped her?" W. Wilson Humphries's wrinkled face looked absolutely astonished. "A Nobel Prize scientist? You kidnapped her?"

"I've brought her here, to my home," Humphries said, holding himself rigidly erect in his chair, exerting every gram of willpower he possessed to keep from squirming. "I couldn't let her warn Randolph."

The conversation between father and son was being carried by a tight laser beam, directly from Humphries Space System's communication center on the top of Alphonsus crater's ringwall mountains to the roof of the senior Humphries's estate in Connecticut. No one could eavesdrop unless they tapped into the laser beam itself, and if someone did, the drop in the beam's output at the receiver would be detectable.

"Killing Randolph isn't bad enough," grumbled the old man. "Now you're going to have to kill her, too."

"I haven't killed anybody," Humphries said tightly. "If Randolph has any brains at all he'll turn back."

It took nearly three seconds for his father's reply to reach him. "Sloppy work. If you want to remove him, you should have done it right."

Humphries's temper flared. "I'm not a homicidal maniac! Randolph is business, and anyway, if he dies it will look like an accident. His ship fails out there in the Belt and he and his crew are killed. Nobody will know what happened and nobody will be able to investigate, not for months, maybe years."

He tried to calm himself as he waited for his father's response.

"Gaining Astro Manufacturing is worth the risk," the old man agreed. "Especially since no one can connect you with the . . . uh, accident."

"She can."

Humphries knew what his father was going to say.

"Then you'll have to get rid of her."

"But that doesn't mean I have to kill her. I don't want to do that. She's a valuable asset. We can use her."

It wasn't a spur-of-the-moment decision, Humphries told himself. Dr. Cardenas and her knowledge of nanotechnology had been part of his long-range plan all along. It's just that this crisis has forced me to move faster than I'd originally planned to, he told himself.

"Use her?" his father snapped. "How?"

Waving a hand in the air, Humphries said vaguely, "Nanotechnology. She's the top expert. Without her it would've taken years to build that fusion rocket."

His father cackled. "You don't have the guts to take her out."

"Don't be an idiot, Dad! She's much more valuable to me alive than dead."

"You want her to be part of your team, then," his father replied.

"Yes, of course. But she's having this goddamned attack of integrity. She's got cold feet about Randolph, and if I don't stop her, she'll tell everyone about the sabotage, even though she's a party to it."

The old man chuckled when he heard his son's complaint. "An attack of integrity, eh? Well, there are ways to get around that."

"How?"

It was maddening to have to wait nearly three seconds for his father's response.

"Make her an offer that she can't accept."

"What?"

Again the interminable wait. Then, "Offer her something that she really wants, but can't agree to. Make her an offer that really tempts her, but she'll have to reject. Then you've shown yourself to be reasonable, and she's being the difficult one. Then she'll be more willing to agree to your next offer."

Humphries was impressed. "That's ... Machiavellian."

When his father answered, his seamed, sagging face was strangely contorted, as if he were suppressing a guffaw. "Yes, it is, isn't it? And it works."

Humphries could only sit there and admire the old bastard.

More thoughtfully, his father asked, "What's her weak point? What does Cardenas want that she can't get unless you give it to her?"

"Her grandchildren. They'll be our hostages. Oh, I'll do it in a nice, elegant manner. But I'll let her know that either she works for me or her grandchildren suffer. She'll do what I want."

"You really want to be emperor of the world, don't you, Martin?"

Humphries blanched. "*Your* world? God forbid. Earth is a shambles and it isn't going to get any better. You can have it. You're welcome to it. If I make myself emperor, it'll be up here: Selene, the Moon, the asteroids. That's where the power is. That's where the future lies. I'll be emperor of these worlds, all right. Gladly!"

For long moments his father said nothing. At last the old man muttered, "God help us all."

STARPOWER 1

ars Fuchs was scowling as he peered at the display screen.

"Well?" Dan prompted.

The two men stood in the cramped sensor bay, where Fuchs had rigged a makeshift laboratory by yanking one of the ship's mass spectrometers from its mounting and putting it on the repair bench where he was using it to examine the sample of dull gray wire that Pancho had brought in. A thin sky-blue coolant tube lay alongside the wire. Dan knew the wire had originally run through the tube, like an arm in a sleeve.

"There is no leak in the coolant line," Fuchs said. "I drove pressurized nitrogen through it and it didn't leak."

Dan felt puzzled. "Then what's causing the hot spot?"

Pointing to the tangle of curves displayed on the screen, Fuchs said, "The composition of the wire seems to match the specifications quite closely: yttrium, barium, copper, oxygen—all the elements are in their proper proportions."

"That doesn't tell us diddley-squat," Dan groused.

Fuchs's frown deepened as he studied the display. "The copper level seems slightly low."

"Low?"

"That might be a manufacturing defect. Perhaps that's the reason for the problem."

"But there's no leak?"

Fuchs rubbed his broad, square chin. "None that I can detect with this equipment. Really, we don't have the proper equipment for diagnosing this. We would need a much more powerful microscope and—"

"Dan, we're receiving a call for you," Amanda's voice came through the speaker in the sensor bay's overhead. "It's from George Ambrose, marked urgent and confidential."

"I'd better get back up to the bridge," Dan said. "Do the best you can, Lars, with what you've got."

Fuchs nodded unhappily. How can a man accomplish anything without the proper tools? he asked himself. With a heavy sigh, he turned back to the display screen while Randolph ducked through the hatch and headed forward.

What other sensors can I take from the set we have to examine this bit of wire? Everything we have here has been designed to measure gross chemical composition of asteroids, not fine details of a snippet of superconducting wire.

With nothing better that he could think of, Fuchs fired up the mass spectrometer again and took another sampling of the wire's composition. When the curves took shape on the display screen his eyes went wide with surprised disbelief.

George held one meaty hand over the earphone clamped to the side of his head, listening intently to Dan Randolph's tense, urgent voice. There was no video transmission; Dan had sent audio only.

"... you go with Blyleven to Stavenger himself and tell him what's happened. Stavenger can bypass a lot of red tape and get Selene's security people to turn the place upside down. You can't hide much in a closed community like Selene. A really thorough search will find Dr. Cardenas...or her body."

George nodded unconsciously as he listened. Once, ten years earlier, he had lived as a fugitive on the fringes of Selene, an outcast among other outcasts who called themselves the Lunar Underground. But they had survived principally on the sufferance of Selene's "straight" community. They could exist on the fringes because nobody cared about them, as long as they didn't make nuisances of themselves.

George agreed with Dan, up to a point. If Selene's security cops wanted to find a person, there wasn't much chance of hiding. But a dead body could be toted outside, concealed in a tractor, and dumped in the barren wilderness of the Moon's airless surface.

"Okay, Dan," he half-whispered into the pin-mike at his lips. "I'll get to Stavenger and we'll find Dr. Cardenas, unless she's already dead."

Frank Blyleven was head of Astro corporate security. A round, florid-faced, jovial-looking man with thinning straw-colored hair that he wore down to his collar, Blyleven seemed to have a grandfatherly smile etched permanently on his face. It unnerved George to see the security director smiling as he explained about Dr. Cardenas's disappearance.

"This is way out of our league," he said, without the slightest change in expression. "I mean, I only have half-a-dozen people in my group. We chase down industrial espionage and petty theft, for the lord's sweet sake, not kidnappings."

George knew how well Astro's security team chased down petty theft. The Lunar Underground lived on small "borrowings" from corporate storerooms.

"Dan said we should go to Stavenger," said George.

Nodding cheerfully, Blyleven turned to his desktop phone and asked for Douglas Stavenger.

When George and Blyleven were ushered into Stavenger's office, up in the Grand Plaza, a fourth man was sitting in front of Stavenger's broad, glistening desk. Stavenger introduced him as Ulrick Maas, director of security for Selene. Maas looked like a real cop to George: muscular build, dark, suspicious eyes, scalp shaved bald.

"You realize that this may be nothing to get alarmed about," Stavenger said once all four men were seated. "But Kris Cardenas isn't the kind of woman who suddenly goes into hiding, so I think we ought to try to find her."

"She's in Humphries's place, down at the bottom level," George said flatly.

Stavenger leaned back in his desk chair. Maas stared at George through narrowed eyes; Blyleven looked as if he were thinking about much more pleasant things. Through the office windows George could see the broad expanse of the Grand Plaza. A couple of kids were flying above the greenspace like a pair of birds, flapping their brightly-colored rented plastic wings.

Grimacing, Stavenger asked, "You're certain of that?"

"It's Humphries she was scared of," George replied. "Where else would he stash her?"

"That area down there is the property of the Humphries Trust," Maas pointed out. "Selene doesn't have legal authority to go in and search it."

"Not even if her life's on the line?" George asked.

Stavenger said to Maas, "Rick, I think you'll have to initiate a search."

"Of Humphries's place?" George asked.

"Of all of Selene proper," Stavenger said. "Humphries's place is a different matter." He turned to the phone and asked it to connect him with Martin Humphries.

* * *

"Dr. Cardenas?" Martin Humphries said to Stavenger's image on his patio wallscreen. "You mean the scientist?"

"Yes," said Stavenger, looking strained. "She's missing."

Humphries got up from the chaise longue on which he'd been reclining while he reviewed his father's holdings in Libya.

"I don't understand," he said to Stavenger's image, trying to look puzzled. "Why are you telling me about this?"

"The security office has initiated a search for her throughout Selene. I'd appreciate it if you allowed them to search your premises, as well."

"My home?"

"It's just a formality, Mr. Humphries," Stavenger said, with an obviously false smile. "You know security types: they want to dot every eye and cross every tee."

"Yes, I suppose they do," Humphries replied, smiling back. "I suppose someone could hide out in the gardens, couldn't they?"

"Or inside the house. It's rather large."

"H'mm, yes, I suppose it is—by Selene standards." He took a breath, then said reluctantly, "Very well, let them send a team down here. I have no objections."

"Thank you, sir."

"You're welcome," said Humphries. He snapped his fingers to shut down the connection. Then he went into the house, walking swiftly to his office.

He snapped his fingers as he entered the office. The phone screen lit up. "Get Blyleven down here on the double. I've got a job for him."

MARE NUBIUM

he tractor plodded slowly along the bleak, empty expanse of *Mare Nubium*, heading away from the ringwall mountains that marked Alphonsus and the site of Selene.

Kris Cardenas fought to keep the terror from overcoming her. She could feel it, trembling deep inside her, crawling up into her throat, making her heart race so hard she could hear its pulse thundering in her ears.

"Where are you taking me?" she asked, her voice muffled by the helmet of the spacesuit they had put her into.

No response from the driver. Of course, Cardenas thought. They've disabled my suit's radio. A neat, high-tech way of gagging me.

The two goons who had picked her up the night before had brought her down to Humphries's extravagant place in Selene's lowest level. Martin Humphries had not deigned to meet her, but she knew whose place it was. The servants had been very polite, offering her food and drink and showing her to a comfortable guest suite where she'd spent the night. The door to the corridor had been locked, of course. She was a prisoner and she knew it, no matter how sumptuous her cell.

Strangely, she slept well. But thinking over the situation the next morning, after a maid had brought a breakfast tray into her sitting room, Cardenas reasoned that Humphries was going to murder her. He'll have to, she thought. He can't let me go and let me tell everyone that he's killed Dan Randolph.

With my help, she added silently. I'm an accomplice to murder. A blind, stupid, stubborn fool who didn't see what she didn't want to see. Not until it was too late.

And now I'm going to be murdered, too. Why else would they be taking me all the way out into the godforsaken wilderness?

The thought of being killed frightened her, intellectually, in the front lobe of her brain. But being outside on the surface of the Moon, out in the deadly vacuum with all the radiation sleeting in from deep space, out here where humans were never meant to be—that terrified her deep in her guts. This tired little tractor had no pressurized cabin, no crew module; you had to be in a spacesuit to survive for a minute out here.

This is a dead world, she thought as she looked through her helmet visor. The gray ground was absolutely dead, except for the cleated trails of other tractors that had come this way. No wind or weather would disturb those prints; they would remain in place until the Moon crumbled. Behind them, a lazy rooster tail of dust floated in the soft lunar gravity.

And beyond that, nothing but the gently undulating plain of barren rock, pockmarked with craters, some the size of finger-pokes, some big enough to swallow the tractor. Rocks strewn everywhere, like the playroom toys of careless children.

The horizon was too close. It made Cardenas feel even

jumpier. It felt wrong, dangerous. In the airless vacuum there was no haze, no softening with distance. That abrupt horizon slashed across her field of view like the edge of a cliff.

She saw that the ringwall mountains of Alphonsus were almost below the horizon behind them.

"Where are we going?" she asked again, knowing it was useless.

Beside her, Frank Blyleven was no longer smiling. He sweated inside his spacesuit as he drove the tractor. When he'd made his deal with Martin Humphries, it had been for nothing more serious than allowing Humphries to tap into Astro Corporation's communications net. A good chunk of money for practically no risk. Now he was ferrying a kidnapped woman, a Nobel scientist, for the lord's sweet sake! Humphries was going to have to pay extra for this.

Blyleven had to admit, though, that Humphries had smarts. Stavenger wants to search for Dr. Cardenas? Okay. Who better to spirit her out of Selene for a while than the head of Astro's security department? Nobody asked any questions when he showed up at the garage already suited up, with another spacesuited person alongside him.

"Got to inspect the communications antennas out on Nubium," he told the guard checking out the tractors. "We'll be out about six hours."

Sure enough, three hours into his aimless wandering across the desolate *mare,* he got a radio signal from Humphries's people. "Okay, bring her back."

Smiling again, he leaned his helmet against Cardenas's so she could hear him through sound conduction.

"We're going back now," he said. "They'll have a team to meet you. You behave yourself when we get to the garage."

Kris Cardenas felt a huge surge of gratitude well up inside her. We're going back. We'll be safe once we're back inside.

Then she realized that she was still Humphries's prisoner, and she wasn't really safe at all.

* * *

Dan felt simmering anger as he watched George's report on the wallscreen of the ship's wardroom.

"I was in on th' search of Humphries's place. It's big enough to hide a dozen people. We din't find Dr. Cardenas or any trace of her," George ended morosely.

"She must still be alive, then," Dan said. Then he blew out an impatient huff of breath as he realized that George wouldn't hear his words for another twenty minutes or so.

Pancho was sitting beside him in the wardroom, looking more puzzled than worried as George's image faded from the wallscreen.

"If they haven't found her body," Dan said to her, "it means she's probably still alive."

"Or they've stashed the corpse outside," Pancho suggested.

Dan nodded glumly.

"Why would Humphries want to kill Dr. Cardenas?" Pancho asked.

"Because she found out something that she wanted to tell me; something that Humphries doesn't want me to know."

"What?"

"How should I know?" Dan snapped.

Pancho grinned lamely. "Yeah, I guess that was a pretty dumb question."

Dan rubbed his chin, muttering, "Humphries knew the security people were coming to search his place so he just moved her somewhere else until the search was over. I'll bet a ton of diamonds she's back inside his house now. He'll want to keep her close."

"Prob'ly," Pancho agreed.

"I wish there was a way we could get somebody into Humphries's place without him knowing it," Dan mused.

Pancho sat up straighter. "There is," she said, with a sly smile.

* * *

George counted it as a sign of Doug Stavenger's respect for Dr. Cardenas that he agreed to a private meeting.

"Invisible?" Stavenger looked shocked. "A cloak of invisibility?"

"I know it sounds nutty," George said, "but Dan told me that—"

"It's not nutty," Stavenger murmured, steepling his fingers before his face. "I'm stunned, though, that Ike Walton told anyone about it."

"You mean it's real? A cloak of invisibility?"

Stavenger eyed the big Aussie from behind his desk. "It's real, all right. But I doubt that it comes in your size. We're going to have to put the loose-lipped Mr. Walton back to work."

The worst part about this, Dan fumed silently, is being so far apart that we can't talk in real time.

He had paced the length of the crew module several times, from the bridge where Pancho and Amanda chatted amiably while monitoring the ship's highly automated systems to the sensor bay at the far end of the passageway, where Fuchs was bent over the sample of superconducting wire.

George's last message had an almost fairy-tale quality to it. "Stavenger's got the guy who made the cloak enlarging it to fit me. He's over in th' nanotech lab now, doin' it. He says I'll be able to sneak into Humphries's place sometime tomorrow morning, if he doesn't run into any snags."

Rumpelstiltskin, Dan thought as he prowled along the passageway. No, he was the guy who spun straw into gold. Who had the cloak of invisibility?

Pancho, he answered himself. Of all the sneaky con artists in the solar system, she's the one who comes up with a cloak of invisibility. Well, chance favors the prepared mind, they say. Pancho was smart enough and fast enough to use what chance offered her.

He found himself at the sensor bay again. There wasn't room for a chair. Fuchs was standing, staring at the same display screen he'd been staring at the last time Dan had looked in at him.

"Anything interesting?" Dan asked him.

Fuchs stirred as if being awakened from a dream. But from the worried expression on his face, Dan thought it might have been a nightmare.

"What is it, Lars?"

"I've found what created the hot spot in this section of wire," Fuchs said, his voice grave, solemn.

"Good!" said Dan.

"Not good," Fuchs countered, shaking his head.

"What is it?"

Pointing to the curves traced across the display screen, Fuchs said, "The amount of copper in the wire is diminishing."

"Huh?"

"The wire is superconducting only if its composition remains constant."

"And it stays cooled down to liquid nitrogen temperature," Dan added.

"Yes, of course. But this length of wire . . . its copper content is diminishing."

"Diminishing? What do you mean?"

"Look at the curves!" Fuchs said, with some heat. Rapping his knuckles on the display screen he said, "In the past two hours the copper content has gone down six percent."

Dan felt baffled. "How could—"

"As the copper content dwindles, the wire goes from a superconducting state to a normal state. It begins to heat up. The hot spot boils off some of the nitrogen coolant. The hot spot grows. It was only microscopic at first, but it eventually became large enough for the monitoring sensors to detect it."

Dan stared at him.

"There is only one agency that I can think of that could selectively remove copper atoms from the wire."

"Nanomachines?" Dan squeaked.

Fuchs nodded solemnly. "This length of wire was seeded with nanomachines that remove copper atoms and release them into the liquid nitrogen coolant. Even now they are removing copper atoms and letting them flow into the air of this compartment."

"Jesus H. Christ on a bicycle," Dan said, his insides suddenly hollow. "That's why Humphries grabbed Cardenas. She's the nanotech expert."

"We are infected," Fuchs said.

"But you caught it in time," Dan countered. "It's only this one length of wire that's infected."

"I hope so," Fuchs said. "Otherwise, we're all dead."

HUMPHRIES TRUST RESEARCH CENTER

George stood to one side of the walkway leading into Humphries's house. It had been eerie, riding down the escalators wearing the enlarged stealth suit that Ike Walton had cobbled together for him. George couldn't see his own feet. At one point, he nearly tripped and tumbled down a flight of escalator stairs.

Walton had looked like a naughty little kid caught peeking at dirty pictures when Stavenger had confronted him in his office and ordered him to enlarge the stealth suit to fit George.

Red-faced, Walton had stammered that he'd need help from the nanolab technicians, and that would ruin the secrecy that had shrouded the stealth suit since he'd first invented it.

"That can't be helped," Stavenger had replied tightly. "Secrecy's already been breached."

In the end, Stavenger himself went with Walton and George to the nanolab and asked the chief technician to clear out the lab and work with Walton by herself. In total secrecy.

Once she understood that Dr. Cardenas's life might be at stake, she quickly agreed.

"I'd heard rumors about a stealth suit, off and on," she marveled, once Walton explained what was needed.

"Don't add to them," Stavenger pleaded.

Walton had the programs for the nanomachines buried in his personal files. Within hours, he and the chief technician were watching a spread of darkly-glittering stealth cloth growing on a lab table. George stood slightly behind them, eyes goggling as the invisible virus-sized machines busily turned bins of metal shavings into his new suit.

Now he stood at the entrance to Humphries's house at high noon, trying to figure out a way to get through the front door without being detected. The huge cavern was in its daylight mode, long strips of full-spectrum lamps shining brightly. Wondering if the people inside the house came out for lunch, George edged closer to the door.

It swung open, surprising him, and a pair of Humphries's research scientists came out, deep in earnest conversation. George knew they were scientists from their costumes: the guy wore a shapeless open-necked shirt and faded jeans; he had a long ponytail down his back as well. The woman was in a light sweater and loose, comfortable slacks. They were talking about the life cycle of some Latin-named species.

George slipped behind them as the door started to close and held it halfway open with one extended arm. The two scientists went on their way, chattering intently. George pushed the door open a little more and peered inside. Two hefty men in blue security uniforms stood inside, looking bored. George slipped through the door and then let it swing shut. The two guards never noticed. They were talking about last night's football tournament, videoed live from Barcelona.

An older man in a dark suit came out of a doorway halfway down the hall. He had the frozen-faced expression of a trained butler. George tiptoed past the guards, peeking into each open doorway as he went. He could hear voices from his left, and found a doorway that opened onto a long corridor, with plenty of people shuttling from one office to another along its length. That must be where the research staff works, he thought. Don't they break for lunch?

It was difficult to pick up odors from inside the suit's face mask, but George caught the unmistakable scent of steaks on the griddle, something he hadn't smelled since he'd been on Earth. Steaks! he thought. Humphries doesn't mind spendin' his fookin' money on hauling steaks up here.

The hallway ended in a busy, stainless-steel kitchen big enough to keep a good-sized restaurant going. The staff eats in, George realized. At least they do for lunch. Cooks and assistants were scurrying back and forth, pots were boiling steam, and an industrial-sized grill was sizzling with thick steaks. George counted eleven of them. A banker's dozen, he said to himself.

One of the dark-uniformed maids was putting together a much more modest meal on a large teak tray: a crisp salad, a small sandwich, a slice of melon and a pot of tea. A woman's lunch, George thought.

He followed the maid as she carried the tray past him, down the hallway, and up the stairs to the second floor. One of the doors along the upstairs hall was guarded by a bored-looking young man in a gray business suit. He saw the maid approaching and opened the bedroom door.

"Lunch is here, Dr. Cardenas," he said.

George stopped as the maid went through the bedroom door and came out again less than a minute later, the tray empty at her side. She closed the door. George heard the lock click. The guard gave her a smile and she smiled back, but neither of them said anything as she headed back for the stairs.

George leaned against the wall a half-dozen meters from the lethargic guard, who sat on a wooden chair and pulled a palmcomp from inside his jacket. From the beeps and peeps, George figured the guy was playing a game to pass the time.

Okay, George said, folding his arms across his chest. Cardenas is in there. She's still alive. Now how do I get her out—alive?

He spent the better part of an hour prowling along the upstairs hall, checking out the stairway, studying the lone guard. Humphries apparently insisted on a dress code for his servants: the guards wore suits, the maid and the kitchen help wore uniforms. The scientists stayed on the other side of the house. They'd be no problem, George decided.

The maid returned with the empty tray, went into Cardenas's room, and came out with the lunch dishes. George thought Cardenas might be on a hunger strike; she had hardly eaten anything.

Shortly afterward, Humphries himself came up the hall. He was dressed casually: a white velour pullover and navy blue well-creased slacks. The guard snapped to his feet and stuffed his still-beeping palmcomp into his side pocket. Humphries frowned at him and motioned impatiently for him to open the door.

The door's kept locked, George realized, as Humphries stepped into the room. He waited until the door was almost shut, then tiptoed to it and pushed it slowly open. The guard paid no attention, engrossed once more in his video game. George let the door swing halfway open, then deftly slipped into the room.

Humphries noticed it. Frowning, he marched to the door and snapped at the guard. "Can't you close a goddamned door properly?" Then he slammed it shut.

Suppressing a chuckle, George edged into a corner of the room. Dr. Cardenas was standing tensely by the only window. It was a super room, George thought: big pieces of furniture made from real wood. Hauling it up to Selene must have cost more than the whole kitchen staff's salaries for ten years.

"How do you feel today?" Humphries asked Cardenas, crossing the oriental carpet toward her.

"I want to go home," she said flatly, as if it were a request that they both knew would be ignored.

Sure enough, Humphries acted as if he hadn't heard her. "I'm sorry that we had to take you outside. I understand that you don't like that."

"I want to go home," Cardenas repeated, stronger. "You can't keep me locked up here forever."

"I have a proposition to offer you. If you agree to it, you could go back to Earth and be with your grandchildren."

She closed her eyes wearily. "I simply want to go back to my quarters here at Selene. Let me go. Now."

Humphries sighed dramatically and sat on the upholstered chair near the window. "I'm afraid that's impossible, at this precise moment. Surely you can understand why."

"I won't say a word to anyone," Cardenas replied, walking uncertainly toward the sofa that faced his chair. "I simply want to return to my normal life."

"Without warning Randolph?"

"It's too late to warn Dan by now," she said. "You know that."

Humphries spread his hands. "Really, the best option for you is to return to Earth. You'll be in very comfortable quarters and I'll personally guarantee that your daughters and grandchildren will be brought to you."

"The way I was brought here?"

"You haven't been harmed, have you? You've been treated with great care."

"I'm still a prisoner."

It seemed to George that Humphries was working hard to control his temper. "But if you'll only do what I ask," he said, tightly, "you can return to Earth and be with your family. What more could you ask for?"

"I don't *want* to go to Earth!" Cardenas burst. "I won't be a part of your scheme!"

"You haven't even heard what my . . . scheme, as you put it, is."

"I don't care. I don't want to hear it."

"But it will stop the greenhouse warming. It will save the Earth."

"Nothing can save the Earth and you know it."

He hung his head for a moment, as if trying to find the right words. At last he looked up at her again. "You can save the Earth, Dr. Cardenas. That's the real reason why I brought you here. I need you to run the operation. I need the absolute best person there is. That person is you. No one else could make it work."

"Whatever it is, I won't do it," Cardenas said flatly.

"Not even to save the Earth?"

She gave him a withering look. "What makes you think I want to save the Earth?"

"Not even to save your grandchildren?" He said it with a smile.

Cardenas gasped when she realized what he meant. "You're threatening my family?"

He put on an innocent air. "Did I make a threat?"

"You're despicable!"

Humphries slowly got to his feet, like a man weary of dealing with an obstinate child. "Dr. Cardenas," he said slowly, "your options are few. Please hear me out."

"I won't say a word to anyone."

"I'm not talking about that now."

She started to reply, then thought better of it.

"At least listen to what I have to say."

She stared at him.

"Think of your grandchildren back there on Earth," Humphries coaxed. "Their future is in your hands."

Still without saying a word, Cardenas slowly sat on the sofa, facing Humphries.

"That's better," he said smiling. "We're both reasonable people. I'm sure we can work this out."

George walked softly toward them, listening intently.

STARPOWER 1

S itting in her command chair on the bridge, Pancho asked, "How do we know the bugs ain't chewin' away at us now?"

Dan had never before seen Pancho look morose. Her long, lantern-jawed face was deadly serious now; her usual cocky grin had vanished.

"They were eating copper," Dan replied. "We got rid of the wire sample. The bugs went out the hatch with it."

"You hope."

"Fervently," said Dan.

"Well, the ship's wiring doesn't use any copper," Pancho said hopefully.

"It's all fiber optic. I know."

"There's plenty of copper here and there, though," Pancho went on. "Maybe only trace amounts, but if we got nanobugs eatin' copper, they could knock out half the microprocessors on board."

"That's great," Dan groused.

"The MHD channel!" she blurted. "It's got a superconducting magnet wrapped around it!"

"Holy Christ!"

"If that goes, the magnet'll dump all its energy—"

"It'll explode?"

"Like a frickin' bomb," Pancho said.

"Great. Just perfect," Dan muttered. "And there's not a double-damned thing we can do about it, is there?"

She shook her head. "Just hope it hasn't been infected."

Dan felt shaky inside. He had to swallow before he could speak. "Not much we can do if it has been."

"Could be worse," Pancho said, with false jollity. "If we had bugs that ate carbon, they'd be chewin' on us."

Dan saw no humor in that. "Where's Amanda?" he asked, pointing to the empty co-pilot's chair. "Shouldn't she be on duty up here?"

"She's back with Lars."

"In the sensor bay?"

"Yup. He's tryin' to jury-rig the electron microscope to get nanometer resolution."

"So he can see nanobugs?"

"If there're any to be seen, right."

"Those two seem to spend a lot of time together," Dan grumbled.

"Come to think of it, that's true."

Dan said nothing. He didn't like the idea of Amanda and Fuchs playing around together, but he had no evidence that they were. Fuchs seemed like a pretty stiff straight arrow. But you never know, Dan said to himself. Amanda certainly seems to enjoy being with him.

Pancho jabbed a finger toward one of the touchscreen displays. "Well, at least the magnetic shield's holdin' up okay. We're safe from radiation storms . . . for th' time being."

For the time being, Dan echoed silently.

"And the MHD channel?"

She tapped at a screen. "Normal as pie."

"The bugs haven't infected it, then."

"Maybe not."

"I think I'll go back to the sensor bay," Dan muttered. "See how those two are getting along."

"Gonna be their chaperon?" Pancho teased.

"Am I that obvious?"

"You sure are, boss. A real worrywart."

"Do you think they need a chaperon?"

"Prob'ly not. Mandy can take care of herself. Lars isn't like Humphries."

Nodding his agreement with Pancho's assessment of the situation, Dan said, "So I'll see how he's doing with the electron microscope."

"Good excuse," Pancho said, laughing.

Wishing he could forget his fears of the nanobugs, Dan left the bridge, poured himself a mug of coffee in the wardroom, and then headed along the passageway to the sensor bay. He could see them through the open hatch to the cramped little compartment, standing amid the humming instruments and flickering display screens, deep in earnest conversation.

My god, they look like Beauty and the Beast, Dan thought. Even in rumpled tan coveralls, with her shining blonde hair pinned up in a sensible, no-nonsense fashion, Amanda looked gorgeous. Her big blue eyes were totally focused on Fuchs. In his usual dead-black pullover and slacks, his barrel-chested thickset body made him look like a feral animal out of some wildlife vid: a boar or a black bear. But he wasn't growling or snarling at Amanda. Far from it.

"How's it going?" Dan asked as he stepped through the open hatch.

They looked startled, as if they hadn't seen him approaching.

Pointing to the gray tube of the miniaturized electron microscope, Dan forced a grin and asked, "Find any nanobugs?"

Fuchs turned away from Dan, toward the microscope.

"No, it's hopeless. This machine will never resolve nanometer objects."

Dan wasn't surprised. "It wasn't designed to."

"I had thought perhaps I could boost its power," Fuchs went on, "but that was an idle hope."

"We've been reviewing the long-range sensor data," Amanda said, her cheeks slightly red. "Looking for a suitable asteroid, you know."

"And?"

Fuchs broke into a happy grin. It was so unusual that Dan was taken aback.

"We have an embarrassment of riches," he said, tapping at one of the touchscreens. "There are more than a dozen metal-rich bodies within a day's flight of us, or less."

Amanda said, "We've been trying to decide which one we should aim for."

Dan smiled at her. "That's easy. Go for the biggest one."

George held his breath as he edged closer to the corner of the big bedroom where Humphries and Dr. Cardenas sat. They both looked tense, although he seemed strung high with anticipation, while fear and anger glowered clearly on Cardenas's face.

George knew that they couldn't see him, yet he felt anxious, almost frightened to be this close to them, invisible or not. Don't sneeze, he warned himself. Don't fookin' breathe.

"All right," Cardenas said tightly. "I'm listening."

Leaning slightly toward the sofa on which Cardenas sat, Humphries clasped his hands together and began, "Suppose I set you up in your own laboratory in some remote location on Earth. My father has holdings in Libya, for example. We could bring your grandchildren there, to be with you."

"And what would I be expected to do at this remote laboratory?" Cardenas asked. Her voice was without inflection, like an automaton's, her face a frozen mask.

"Nanomachines could be made to take carbon dioxide out of the atmosphere, can't they? Break the molecules down into carbon and oxygen atoms. The carbon could be buried, the oxygen released back into the air or sold as an industrial gas, whatever. That could stop the greenhouse warming in a year or two!"

Cardenas's expression did not change. "Nanotechnology is banned, you know that. No matter how you want to use it, you can't make nanomachines anywhere on Earth. You'd have the GEC, the world government, every religious nut on Earth going crazy if you even hinted that you're thinking of using nanotechnology."

Humphries smiled patiently. "We won't tell them, for god's sake. We just start doing it. In secret. Out in the Sahara or the middle of the ocean or Antarctica, anywhere. In a year or maybe even less, they'll start noticing the carbon dioxide levels going down. We can take out the other greenhouse gases, as well. They'll see that the greenhouse warming is lessening. *Then* we'll have them all by the balls! They'll have to accept what we're doing. They'll have no choice."

"And what happens if these nanomachines don't work exactly right? What happens if they start taking other carbon compounds apart? Like *you*, for instance. You're made of carbon atoms, aren't you?"

"That won't happen."

"I know it won't happen," she said. "Because I won't do it. It's an absurd scheme."

"What's absurd about it?" Humphries demanded.

A slight, sardonic smile cracked Cardenas's facade. "You don't have any idea of how enormous Earth's atmosphere is. Do you know how many tons of carbon dioxide you'd have to remove? Billions! Tens of billions, at least! You'd have to cover Africa with nanomachines to remove that much carbon dioxide!"

"I'm sure that's an exaggeration," Humphries muttered, scowling.

Cardenas shot to her feet, startling George. "All right, you'd merely have to cover the Sahara desert. It's still beyond belief!"

"But—"

"And you'd never be able to keep it secret. Not a program of that scale."

"But it could be done, couldn't it?"

"It could be started," she admitted. "Until some fanatic drops a nuke on us. Or laces our drinking water with plague bacillus."

"I can protect you against terrorists," Humphries said.

Cardenas paced to the window, obviously thinking furiously. Turning back to Humphries, she said, "Using nanomachines on that scale is an invitation to disaster. Some fruitcake could steal a handful and reprogram them to take apart . . . plastics, for example. Or petroleum. Or use them as assassination weapons. You're talking about gobblers, for Christ's sake!"

"I know that," Humphries said coldly.

Cardenas shook her head. "It won't work. Aside from the sheer physical scale of the project, the authorities on Earth would never grant approval for using nanomachines. Never! And I can't say that I'd blame them."

Humphries slowly got to his feet. "You refuse to even try?"

"It's a hopeless task."

He sighed theatrically. "Well, I've tried to be reasonable. I thought we might be able to work something out."

"Let me go," Cardenas said, with a pleading note in her voice.

"I thought it would be a way for you to be with your grandchildren, as you want to be."

"Just let me go."

He gave her a sad look. "You know I can't do that. It's too great a risk for me."

"You can't keep me here forever!"

With a small shrug, Humphries asked, "What do you propose as a way out of this impasse?"

She stared at him, open-mouthed.

"I mean, you can see my problem. I know you can. How can I let you go when there's every chance that you'll tell people that I'm responsible for Dan Randolph's death?"

"But I'm responsible, too."

"Yes, I know. But you'd confess to it, wouldn't you?"

"I . . ." she hesitated, then said in a low, defeated voice, "I suppose I would, sooner or later."

"There you are," Humphries said softly. "The problem remains."

"You're going to have to kill me."

"I don't want to do that. I'm not a cold-blooded murderer. In fact, I'd like to see you reunited with your grandchildren, if it's at all possible. There must be some way we can work together, some way we can find around this problem."

"I don't see any," Cardenas whispered.

"Well, think it over," Humphries said, heading for the door. "I'm sure you can come up with a solution, if you just put your mind to it."

He smiled as he opened the door and left. George saw the guard standing out in the hallway before Humphries closed the door and its lock clicked shut.

As he strode down the hallway, Humphries mused to himself, It *could* work! If we could spread enough nanomachines I could break the greenhouse warming in a couple of years. They'd be on their knees with gratitude.

He decided to put a small team of experts together to study the possibilities dispassionately. Cardenas isn't the only nanotechnology guru in Selene, he assured himself.

BREAKOUT

Kris Cardenas stared at the locked door for several silent
moments after Humphries left, then she suddenly broke
into racking sobs. Face buried in her hands, body bent,
she stumbled to the bed and threw herself onto it, crying inconsolably.

George stood uncertainly in the far corner of the bedroom, wondering what he should do. She's already hysteri-
cal, he said to himself. If I go and tap her on the shoulder
and say, "Hi! I'm an invisible man!" she'll probably freak
out altogether.

So he waited, fidgeting unhappily, until Cardenas stopped
crying. It didn't take long. She sat up on the bed, took a deep
breath, then got to her feet and went to the lavatory. When
she came out again, it was obvious to George that she had
washed her face and put on some makeup. But her eyes were
still red, puffy.

Well, you can't stand here like a fookin' idiot forever,
George told himself. Do something!

Before he could decide what to do, Cardenas walked to the window and pressed her fingers against the glass. Then she turned and seemed to survey the room. With a slight nod, she walked to the bare little desk and picked up its wooden, cushioned chair. It seemed heavy for her, but she carried it, tottering slightly, to the window.

She wants to crash the window and jump out of here, George realized. She'll just end up hurting herself.

He touched her arm lightly and whispered, "Excuse me."

Cardenas flinched and let the chair thump to the carpeting. She blinked, stared, saw nothing.

"Excuse me, Dr. Cardenas," George whispered.

She spun around in a complete circle, eyes wide.

"Who said that?"

George cleared his throat and replied, a little louder, "It's me, George Ambrose. I'm—"

"Where the hell are you?"

George felt slightly embarrassed. "I'm invisible."

"I'm going crazy," Cardenas muttered. She sank down onto the chair, right there in the middle of the room.

"No you're not," George said, still keeping his voice low. "I'm here to get you out of this place."

"This is a trick."

"Is this room bugged? Do they have any cameras in here?"

"I . . . don't think so . . ."

"Look," George said, then immediately realized it was a foolish term to use. "I'm gonna take off me hood so you can see me face. Don't get scared now."

Cardenas looked more suspicious than frightened. George yanked the hood off his head and pulled off his face mask. It felt good to feel cool air on his skin.

She jumped out of the chair. "Christ almighty!"

"No, it's just me," he said, with a slight grin. "George Ambrose. I work for Dan Randolph, y'know."

Comprehension lit her eyes. "Walton's stealth suit! He didn't destroy it, after all."

"You know about it."

"Me, and four other people."

"There's a few more now," George said.

"How in the world did you ever—"

"No time for that now. We've got to get you out of here."

"How?"

George scratched at his beard. "Good question."

"You didn't bring along a suit for me, did you?" Cardenas said.

"Should have, shouldn't I? We just didn't think of it. We weren't certain where you were."

"So what do we do?"

George thought it over for a few moments. "They keep you in this room all the time?"

Cardenas nodded.

"Door's locked, isn't it?"

"Yes. And there's a guard outside...at least, every time they've brought a meal in to me there's been a guard out in the hall. I imagine he's armed."

George's face lit up. "When do they bring you meals? When's the next one coming?"

Several hours later there was a single rap on the door, and then Cardenas heard the lock click. She glanced swiftly about the room but could no longer see George.

The door opened and the same silent, sour-faced woman in dark uniform came in, carrying a dinner tray. Cardenas could see a wiry young man standing on the other side of the doorway. The woman deposited the tray wordlessly on the coffee table in front of the sofa and then departed, still silent and dour. The guard closed the door and locked it again.

Cardenas sat on the sofa. For the first time in days she had an appetite. She felt George's bulk settling on the cushions beside her.

"Smells good," George said.

She took the lid off a platter of fish fillets and vegetables.

"Looks good, too," George added.

"You're hungry," she said.

"Haven't eaten since breakfast."

"Help yourself."

George didn't wait to be coaxed. He lifted off his face mask again and dug in. Cardenas watched as fork and knife moved seemingly by themselves and chunks of dinner rose to his face, which seemed to be floating in midair. She found that if she looked hard enough, directly at him, she could see a faint flickering glitter, almost subliminal. Reflection of the ceiling lights scattered by the chips, she thought. But you have to know he's there to see it, and even then it's almost below the perception level.

"Don't you want any?" George asked.

"No, you go ahead."

"Eat the veggies, at least."

"I'll take the salad."

The meal was finished in a few minutes. George put his mask on again and completely disappeared.

"D'you tell 'em you're finished or do they send the maid back for the tray automatically?"

"I tell the guard. He sends for the maid."

"Okay. Tell the guard you're finished and ask him to take the tray."

"He'll send for the maid."

"Tell 'im you don't want to wait for her. Make some excuse."

Cardenas nodded, got up from the sofa, and went to the door. She could sense George's body warmth as he padded along beside her.

She banged on the door with the flat of her hand. "I'm finished. Could you please take the tray?"

"I'll call the kitchen," came the guard's muffled voice.

"I can't wait! I've got to get to the toilet right away! I'm sick to my stomach. Please take the tray."

A moment's hesitation, then they heard the lock click. The door swung open and the guard stepped in, looking concerned.

"What's the matter? Something in the—"

The punch sounded like a melon hitting the pavement from a considerable height. The guard's head snapped back and his eyes rolled up. He crumpled to the floor. Cardenas saw his arms yanked up into the air and his body dragged into the room.

"Come on, now," George whispered to her.

They stepped out into the hallway. The door shut, seemingly by itself, and locked. She felt his hand engulf half her upper arm as George led her down the hallway to the stairs. The house seemed quiet at this hour, although a glance out the windows showed that the cavern outside was still lit in daytime mode.

The downstairs hall was empty, but Cardenas could hear the sounds of conversation floating through from somewhere. Neither of the voices sounded like Humphries's to her. They got to the foyer just inside the front door. Two young men in gray suits looked surprised to see her approaching them.

Frowning, the taller of the two said, "Dr. Cardenas, what are—"

George's punch spun him completely around. The other guard stared, frozen with surprise, until he was lifted off his feet by a blow to the midsection. Cardenas heard a bone-snapping *crunch!* and the guard fell limply to the tiled floor.

The front door jerked open and George hissed, "Come on, then!"

Cardenas ran out of the house, up the path that wound through the garden, and through the hatch that opened into Selene's bottommost corridor. She could hear George panting and puffing alongside her. Once they were through the hatch, George's hand on her arm brought her to a stop.

"I don't think anybody's followin' us," he said.

"How long do you think it will take for them to realize I'm gone?" she asked.

She sensed him shrugging. "Not fookin' long."

"What now, then?"

"Lemme get outta this suit," George muttered. "Hot enough inside here to cook a fella."

His face appeared, then his entire shaggy head. Within a minute he stood before her, sweating and grinning, a big red-haired mountain of a man in rumpled, stained olive-green coveralls.

"That's better," George said, taking a deep breath. "Could hardly breathe inside that suit."

As they started walking swiftly along the corridor toward the escalator, Cardenas asked, "Where can I go? Where will I be safe? Humphries will turn Selene upside-down looking for me."

"We could go to Stavenger and ask him to take care of you."

She shook her head. "Don't put Doug in the middle of this. Besides, Humphries probably has his own people planted in Selene's staff."

"H'mm, yeah, maybe," George said as they reached the escalator. "Inside Astro, too, for that matter."

Suddenly frightened at the possibilities, Cardenas blurted, "Where can I go?"

George smiled. "I got the perfect hideout for ya. Long as you don't mind sharin' it with a corpsicle, that is."

BONANZA

t's a beauty," Dan breathed, staring at the image on the control panel's radar screen.

"Purty ugly-lookin' beauty," Pancho countered.

The radar image showed an elongated irregular lump of an asteroid, one end rounded and pitted, the other dented by what looked like the imprint of a giant mailed fist.

"It looks rather like a potato," said Amanda, "don't you think?"

"An iron potato," Dan said.

Fuchs came through the hatch, and suddenly the bridge felt crowded to Dan. Lars isn't tall, he said to himself, but he fills up a room.

"That is it?" Fuchs asked, his eyes riveted to the screen.

"That's it," Pancho said, over her shoulder. She tapped at the keyboard on her left and a set of alphanumerics sprang up on the small screen above it. "Fourteenth asteroid discovered this year."

Amanda said, "Then its official name will be 41–014 Fuchs."

"How's it feel to have your name on an asteroid, Lars?" Pancho asked.

"Very fine," Fuchs said.

"You're the first person to have his name attached to a newly-discovered asteroid in *years*," Amanda said. She seemed almost aglow, to Dan.

"Most of the new rocks have been found by the impact searchers," Pancho said. "Those li'l bitty probes don't get their names into the record."

"Asteroid 41–014 Fuchs," Amanda breathed.

He smiled and shrugged—squirmed, almost, as if embarrassed by her enthusiasm.

"The official name's one thing," Dan said. "I'm calling her Bonanza."

"Her?" Fuchs asked.

"Asteroids are feminine?" Pancho challenged.

Dan held his ground. "Hey, we speak of Mother Earth, don't we? And they call Venus our sister planet, don't they?"

"What about Mars?" Pancho retorted.

"Or Jupiter," said Amanda.

Pointing to the lump imaged on the radar screen, Dan insisted, "Bonanza's going to make us all rich. And very happy. She and her sisters are going to save the world. She's a female."

"Sure she's female," Pancho said laconically. "You want to dig into her, don't you?"

Fuchs sputtered and Amanda said, "Pancho, really!"

Dan put on an innocent air. "What a dirty mind you have, Pancho. I admire that in a woman."

Within three hours they were close enough to Bonanza to see it for themselves: a dark, deformed shape glinting sullenly in the wan light of the distant Sun. The asteroid blotted out the stars as it tumbled slowly end over end in the cold empty silence of space.

"...eighteen hundred and forty-four meters along its long axis," Amanda was reading out the radar measurements. "Seven hundred and sixty-two meters at its maximum width."

"Nearly two kilometers long," Dan mused. He hadn't left the bridge all during their approach to the metallic asteroid.

"Killing residual thrust," Pancho said, her attention focused on the control displays.

"Throttling down to zero," Amanda confirmed.

The asteroid slid out of view as the pilots established a parking orbit around it. Dan felt what little weight remaining dwindle away to nothing. He floated up off the deck, stopped himself with a hand against the overhead.

He felt Fuchs come through the hatch behind him.

"Lars, we're going to be in zero g for a while," Dan said.

"I know. I think I'm getting accustomed to it."

"Good. Just don't make any sudden head movements and you'll be fine."

"Yes. Thank—*mein gott!* There it is!"

The dark lopsided bulk of Bonanza rose in front of the bridge windows like some pitted, pockmarked monster, huge, overawing, menacing. Despite himself, Dan felt a wave of unease surge through him. It's like confronting an ogre, he thought, a giant beast from a fairy tale.

"Look at those striations!" Fuchs said, his voice vibrant with excitement. "This must have been broken off from a much larger body, perhaps a planetesimal from the early age of the solar system! We've got to get outside and take samples, drill cores!"

Dan broke into laughter. Fuchs turned toward him, looking confused. Even Pancho glanced over her shoulder.

"What so funny, boss?"

"Nothing," Dan said, trying to sober himself. "Nothing." Inwardly, though, he marveled that the same sight that brought back to him memories of childhood dread stirred Fuchs into a frenzy of scientific curiosity.

"Come on," Fuchs said, ducking past the hatch. "We've got to suit up and go outside."

Dan nodded his agreement and followed the scientist. *He's forgotten about zero-g,* Dan realized. *He's not worried about upchucking now, he's got too much work that he wants to do.*

Amanda remained on the bridge as Pancho followed Dan down to the airlock.

"You're not thinkin' of goin' EVA, are you?" she asked Dan.

"I've been a qualified astronaut since before you were born, Pancho."

"You've been redlined. You can't go outside."

"And rain makes applesauce."

"I mean it, Dan," Pancho said, quite seriously. "Your immune system can't take another radiation dose."

"Fuchs can't go out there by himself," he countered.

"That's my job. I'll go with him."

"Nope. You stay here. I'll babysit him."

"I'm the captain of this craft," Pancho said firmly. "I can order you to stay inside."

He gave her a crooked grin. "And I'm the owner. I can fire you."

"Not till we get back to Selene."

Dan huffed out an impatient sigh. "Come on, Pancho, stop the chickenshit."

"Your medical records say—"

"Dammitall to hell and back, I don't care what the medical records say! I'm going out! I want to *see* this sucker! Touch her with my own hands."

"No gloves?"

They had reached the airlock, where the spacesuits hung in racks like suits of armor on display. Fuchs was sitting on the bench that ran in front of the racks, already into the lower half of his suit, sealing the boots to the cuffs of his leggings. Dan reached for the suit that bore his name stenciled on its chest.

"I thought you were scared of the radiation," Pancho said.

"I'll be okay inside the suit," Dan said. "The weather's calm out there; no radiation storm."

Fuchs looked up at them, said nothing.

"The regulations say—"

"The regulations say you're not supposed to bring pets aboard," Dan said, grinning again as he pulled the lower half of his suit from its rack and sat down beside Fuchs. "But I've got to look into my shoes every morning to make sure your damned snake isn't curled up inside one of them."

"Snake?" Fuchs yelped, looking alarmed.

Pancho planted her fists on her hips and glared down at Dan for a long moment. Then she visibly relaxed.

"Okay, boss," she said at last. "I guess I can't blame you. But I'm gonna monitor your vitals back on the bridge. If I say come in, you come in. Right then. No arguments. Agreed?"

"Agreed," Dan replied instantly. A voice in his head was laughing mockingly. Are you satisfied? the voice asked. You've shown her that you're not a sick old man. Big deal. How are you going to feel when the cold clamps down on you and your bones start hurting again?

Doesn't matter, Dan answered himself. I'm not going to stay cooped up in here like a cripple. To hell with it; I don't really give a damn. If I've got to die, I'd rather wear out than rust out. What difference does it make?

"Clear for EVA." Amanda's voice came through the speaker in Dan's helmet.

He was in the airlock, sealed in his suit, feeling like a robot in a metal womb.

"Opening outer hatch," he said, pressing a gloved finger on the red light of the control panel.

"Copy, outer hatch."

The hatch slid open and Dan felt his pulse start to quicken. How long has it been since I've been outside? he asked himself. That sardonic voice in his head answered, Not since you got the radiation overdose, jiggering comm-sats in the Van Allen Belt.

Ten years, Dan realized. That's a long time to be away from all this.

He pushed himself through the hatch and floated in empti-ness. The universe hung all around him: stars solemn and unwinking, staring at him even through the heavy tinting of his fishbowl helmet. Turning slowly, he saw the Sun, strangely small and pale, with its arms of faint zodiacal light outstretched on either side of it.

Freedom. He knew he was confined inside the spacesuit and he couldn't survive for a minute without it. Yet hanging there weightlessly in the silent emptiness of infinity, Dan felt free of all the world, alone with the cosmos, in tune with the ethereal music of the spheres. Glorious freedom. Radiation be damned; he felt he could soar out into the universe for-ever and leave the petty lusts and hates of humankind far be-hind. It wouldn't be a bad way to die.

Then the asteroid slid into his view. Massive, ponderous, an enormous pitted dark looming reality hanging over him like an ominous cloud, a mountain floating free in space. *Starpower 1* looked pitifully small and helpless alongside the two-kilometer-long asteroid; like a minnow next to a whale. Dan suddenly understood how Jonah must have felt.

You can't scare me, he said to the asteroid. You're two kilometers of high-grade iron ore, pal. You're going to look beautiful to a lot of people on Earth. Money in the bank, that's what you are. Jobs and hope for millions of people. Bonanza: that's your name and that's just what you are.

"Ready for EVA." Fuchs's voice broke into Dan's silent monologue.

"Clear for EVA. Lars," he heard Amanda reply.

Dan squeezed the right handgrip on his maneuvering controls with the lightest of touches. The cold gas jet on the backpack squirted noiselessly and he turned enough to be looking back at the ship. *Starpower 1* glinted nicely in the starlight. She still looked brand-new, shining, not a pit or a scratch on her. The airlock hatch slid open and a spacesuited figure stood framed in it.

"Exiting the airlock," Fuchs said, his voice trembling slightly.

"Come on, Lars," Dan called. "Isn't she a beauty?"

Fuchs jetted toward him. Dan saw that his suit was bristling with hammers and drills and all sorts of equipment.

"It's enormous!" He sounded awestruck.

"She's just an average-sized chunk of metal," Dan said. "And as soon as you chip a piece off her, we can claim her."

Fuchs showed no hesitation at all, although he seemed a bit clumsy working the controls of his maneuvering thrusters. For a moment Dan thought he was going to ram into the asteroid, but at the last instant Fuchs fired a braking blast and hovered a scant few meters above its pitted, pebbly surface.

Dan jetted toward him, and with a bare touch of the handgrip controls lowered himself to the surface of the asteroid. He felt his boots make contact and then recoil slightly. Not much gravity, he thought, as he puffed down again and finally stood on the surface of Bonanza. Clouds of dust rose where his boots made contact with the surface; they just hung there, barely moving in the minuscule gravity.

It took Fuchs three tries to get firmly onto the surface; he kept coming down too hard and bouncing off. In the end, Dan had to reach out and yank him down.

"Don't try to walk," he told Fuchs. "The gravity's so light you'll float up and away."

"Then how—"

"Slide your boots along." Dan demonstrated a couple of steps, shuffling up even more dust. "Like you're dancing."

"I don't dance very well," Fuchs said.

"This isn't the smoothest dance floor in the solar system, either."

The asteroid's surface was rough and uneven, covered with a powdery coating of dust, much like the surface of the Moon. Dan thought it was more like standing on the deck of a boat, though, than on solid ground. There wasn't really a horizon; the rock just *ended.* Pinhole craters peppered the surface, pebbles and fist-sized rocks littered it, and out along its far end, Dan could see a more sizeable crater, a big depression with a raised rim all around it.

"How much iron do you think we've got here?" Dan asked.

"We'll have a good measure of its mass by the time we return to the ship," Fuchs said. "With the ship orbiting the asteroid we have a classic two-body system. It's simple Newtonian physics."

Dan thought to himself, He's a scientist, all right. Ask him a simple question and you get a dissertation. Without the answer to your question.

"Lars," he said patiently, "can't you give me some idea of this lump's mass?"

Fuchs spread his hands. In the spacesuit, he looked like a bubble-topped fireplug with arms.

"A back-of-the-envelope guesstimate?" Dan coaxed.

"Oh...considering its dimensions...nickel-iron asteroids are typically no more than ten percent nickel...it must be somewhere in the neighborhood of seven or eight billion tons of iron and eighty million tons or so of nickel."

Dan's eyes went wide. "That's five or six times the world's steel production in its best year! Before the floods and all!"

"There are impurities, of course," Fuchs warned. "Platinum, gold and silver, other heavy metals."

"Impurities, right," Dan agreed, cackling. His mind was spinning. One asteroid is enough to supply the world's steel industry for years and years! And there are thousands of these chunks out here! It's all true! Everything I hoped for, all those wild promises I made—they're all going to come true!

Fuchs seemed oblivious to it all. "I want to look at those striations," he said, turning toward the far end of the asteroid. His effort made him rise off the surface and Dan had to yank him down again.

"Take a sample here, first," Dan said. "Then we can claim it."

The light was so dim that Dan could see Fuchs's head outlined inside his bubble helmet. He nodded and slowly, very slowly, got down into a kneeling position. Then he pulled a rock hammer from his equipment belt and chipped off a bit of the asteroid. The effort raised more dust and lifted him off the surface again, but this time he clawed at the ground with one gloved hand and pulled himself back down.

"Anchor yourself, Lars," Dan said. "Hammer a piton in and tether it to your belt."

"Yes, of course," Fuchs answered, fumbling with the equipment clipped to his waist.

Dan said, "Record this, Amanda, and mark the time. Starpower Limited has begun taking samples of asteroid 41–014 Fuchs. Under the terms of the International Astronautical Authority protocol of 2021, Starpower Limited. claims exclusive use of the resources of this asteroid."

"I've got it," Amanda's voice replied. "Your statement is being beamed to IAA headquarters on Earth."

"Good," Dan said, satisfied. He recalled from his school days the story of the Spanish explorer Balboa first sighting the Pacific Ocean. From what he remembered of the tale, Balboa waded out into the surf and claimed the whole bloody ocean and all the lands bordering on it for Spain. They thought big in those days, Dan said to himself. No pissant IAA to worry about.

Fuchs got the knack of shuffling along the surface of the

asteroid, and started chipping out samples and making stereo videos. Dan worried about the dust they were kicking up. It could get into the joints of our suits, he thought. Damned stuff just hangs there; must take a year for it to settle back again.

He saw a bulge off to his right, like a small knoll or a rounded hill. That must be the tail end of this rock, Dan told himself. Looking back at Fuchs, he saw that the scientist had finally anchored himself to the ground and was busily chipping away, raising lingering clouds of dust.

"I'm going to go up to that ridge," he told Fuchs, pointing, "and see what's on the other side."

"Very well," said Fuchs, still bent over his sampling.

Dan shuffled carefully along, worrying about the dust. On the Moon, dust raised from the ground was electrostatically charged; it clung stubbornly to the suits and helmet visors. Probably the same thing here.

He started up the slight rise. Something didn't feel right. Suddenly his boots slid out from under him and he tumbled, in dreamlike slow motion, face forward. His fall was so gentle that he could put out his hands and stop himself, but he bounced off the dusty ground and found himself floating *up* the rise like a hot-air balloon gliding up the side of a mountain.

Dan's old astronaut training took over his reflexes. In his mind he saw clearly what was happening. The gravity on this double-damned rock is so low that I'm floating off it! He saw the bulbous end of the asteroid sliding slowly beneath him and, beyond it, the star-strewn infinity of space.

Twisting his body so that he pointed himself back toward the asteroid's bulk, Dan squirted his maneuvering jets and lurched back to the asteroid. Gently, tenderly, he touched down again on its surface. Fuchs was still tapping away with his sampling hammer, rising off the ground with every blow, his anchored tether pulling him back again for another crack.

Dan was breathing hard, but otherwise no worse the wear for his little excursion. With even greater care than before he shuffled back to stand beside Fuchs and help bag the samples he'd chipped out.

At last Pancho said sternly, "Time to come in, guys."

"Just one more sample," Fuchs replied.

"*Now,*" Pancho commanded.

"Aye-aye, cap'n," said Dan. He rapped his gloved knuckles on Fuchs's helmet. "Come on, Lars. You've done enough for one day. This rock isn't going to go away; you can come back another time."

Amanda was at the airlock to help them take off their backpacks and dust-spattered spacesuits. Dan caught a strange, pungent smell once he removed his helmet. Not like the sharp firecracker odor of the lunar dust; this was something new, different.

Before he had time to puzzle out the dust's odor, Pancho came down to the airlock area, looking so somber that Dan asked her what was the matter.

While Fuchs chattered happily with Amanda, Pancho said, "Bad news, boss. Another section of the superconductor is heating up. If it goes critical it could blow out the whole magnetic shield."

Dan felt his jaw drop open. Without the shield they'd be cooked by the next solar radiation storm.

"We've gotta get back to Selene pronto," Pancho said. "Before another flare breaks out."

"What're our chances?" Dan asked, his throat dry.

She waggled a hand. "Fifty-fifty . . . if we're lucky."

TEMPO 9

W e won't have to go outside, will we?" Cardenas asked nervously.

She was following George through the maze of pumps and generators up on the topmost level of Selene. Color-coded pipes and electrical conduits lined the ceiling; Cardenas wondered how anyone could keep track of which was which. The air hummed with the subdued sounds of electrical equipment and hydraulic machinery. On the other side of the ceiling, she knew, was the grassy expanse of the Grand Plaza—or the bare dusty regolith of the Moon's airless surface.

"Outside?" George echoed. "Naw, there's a shaft connectin' the tempo to the tunnel...if I can find th' fookin' tunn—ah, there it is!"

He pulled a small hatch open and stepped over its coaming, then reached a hand back to help Cardenas. The tunnel was dark, lit only by the hand-torch George carried. Cardenas expected to see the evil red eyes of rats in the darkness, or hear the slithering of roaches. Nothing. Selene is clean of vermin, she thought. Even the farmlands have to be pollinated artificially because there aren't any insects here.

Not yet, she thought. Sooner or later, though. Once we start allowing larger numbers of people up here, they'll bring their filth and their pests with them.

"Here we are," George said.

In the circle of light cast by his torch, she saw the metal rungs of a ladder leading up along the wall of the tunnel.

"How much farther does the tunnel go?" she asked in a whisper, even though she knew there was no one else there.

"Another klick or so," George answered. "Yamagata people wanted to drill all the way through the ringwall and out to *Mare Nubium.* Got too expensive. The cable car over the top was cheaper."

He scampered up the ladder, light and lithe despite his size. Cardenas started to follow him.

"Wait a bit," George called down to her. "Got to get this hatch unstuck."

She heard metal groan. Then George said, "Okay, up with you, now."

The ladder ended in an enclosed area about the size of her apartment unit down inside Selene. It was a cylindrical shape, like a spacecraft module.

"We're on the surface?" Cardenas asked, trying to keep her voice from shaking.

"Buried under a meter of dirt from the regolith," George said happily. "Safe as in church."

"But we're outside."

"On the slope of the ringwall. Just below the cable-line. The original idea was, if there's an emergency with the cable-trolley, people could stay in here till help arrives."

She looked around the shelter warily. A pair of double-decker bunks stood at the far end, the hatch of an airlock at the other. Inbetween was a small galley with a freezer, microwave oven, and sink; some other equipment she didn't recognize; two padded chairs; a desk with a computer atop it and a smaller chair in front of it . . .

And a big metal cylinder sitting in the middle of the floor, crowding the already-cramped quarters. One end of the cylinder was attached to a large pair of tanks and a miniaturized cryostat.

"Is that a dewar?" Cardenas asked.

George nodded. "Had to hide the woman inside it from Humphries."

"She's dead?"

"Preserved cryonically," George said. "There's hopes of reviving her."

"She won't be much company."

"'Fraid not. But I'll pop back here every few days, see that you're okay."

Stepping toward the desk, trying to hide her anxiety, Cardenas asked, "How long will I have to stay here?"

"Dunno. I'll have a chat with Dan, see what we should do."

"Call Doug Stavenger," she said. "He'll protect me."

"I thought you didn't want to put him in the middle of this scrape."

She wrapped her arms around herself, trembling with cold fear. "That's before I knew you were going to put me out here."

"Hey, this isn't so bad," George said, trying to sound reassuring. "I useta live in tempos like this for months at a time."

"You did?"

"Yup. Me and my mates. This is like home-sweet-home to me."

She looked around the place again. It seemed smaller than her first view of it. Closing in on her. Nothing between her and the deadly vacuum outside except the thin metal of the shelter's cylinder and a heaping of dirt over it. And a corpse in the middle of the floor, taking up most of the room.

"Call Stavenger," she pleaded. "I don't want to stay here any longer than I have to."

"Sure," said George. "Lemme talk to Dan first."

"Make it quick."

"The magnetic shield is going to blow up?" Dan asked, for the thirtieth time.

Pancho sat across the table from him in *Starpower 1*'s wardroom. Amanda was on the bridge as the ship raced at top acceleration back toward Selene. Fuchs was in the sensor bay, assaying the samples he'd chipped from Bonanza.

"You know how superconductors work," Pancho said, grimly. "They have to stay cooled down below their critical temperature. If they go above that temperature all the energy in the coil gets dumped into the hot spot."

"It'll explode," Dan muttered.

"Like a bomb. Lots of energy in the superconductor, boss. It's a dangerous situation."

"There's more than one hot spot?"

"Four of 'em so far. Wouldn't be surprised if more of 'em crop up. Whoever bugged this ship didn't want us to get back home."

Dan drummed his fingers on the table top. "I can't believe Kris Cardenas would do this to me."

"It's Humphries, pure and simple," said Pancho. "He could kill you with a smile, any day."

"But he'd need Kris to do this."

"Look," Pancho said, hunching forward in her chair. "Doesn't matter who spit in whose eye. We got troubles and we've gotta figger out how to save our necks before that magnetic coil goes up like a bomb."

Dan had never seen her look so earnest. "Okay, right. What do you recommend?"

"We shut down the magnetic field."

"Shut it down? But then we'd have no radiation shield."

"Don't need it unless there's a flare, and we can prob'ly get back to Selene before the Sun burps another one out."

"Probably," Dan growled.

"That's the chance we take. I like those odds better'n letting the coil's hot spots build up to an explosion that'd rupture the ship's skin."

"Yeah, you're right," Dan said, reluctantly.

"Okay, then." Pancho got up from the table. "I'm gonna shut it down now."

"Wait a minute," said Dan, reaching for her wrist. "What about the MHD channel?"

Pancho shrugged. "No problems so far. Prob'ly hasn't been bugged."

"If it goes, we're dead, right?"

"Well . . ." She drew the word out. "We *could* dump the coil's energy in a controlled shutdown. That wouldn't affect the thrusters."

"But we'd lose our electrical power."

"We could run on the fuel cells and batteries—for a while."

"Long enough?"

Pancho laughed and headed for the hatch. "Long as they last, boss," she said over her shoulder.

"Murphy's Law," Dan growled after her.

If anything can go wrong, it will: that was Murphy's Law. Now I can add Randolph's corollary to it, he thought: If you turn off your radiation shield, you're certain to be hit by a solar flare.

George shooed everyone out of the mission control center, except for the chief who insisted hotly that the center must have at least one human controller on duty at all times.

If he'd been a man, George would have simply picked him up and heaved him through the door out into the corridor. Instead, the chief on this shift was a rail-thin, pasty-faced, lank-haired woman with the personality of an Arkansas mule. She would not leave the center.

Restraining the urge to lift her off her feet and carry her out to the corridor, George pleaded, "I've got to send a private message to Dan Randolph. I can't have anybody listenin' in on it."

"And why not?" she demanded, hands on hips, narrow nostrils flaring angrily.

"None of your fookin' business," George snarled. "That's why not."

For long moments they glared at each other, George towering over her, but the woman totally unfazed by him.

"It's Dan's own orders," George said at last, stretching the truth a little. "This is ultra-sensitive stuff."

The woman seemed to think that over for a second, then said more reasonably, "You take the console over there, on the end. I'll set you up with a private channel. Nobody else in here but you and me, and I won't eavesdrop. Okay?"

George started to say no, but realized that this was the best he could accomplish, short of physical mayhem.

Before he could agree, though, Frank Blyleven pushed through the double doors, his normally smiling face wrinkled into a puzzled frown.

"What's going on here?" the security chief demanded, walking up the aisle between the consoles. "I got a report that you're throwing controllers out of the center."

Heaving an impatient sigh, George explained all over again that he had to get a message through to Dan. "In private," he said. "Nobody listenin' in."

Blyleven crossed his arms over his chest and tried to look authoritative. It didn't work. To George he looked like a red-faced shopping mall Santa in mufti.

"Very well," he said. "Send your message. I'll sit by the corridor door and make certain nobody disturbs you."

Surprised, George thanked him and headed for the console that the chief controller had indicated. Blyleven went to the last row of consoles and sat down at the one closest to the door. Surreptitiously, he tapped the keyboard a few times. When George finished his message and erased it from the comm system's memory core, Blyleven had a copy that he could pawn to Humphries.

Dan felt nervous as he watched Pancho and Amanda shut down the radiation shield. Dumping all that electromagnetic energy didn't bother him; it was the idea that now they had no protection against another solar storm except the thin hull of the ship itself.

"...shutdown complete," Pancho announced. "Magnetic field zeroed out."

"Zero field," Amanda confirmed.

"Naked to mine enemies," Dan murmured.

"How's that, boss?" Pancho asked, looking up over her shoulder toward him.

"I feel naked," Dan said.

"Don't worry. Sun looks calm enough for the time being. Even if it shoots out a flare, we can always get into our suits and go for a swim in one of the fuel tanks."

"That wouldn't be very helpful," Amanda pointed out, not realizing that Pancho was joking. "The high-energy protons would set off all sorts of secondary particles from the fuel's atoms."

Pancho frowned at her. Amanda looked from her to Dan and then back to her control panel.

"I think I'll go back and see how Lars is doing," she said, getting up from her chair.

"Have fun," Pancho said.

Dan watched her step through the hatch, then slid into her vacated chair.

"Don't look so glum, boss. We're battin' along at one-third *g* with no sweat. Be back in lunar orbit in less'n four days."

"I had wanted to stop to sample those other two rocks," Dan said.

"Can't take the chance. Better to—hold on. Incoming message from Selene. George Ambrose."

"I'll take it here," said Dan. "By the way, have you told mission control that we've shut down the shield?"

"Not yet, but they'll see it on the telemetering. It's recorded automatically."

Dan nodded as George's bushy red-maned face appeared on the screen. Quickly, in a worried whisper, George explained how he'd located Cardenas and spirited her off to the temporary shelter.

"She wants t'see Stavenger," George concluded. "I told her I'd talk to you first. She'll be perfectly okay in the tempo for a coupla weeks, if we need to keep her stashed there. So ... what d'you want me to do, Dan?"

George's image on the screen froze. Dan could see that he must have been at the mission control center when he'd sent the message. Good. He must've cleared out the place to make sure nobody could eavesdrop.

Now I've got to send him a reply that just about anybody can listen to, Dan thought. This is going to be like an old-time mafioso speaking into a tapped telephone.

"George, I think she's right. Do as she asks ... as carefully as you can. She's important to us; there's a lot she and I have to talk about when I get back. We've got some problems here on the ship and we're heading back home. If all goes well, we should be back in lunar orbit in less than four days. I'll keep you informed, and you let me know how things are going there."

Dan reviewed his own message, decided there was nothing he needed to add to it, then touched the SEND button on the comm panel.

He started to get up from the co-pilot's seat when the comm unit pinged.

"'Nother message comin' in," Pancho said needlessly.

A young man's face appeared on the screen. He looked annoyed. "General notice to all spacecraft and surface vehicles. A class-four solar flare has been observed by the early-warning sensors in Mercury orbit. Preliminary calculations of the interplanetary field indicate the resulting radiation storm has a ninety percent chance of reaching the Earth–Moon system within the next twelve hours. All spacecraft in cislunar space are advised to return to the nearest safe docking facility. All activities on the lunar surface will be suspended in six hours. Anyone on the surface is advised to seek shelter within six hours."

Dan sagged back into the chair.

Pancho tried to smile. "You called it, boss: Murphy's Law."

STORM SHELTER

F our worried people clustered around the table in *Star-power 1*'s wardroom. The wallscreen showed a chart of the solar system, with the radiation cloud that the solar flare had belched out appearing as a shapeless gray blob twisted by the interplanetary magnetic field. It was approaching Earth and the Moon rapidly. Deep in the Asteroid Belt a single pulsating yellow dot showed where their ship was.

Dan said to the computer, "Show the projections for the next two days."

The cloud grew and thinned, but surged out past the orbit of Mars and then engulfed the inner Belt and overran the blinking dot that marked *Starpower 1*'s position.

Pancho made a sound halfway between a sigh and a snort. "No way around it. We're gonna get hosed."

Amanda looked up from her palmcomp. "If we could pump all our remaining fuel into one tank, it could serve as a shelter . . . of sorts."

"I thought the secondaries would get us," Dan muttered.

"They'd be high," Amanda admitted, "but if we could pressurize the fuel it might absorb most of the secondary particles before they reached us."

"If we're plumb in the middle of the tank," Pancho said.

"Yes. Inside our suits, of course."

"Can the suits handle the temperature? We're talking about liquid hydrogen and helium; damned close to absolute zero."

"The suits are insulated well enough," Pancho said. Then she added, "But nobody's ever tried a dunk in liquid hydrogen with 'em."

"And we'd have to be dunked for god knows how many hours," Dan muttered.

Fuchs had not said a word. His head was bent over his own palmcomp.

"How much protection would the fuel give us?" Dan asked glumly.

Amanda hesitated, looked down at her handheld screen, then said, "We'd all need hospitalization. We'd have to set the flight controls to put us into lunar orbit on automatic."

"We'd all be that sick?" Pancho asked.

Amanda nodded solemnly.

And I'd be dead, Dan thought. I can't take another radiation dose like that. It would kill me.

Aloud, he tried to sound reasonably hopeful. "Well, it's better than sitting here with our thumbs jammed. Pancho, start transferring the fuel."

"How high can we pressurize one of the tanks?" Amanda wondered.

"I'll check the specs," said Pancho. "Come on, we've got to—"

"Wait," Fuchs said, looking up at them. "There is a better way."

Dan looked hard at him. Fuchs's eyes were set so deep that it was difficult to see any expression in them. Certainly he was not smiling. His thin slash of a mouth looked tight, hard.

"Computer," Fuchs called, "display position of asteroid 32–114."

A yellow dot began blinking near the inner edge of the Belt.

"That's where we must go," Fuchs said flatly.

"It's half a day off our course home," Pancho objected.

"Why there, Lars?" Amanda asked.

"We can use it for a storm shelter."

Dan shook his head. "Once the cloud runs over us, the radiation is isotropic. It comes from all directions. You can't hide behind a rock from it."

"Not behind the rock," Fuchs said, with growing excitement. "Inside it!"

"Inside the asteroid?"

"Yes! We burrow into it. The body of the asteroid will shield us from the radiation!"

"That would be great," Dan said, "if we had some deep drilling equipment aboard and a few days to dig. We don't have either."

"We don't need them!"

"The hell we don't," Dan shot back. "You think we're going to tunnel into that rock with your little core sampler?"

"No, no, no," Fuchs said. "You don't understand. That rock is a chondritic asteroid!"

"So what?" Pancho snapped.

"It's porous! It isn't a rock, not like Bonanza. It's an aggregate of chondrites—little stones, held together by gravity."

"How do you know that?" Dan demanded. "We haven't gotten close enough to—"

"Look at the data!" Fuchs urged, waving a thick-fingered hand at the wallscreen.

"What data?" The screen still showed the chart with the radiation cloud.

Fuchs pointed his palmcomp at the screen like a pistol and the wall display suddenly showed a long table of alphanumerics.

"Look at the data for its density," Fuchs said urgently. He jumped up from his chair and bounded to the screen. "Look! Its density isn't much more than that of water! It *can't* be a solid object! Not with such a density. It's porous! An aggregation of stones! Like a..." he searched for a word, "...like a pile of rubble...a beanbag chair!"

Dan stared at the numbers, then looked back at Fuchs. The man was clearly excited now.

"You're sure of this?" he asked.

"The numbers don't lie," Fuchs said. "They can't."

Pancho gave out a soft whistle. "Shore wish we had somethin' more'n numbers to go on."

"But we do!" Fuchs said. "Mathilde in the Main Belt, and Eugenia—several C–class bodies among the Near-Earth Asteroids—they are all aggregates, not solid at all. Microprobes have examined them, even gone inside them!"

"Porous," Dan muttered.

"Yes!"

"We can dig into them without drilling equipment?"

"They are probably highly-tunneled by nature."

Dan stroked his chin, trying to think, trying to decide. If he's right, it'd be better than dunking ourselves in a pool of liquid hydrogen for hours on end. If Fuchs is right. If we can burrow into the asteroid and use it for a storm shelter. If he's wrong, we're all dead.

Pancho spoke up. "I say we go for the asteroid, boss."

Dan looked into her steady light brown eyes. Is she saying this because she knows I won't make it otherwise? Is she willing to take the chance with her own life because it's the only chance we've got to save mine?

"I agree," Amanda said. "The asteroid is the better choice."

He turned back to Fuchs. "Lars, are you absolutely certain of all this?"

"Absolutely," Fuchs replied, without an instant's hesitation.

"Okay," Dan said, feeling uneasy about it. "Change course for—which one is it?"

"Asteroid 32–114," Fuchs and Amanda answered in unison.

"Point and shoot," Dan said.

Dan tried to sleep while *Starpower 1* raced to the chondritic asteroid, but his dreams were troubled with faces and visions from the past and a vague, looming sense of dread. He awoke feeling more tired than when he'd crawled into his bunk.

He felt stiff and sore, as if every muscle in his body were strained. Tension, he told himself. But that sardonic voice in his mind retorted, Age. You're getting to be an old man.

He nodded to his image in the lav mirror. If I live through this I'm going to start rejuve therapy.

Then he realized what he'd said: *if* I live through this.

He put on a fresh set of coveralls and grabbed a mug of coffee on his way to the bridge. Amanda was in the command chair, with Fuchs sitting at her right.

"Pancho's sleeping," Amanda said before Dan could ask. "We'll be making rendezvous with 114 in..." she glanced at one of the screens, "...seventy-three minutes. I'll wake her in half an hour."

"Can we see the rock yet?" Dan asked, peering into the black emptiness beyond the windows.

"Telescopic view," said Amanda, touching a viewscreen.

A lumpy, roundish shape appeared on the screen. To Dan it looked like a partially-deflated beach ball, dark gray, almost black.

"We're getting excellent data on it," Fuchs said. "Mass and density are confirmed."

"It's porous, as you thought?"

"Yes, it has to be."

"It's certainly no beauty," Amanda said.

"I don't know about that," replied Dan. "It looks pretty good to me. In fact, I think I'll call it Haven."

"Haven," she echoed.

Dan nodded. "Our haven from the storm." Silently he added, If those numbers for its density mean what Fuchs says they do.

The worst part of being alone in the temporary shelter was the waiting. There was nothing to do in the tempo except pace its length—an even dozen strides for Kris Cardenas—or watch the commercial video broadcasts that the shelter's antenna pulled in from the relay satellites.

Maddening. And there was the high-tech sarcophagus in the middle of the floor with the frozen woman inside its gleaming stainless steel cylinder. Not much company.

When the hatch in the floor suddenly squeaked open, Cardenas jumped with surprise so hard she nearly banged her head on the shelter's curving roof. For an instant she didn't care who was coming through the hatch; even an assassin would be a welcome relief from the boredom of the past night and day.

But she puffed out a big sigh of relief when she saw George Ambrose's brick-red mane rising through the open hatch. George climbed through and grinned at her.

"Dan says I should take you to Stavenger."

Cardenas nodded. "Yes. Fine."

Doug Stavenger was not happy to see her. He sat behind his desk and eyed her with raw disappointment showing in his expression. Cardenas sat in the cushioned chair before the desk like an accused criminal being interrogated. George stood by the office door, beefy arms folded across his chest.

"You seeded Randolph's ship with gobblers?" he said, his voice hollow with shocked disbelief.

"Specifically tailored to take apart copper compounds," Cardenas admitted, feeling shaky inside. "Nothing more."

"Isn't that enough?"

"It was meant to cripple the ship's radiation shield," she said defensively. "Once they found out about it they'd abort their mission and return here."

"But they didn't find out about it until they were deep in the Belt," Stavenger said.

George added, "And now they're sailing into a fookin' radiation storm without a shield."

"This could become a murder," Stavenger said. "Four murders."

Cardenas bit her lip and nodded.

"And Humphries was behind this scheme," Stavenger said. It was a statement, not a question.

"He wanted Randolph's mission to fail."

"Why?"

"Ask him."

"He's a major investor in the project. Why would he want it to fail?"

"Ask him," she repeated.

"I intend to," said Stavenger. "He's already on his way here."

As if on cue, Stavenger's phone chimed. "Mr. Humphries here to see you," said the phone's synthesized voice.

"Send him in," Stavenger said, touching the stud on the rim of his desk that opened the door.

George stood aside, clearly glowering through his beard as Humphries walked in. Humphries looked at Cardenas, half turned in her chair, then at Stavenger. With a slight shrug he took the other chair in front of the desk.

"What's this all about?" he asked casually as he sat down. "What's going on?"

"It's about attempted murder," Stavenger said.

"Murder?"

"Four people are caught in a solar storm out in the Belt without a working radiation shield."

"Dan Randolph, you mean." Humphries almost smiled. "That's just like him, barging ahead like a bull in a china shop."

Stavenger bristled. "You didn't get Dr. Cardenas here to seed Randolph's ship with gobblers?"

"Gobblers?"

"Nanomachines. Disassemblers."

Humphries glanced at Cardenas, then said to Stavenger, "I asked Dr. Cardenas if there was any way that Randolph's ship could be... er, disabled slightly. Just enough to get him to turn back and abort his flight to the Belt."

Cardenas started to reply, but Stavenger said heatedly, "If they die—if any one of them dies—I'll have you arraigned for premeditated murder."

Humphries actually smiled at Stavenger. "That's so far-fetched it's ludicrous."

"Is it?"

"I had Randolph's ship sabotaged so he would abort his flight and come back to Selene. I admit to that. Any sane man would have turned around and headed for home as soon as he found the sabotage. But not Randolph! He pushed on anyway, knowing that his radiation shield was damaged. That's his decision, not mine. If there's a crime in this, it's Randolph committing suicide and taking his crew with him."

Stavenger barely held on to his composure. His fists clenched, he asked through gritted teeth, "And just why did you want to sabotage his ship?"

"So the stock in Astro Corporation would drop, why else? It was a business decision."

"Business."

"Yes, business. I want Astro; the lower its stock, the easier for me to buy it up. Dr. Cardenas here wanted her grandchildren. I offered to get her together with them in exchange for a pinch of nanomachines."

"Gobblers," Stavenger said.

"They weren't programmed to harm anyone," Cardenas protested. "They were specifically set to attack the copper compound of the superconductor, nothing more."

"My father was killed by gobblers," Stavenger said, his voice as cold and sharp as an icepick. "Murdered."

"That's ancient history," Humphries scoffed. "Please don't bring your family baggage into this."

Visibly restraining himself, Stavenger stared at Humphries for a long, silent moment. Electricity crackled through the office. George decided that if Stavenger came around the desk and started beating up on Humphries, he would keep the door closed and prevent anyone from coming to the bastard's aid.

At last Stavenger seemed to win his inner struggle. He took a shuddering breath, then said in a low, seething voice, "I'm turning this matter over to Selene's legal department. Neither of you will be allowed to leave Selene until their investigation is finished."

"You're going to put us on trial?" Cardenas asked.

"If it were up to me," Stavenger said, "I'd put the two of you into leaky spacesuits and drive you out into the middle of *Mare Nubium* and leave you there."

Humphries laughed. "I'm glad you're not a judge. And, by the way, Selene has no capital punishment, does it?"

"Not yet," Stavenger growled. "But if we get a few more people like you here, we'll probably change our laws on that point."

Humphries got to his feet. "You can threaten all you like, but I don't think your courts will take this as personally as you are."

With that, he strode to the door. George stepped aside and let him open it for himself. He noticed that there was a thin sheen of perspiration on Humphries's upper lip as he left the office.

The instant the door closed again, Cardenas broke into sobs. Half doubled over in her chair, she buried her face in her hands.

Stavenger's icy composure melted. "Kris...how could you do it? How could you let him..." He stopped and shook his head.

Without looking up at him, Cardenas said in a tear-choked voice, "I was angry, Doug. Angrier than you can know. Angrier than I myself knew."

"Angry? At Randolph?"

"No. At *them*. The crazies who let this greenhouse cliff ruin the world. The fanatics who've exiled us, who won't let me come to Earth to see my children, my grandchildren. And they won't come here, not even for a visit. I wanted to punish them, get even with them."

"By killing Randolph?"

"Dan's trying to help them," she said, looking up at him at last, her face streaked with tears. "I don't *want* them helped! They made this mess. They shut me out of their lives. Let them stew in their own juices! They deserve whatever they get."

Stavenger shook his head, bewildered. He handed Cardenas a tissue and she dabbed at her reddened eyes.

"I'm going to recommend that you be placed under house arrest, Kris. You'll be able to go anywhere in Selene except the nanotech lab."

She nodded wordlessly.

"And Humphries?" George asked, still standing by the door.

"Same thing, I suppose. But he's right, the smug slime-bag. We don't have capital punishment; we don't even have a jail here in Selene."

"House arrest for him would be a lark," George said.

Stavenger looked disgusted. But then his chin came up and his eyes brightened. "Unless we take it out on his wallet."

"Huh?"

With a slow smile spreading across his youthful face, Stavenger said, "If he's found guilty of murder, or even attempted murder, maybe the court can divest him of his share of Starpower and keep him from taking over Astro Corporation."

George huffed. "I'd rather punch his ribs in."

"So would I," Stavenger admitted. "But I think he'd *rather* have his ribs punched in than to have to give up Astro and Starpower."

HAVEN

here it is," Pancho sang out. "How's that for navigation?"

Dan crouched slightly behind the command chair and peered through the window. The asteroid was visible to their naked eyes now against the distant glow of the Sun's zodiacal light, a dumbbell-shaped dark mass tumbling slowly end over end.

Fuchs stood beside Dan, his hands on the back of Amanda's chair.

"It's two bodies in contact," he said. "Like Castallia and several others."

"Looks like a peanut," said Dan.

"A peanut made of rock," Pancho said.

"No, no," Fuchs corrected, "a peanut made up of thousands of little stones, chondrules, that are barely holding together in their very weak mutual gravitational attraction."

"Uh-huh."

"Look, you can see craters on the surface."

Dan strained his eyes. How in hell can he see craters on that black slug in this dim lighting?

"They have no rims," Fuchs went on, talking fast in his excitement. "Smaller objects have collided with the asteroid but they don't make impact craters as they would on a solid body. They simply burrow into the loose rubble."

"Same as we're gonna do," Pancho said.

"Our storm cellar," Amanda added, glancing up at Fuchs.

It's our storm cellar only if he's right, Dan added silently. If that chunk out there really is a beanbag and we can dig into it until the storm's over.

Aloud, he asked, "How long before the radiation starts to build up?"

"Four hours, plus a few minutes," Pancho said. "Plenty of time."

You hope, Dan said to himself.

She established *Starpower 1* in a close orbit around the tumbling asteroid, and then the four of them floated weightlessly down to the airlock, where Dan and Fuchs had already assembled six emergency tanks of air. As they wriggled into their spacesuits Fuchs begged to go out the airlock first, but Dan overruled him.

"Pancho goes first, Lars. You're still a tenderfoot out there."

Through his fishbowl helmet, Fuchs's broad face frowned in puzzlement. "But my feet are fine," he said. "Why are you worried about my feet?"

Dan and Pancho both laughed, but Amanda shot an annoyed glance at Dan and said, "It's an American expression, Lars. From their western frontier, long ago."

"Yep," Dan conceded. "I learned it from Wild Bill Hickok."

Getting serious, Pancho said, "We can go together, Lars and me—whenever you guys are ready to stop horsin' around."

"Aye-aye cap'n," said Dan, touching his helmet with a gloved hand in a sloppy salute.

Pancho and Fuchs went through the airlock and, once it cycled, Dan and Amanda. While he stood in the cramped metal chamber, listening to the air-pump's clatter dwindling to silence, he heard Fuchs's excited voice through his helmet speaker:

"It's like a sandpile!"

Dan offered a swift thanks to whatever gods there be. Maybe we'll all live through this, after all.

With Amanda, he went through the airlock and then jetted the hundred meters or so separating the ship from the asteroid. It sure looks solid, Dan thought, staring at the black, slowly tumbling mass as he approached it. And yes, there were craters here and there with no rims to them; just holes, as if some giant had poked his fingers into the asteroid.

Then he saw Fuchs's helmet and shoulders; the rest of him was in some sort of a pit. He's digging like a kid in a sandbox, Dan saw.

As he got closer, Dan saw that the surface of the asteroid looked hazy, blurred. Is he stirring up that much dust? Dan asked himself. No, it's not just where Fuchs is digging. It's everywhere. The whole surface of the asteroid is blurry. What the hell is causing that?

"Are my eyes going bad or is the surface blurred?" he said into his helmet microphone.

"Dust," came Fuchs's immediate reply. "Particles from the solar wind give the dust an electrostatic charge. It makes the dust levitate."

"That doesn't happen on the Moon," Dan objected.

'The Moon is a very large body," said Fuchs. "This asteroid's gravity is too weak to hold the dust on the surface."

Just then Dan touched down on Haven. It was like stepping on talcum powder. His boots sank into the dark dust almost up to his ankles even though he came down with a feather light touch. Cripes, he thought, it's like one of those black sand beaches in Tahiti.

Dan turned and saw Pancho, long and lean even in her spacesuit, gliding across the asteroid's dusty surface toward him.

"Bring out the air tanks, Mandy," Pancho said.

Amanda soared weightlessly to *Starpower 1*'s airlock, then emerged again towing a string of six tall gray cylinders behind her. In her gleaming white spacesuit she looked like a robot nurse followed by a half-dozen unfinished pods.

"Better start diggin', boss," Pancho said.

Dan nodded, then realized that she might not be able to see the gesture. There wasn't all that much light out here, and they had decided to keep their helmet lamps off to save their suit batteries.

"We go with the buddy system," Dan said as he unlimbered the makeshift shovel he had carried with him. "You and me, Pancho. Amanda, you stay with Lars."

"Yes, of course," Amanda replied.

It wasn't quite like digging at the beach. More like working on a giant, black hunk of Swiss cheese, Dan thought. There were holes in the surface, tunnels that had apparently been drilled by stray chunks of rock hitting the asteroid. There was no bedrock, just a loose rubble of black rounded grains, the largest of them about the size of a small pebble. It's a wonder they hold together, Dan thought.

"Here's a ready-made tunnel for two," Pancho called to him. He saw her slowly disappearing into one of the tunnels.

It was wide enough for the two of them, just barely.

"How far down does it go?" Dan asked as he gingerly slid over the lip of the crater, careful not to catch his backpack.

"Dunno," Pancho answered. "Deep enough to ride out the storm. Better start fillin' in the hole."

He nodded inside his helmet and took a tighter grip on his improvised shovel: it had been a panel covering an electronics console. They had to cover themselves with at least a meter of dirt to protect against the oncoming radiation.

As he dug away at the sides of the sloping tunnel, Dan expected the gritty dirt to slide down into their hole. That's what would have happened on Earth, or even on the Moon. But Haven's gravity was so slight that the tunnel walls would not cave in no matter how furiously he dug into them.

In short order he and Pancho, working side by side, had buried themselves as deep as their waists. Not enough, Dan knew. Nowhere near enough, not yet.

"How're we doing . . . on time?" he asked Pancho, panting from the exertion of digging.

She straightened up. "Lemme see," she said, tapping at the keyboard on her left forearm. Dan could see a multicolored display light up on her bubble helmet.

"Radiation level's not up much over ambient yet," she said.

"How soon?" Dan asked impatiently.

The lights on her helmet's inner face flickered, changed. "Hour and a half, maybe a little less."

Dan went back to digging, blinking sweat out of his eyes, wishing he could wipe his face or just scratch his nose. But that was impossible inside the suit. Should have worn a sweat band, he told himself. Always did when I went outside. Been so long since I've done any EVA work I forgot it. Hindsight's always perfect.

"Y'know we're gonna need at least a meter of this dirt over us," Pancho said, digging alongside him.

"Yep."

"And then dig our way out, after the cloud passes."

"Yep," Dan repeated. It was the most he could say without stopping work. His muscles ached from the unaccustomed exertion.

It seemed like hours later when he heard Pancho's voice in his helmet speaker. "How're you guys doin', Mandy?"

"We're fine. We found a lovely cave and we have it almost completely filled in."

"Once you're all covered over it's gonna degrade our radio link," Pancho said.

"Yes, I'm sure it will."

"Got your air tanks in there with you?"

"Yes, of course."

Dan saw that their air tanks were still lying out on the surface, more than arm's reach away.

"Okay, keep your radio open. If we get completely cut off, you stay in the hole for fourteen hours. Got that?"

"Fourteen hours, check."

"Time count starts now."

"Fourteen hours from now," Amanda confirmed.

"Have a nice day."

"We'll see you in fourteen hours," Fuchs said.

"Right," said Dan, silently adding, Dead or alive.

To Pancho, he said, "I'd better drag the air tanks in here." Before she could object he pushed himself out of the hole and soared up above the dark, uneven ground. Dan glanced around but could not find the shelter that Amanda and Fuchs had dug for themselves. They did a good job, he thought as he tapped his jet thruster controls to push himself back to the surface.

The cylinders weighed next to nothing, but still he was careful with them as he slid them down into the pit. They still have mass, and inertia, Dan knew. I could break open Pancho's helmet or spring her suit's joints if I let one of these things bang into her.

By the time he wormed himself back into the pit beside her, Dan was bathed in cold sweat and puffing hard.

"You're not used to real work, are you, boss?" Pancho teased.

Dan shook his head inside his helmet. "Soon as we get back to Selene I'm going in for rejuvenation therapy."

"Me too."

"You? At your age?"

"Sooner's better'n later, they claim."

Dan humphed. "Better late than never."

"Radiation level's starting to climb," Pancho said, starting to paw at the sides of their pit again. "We better get ourselves buried or neither one of us'll get any younger."

"Or older," Dan muttered.

Buried alive. This is like something out of an Edgar Allan Poe story, Dan said to himself. He knew Pancho was mere centimeters from him; so were the air tanks. But he could see nothing. They were buried under nearly a full meter of loose rubble, curled fetally, nothing to see or hear or do except wait.

"...are you doing?" He heard Amanda's voice, scratchy and weak, through his helmet's speaker.

"We're okay," Pancho said. "I've been thinkin' we oughtta organize a square dance."

Dan suppressed a groan. That's just we need, he thought, redneck humor. Then, surprisingly, he laughed. He hadn't heard the term "redneck" since he'd been in Texas, long ages ago. There are no rednecks off-Earth, Dan realized. You don't get sunburned out here. Cooked, maybe. Fried by radiation. But not tanned, not unless you sit under the sunlamps in the gym at Selene.

He wiggled his right hand through the loose rubble encasing him and felt for the keyboard on his left forearm. By touch he called up the ship's sensor display. They had programmed the suits to show the displays on the inner surfaces of their bubble helmets. Nothing but streaks of colored hash. Either the pile of dirt atop them or the radiation storm was interfering with their link to the ship. Probably a combination of both, he thought.

"What's the time?" Dan asked.

At least he could talk with Pancho. Even if the radio link broke down completely, they were close enough to scrunch through the dirt and touch helmets so that they could talk through sound conduction.

"More'n thirteen hours to go, boss."

"You mean we've been down here for less than an hour?"

"Forty-nine minutes, to be exact."

"Shit," Dan said, with feeling.

"Take a nap. Best way to spend the time."

Dan nodded inside his helmet. "Nothing else to do."

He heard Pancho giggle softly.

"What's funny?"

"Mandy and Lars. I bet they're tryin' to figger out how to get the two of them into one suit."

Dan laughed, too. "Maybe you and I ought to try that."

"Boss!" Pancho cried in mock shock. "That's sexual harassment!"

"Nothing else to do," he repeated. "I can't even jerk off inside this double-damned suit."

"I can," Pancho teased.

"Now *that's* sexual harassment," Dan grumbled.

"Nope. Just better design."

Dan licked his lips. He felt thirsty, chilled, yet he was sweating. His stomach was queasy.

"How do you feel, Pancho?"

"Bored. Tired. Too jumpy to sleep. How 'bout you?"

"The same, I guess. Every part of me aches."

"How's your blood pressure?"

"How in hell would I know?"

"You hear your pulse in your ears?"

"No."

"Then you're okay, I guess."

"Thank you, Dr. Pancho."

"Go to sleep, boss. That's what I'm gonna try to do."

"I thought you said you were too jumpy."

"Yeah, but I'm gonna give it a try. Close my eyes and think pleasant thoughts."

"Good luck."

"You try it, too."

"Sure."

Dan closed his eyes, but his thoughts were far from pleasant. Opening them again, he fumbled with his wrist keyboard until he got the suit's radiation sensor displayed on his helmet. The graph was distorted by the curve of his helmet, and blurry. He tried to focus his eyes on it. Looks okay, he said to himself. Curve's going up, but the slope is low and it's a far distance from the red zone.

Try to sleep. He was certainly tired enough for it. Relax! Think about what you're going to do when you get back to Selene. I'd like to personally punch out Humphries's lights. Dan pictured Humphries's surprise when he broke his nose with a good straight right.

Somewhere in his mind an old adage sounded: Revenge is a dish best taken cold.

Punching in Humphries's face would be fun, but what would *really* hurt the bastard? He's tried to kill me. He may succeed yet; we're not out of this. If I die he'll move in and take over Astro. How can I prevent him from doing that? How can I stop him, even from the grave?

Dan chuckled bitterly to himself. I'm already in my grave, he realized. I'm already buried.

NANOTECHNOLOGY LABORATORY

harley Engles looked worried, upset. He nervously brushed his sandy hair back away from his forehead as he said, "Kris, I'm not supposed to let you in here."

It was well past midnight. Cardenas was surprised that anyone was still working in the lab complex. Selene's security people hadn't bothered to change the entry code on the main door; she had just tapped it out and the door had obligingly slid open. But Engles had been working in his cubicle, and as soon as he saw Cardenas striding determinedly past the empty work stations toward her own office, he popped out of his cubbyhole and stopped her.

"We got notified by security," he said, looking shamefaced. "You're not allowed in here until further notice."

"I know, Charley," she said. "I just want to clear out my desk."

Charles Engles was a young grad student from New York whose parents had sent him to Selene after he'd been crippled in a car crash. Even knowing that he could never return to them once he'd taken nanotherapy, his parents wanted their son's legs repaired so he could walk again.

"The cameras..." Engles pointed to the tiny unwinking red lights in the corners of the ceiling. "Security will send somebody here once they see you."

"It's all right," she said, trying to mask her inner tension. "I'll only be here a few minutes. You can go back to your work."

Instead, he walked with her as she headed for her office.

"What's this all about, Kris? Why do they want to lock you out of your own lab?"

"It's a long story and I'd rather not go into it right now, Charley. Please, I just need a few minutes in my office."

He looked unhappy, almost wounded. "If there's anything I can do to help..."

Cardenas smiled and felt tears welling in her eyes. "That's very kind of you, Charley. Thanks."

"I mean, I wouldn't be able to walk if it weren't for you."

She nodded and added silently, And now that you can walk you'll never be allowed to return to Earth.

"Well..." he shifted uneasily from one foot to the other. "If there's anything you need, anything at all, just let me know."

"Thanks, Charley. I'll do that."

He stood there for another awkward moment while Cardenas wondered how long it would take Security to send someone to apprehend her. Finally he headed reluctantly back to his own cubicle. She walked slowly toward her office.

Once Charley stepped into his cubicle, though, Cardenas swiftly turned down a side passageway toward the rear of the laboratory complex. She passed a sign that proclaimed in red letters AUTHORIZED PERSONNEL ONLY BEYOND THIS POINT. This was the area where newly developed nanomachines were tested. The passageway here was lined with sealed, airtight chambers, rather than the cubicles out front. The door to each chamber was locked. The passageway itself was

lined with ultraviolet lamps along its ceiling. Each nanomachine type was designed to stop functioning when exposed
to high-intensity ultraviolet light: a safety precaution.

Cardenas passed three doors, stopped at the fourth. She
tapped out its entry code and the steel door opened inward a
crack. She slipped into the darkened chamber and leaned her
weight against the heavy door, closing it. With a long, shuddering sigh, she reset the entry code from the panel on the
wall, effectively locking the door to anyone who might try to
get in. They'll have to break the door down, she told herself,
and that will take them some time.

By the time the get the door open I'll be dead.

Dan dreamed of Earth: a confused, troubled dream. He was
sailing a racing yacht, running before the wind neck-and-
neck with many other boats. Warm tropical sunlight beat
down on his shoulders and back as he gripped the tiller with
one hand while the boat's computer adjusted the sails for
every change in the breeze.

The boat knifed through the water, but suddenly it was a
car that Dan was driving at breakneck speed through mur-
derously heavy traffic. Dan didn't know where he was; some
city freeway, a dozen lanes clogged with cars and buses and
enormous semi rigs chuffing smoke and fumes into the dirty
gray, sullen sky. Something was wrong with the car's air
conditioning; it was getting uncomfortably hot in the driver's seat. Dan started to open his window but realized that
the windows had to stay shut. There's no air to breath out
there, he said to himself, knowing it was ridiculous because
he wasn't in space, he was on Earth and he was suffocating,
choking, coughing.

He woke up coughing with Pancho's voice blaring in his
ears, "Recharge your backpack, boss! You're runnin' low on
air."

Blackness. He couldn't see a thing. For a moment he felt

panic surging through him, then it fell into place. Buried in the asteroid. Time to refill his backpack's air tank. In the dark. By touch.

"Lemme help you," Pancho said.

Dan sensed her beside him. The gravelly dirt shifted, crunched. Something bumped into his side.

"Oops. 'Scuse me."

Dan pushed one hand through the gritty stuff, remembering where he'd put the cylinders.

"I've got the hose," he said.

"Okay, good. That's what I was lookin' for."

"Groping for, you mean."

"Whatever. Hand it to me now."

Dan felt her hand pushing against his side. "I can do it," he said.

"Better let me," said Pancho. "You're tired and fatigue makes you sloppy, causes mistakes."

"I'm all right."

'Sure. But just lemme do it, huh? Tired astronauts don't live long."

"And rain makes applesauce," he mumbled, pushing the end of the hose into her waiting hand.

"Don't open it up yet," Pancho warned. "Don't want grit or dust contaminating the air."

"I know," he groused.

It seemed to take hours. Dan tried to keep from coughing but the air in his suit seemed awfully thick; his chest was hurting. He pictured old pantomime comedy routines as he and Pancho haltingly fumbled with the air hose, working blindly, and refilled each other's suit tanks. They filled Dan's backpack first, and within a minute he could take a deep breath again without it catching in his throat.

Once they filled Pancho's backpack he heard her inhale deeply. "Best canned air in the solar system," she announced happily.

"What time is it? How long do we have to go?"

"Lemme see . . . seven and a half hours."

"That's how long we've been down here?"

"Nope, that's how long we still have to go," Pancho answered.

"Another seven and a half hours?"

Pancho laughed. "You sound like a kid in the back seat of a car."

He huffed, then broke into a chastened grin. "I guess I was whining, wasn't I?"

"A little."

A new thought struck Dan. "After the time's up, how do we tell if the radiation's really gone down enough for us to get back to the ship?"

"Been thinkin' about that. I'll worm my extensible antenna wire up to the top of this rubble heap and see if we can link with the ship. Then it'll be purty simple to read the ship's sensors."

"Suppose the ship's comm system's been knocked out by the radiation."

"Not likely."

"But what if?"

Pancho sighed. "Then I'll just hafta stick my head out and see what my suit sensors read."

"Like an old cowboy video," Dan said. "Stick your head out and see if anybody shoots at you."

"Hey, boss, you really did learn a lot from Wild Bill Hickok, didn't ya?"

This late at night there was only one man on duty monitoring Selene's security-camera network. He was a portly, balding former London bobby who had spent his life's savings to bring himself and his wife to the Moon and live in comfortable, low-gravity retirement. He'd found retirement so boring, however, that he pleaded with Selene's personnel department to allow him to work, at least part-time.

The uniform they gave him wasn't much; just a set of glorified coveralls with an insignia patch on the left shoulder and his name badge clipped over its breast pocket. But at least he could spend three nights each week sitting alone and content, watching the videos his wife always complained about while still feeling that he was doing something worthwhile. He half-dozed, leaning back in his padded swivel chair, as the twenty display screens arranged in a semicircle around his desk flashed views from Selene's hundreds of security cameras. Actually, only nineteen of the screens showed the cameras' scenes; the screen directly in front of the desk was showing the football match from Vancouver, live. But with the sound well-muted, of course.

The computer did all the real work. The toffs in the main office programmed the computer with a long list of things that would be considered questionable or downright illegal. If the computer detected any such activity it sounded an alarm and indicated where and what was going on.

With the score still tied and only four minutes left in the final period, the blasted computer buzzed.

The guard frowned with annoyance. His central screen winked out for an instant, then displayed a ceiling-eye-view of a woman walking through one of the labs. UNAUTHORIZED PERSON blinked in red across the bottom of the screen.

It took a few minutes to coax the information out of the computer, but finally the guard phoned the security chief, waking him of course, with the news that Dr. Kris Cardenas had entered the nanotechnology laboratory. The chief grumbled and cast a bleary eye at the guard, but at least had the good grace to say, "Thanks. I'll send somebody down there."

Then he hung up and the guard went back to watching the football game. It was going into overtime.

HAVEN

T ry as he might, Dan could not get back to sleep. Pancho
had attempted to call Amanda and Fuchs, but there was
no response from them.

"Must be a lotta sizzle outside," she said.

Dan thought she sounded worried. Not her usual
sassy self. Or maybe she's just tired. Or bored.

How can anybody be bored with this storm only a meter
over our heads? Dan asked himself. Some storm. No thunder
and lightning. No noise at all, unless you count the crackle
and hiss when you try to use the radio.

Quiet. Deadly quiet.

Dan found the water nipple in his suit's collar and took a
sip. Flat and warm. Like recycled piss.

More than seven hours to go. I'll go bonkers by then:
stark, raving nutty.

Then he tasted blood in his mouth.

It was like an electric shock. His entire body flinched.
Everything else disappeared from his mind.

Bleeding gums, he thought, trying to fight down the terror rising in him. One of the prime symptoms of radiation sickness.

Or maybe you accidentally bit your tongue, he told himself.

Yeah, sure, answered that sardonic voice in his head. You've had a bout of radiation sickness before, you know the drill. Only this time there's no place to go to, nothing to do except sit here in this grave and let the radiation do its job on you.

"Pancho," he croaked, surprised at how dry his throat was.

"Right here, boss."

"Can you turn on your suit's recorder?"

"Yeah, I think so..."

Dan sensed her fumbling in the dirt. This must be the way moles live, he thought, depending on touch instead of sight. His stomach was fluttering, nauseous. Christ, don't let me toss my cookies inside the double-damned helmet, he begged silently.

Pancho said, "Testing, one, two, three." A moment later he heard the words repeated.

"Okay, the recorder's workin'."

"Good," said Dan. "Get this down." He cleared his throat. It felt raw, raspy. Then, in as normal a voice as he could produce, he pronounced:

"I am Dan Randolph, CEO of Astro Manufacturing Corporation. This is my last will and testament. The recording equipment will automatically mark this statement with the date and time."

"That's right," Pancho said.

"Don't interrupt, kid. Where was I? Oh, right, last will and testament. I hereby bequeath all my stock in Astro Corporation to my friend and loyal employee, Priscilla Lane, together—"

Pancho was so shocked she didn't even bristle at the use of her proper name. "To me? Are you loco?"

"Don't interrupt!" Dan snapped. "All my Astro stock to Priscilla Lane, together with all my personal belongings and possessions." He had to stop and take a few breaths. Then, "And I nominate Priscilla Lane to take my place on the board of directors of Astro Corporation."

He thought about it for a few moments, then nodded, satisfied. "Okay, that's it. You can turn off the recorder now."

"What'd you do that for? How come you—"

"I'm not going to make it, kid," Dan said tiredly. "The radiation's getting to me. I want you to take my place on the board of directors and fight that sumbitch Humphries with every gram of strength you've got."

"Me? I'm just a hick engineer . . . a rocket jock, for cryin' out loud."

"You're my heir, Pancho. Like a daughter. I don't have any family to leave anything to, and besides, you know Astro as well as anyone does."

"Not the board of directors."

Dan laughed weakly. "You'll roll right over them, kid. The board needs some fresh, young blood. You'll have to fight Humphries, of course. He'll want to be made chairman once I'm gone."

In a quieter voice, Pancho asked, "You're talkin' like you're at death's door."

"I think I am. My gums are bleeding. I feel woozy. My ears are ringing. I just hope I don't get the shits."

"The storm's almost over," she said.

"So am I."

"Once we get back into the ship we can zip back to Selene in a couple of days. Maybe faster! I can goose her up to maybe half a *g*."

"And how will you brake her? Impact? Dive right into Alphonsus?"

Pancho fell silent for several moments. Dan was glad she couldn't see him. The way his insides felt, his hands would probably be shaking like a palsied old man's if they weren't buried in the asteroid's rubble.

"They can cure radiation sickness back at Selene," Pancho said at last. "Use nanomachines."

"If I make it back to Selene."

"Only about seven hours to go," she said. "Radiation's levelin' off."

"Not as deep as a well," Dan quoted, "or as wide as a church door, but it's enough. It'll do."

"You goin' delirious?"

"No, that's just Shakespeare. *Romeo and Juliet.*"

"Oh. Yeah, right."

"I'm going to take a nap, kid. I feel pretty tired."

"Good idea, I guess."

"Wake me when it's over."

Kris Cardenas was surprised at how her hands trembled as she worked. Programming nanomachines to disassemble carbon-based molecules was a snap, a no-brainer. Just a slight modification to the procedure they used every day to build diamond mechanisms out of bins of soot.

It wasn't the difficulty of the work. As she sat at the lab bench, peering intently at the desktop screen that displayed what the atomic force microscope was showing, she thought about the consequences.

Gobblers. I'm deliberately creating a batch of gobblers. If they get loose . . .

Calm down! she scolded herself. Go through this logically, step by step.

Okay, they'll break in and find me dead. Lying on the floor. I'll leave a note on the computer screen. Put it in big red letters, so they can't miss it. I'm only making a microsample of gobblers and I'm disabling their assembly capabilities. They can't reproduce. They'll be contained inside my body.

But what if they get outside your body? They'll be taking you apart from the inside. What's to stop them from getting out?

Nothing, she told herself. So I'll turn on the UV overheads before I swallow the bugs. That will destroy them once they get outside my body.

A knock on the door startled her.

"Dr. Cardenas? We know you're in there. Open up, please."

She wiped the display from the AFM and began hurriedly typing her suicide note.

"Warning. I have ingested a microgram of nanomachine disassemblers. They are programmed to take apart carbon-based molecules. Do not allow them to go beyond the confines of this laboratory. Disinfect the lab with high-intensity ultraviolet light before moving my body or touching anything in this room. Notify—"

Someone banged on the door, hard. "Kris! It's Doug Stavenger. You don't have to do this. Come on out."

She scanned the red block letters on the display screen and erased the final word; no need to notify Doug, he's already here.

"Kris, it's not your fault." Stavenger's voice was muffled by the heavy steel door, but she heard the urgency in it well enough. "Come out and talk this over with me."

She got off the spindly-legged stool and went to the sampling site at the end of the bench. A gleaming cup of lunar aluminum sat there, half full of water that contained the nanomachines that were going to kill her.

"Kris," Stavenger called, "you've spent your life developing nanotechnology. Don't throw it all away. Don't give them another reason to say nanomachines are killers."

She picked up the cup and held it in both hands, thinking, I can't live with this guilt. I've committed murder. I've killed four people.

Stavenger was shouting through the locked door, "That's

what they'll say. You know that. They'll say that nanomachines killed the foremost researcher in the field. They'll use it to show how dangerous nanomachines are, how right they've been all along to ban them."

She looked from the cup to the closed, locked door. It was Humphries's idea, but I did it. Willingly. He pulled my strings and I danced like a blind, obedient little puppet.

"Don't throw your life away, Kris," Stavenger pleaded. "You'll be destroying everything you've worked for. You'll be giving them the excuse they need to come back here and force us to obey their laws."

Humphries, she thought. Once I'm dead he'll be able to blame the whole thing on me. His lawyers will talk his way out of it. He'll walk away from this. From four murders. Five, counting me.

Cardenas carried the cup back to the sampling site and sealed its aluminum top to its rim. Once the top clicked into place she placed the cup in the disposal oven and closed its door. The inner walls of the oven fluoresced as its ultraviolet lamps bathed the cup.

Why should I die for Martin Humphries? she asked herself. Someone's got to stand up to him. Someone's got to tell the truth about this. No matter what it costs, I've got to face him, face all of them.

"Come on, Kris. Open the door."

They're watching me through the security camera, Cardenas knew. She went back to the computer and erased her message. One of the staff people can destroy the gobblers tomorrow, she told herself. They're safe enough in the oven for now.

Slowly she walked to the door, then stopped at the keypad on the wall next to it.

"Doug?" she called.

"I'm right here, Kris. Open the door, please."

"This is silly," she said, feeling stupid, "but I don't remember the sequence I used to reset the lock."

A mumble of voices on the other side of the door. Then Stavenger, sounding relieved, replied, "Okay, Kris. Security's bringing an analyzer down anyway. We'll have it open in a few minutes."

"Doug?" she said again.

"Yes."

"Thanks."

"*Da nada,*" he answered.

By the time they got the door unlocked, Cardenas was surprised at how calm she felt. She had looked death in the face and discovered that she was strong enough to go on living.

The passageway outside was crammed with men and women in security coveralls, half-a-dozen of her own nanotech people, several medics in white, and Doug Stavenger.

"Are you all right?" Stavenger asked worriedly.

Cardenas felt herself smile a little. "I am now," she said.

DEATH

"'mon, boss, wake up!"

Pancho's voice, muffled, distant. Dan's eyes were gummy, bleary; it took an effort to open them. He tried to wipe them but his hands were still buried in the loose rubble of the asteroid.

"Dan! Wake up!"

He heard the urgency in her voice.

"Yeah. Okay . . ." His stomach heaved.

"Radiation level's down almost to normal," Pancho said. "You okay?"

"Sure," he lied. He felt too weak to move, too tired to care.

"Time to get outta here." She was scrabbling, clawing through the gravelly dirt. Dan wanted to help her but he could barely move his arms. All he wanted to do was sleep. Then his guts suddenly lurched and a wave of nausea swept over him.

"We're up, in the open." Amanda's voice came through his helmet speaker.

"I'm gonna need some help here," Pancho replied. "Dan's in a bad way."

Dan was concentrating on not vomiting. Get me to a toilet, he begged silently. I don't want to let loose inside the suit. Even in the depth of his misery, though, somewhere in the back of his mind he laughed bitterly at himself. It all boils down to this, he thought. Everything you've done in your life doesn't amount to a teaspoon of applesauce. All that's really important is not upchucking or losing control of your bowels.

He sensed somebody digging frantically above him, and then strong arms lifting him, dragging him free of the rubble-filled tunnel. Fuchs. He overdid it, and the two of them went tumbling completely off the asteroid, spiraling crazily in space. Dan saw *Starpower 1* slide past his field of view and then an unstoppable surge of bile rose into his throat and he vomited, spattering his stomach's contents noisomely all over his fishbowl helmet. The stench was overpowering. He groaned and retched again.

"Hang in there, boss," Pancho said. "I gotcha."

Dan thought he heard someone else retching, too. Nothing like the sound of vomiting to make you upchuck, too. I could get the whole Vienna Boys Choir tossing their cookies this way.

He wavered in and out of consciousness, thinking, That's the way they get you. They make you so miserable that you'll be glad to die. He squeezed his eyes shut and tried not to breathe. He desperately wanted to wipe his face but inside the suit and helmet it was impossible.

"Okay, the lock's cycling," he heard Pancho say.

"Bring him inside." Amanda's voice.

"Take him to his own bunk."

"Yes. Careful now."

He didn't dare open his eyes. At one point he heard Pancho say, "You get him out of his suit. I gotta see how much damage the storm did to the ship's systems."

After a while he felt something cool and soothing wiping his face. Opening his eyes at last, Dan saw a blurred image of Amanda bending over him, with Fuchs beside her. They book looked worried, grim.

"How do you feel?" Amanda asked.

"Lousy," he croaked.

Fuchs said, "We are under way. Pancho is accelerating to one-third *g*."

"The ship's okay?"

"Some of the sensors were damaged by the radiation," Fuchs said. "And the communications equipment, too. But the fusion power plant is functioning properly."

"The nanobugs didn't get to the MHD generator's superconductor?" Dan asked. It took most of his strength to get the words out.

"No, they seem perfectly in order," Fuchs answered. Then he added, "Thank god."

We're on our way home, Dan thought. He closed his eyes. On our way home.

"Until you get him here where we can give him proper medical treatment," Selene's chief radiation therapist was saying, "there's nothing you can do for him beyond the chelation pills and antioxidants you're already giving him."

Pancho watched the medic's unhappy image as she sat disconsolately in the command pilot's chair. It had taken more than an hour to contact Selene. *Starpower 1*'s high-gain antenna had been knocked out by radiation damage and she'd had to use the backup laser comm system. Otherwise the ship was running okay, some radiation damage here and there; nothing vital. The nanobugs hadn't gotten to the superconducting coil of the MHD generator, thank whatever gods there be.

But Dan was in a bad way, and the sad-assed medics at Selene couldn't do any more for him than a bunch of witch doctors. Bring him in as fast as you can. Well, sure! That's what I'm doin'. But will it be fast enough?

And Elly was dead. Just before they had abandoned the ship she had left the snake in her box and put the box in the refrigerator, knowing the cold would put Elly into a torpor, hoping that the fridge would provide enough shielding to save the krait. I should've carried her inside my suit, Pancho berated herself. Even if she bit me, I should've brought her with me. The radiation had killed the krait, along with the one remaining mouse.

Her thoughts returned to Dan. He's got it bad. We all took a dose, we'll all need medical attention once we get back to Selene. The chelation pills are helping, but Dan might not make it. He looks half-dead already.

Amanda came into the bridge and slipped into the right-hand seat.

"How is he?" Pancho asked.

"We cleaned him up and he's sleeping now." She made a strange face. "His hair is coming out. In clumps."

Pancho fought down the urge to go back to Dan's compartment. Nothing you can do there, she told herself.

She asked Amanda, "How's Lars?"

"He seems to be fine."

"Did he take the pills?"

"Yes, of course. He's working on the high-gain antenna."

"That circuitry's supposed t'be hardened against radiation," Pancho said angrily. "We oughtta sue the manufacturer when we get back."

"Oh, Pancho, it was exposed to such a high level of radiation. That was an intense storm."

She nodded, but said, "Yeah, but still that comm gear has gotta work right."

"You need a rest," Amanda said.

"We all do."

"I'll take the conn. Go back and catch some sleep."

"Maybe you're right."

"Do it, Pancho."

She looked at Amanda for a brief moment, then made up her mind and slowly got to her feet, surprised at how stiff she felt. "If I'm not back in two hours, wake me up."

Amanda nodded.

"I mean it, Mandy. Two hours."

"Yes. I will."

Satisfied, Pancho made her way back through the ward-room. She hesitated at the door to her privacy compartment, then went a further few steps to Dan's door.

She slid it open a crack. Dan was still sleeping, lying on the bunk, his body sheened with perspiration, the shorts and tee-shirt they had put on him stained by his sweat. His scalp was dotted with bald spots where tufts of hair had come out. God, he's in a bad way, she said to herself.

He opened his eyes and focused on her.

"Hi, kid," he breathed.

"How're you feelin', boss?"

"Not good."

"Anything I can bring you? I could fix some broth or somethin'."

"I'd just chuck it all over myself," he said.

"We'll be in Selene in another day and a half. Just rest yourself and we'll get the medics—"

"Did you send my last will and testament to them?" Dan asked.

Pancho shook her head. "Havin' troubles with the main antenna. Lars is workin' on it."

"How's the laser?"

"The backup? It's okay. We're usin' it to—"

"Send my will," Dan said.

"We don't hafta do that. You're gonna be fine."

"Send it," he insisted. He tried to raise himself on one elbow and failed. "Send it," he whispered.

"You sure you wanta leave everything to me?"

"Will you fight Humphries?"

She nodded solemnly. "Yep. That's a promise, boss."

"Good." He smiled weakly. "Send it. Now."

With a reluctant sigh, Pancho said, "Okay, if that's what you want."

"That's what I want," he whispered. "And put in our claim to Haven, too."

She nearly smiled. That's more like Dan Randolph, she thought.

"One more day," said Fuchs.

He and Amanda sat side by side in the wardroom. Fuchs was picking halfheartedly at a breakfast of prepackaged eggs and soymeat. Amanda hardly looked at her cereal and fruit.

"One more day," she repeated glumly.

"You're not happy."

"Humphries is in Selene. It will start all over again once we get back."

"Not if you're married to me," Fuchs blurted.

She stared at him. He looked totally serious, almost solemn. But then his thin lips curved slowly into a hopeful smile.

Before she could think of anything to say, Fuchs went on, "I love you, Amanda. I'm not proposing to you merely to protect you from Humphries. I love you, and more than anything in the universe I want you to be my wife."

"But Lars, we've only known each other a few weeks. Not even that long."

"How long does it take?" he asked. "I've fallen hopelessly in love with you. It happened in an instant."

She felt stunned. This steady, capable, thoughtful, intelligent man was looking at her expectantly, his whole life shining in his pale blue eyes. He loves me? Amanda wondered. We haven't even kissed and he believes he loves me? Do I love him?

Fuchs licked his lips nervously and asked, "I know I'm only a graduate student and my financial prospects aren't very wonderful, but could you—I mean to say, do you think..."

He seemed to run out of words. He simply sat there, gazing at her as if afraid to say anything more.

She thought swiftly, never taking her eyes from his. He's strong. He's steady. He's wanted to come on to me, I've felt that often enough. Yet he didn't. He never even touched me, never said a word until now. He's honorable.

It seemed like an eternity before she heard herself whisper, "Yes, Lars. I'll be happy to marry you."

You can learn to love him, Amanda told herself. You know you can trust him, you know he's gentle and sweet. He'll protect you from Humphries.

Fuchs leaned toward her and slid a strong arm around her waist. Amanda closed her eyes and they kissed, softly, tenderly at first. But she felt him clutch her to him, felt real strength and passion in the lingering kiss. She wound her arms around his neck.

After several minutes they separated slightly. Amanda felt breathless.

Fuchs was beaming like a thousand lasers. "We've got to tell Pancho!" he exclaimed, jumping to his feet. "And Dan!"

Laughing, he took Amanda's arm as she rose to her feet. He let her duck through the hatch to the bridge, then followed right behind her.

"Pancho, Lars has asked me to marry him!"

Pancho turned halfway around in her command chair and grinned at them. "'Bout time," she said. "I was wonderin' when you two would figger it out."

"We've got to tell Dan!"

Pancho nodded, scanned the instrument panel and saw that the ship's systems were performing adequately, then got up and started back with them.

"We oughtta perform the ceremony right here, get you legally hitched before we get back to Selene," she said.

"Oh! Could you?"

"Is the captain of a spacecraft legally empowered to perform marriages?" Fuchs asked.

"Oughtta be," Pancho said, shrugging.

They reached Dan's compartment and softly slid the accordion door back. Dan was lying on his back, his eyes closed, a sweaty sheet covering the lower half of his body.

"He's sleeping," Amanda said.

Dan's eyes popped open. "How can a sick man sleep with all the racket you're making?" he said, barely above a whisper.

Amanda's hands flew to her face. Fuchs started to apologize.

Dan waved a feeble hand to silence him. "If you can establish a comm link, you can get somebody on Earth to perform the ceremony."

"Hey, that's right," Pancho said.

Licking his dry, cracked lips, Dan asked, "You want the Pope in Rome? I've got some connections." Looking at Amanda, he added, "How about the Archbishop of Canterbury?"

"One of the ministers in Selene will do," Amanda said softly.

"I get it," Dan said. "You're in a hurry."

Fuchs turned red.

"I want to give the bride away," Dan said.

"Sure. Fine," said Pancho. "I'll set up the comm link." She headed back toward the bridge.

It took longer to make the arrangements than to perform the ceremony, even with a twelve-minute lag between the ship and Selene. Amanda and Fuchs stood by Dan's bunk with Pancho behind them. They had no flowers, no wedding attire except the coveralls they'd been wearing. The minister appeared on the wall screen opposite Dan's bunk. He was the pastor of Selene's interfaith chapel, a Lutheran: an ascetically thin young German with hair so blond it looked nearly white. Amanda could see that he was in his office, not the chapel itself. That didn't matter, she told herself. He conducted the brief rite in English and with great dignity, despite the time lag between them.

"Do each of you take the other for your lawful spouse?" the young minister asked.

"I do," said Fuchs immediately.

"I do," Amanda said.

They stood there feeling foolish and fidgety for the six minutes it took their response to reach the minister and the six additional minutes it took his words to reach them.

At last he said, "Then I pronounce you husband and wife. Congratulations. You may kiss the bride."

Amanda turned to Fuchs and they embraced. Pancho thanked the minister and cut the electronic link. The wall screen went dark.

They turned to Dan, lying in his bunk.

"He's fallen asleep," Amanda whispered. But she stared at Dan's sweat-stained tee-shirt. His chest didn't seem to be moving.

Fuchs leaned over the bunk and pressed two fingers against Dan's carotid artery.

"I don't feel a pulse," he said.

Pancho grabbed Dan's wrist. "No pulse," she agreed.

"He's dead?" Amanda asked, feeling tears welling up in her eyes.

Fuchs nodded solemnly.

Pancho's heart was thumping, and not merely from the heavier gravity of Earth. The quarterly meeting of Astro Corporation's board of directors was about to begin. Would they follow Dan's wishes and vote her onto the board? And what if they do? What do I know about directing a big corporation? she asked herself.

Not much, she admitted. But if Dan thought I could do it, then I gotta at least give it my best shot.

She stared at the other directors as they milled around the sideboard of the luxurious meeting room, pouring drinks for themselves and picking out delicate little sandwiches and stuff. They all looked old, and dignified, and wicked rich. Most of the women wore dresses, by jeeps, or suits with skirts. Expensive clothes. Lots of jewelry, too. Pancho felt shabby in her best pantsuit and no adornments except for a bracelet and pendant earrings of lunar aluminum.

They were ignoring her. They clumped together in twos and threes, talking to each other in low voices, not whispers exactly, but little buzzing heads-together conversations. Nobody even looked her way, yet Pancho got the feeling that were all talking about her.

Not even the plump oriental woman in the bright red dress spoke to her. She must know what it's like to be an outsider, Pancho thought. But she's keeping her distance, just like all the others.

Martin Humphries strode into the board room, decked out in a sky-blue business suit. Pancho clenched her fists. If he's in mourning for Dan he sure ain't showing it, she thought. None of them are.

Humphries nodded here and there, saying hello and making small talk as he made his way past the sideboard toward Pancho. He glanced once out the long window above the sideboard and seemed almost to wince at the view of the sea out there. Then he turned and came toward Pancho. Stopping a meter or so in front of her, Humphries looked Pancho up and down, the expression on his face pretty close to a sneer.

"Do you honestly think we're going to allow a roughneck grease monkey to have a seat on this board?"

Suppressing an urge to punch him out, Pancho said tightly, "We'll see purty soon, won't we?"

"We certainly will."

He was wearing his lifts, Pancho saw; still, Humphries was several centimeters shorter than she.

"What puzzles me," she said looking down into his ice-gray eyes, "is how they can allow a convicted murderer t' stay on the board."

"I wasn't convicted of murder!" Humphries snapped, keeping his voice low.

Pancho made a small shrug. "They found you guilty of causin' Dan Randolph's death, didn't they?"

"I pleaded guilty to involuntary manslaughter. That was the deal my lawyers set up for me."

"Selene's court was way too easy on you. I would've hanged you. And not by the neck, either."

"They made me divest my holdings in Starpower!" he snarled. "Made me turn over my one-third to them!"

"And Astro," Pancho corrected. "You can still make money off Dan's dead body outta the profits Astro's gonna be pullin' in."

"And they exiled me! Threw me out of Selene. Forbade me from returning for twenty years." He glanced over his shoulder at the view of the sea through the long sweeping window like a man looking back at something chasing him.

"You got off light," said Pancho. "Dr. Cardenas got a life sentence. She'll never be allowed to work in her own nanolab again."

"She was just as responsible for his death as I was. And so are you, for that matter."

"Me?"

"You were the captain of the vessel. You could have turned back once you realized the radiation shield was failing."

"Thanks to you."

Humphries smirked at her. "If Randolph had brought a proper medical man aboard, if he hadn't taken the ship before the IAA approved the flight—"

"That's right," Pancho growled, "blame the victim for the crime."

"You didn't even freeze him once he died. You didn't even try to."

"Wouldn't have done any good," Pancho said. "We couldn't've got his core temperature down quick enough."

They had thought about it, she and Mandy and Fuchs. They had even considered putting Dan's body into a spacesuit and dunking him into one of the fuel tanks. But a quick calculation showed the cryogenic fuel would be used up by the time they reached the Moon and Dan's body would thaw before they could transfer him to a proper dewar.

Humphries smiled slyly. "Or maybe you *wanted* him dead, so you could inherit from him?"

Pancho had her right fist cocked before she realized it. Humphries threw his hands up and scuttled several steps back from her. Everything stopped. The board room went absolutely quiet. All faces turned toward them.

With a deep, deliberate breath, Pancho put her hand down. Humphries straightened up, looking sheepish. The other directors turned back to their own conversations, trying to pretend that nothing had happened.

Scowling angrily, Humphries walked away from her. Pancho saw that most of the directors moved out of his way as he approached the sideboard. As if they didn't want to be close enough to touch him or even have him breathe on them.

"I think we'd better start the meeting," said a petite red-haired woman in a forest-green skirted suit.

The directors went to the long polished table in the middle of the room and began to take their chairs. Pancho watched uncertainly for a moment, then saw that two chairs were unoccupied: one at the head of the table and another at its foot. Remembering her childhood bible classes, she took the lowest chair. The redhead sat to the right of the empty chair at the table's head; Humphries sat opposite her, his back to the window.

Everyone looked around, as if wondering what to do next. The redhead slowly got to her feet.

"For those of you who don't know me," she said, looking down the table toward Pancho, "my name is Harriet O'Banian. As vice-chair for the board, I guess I'll have to run this meeting until a new chairperson is elected."

They all nodded. Pancho saw that a small display screen was built into the gleaming surface of the table in front of each place. It showed an abbreviated agenda.

"I'm going to dispense with the usual formalities," O'Banian said, "and proceed directly to—"

"May I interrupt?" Humphries asked, holding up his hand like a schoolboy.

O'Banian murmured, "Of course."

Rising to his feet, Humphries said earnestly, "I wasn't able to attend the emergency meeting of the board that was called when news of Dan Randolph's unfortunate death was revealed."

Unfortunate? Pancho snarled inwardly.

"You all know that his death was partially my own fault. I played too rough, and I've seen the consequences. Please believe me, I never wanted to have Dan die."

The hell you didn't, Pancho said to herself. Looking along the table, though, she was shocked at the sympathetic expressions on many of the directors' faces.

"My real crime," Humphries went on, "was wanting to run Astro Corporation. And I let that ambition override my common sense. I saw Dan driving this fine organization into bankruptcy, and I knew that I could do better."

He stopped, hung his head for a moment. Pancho thought, The sumbitch should've been an actor.

"I'm truly sorry that Dan is dead. I feel a great weight of responsibility for it, even though that is not what I intended. I'll pay the price for my mistake for the rest of my life."

Pancho could barely keep herself from throwing something at him. But the other directors seemed calm, accepting.

Humphries wasn't through. "I know we can pull Astro through its current crisis. Despite Dan's unfortunate death, the mission to the Asteroid Belt was actually a success. Starpower Limited now has rights to two asteroids that are worth several trillion international dollars on today's commodities markets. And Astro, of course, owns one third of Starpower."

"One half," Pancho snapped.

Humphries stared at her for a long, speechless moment. "One half," he admitted at last. "That's right. Astro now owns half of Starpower."

"And Selene owns the other half," said Pancho.

Humphries bristled. Pancho grinned at him, thinking, I hope you choke on the money you'll be makin'.

Hattie O'Banian broke the tension-filled silence. "Thank you, Mr. Humphries. At this time, before we go on to the regular agenda, I would like to welcome Ms. Priscilla Lane to the board."

Pancho watched Humphries raise an eyebrow. Immediately, the oriental woman, sitting across the table from him, said, "Ms. Lane hasn't yet been elected to the board."

"I'm sure we can do that by acclamation," O'Banian said. "After all, Dan specifically—"

"It's customary to vote on a new member," said a florid-faced man with a full gray beard sitting a few chairs down from Humphries. "After all, a position on the board isn't hereditary," the florid man grumbled. He reminded Pancho of Santa Claus, except that he was nowhere near being jolly. "You can't inherit board membership just because a dying man willed it to you."

Pancho understood the implication. Cripes, they think I was sleepin' with Dan and that's why he named me to the board.

O'Banian looked displeased. "Very well, then. In that case, I believe we should allow Ms. Lane to say a few words about herself."

All faces turned toward Pancho. Thinking furiously, she got slowly to her feet.

In her mind she heard Dan telling her, *My personnel people think you're a flake, Pancho. The rap on you is that you're not serious.* She knew that each member of the board had seen her personnel file. Okay, Pancho, she said to herself, time to grow up and start bein' serious. You're in the big leagues now. You gotta show them your best.

She took a deep breath, then started, "I was just as surprised as any of you when Dan Randolph said he wanted me to take his place on this board. I'm an engineer and pilot, not a banker or a lawyer. But Dan said the board needed some fresh blood, and he picked me. So here I am."

Surveying the men and women watching her, Pancho went on, "I think I know why Dan wanted me here—and it wasn't for my good looks, either."

A few chuckles. O'Banian smiled broadly.

"With all due respect to you, I think this board could use somebody who has some practical experience in Astro's activities. Dan sure did, but I don't think any of you have been involved in the company's actual operations. I've been flyin' Astro spacecraft for nearly seven years now. I've been out to the Belt and back. That's where our best chance of makin' real profits lies: out in the Belt. I know what it takes to get the job done. I think I can help this board to make the right decisions as we start to tap the resources of all those asteroids. Thank you."

She sat down. No one applauded. Humphries gave her a hard stare, then swept his eyes along the table, trying to fathom the opinions of the other directors.

"Oh, one more thing," Pancho said, without getting up from her chair. "If you do elect me to the board, I intend to vote for Ms. O'Banian as the new chairman."

Now Humphries scowled openly.

O'Banian said, "Very well. Let's vote, shall we? All in favor of Ms. Lane, raise your hands."

Two hours later, as the meeting broke up, Humphries accosted Pancho.

"Well, now you're a board member," he said "By the margin of two votes."

"And Ms. O'Banian is the chairman of the board."

Humphries scoffed, "Do you think that's going to stop me from taking control of Astro?"

"It won't stop you from tryin', I know that."

"I'll get Astro," he said firmly. "And Starpower, too, eventually."

"Maybe," said Pancho. "And maybe not."

He laughed at her.

"Lissen, Humpy," Pancho growled. "I don't give a shit how your lawyers wiggled you out of it, you killed Dan Randolph. I'm gonna make sure that he haunts you for the rest of your natural days."

"I don't believe in ghosts," said Humphries.

Now Pancho laughed. "You will, Humpy. You surely will."